T0243673

One
SHINING
Soul

WAYNE L. WILSON

ONE SHINING SOUL

© 2024, Wayne L. Wilson

Print ISBN: 979-8-35096-125-6
eBook ISBN: 979-8-35096-126-3

DEDICATION

To my father, Charles,
for teaching me the value of a strong work ethic.

To my mother, Shirley,
for giving me immeasurable love and support.

To my daughter, India,
for filling my life with her joyful spirit and endless inspiration.

Prologue

S adly, they didn't see that by attacking Olisa they were laying down paint on the wrong canvas. The person they perceived as a detriment to their aims was the same person whose sole purpose in life was to weave a spiritual quilt among all people in an effort to eliminate racism, sexism, and any other obstacles that got in love's way. Unfortunately, I suppose it was difficult for these groundskeepers of glory to focus upon something so simple and pure.

"Once you commit to ridding yourself of all self-absorption and hatred, then you begin to discover how much easier it is to feel compassion toward others. I feel nothing but love toward the Reverend Pocock," Olisa was quoted as saying in a *New York Times* interview with Theo Balanis in response to the vicious and personal attacks mounted by Walter Pocock.

"But you must admit, Olisa," Balanis commented, "some of the things he says are libelous, scathing, and defamatory attacks on your character."

"It doesn't bother me. I know who I am. Does he know himself?"

Chapter 1

Fatalism—a doctrine that events are fixed in advance for all time in such a manner that human beings are powerless to change them.

Sooner or later, it was bound to happen. I guess I should be grateful that nothing occurred while my daughter, Olisa, was out of the country. However, it did transpire at Venice Beach on the Fourth of July days after she returned home.

It was early evening, and our soul food restaurant was packed. A twenty-minute wait increased to sixty minutes as couples and families with restless and hungry children waited for a table.

My sister, Wilma, scolded one of the new waiters in the kitchen about his billing mistakes, while I was absorbed in my own concerns. It didn't look like I'd ordered enough chicken for the night. Meanwhile, the phone begged to be answered. Valerie, our hostess, called in late, so we were also shorthanded.

Gently lifting the phone I wanted to rip out of the wall, I affably answered, "Soul of Venice."

"Unc, is that you? Aww, man . . . you didn't answer your cell phone! I've been trying to reach you!"

"Gumbo? Anybody tell you it's the Fourth of July? We're shorthanded and things are insane! What's up? You need to talk to your mother?"

"No, no, Uncle Joe, I gotta talk to you."

"You sound like you've been running the decathlon. Everything all right?"

"Yeah, well, no . . . Uh, I mean everything is all right now, except . . ." He trailed off.

"Alton, I can't understand a word you're saying. Speak louder! What's going on?"

Wilma stood impatiently next to me, a hand on her hip as she waited for the authorization machine to clear a Visa card. She mouthed, "What's wrong?"

I shrugged my shoulders and covered my ear with the other hand to muffle the cacophony of voices, and clanking plates and silverware.

"Unc, you still there?"

"Yeah, Alton, 'cept I can barely hear you. Where are you now?"

"Your house . . . with Olisa."

Right away I felt riddled by a surge of panic. "She okay?"

"Oh yeah, she's fine. She's asleep right now."

"At seven?"

"Well, that's why I called, Uncle Joe . . . Some stuff went down at the beach today."

"Like, what stuff?"

He sighed. "Uncle Joe, this ain't something I can talk about over the phone. Any way you can come back to the house? I know it's crazy there. Should I try Aunt Grace at the hospital?"

"No, no, you'll be waiting on that phone forever. I'm on the way. Give me about fifteen minutes."

"Hey! Uncle Joe, before you hang up . . ."

"Yes?"

"Don't talk to anyone."

"What's that mean?"

"Don't speak to any reporters."

"Huh? Reporters? It's like that?"

"Yes, sir. Don't say nuthin' to nobody until you talk with me, okay? I'll explain when you get here."

I hung up the phone. Wilma immediately handed me the keys.

"I'm sorry. Something's up. Gumbo wants me to come home."

"Then you better leave. My son wouldn't ask unless it's important. We'll be fine. Valerie came in while you were on the phone."

"Okay, thanks, sis. I promise I'll be back as soon as I can."

"Uh-huh . . . I got a feeling that ain't a promise you'll be keeping. And judging by that frown on your face, it certainly won't be tonight."

I split out the back door, pausing for a second before climbing into my black Lexus GX 460. The underbelly of the clouds looked like pink cotton candy as the sun set. Something big was up. Wilma was right. Gumbo was too conscientious to bother me at the restaurant unless it was serious. All I could think about was what Gumbo said: "Some stuff went down . . ."

My hand trembled as I turned the ignition switch and raced the engine. I had been waiting for this. I could sense whatever happened was going to significantly change the course of our lives forever. I remember the first time our lives consequentially changed April 30, 1992, the day our daughter Olisa was born. She was born early that morning in the midst of one of the worst periods of unrest in our nation's history—the Los Angeles riots. The event seared its way into international recognition.

The activity and damage done to LA streets were eerily similar to what James Baldwin described visiting Watts after the riots in August of 1965:

> Watts doesn't immediately look like a slum, if you come from New York: but it does if you drive from Beverly Hills . . . Over it hangs a miasma of fury and frustration, a perceptible darkening, as of storm clouds, of rage and despair, and the girls move with a ruthless, defiant dignity, and the boys move against the traffic as though they are moving against the enemy. He is not there, of course, but his soldiers are in patrol cars.

MC Hammer's song "This Is the Way We Roll" blasted the air waves.

"Junior, turn that damn music off!" my father-in-law, Harold Willis, whispered furiously.

Junior only stared out the car window, mesmerized.

A solemn-faced Mr. Willis exasperatedly reached out and turned off the car radio. He nervously clutched the steering wheel as all three of us, bunched together in the front seat of the Jeep Grand Cherokee, slowly and deliberately drove south down Western Avenue. Carefully, we dodged roving bands of Black teenagers haphazardly sprinting across the streets, screaming and hollering, sweaty faces against the windshields of cars, obstructing traffic and stoning every police car whizzing down the street.

It was around 7:00 p.m. in the evening of April 29, 1992, about four hours after the Rodney King verdict had been read and the four officers were intolerably acquitted. The weather was moderate outside, but inside the car it was hot, incredibly hot, and our sticky shirts were plastered against our skin. The acrid smell of smoke in the air was stultifying. Los Angeles was entrenched in a fiery war of the people. There was no call to arms, no propaganda, no draft notices. The reactions were spontaneous, instinctual . . . an emotional response to the deep frustration inflicting a community. We found ourselves unwilling participants trapped in a maelstrom of violence, desperate to navigate our way home. Dense clouds of black smoke billowed into the sky, making it difficult to discern the natural course of nature's sunset.

Cars keeled over like dominoes as we watched Brown and Black hands rocking them until their resistance weakened. Eventually they succumbed, tumbling over amidst loud triumphant cheers, finally bursting into fire as they were showered by Molotov cocktails. Darkness moved quickly upon us as we drove with our inside light on, advice that came courtesy of a teenager peering inside of our car with a pistol blatantly in the front part of his pants. "Hey, y'all, it's gettin' dark. Better turn your inside light on so we know who you is, brothas! Know what I'm sayin'? We burnin' this muthafucka down! The revolution *will* be televised! Ha! Ha!"

A moment later, shattering glass forced Mr. Willis to slam on his brakes as Junior and I jerked forward like test dummies slapping our hands against the dashboard.

"Shit! Everybody all right?" yelled Mr. Willis nervously, rubbing the bald spot on his head. The noise was so loud it sounded like *our* windows exploded, but they were still intact. Turned out it was the vehicle next to us as more bricks smashed its windows and shards of glass prickled our car.

A young Caucasian couple sat trapped in their Escalade, eyes stricken with terror as they fought off clawing Black hands reaching into the broken windows of their car. The man feverishly worked to start his Cadillac again, struggling with the ignition, futilely pumping the peddle of a gasping, flooded car. Derisive laughter accompanied his every effort as several people pounced upon his hood and bumper, dancing on the car and furiously beating it with sticks, bats, bricks, cement blocks, and anything else they could lay hold of.

"Kill whitey!" came the frenzied cry that consumed the air. "Hey, peckerwoods, bet you muthafuckas ain't gon be coming through here no more, huh? Get yo asses out the car!"

"Oh my God," whispered Mr. Willis as we sat glued in place.

They yanked the couple from the car and flung them to the ground. The man looked like some kind of account executive. They beat him so bad his clothes shredded from his body, their muffled cries stinging my ears as a mob of people engulfed them.

Somehow, by the grace of God, they actually popped out and managed to escape, fleeing down the street toward a police barricade. The mob overturned their car, torched it, and moved forward like a cloud of locusts. Western Avenue had always been a heavily traveled street with many Whites avoiding the traffic on the freeways by heading north to Hollywood and downtown or south to Gardena, Torrance, and Rancho Palos Verdes. There had always been latent worries about being attacked when they passed through the Black sections, but their fears of a stereotypical jungle were never actualized.

Until now . . .

But these weren't normal times.

In the aftermath, it was poetically referred to as an uprising, a revolution, a rebellion . . .

Damn that! It was chaos, a world gone mad! I saw cops chasing rioters, rioters chasing cops, citizens raiding stores, and arsonists boldly showcasing their work.

Rebellions can make strange bedfellows. Elderly people exhorted youngsters to perpetrate crimes and wreak havoc, kids they'd ordinarily feared, alone, on a dark street with their purse or wallet. Now they were teammates. I watched young hoods boldly break into stores followed by senior citizens sharing the dividends. Young and old broke into stores looting anything that could be carried. On their faces, I saw years of pent-up emotions, hurt, and pain, now relieved by the big paycheck! "Fuck it! Burn it up and start all over again" appeared to be the agenda.

A world gone mad!

In the meantime, Mr. Willis sat at the steering wheel immobile.

In a surge of dread, I visualized my wife bearing our child alone.

"Mr. Willis! Harold! Let's go! Come on now. *Drive!* We need to get the hell out of here! Not much time left. We've gotta get home and make sure everyone's good! Remember, Grace is going to have a baby, your grandchild!"

"Yeah, yeah, I know, I know . . . I just ain't never seen nothing like this . . . and I was in Nam. Those poor people. What are we doing? I never thought I'd see something like this again since the Watts riot. This time they got Blacks *and* Latinos out there looting!"

I thought I'd have to take over the wheel as he just sat there, still dressed in his postal uniform, perspiration coagulating and then rolling down his distressed face. Fortunately, his clouded eyes became lucid again as he punched his foot against the accelerator. The car screeched forward barreling toward home.

Junior punched the radio. Public Enemy's song "Shut 'Em Down" played loudly. Harold shot him a look.

"Pops, ain't nobody gonna mess with us as long as we playin' this!"

This time, Mr. Willis didn't bother yelling at him.

On my right, I noticed there was all kinds of activity.

The only one of us who seemed to have a sense of calm in this turbulence was my sixteen-year-old brother-in-law, Junior. He was the essence of cool as his eyes darted back and forth, engrossed in all of the action. Though he never said a word, I figured there had to be an emotional wrestling match going on as he watched his peers engaged in total anarchy. Junior wasn't the type to be involved in violence, but I didn't think he'd mind picking up a little stereo equipment. He probably needed to be sitting between us because I wondered what choice he would have made if we hadn't been there to keep him psychologically bolted to his seat.

To my right there was all kind of activity at a Chevron gas station. The convenience store attendants had vanished from the victimized station as rioters broke in and freely distributed the spoils of war, generously filling soda pop bottles, wine bottles, and beer cans with gasoline, stuffing them with rags, and charging back into the fray, whooping and hollering like it was a rodeo.

Scores of fire trucks and police cars flew by, sirens squealing and helicopters whirring overhead as blazing fire after fire scorched the darkness. Even where no actual rioting took place, hundreds of people lined up in the streets, some out of curiosity, others awaiting their moment. It was safe to assume what happened thus far was only the tip of the proverbial iceberg.

The only thing I cared about at this point was getting home to Grace as quickly as possible. We were only half a mile away when cars started bucking and driving helter-skelter. One veered onto the sidewalk to avoid whatever was ahead of it, while another spun out of control, twirling like a marble as it crashed into a telephone pole. Its White inhabitants spilled out the car, scattering in all directions.

Much to my chagrin Mr. Willis abruptly braked, and our car screeched to a halt. He uttered, "What the hell . . ."

Up ahead a group of thugs straddled an older White man, pinning him to the ground. The voice crying out in the din was painfully familiar as my body began shaking involuntarily. Imagine the depths my heart sank to when I witnessed my very pregnant wife in the midst of a huge angry crowd, wrestling with all her might to free this man from their grasp. She raced from side to side, pulling at the thrashing arms of this giant spider of bodies unleashed upon him. Grace's mother, Katherine, and her grandmother, Mama Willis, followed closely behind, failing miserably in their attempts to restrain her. Grace was frantic, periodically holding her stomach as her screaming pleas for sanity were deflected by howls of contemptuous laughter.

"Stop it! Stop it! Leave him alone; he hasn't hurt anybody! Beating him up is not going to solve anything. You're defeating your own purpose! Mr. Kaplan has always tried to help everyone in this community. He's a good man!"

I propelled myself from the car, wrapping myself around Grace as I pulled her away. I heard Mama Willis say, "Thank you, Jesus."

When Grace realized it was me, she burst into hysterical tears yanking on my arms. "Joseph, stop them. They're going to kill our neighbor, Mr. Kaplan. We were driving home from the drugstore and saw them dragging him out of his motel . . . like he was some kind of animal. Oh God, they're going to kill him . . ."

Helmeted officers arrived, whipping out their clubs as the rioters vanished into the arms of the crowd who lashed at the police with a flurry of epithets. I felt so bad seeing Ron Kaplan in a daze as he struggled to get up. One of the African American policemen offered him a hand. Recoiling in fear, eyes bulging, he backpedaled like he was being stalked by Godzilla. He clumsily ran away vanishing into his motel building.

The demonstrators cackled with laughter as they closed in upon the small band of officers and screamed obscenities. However, they reserved a shit load of venom for the two Black officers who stood with the other cops.

"Look at them Uncle Toms over there! What you traitors doing here? Fucking pigs! You ought to be ashamed! Wearing those uniforms makes you no better than those blue-eyed devils! What you need to do is take off those uniforms and stand united with us. This is where you belong, not holding hands with those honkeys! Better recognize!"

While the crowd spewed their vitriol on the police, Mr. Willis signaled with his hand and waved for us to head toward the motel.

"Where the hell do you think you people are going?"

A White and well-built policeman clamped his hand down on Mr. Willis' arm like a steel vise. The other hand held a baton poised to strike as he jerked Mr. Willis' arm. The smirk on his face spread as he became more encouraged by the multitude of officers arriving on the scene. The growing crowd of police incensed the crowd even more.

Mr. Willis casually glanced sideways at the hand gripping his arm.

"Before you laid your hands on me, I planned on going to our neighbor's assistance to see if he's okay."

"Your neighbor? That's how you people treat your neighbor?" he snorted. "No, I don't think so. Why don't you come along with me." The young naïve and well-muscled cop eagerly tried to assert his authority in front of the crowd, mistakenly thinking that this show of force was enough to intimidate the amassing crowd.

"Sir, please let me go. The 'you people' you are referring to are some young hoodlums who are probably using some other victim as a trampoline right now. We're not all criminals."

"Says who?" the stone-faced officer responded sarcastically, staring at Mr. Willis with a look that spoke volumes about the insensitivity, brutality, and lack of communication that characterized the relationship between the police force and the community. Mr. Willis winced in pain when his other arm was snatched and the officer pinned him against the police car, as he reached for his handcuffs.

"Dick, put those handcuffs away, you damn fool. Let him go, *now!*" sternly whispered the veteran officer standing next to him. Dick was oblivious to the mob inching closer and closer to them. They were ten officers facing a hostile crowd that was growing exponentially.

"Get your hands off the mailman, pigs! What the fuck did *he* do to you? Free him! See, you muthafuckas is always starting shit like this!"

"I'd advise you to take a clear look at your surroundings and let go of me before things get too out of hand," Mr. Willis calmly advised.

It was already too late. Rocks, stones, bricks, and pieces of concrete showered the police officers mercilessly. The rookie instantly released Mr. Willis' arms, shielding himself as fear started to shape itself on his formerly smug face.

I instinctively shielded Grace with my body as I pushed her out of the line of fire. Several fire trucks roared by, crying like babies as smoke drifted into the sky and the area was set ablaze. Next, we heard the terrifying sounds of gunshots as chunks of cement popped up from the ground. Everyone hit the turf as the police tore off in the direction of the fire engines, followed by crossfire ricocheting from every direction. One officer, hit by a bullet, tumbled to the ground holding his leg as his partner scooped his arms around his shoulders and helped him get away.

We fled to the Kaplan Motel on the other side of the street for shelter. Mr. Willis and I assisted Grace as she struggled to catch her breath.

"Honey, are you all right?" I held my breath awaiting her answer.

"All right as can be considering my labor pains have started."

"What?"

"Yes," she gasped, holding her stomach.

"We've got to get to a hospital now! Where's the car?" I screamed.

The horrid sounds of gunfire afflicted my ears.

"What car?" Mr. Willis cried. His mouth hung open in shock.

The rioters overturned several police cars, smashing them with Molotov cocktails and exuberantly cheering when they exploded into huge balls of fire. Mr. Willis' car was parked too close to the overbearing heat. Sparks tickled the hood of his car, blowing up into waves of dancing orange flames as they lit ghastly shadows on our dismayed faces.

"Motherfuckers! Motherfuckers! Can you believe these stupid motherfuckers! Shit! These crazy ass fools, mad at the world, not only burn up my fucking car, but my goddamn city! What kind of fucking shit is this?"

"What are we going to do?" I asked, completely alarmed as I watched the carnage unfold before my eyes. The rioters looted Dee's liquor store, carting away cases of beer and wine. Kids nine and ten years old chugged beers like it was soda pop.

"We are going to take this girl inside and let her rest before somebody gets hit with a stray bullet. And then we'll pray this thing blows over soon enough for us to get her to a hospital; that's what we're going to do," Mama Willis replied brusquely, swinging the door open. Katherine Willis shoved past us, whisking Grace into the motel office as we followed sheepishly along.

"If anyone comes a step closer, I will shoot!"

Behind the registration desk stood Mr. Kaplan, shotgun in hand, pointed at us. His white dress shirt was torn and bloody, and cuts and lacerations marred his face. A huge knot protruded from the side of his forehead. His eyes were completely lifeless, and his body shook like a leaf in a Chicago windstorm. His wife and five-year-old son stood behind him.

"Now Mr. Kaplan, put that gun down, buddy, before you hurt someone. You know we don't mean you any harm."

"I *said* don't come any closer! Who the hell are you?"

"Easy, Ron . . . It's Harold, Harold Willis . . . your next-door neighbor. Don't worry; everything is all right . . . We are your friends."

"Ron, honey . . . It's the Willises," his wife remarked shakily.

"Judy, I don't care who it is! We have no friends tonight. We're not *their* brothers and sisters!" he retorted disdainfully. "How do we know they haven't joined up with *their* people out there? How can we trust them? We are their enemies, which makes them ours. I've got to protect my family." He raised the gun to his shoulder. "Now get the hell out of here!"

I couldn't take much more of this; my wife was about to have a baby!

"Be serious, Mr. Kaplan! You know us better than that. We—"

"What I know is I'm telling you for the last time: get the hell out of my place!"

"I also have family in here to protect, Mr. Kaplan. And if I don't sit down soon, this baby is going to drop right down here on the floor."

"Grace, get back!" I shouted. But it was too late to grab her. She stepped in front of him and that shotgun. My heart executed a somersault.

Grace's unexpected move completely flummoxed him as his eyes flitted back and forth, reflecting the turmoil wracking his brain. Rigidly he held the gun as he tried to blink away the moisture collecting in his eyes.

Suddenly there was the sound of little feet. His son, Peter, raced around the counter and hugged Grace's legs.

"Peter, what are you doing? You get back here right now!" Ron Kaplan directed him.

Big blue eyes gazed up at Grace.

"Hi, Grace."

"Hi, Peter."

"Are you really going to have a baby?"

"Yes, Peter, I am," she said tenderly. Grace patted his head. "Maybe tonight. You want to touch my stomach?"

"Sure."

She guided his tiny hands around her stomach as he grinned broadly, fascination brightening his face. Grabbing her hand, Peter led Grace around the counter to his father.

"Hey, Daddy, what's wrong? Do your eyes hurt again? This is not our enemy. It's Grace. And that's the Willises over there. Hi, Junior!"

"What's up, little man?"

"See, Daddy, they're not going to hurt us. These are our neighbors and friends. Did you know Grace is going to have a baby? Daddy, are you listening? Daddy?"

Peter clasped Grace's hand, delightedly pressing it against his face.

"Yes, I'm listening, Peter. And, yes, you're right . . . That is Grace," he replied, smiling wanly. He placed the shotgun under the counter, weariness etching his bruised face. His wife massaged his shoulders. His head dropped as he covered his face with his hands.

"My God, what am I doing? I'm sorry, so sorry . . . I don't know what—"

"No apologies necessary, Mr. Kaplan," Grace gently responded. "After what you've been through, every person in here can relate. You're scared. I'm scared. We're all scared this evening. The world's not quite right tonight. The main thing is you're alive and among friends. We need to get you cleaned up."

She moved toward him but staggered and fell into his ready arms as she doubled over in pain. We rushed her like she was carrying a football. But the women had already taken over the offense.

"She needs to lie down!" Mama Willis bluntly stated.

"Here, let me take her here to this back room," offered Mrs. Kaplan as she ushered Grace into the bedroom with Katherine Willis following closely behind. I tried to follow, but Mama Willis blocked the door like a sentry. She may have only been 5'4", but I wasn't about to step past her.

"Joseph, you men stand guard. When the time's right, we'll call you in here. Ain't no doubt she'll have the baby sometime this evening, but we need you men out front keeping your eye out for trouble. All hell's breaking loose out there!"

"But don't we need a doctor?" I anxiously questioned.

"It'd be nice if one did riot calls, but we don't have that luxury tonight, baby. And with bullets flying around out there, we're not going to try to drive to a hospital. Besides, I don't think we'd make it in time."

"She's that close?"

"She is."

"But who's going to—"

"Child, I've been around enough babies in my life to handle this with my eyes closed. Don't worry; we're blessed. By the grace of God, Mama Willis will take care of everything.

"But—"

The door quietly closed in my face.

I turned and saw Mr. Willis and Mr. Kaplan softly chatting in the corner. I considered how fortunate we were to be able to take shelter in a motel, which wasn't on the top ten lists of places to loot. What were you going to steal, a room? We felt fairly comfortable in our refuge.

Contrarily, life lessons say there is an exception to every rule. It happened after I had finally gained entrance to the forbidden zone, largely due to the screams erupting from Grace demanding that I be in the room with her.

I held Grace's hand as she harshly inhaled and exhaled, perspiration running steadily down her face. Her thick hair was all disheveled. She gripped my hand so tightly I was positive I'd never regain use of it again.

"You just hang in there, Grace. The way I see it, honey, you can bet the farm on that baby arriving in about an hour or so," Mama Willis cooed as she wiped Grace's brow with a hand towel. Mrs. Kaplan and Katherine Willis were busily going back and forth, laying towels on her chair and other bathroom items in preparation for the birth.

I tried to act cool, but I was feeling a little light-headed from not eating all day. Nonetheless, I had to stay strong. It wasn't about me; it was about Grace.

Just at that moment, it sounded like a bomb exploded in the motel's front office.

"Jesus! What was that?" Katherine Willis asked, practically ripping my shirt as she clutched my arm. Grace's doe eyes widened and then closed as she continued to focus on breathing rhythmically.

"I don't know, but I'll check it out." I kissed Grace on the forehead and raced into the front office.

Junior stepped inside the door, a worried look on his normally placid face. "Daddy, trouble's heading our way!"

"Damn, I wondered how long it would take," Harold Willis peeked out the curtained window, sucking on his lower lip. He picked up one of the bricks surrounded by glass particles that had been thrown through the window and quickly examined it. "Ron, do you trust me?" he asked quietly as he walked over to the counter, pulled out the rifle underneath it, and placed it on the registration desk facing the door.

"Of course, Harold. I mean what happened earlier has no bearing on—"

"Then I need you and Peter to get out of sight, right now! Let us deal with this."

"Okay, Harold," he said, reluctantly, as he ushered Peter into the back room. Before following him, he turned and gave Harold a concerned look. "Harold . . ."

"Yes?"

"The rifle was never loaded."

"Ok, so where's the ammunition for it?"

"It doesn't work."

"Great."

A second after Ronald closed and locked the door to the backroom, a foot kicked the front door of the motel so hard it almost rattled off its hinges. It flew open, causing more glass from the shattered window to tinkle to the floor. They coolly strolled in, glass cracking underneath their feet, bringing with them the smell and sounds of the streets: the smoke, the stifling heat, the musty mix of alcohol and body sweat, and pure undiluted rage. One of them held a portable boombox, price tag dangling defiantly, while Bobby Brown's raspy voice screamed, "It's my prerogative!" The funky bassline made my feet tap involuntarily, even with my life on the line.

"Burn, baby, burn! Ain't that what they used to say?" crowed the one with the high-top fade cut and carrying the boombox.

Four shirtless Black bodies stood in the middle of the room caustically surveying everything in the front office. A couple of them loosely held empty wine bottles in their hand. The tall lanky one wearing a silver and black bandana in the style of Tupac Shakur with a knot protruding from the front of his head displayed more teeth than a barracuda. His eyes exhibited primeval madness, wilder than anything Edgar Allen Poe could have ever imagined. He took a final swig from some malt liquor in a can and flung it to the floor where it banged flatly. The gold grills in his mouth flashed like a radio transmitter when he spoke.

"You brothas ought to be glad we came in here first! We was about to blow this bad boy up until my dude, Shorty, thought he saw some homies up in here!"

Shorty was the one who metronomically rocked the full gas can, spilling some of it on the floor. Short in height but not in width, he looked like Winnie the Pooh with an attitude. The gassy fumes made my eyes water. Rags hung out the back of his pants pocket. He nodded at Junior with a snarl that I think was meant to be a grin.

"So where's that stinky Jew muthafucka?" Bandana barked. "I'm tired of these assholes comin' here stealing our money and not givin' back to the community! We gonna give him another ass whooping and show him what Smokey the Bear is really all about. After that, we gonna burn this mutha to the ground!" His grills levitated in the air when he laughed.

"Tell 'em about it, Smokey!"

"Ain't nobody heard what I axed?" He hitched his trousers and menacingly appraised us. His fingers did a spidery crawl across the handle of the pistol hanging out the front of his belt.

None of us said a word. The only noise was the sound of sirens, intermittent gunfire, and from the boombox, the wailing of Junior Walker's saxophone on the song "Shotgun."

"You niggers must be deaf and dumb. Know what I'm sayin'? Don't let me have to ax you again!"

"Y'all better listen up. He crazy!" warned one of his butt-kiss-ing sycophants.

"We heard every word you said. Now, I hope you'll extend the same courtesy to me and listen to what I have to say," Mr. Will responded as he stood behind the registration counter tapping the shotgun lying on top of it.

Judging by the shock on Bandana's face, it was the first time he laid eyes on it. A slight frown creased his forehead as he remarked in a low baleful voice, "You got the best hand. Play it, Mr. Postman."

"All right, then here's the deal. The man you're looking for is our neighbor and our friend. He's a good man, and we don't want to see him hurt. So, all I'm asking is y'all go on about your business and leave us be."

Mr. Willis was icy cool except for his hands subtly trembling. I bit my lip as I watched Bandana glaring at him like he ought to be gutted.

"Uh, uh . . . I know you ain't protecting that white devil. So I'm gonna ignore what you said, Mr. Postman. We'll call it a miscommunication. Matter of fact, I'm bettin' a smart old man like you knows with one phone call I could bring a hundred niggas in here."

Mr. Willis nodded slowly and then angled the gun on him.

Junior spoke up, "Man, we don't want no trouble. We all down with the cause."

Bandana gave Junior the once-over look. "Well, if you so down with us, bruh, then bring that Jew, Kaplan, out here and we'll be on our way."

Junior shuffled his feet uneasily. "Man, I can't do that."

"Then you need to shut the fuck up! And tell that old man over there, Uncle Tommin, for his Massa to put his shit down and get the fuck out our way so we can take care of *bidness*!" Scowling, he hitched one shoulder as he and his boys stepped forward.

Mr. Willis raised the shotgun and in an even voice said, "I told y'all to move on."

I held my breath.

To my right, I saw an arm quickly rise as one punk who wore a doo rag got ready to sling his bottle at Mr. Willis.

"Mr. Willis, look out!" I screamed.

In a flash, Mr. Willis swung around, and there was a blast as the gun fired, shattering the wine bottle in Doo Rag's hand. He bent over in anguish, grabbing his hand and groaning in pain. Then another shotgun blast as a second bottle exploded.

"Hey, man, you messed up my box!" shouted an anguished Boombox who kept futilely flipping the "on" switch after his music died with the blast.

Mr. Willis looked more shocked than anyone as smoke drifted out of the shotgun.

"Gimme that, Shorty!" Bandana snatched the gas can from him, splashing gasoline all over the floor.

"You muthafuckas want to protect whitey, huh? Then you can burn in hell with his devil ass! Come on, fellas, we outta here!"

"*Noooo*! My wife's in the other room!" I hollered as Bandana lit a match and set one of the torn rags on fire throwing it in the pool of gasoline.

There was a rattlesnake-like hiss as the flame rapidly died.

"Fuck this!" Bandana quickly set another rag on fire, but all of a sudden, all by itself, one of the counter fans kicked into high gear and a burst of air blew out, reversing the direction of the flame and setting Bandana's pants on fire. He tore out the door, belting out a strangled cry as his fellow hoods chased after him. His burning body blazed like a comet as he streaked down the nighttime streets.

Mr. Willis held the shotgun at arm's length, goggling at it like it had leprosy.

The backroom door creaked open, and Mr. Kaplan poked his head out. "Thank God, everyone's okay."

Mrs. Willis burst through the open door, tears streaming down her cheeks and wringing her hands nervously. "Harold? Boys? Are you all right? All that shooting and hollering—"

"It's okay, Katherine . . . It's okay. We're fine," Harold answered, embracing her.

He turned to Mr. Kaplan and said, "Ron, I am so happy to say you were wrong. The gun *was* loaded. It worked fine."

Mr. Kaplan looked absolutely befuddled. "Harold, it can't be fine . . . no way . . . That shotgun hasn't been fired in years. The trigger mechanism doesn't work anymore. Look . . . see?" He flicked the trigger, which was as limp as a rubber band. "The only reason I kept this gun here was to ward off robbers and intruders. When I heard the gunfire, I thought they were doing the shooting."

"If that don't beat all," Mr. Willis shook his head. "It was like the rifle jumped to a life of its own. As I held it, it tugged me along like I was a big trout on a fishing pole. I just moved in whatever direction it pulled me."

Mr. Kaplan shrugged. "Weirdest thing I ever heard."

"Tell me about it. I thought we were goners when he poured gasoline on the floor."

Junior kneeled down and dabbed his finger in the gas spill, raising it to his nose. His face crinkled up. "Daddy, this isn't gasoline; it's just water."

"*What?*"

My stomach felt like tiny snakes were crawling inside. I couldn't breathe. The stress, not eating . . . Thank goodness the front door was open. I felt much better when I stepped outside the door.

Gazing up at the night sky, I spotted high arcing streams of white water gobbled up by hungry black smoke and bright orange flames, flames that formed tiny little crowns of fire on the neighboring telephone pole. If I hadn't been looking up, I never would have noticed the hulking figure perched on top of the high-rise building next door. His back faced me. Either I was seeing an illusion, or the smoke was dimming my vision, but I was positive his feet weren't touching the ground! Almost like an act of levitation. *But that's impossible!*

Nothing is impossible.

The man's enormous frame glowed as it stood silhouetted against the supernaturally reddened sky created by the burning fires. He deliberately pivoted and faced in my direction. Though I couldn't see his face or eyes, I *knew* he was looking at me.

A baby's cry pierced my reverie as I turned around and saw heads snap toward the backroom. *Grace!* Oh, Grace. I scrambled back inside the motel. Smiling family members and friends parted as I rushed through. I was welcomed by Grace's tired yet beaming face as she lovingly cradled the most precious, beautiful, and sweetest baby I had ever seen.

Nestled in a world ravaged by violence, anger, weapons, fire, and screams of injustice existed an oasis of the purest love. Grace tenderly caressed my face as I snuggled beside them in the bed. I was in awe of the tiny little person bundled up before me. I kissed her on the forehead.

"Oh, Joseph, I was so worried . . . Are you okay?"

"Am I okay? You're asking if I'm okay? I'm fine. The question is, how are you?"

"Tired, in pain, and happier than I've ever been."

She placed my hand against her cheek. Tears spilled over my fingers. I couldn't imagine a single poet, alive or dead, who could have accurately described how deeply I loved her.

"Look at her, Joseph. This is your daughter."

"Yeah . . . She's . . . she's beautiful, simply beautiful. Look at all that hair on her head. I thought babies were supposed to be bald."

"Not this one, honey. Would you like to hold her?"

"Hold her? With my hands?" Self-consciously I began brushing the sides of my pants. "I'm filthy; look at me. I mean . . . are you sure? I'm not going to infect her, am I? And now she's crying. I don't know how to, you know . . . she's so small . . . ?"

"Joseph, be quiet. Hold your daughter."

Grace handed her to me as I fumbled awkwardly to position her just right, afraid of harming her, so fragile and so soft. It may be a cliché, but

I was floating on a cloud as I tiptoed around the room, gazing into her innocent little face. The warmth I felt from cushioning her against my chest was indescribable.

"See, Joseph, she's already in love with you. She stopped crying."

"Yeah, she did, didn't she? . . . Aww, she's something, isn't she?"

"She's very special, Joseph, *very* special . . . You just know it."

For a brief instant, I thought I saw a glimmer of a woman staring at us from the side window of the backroom where the curtains were drawn. I did a double take, and she was gone.

"Did you tell Mama Willis about our decision?" I questioned Grace.

A very tired Mama Willis sat on the other side of the bed, head partially bowed. Grace grabbed her arm, which made her sit up straight, and said, "You mean this beautiful lady right here? The one who saw me through my delivery? Grandmother, it came to me months ago in a dream that our child would end up a girl, so we already settled on a name."

"I tried my best to convince her to come up with some boy names as a backup, but she was insistent it was going to be a girl," I added.

"We agreed to name her Olisa, a combination of your first name, Sharlisa, and Grandfather's middle name, Odis. God, how I wish he were alive to see her. You're still okay with that name, right, Joe?"

"Are you kidding? I love the name Olisa. How about you, Mama Willis?"

No answer was forthcoming as she cupped her hands over her trembling mouth. Her eyes, held by wrinkled dark folds, transformed into wading pools.

Fortunately, the rest of the night passed without further incident inside the motel. The sun peeping over the San Gabriel Mountains at sunrise offered a special treat to some tired and weary people. Mr. Willis managed to retrieve his wife's car. We drove Grace and the baby safely to the hospital, traveling through a war-torn city still simmering with anger. Olisa was born in a sea of tumult later known as the 1992 Los Angeles Riots or, to others, the 1992

Los Angeles Uprising and Rodney King Riots. At the time, the significance of that event escaped us owing to being so thrilled to have Olisa in our lives.

Grace and I believed she was a very special baby, but don't most new parents believe that about their firstborn? Except in our case, it didn't take long before we found out how special she really was. And for nearly thirty years, our greatest fear was the world would one day, like us, discover it as well. This was what I contemplated when I arrived home from the restaurant. I waited impatiently in the back alley for the electronic garage door to open. All of a sudden, a woman leaped out of an obscure blue van in the alley like a ninja warrior and made quick strides toward my car. My instincts screamed, "Hurry up! Drive in and let the door close in her face before she catches up to you!" But my curiosity got the better of me, and I waited.

She was Latina, probably in her early twenties, attractive, medium length trendily cut auburn hair, and golden-brown eyes that lit up on cue as she waved to me like she was my BFF. Behind her trailed a burly White man wearing a Yankee baseball cap that covered a crow's nest of lifeless red hair. He had a major case of acne on his sun-parched face and tiredly lugged a handheld camera. She held the microphone down to her side and then lifted it up to my mouth like she was offering me a lick of an ice cream cone.

"Good evening, sir. My name is Eva Sanchez from Station KLSC. Would you mind talking to me for just a minute?" She waved her cameraman into position like it was a done deal.

"About what?" I asked in a monotone voice.

"Well, first, may I ask what your relationship is with Olisa Timmerman?"

"I'm her father."

Her eyes expanded faster than a balloon filling up with helium. "Oh, great!" she replied, barely able to contain her excitement. "Mr. Timmerman, you're just the man I need to talk to! And I'd love to speak with your daughter too!"

"Bottom line. What do you want?"

"Well, I was hoping you could share your thoughts on what happened today."

As the red light on the camera glared at me, my curiosity dissipated. "No comment."

"I don't know if you realize it, Mr. Timmerman, but people see your daughter as a hero. What she did out there this afternoon took guts. It was the most incredible—"

"Look; I don't mean to be rude, but I gotta go. We're done."

"Understood. Here's my card. Maybe we talk later tonight or tomorrow? Call me *any* time! And let me know what you think of my broadcast at eleven tonight."

"Uh-huh."

"Mr. Timmerman, I'd really appreciate it if you'd promise not to speak with anyone else about this. We'd love to keep this as an exclusive, you know?"

I pulled into the garage and pressed the door remote. Before it closed, I saw a girlish pout on Eva Sanchez's face that completely belied her granite-eyed determination. Thankfully, the garage door slammed shut.

Outside the door, she yelled, "Mr. Timmerman, is it true? Can she heal people?"

Chapter 2

Olisa's studio apartment, a detached accessory dwelling unit from the house, was dark. I figured I'd check inside our house first to see if she was there.

Even before I opened the back door, I smelled the aroma of cheddar cheese. Olisa's closest friend, Lara, with her back to me, busily moved about the kitchen. Her coal black hair was piled on top of her head, and feathered earrings swung back and forth. She greeted me with a smile that was like a warm embrace.

"Hello, Uncle Joe."

"Hey there, Little Oak. Whatcha up to?"

"Nothing much. Some green tea?"

"Not right now, kiddo, but thanks. Where are they?"

"Living room," she replied sucking her lower lip. I'm sure she noticed the anxiousness on my face.

"How's she doing?"

"Out like a light."

Lara patted my arm supportively as I passed by.

Olisa was curled up in a fetal position on the couch asleep. I felt her forehead; at least it was cool. I'm sure I gazed at her the same way I did when she was born. Studying her face, I no longer saw the squirrel-cheeked little girl with eyes too big for her face and billowing clouds of curls who let caterpillars crawl up her arms. Now before me lay a quietly beautiful woman who still allowed caterpillars to crawl up her arms. Her thick reddish-brown hair that flowed in large ripples past her shoulders framed a lofty forehead and elegant cheekbones, sheltering her delicately curved indigo eyes. Even asleep, her sienna-brown skin shined like she was escorted by her own personal sun. An exuberant writer for the *Los Angeles Times* would one day write, "If the Gods built a queen from African soil, she would look just like Olisa Timmerman."

Alton sat on the floor in a white tank top and sweat bottoms watching TV with a plate of nachos on his lap. "Hey, Unc! You want some nachos?"

"No thanks, nephew." I sat down in the sofa chair next to Olisa. "So listen, I met your reporter outside, Eva Sanchez?"

"Oh, man, I thought we ditched her. Damn! How did she get this address?"

"They got their ways. You can find anybody these days with the right kind of technology. Thanks for warning me. She ambushed me the minute I pulled up."

"Sorry, Uncle Joe. I got a feeling she's going to be a major pain."

"Me too. So talk to me."

Alton pointed the remote toward the TV set, killing the sound. Lara walked into the living room and sat at the end of the couch next to Olisa. She released her hair from the bun; it tumbled down in waves. Her radiant black hair, so dark it was almost blue, softened a striking face with prominent cheekbones and a strong straight nose. Her face had gained far more mileage than it should have for someone in her early thirties, but she had lived a tough life. She began twisting her hair into a single braid as she lifted her pensive eyes and stared at the muted television screen.

Lara Nelson was half Cherokee and half German. She lost both of her parents in a car crash when she was only eight years old. She was taken in by her father's family and raised on a reservation in Oklahoma. She remained there until she was sixteen, then moved to the San Francisco area and stayed with family there to escape the demons that trailed her. She had been on a path of self-destruction, partying, drinking, and using hard drugs. She fled to the Bay Area because it had been rumored she was targeted for murder by a couple of drug dealers she'd stolen drugs from. Luckily, she found a mentor in an elderly man known as Chief Eaglespeaker who helped her to pull herself together and radically transform her life before the last call.

Lara first met Olisa at UC Santa Cruz where they immediately became college roommates, forging a fast and lasting friendship. I had seen them in the same room for hours, neither one saying a word, absorbed in their own thoughts writing, reading, doing whatsoever, but always enjoying each other's company. Then Lara might depart with a nod, and that would be it. They had an understanding and mutual respect for each other that didn't need to be expressed in words. I admired the depth of their friendship.

Grace and I regarded Lara as family even before she and Gumbo hooked up and fell madly in love. They'd been living together for the past two years. Even though we teased them endlessly about getting officially married all the time, I had never seen two more in love and happier people. I teasingly nicknamed her "Little Oak" because she was originally from Oklahoma, petite, about 5′2″, yet tough and as durable as the tree.

As for my nephew, Alton, I nicknamed him "Gumbo" because he ate so much gumbo in one sitting at an event that it made me seasick. He was 6′5″ and 280 pounds of solid, ripped, angry muscle. The former USC All-American linebacker and first year draft choice for the Tampa Bay Buccaneers pro football team had to abandon his football career when he got into a life-altering car accident, wrapping his car around a telephone pole while driving drunk in Tampa, Florida, after an all-night party binge. He broke both legs, injured several ribs, and suffered facial lacerations. They had to use the Jaws of Life machine to peel him out of his Jaguar, which looked like a metal jellyfish afterwards. The severity of his accident left him with a subtle limp. Nevertheless, it was a blessing he was given a second chance to live life. After months of grueling rehabilitation, Alton focused his attention on building up his body, studying yoga and martial arts. He currently worked part time as a bouncer at a prestigious night club in downtown LA.

"I'm waiting, Gumbo," I firmly announced.

"I know, Unc. I don't even know where to start . . . So much has happened."

"The beginning might work."

He hoisted up a large full Evian bottle and guzzled it down. In between nacho crunches he talked.

"After I finished my workout at Gold's Gym, I figured I'd head down to the Venice Beach Boardwalk and check on Lara and Olisa. The beach was packed. It was hot, but everything was righteous, man. People got their groove on, roller blading, biking, jogging, listening to the live music, dancing, checking out the vendors hustling their wares . . . The day started out smooth. Hey, you know what turned out to be a trip? What do they call it, Lara . . . an iron?"

"Irony."

"Yeah, that's it. Eva Sanchez came over to interview us. She said, 'Hey, guys! I'm Evan Sanchez from KLSC News. Tell us what this lovely fourth of July weekend means to you.' Lara told her, 'It means the winner of the white man's war was free to continue stealing indigenous people's lands.' Ha! That didn't go over too well, so she turns to me and asks the same thing. I told her, 'African Americans were still slaves. Really? Ask me about the Emancipation Proclamation or Juneteenth and we can talk.' That's about the point she signaled cut to her cameraman, and they walked away."

"Where was Olisa?"

"Checking out some native artwork from a new vendor."

"Okay, so go on."

"You know how the tensions have been building again between the Black and Latino gangs in Venice? There've been some shootings here and there, but so far no major incidents that broke the truce. Then BAM! BAM! Next thing I know is there's like a few dudes taking sides, shouting and taunting each other. Brothas versus *eses*, you know. Dawg had been hittin' on *vato's* honey. One thing led to another, they got to smack talking, and before long everybody started gathering up their boys and it was on. At this point, we were kickin' it at the healer's booth. Olisa was giving me a neck massage when the next thing we see is this huge crowd scattering in all directions! They were panicked, man, screaming and running. The gangs are seriously scrapping, fists flying, trash cans, rocks . . . Anything that could be picked up was thrown.

"When the dust settled, there's a Mexican guy lying on the ground next to a big ass blade with his hands over his stomach and blood squirting out of him. Homeboy was in bad shape. The worst part is, not a police officer was in sight as the gangs got ready to knuckle up again, but this time you knew it was going to be Dodge City."

"So then what?"

"So then I see Olisa standing right between the two gangs with her hands up, screaming at them."

My head got so tight I thought it would implode. I had been working overtime to stay cool, but tension had partnered with me ever since the phone call.

"Shit, Gumbo! What in the hell were you thinking about? You let her get past your big ass! She could have gotten killed!"

I recognized my blunder as soon as the words left my lips. Hurt whipped across Alton's face. He would have taken a bullet for his cousin, and I knew that.

His face contorted as he dropped his head and said softly, "You're right, Uncle Joe, I'm sorry . . . I wasn't thinking. I'm really sorry."

"No, no . . . I'm sorry, Gumbo. Sometimes I get real stupid. Wasn't any call for me to yell at you like that. It wasn't your fault. Olisa is a grown woman. You are not responsible for her decisions."

Lara rapidly twisted the end of her braid. "He couldn't have done a thing, Uncle Joseph, even if he tried. Olisa moved fast. I kept shouting at her to move away, but she didn't listen."

"Can't say I'm surprised," I replied, rubbing my forehead.

"But look; she's here, safe and sound, and that's all that matters, right?"

"Yep, Little Oak, that's right."

Meanwhile, Olisa shifted positions as she hugged the couch pillow, eyes tightly shut, just an innocent little girl again. I couldn't imagine her in that chaos . . . yet, I could.

Gumbo continued, "Blew me out, Unc. When it finally hit me what was going down, I ran toward Olisa as fast as I could, but by then, she had those dogs at bay. Tripped me out! Those little punks froze like their mother had busted them, didn't they, Lara?"

"Sure did. Before anyone can react, my girl is sitting on the ground cross-legged. She hoists the unconscious and bleeding teenager's upper body onto her lap. She cradles him as she pulls up his t-shirt and places her hands over the wound . . ." Lara started to get choked up. "Alton, you can tell him the rest."

"He doesn't have to. Like Flash?"

"Yeah, Unc, just like . . ." Alton responded in a faraway voice.

Alton was just a chubby seven-year-old that his cousin Olisa looked up to and absolutely adored. He and some of the other kids in the neighborhood were playing softball in our front yard. Olisa was around six at the time. She sat in chair and firmly held the leash of Alton's Doberman Pinscher, Flash, who whined and strained against it. He intently watched the kids playing softball.

It was late Sunday afternoon. Grace had gone to the store to pick up some dessert. Katherine and Wilma were in the house cooking. I heard a few curse words coupled with the name "Lester" who was Alton's absentee father. I don't think Alton had seen his father more than a couple of times in his life.

Mr. Willis and I were stationed on the front porch, keeping an eye on the kids while playing a cutthroat game of "bones" as dominoes slammed harder on the folding table than a jail cell door. We grooved to Mr. Willis' collection of

Down Home blues: Willie Dixon, Muddy Waters, Sonny Terry, and B. B. King. We were feeling mighty good as we leisurely sipped on cognac like two country gents. Mama Willis rocked on the porch swing with Olisa's little brother, Noel, who was three, in her lap, reading him The Little Engine That Could *picture book. Noel's head jerked periodically as he fought a losing battle to stay awake, his eyes forming tiny slits.*

The front gate clicked, and Grace walked in clasping two grocery bags. The kids stopped playing until she passed through. Once she reached the porch, the game resumed.

"How come you're not out there playing softball with the rest of the kids, Olisa?" Grace asked as she stood on the porch with her bags.

"It's my job to watch Flash so he won't chase the ball," Olisa replied with staunch importance. "No, Flash!" Olisa firmly readjusted her grip on the leash, making it more taut, as the stocky Doberman kept thrusting forward and energetically wagging its docked tail whenever the ball was thrown.

"Looks to me like you're doing a pretty good job!"

"Thank you," Olisa giggled as Flash licked her face to try and convince her to let go of the leash.

"Hey, baby, did you get some sweet potato pie from Alma's Bakery?"

"Of course I did! And some apple and cherry pie!"

"Yay! My favorites! Can I have a tiny piece of cherry now? Please?"

"I think you know better, young lady—after dinner." Grace grinned seeing Noel sound asleep in Mama Willis' lap. "The Sand Man got him, huh?"

Mama Willis tenderly rubbed his head. "Sure did, bless his little heart."

Grace tapped her foot and dangled one of the bags in front of us. "Sure would be nice if one of you handsome gentlemen opened the door so I can help Momma and Wilma finish cooking."

"Handsome? She must be talking about me," grunted Harold. He jumped up and grabbed the bags and opened the door. "And don't be looking at my hand!"

I know I rolled my eyes. "Man, I could care less about your hand. You don't know it yet, but you're already beat."

Flash temporarily ceased struggling and raised his head. His nose crinkled and saliva dripped from his mouth as he inhaled the good smells emanating from the kitchen: fried chicken, ham hocks, barbecue hot links, mac and cheese, sweet potatoes, corn on the cob, black-eyed peas, and greens. Harold Willis burst out of the house bobbing his head to B. B. King's "Why I Sing the Blues." Hard not to move your body with the booming bass line accompanied by stinging blues licks from King's favorite guitar mistress Lucille!

A loud whack supplanting the music made me look up. Alton smacked the ball over the gate. It bounced between two parked cars and rolled to the other side of the street. Panting excitedly, Flash lunged, and the leash ripped in half. The Doberman jumped off the porch despite Olisa and me yelling and streaked through the front yard in pursuit of the ball. He scooted through one boy's legs. Alton dove to tackle, but Flash hurdled over him, leaped over the fence, shot between the two parked cars, and into the street where we could no longer see him. But we did hear Alton's sonic scream.

"Flash! Nooooo!"

Screeching tires and a gut-wrenching thump made everyone freeze. It seemed like the entire Oakwood section of Venice's "Hood" came to a deafening silence until it was shattered by a lone boy's heartbreaking wails.

Grace led the surge of women rushing out of the kitchen and onto the front porch. She cried, "Oh my God, Joseph, what happened?"

I didn't—couldn't answer. All I knew was that we'd find a black-and-tan furry body prostrate on the street.

A deeply stricken Olisa held up the torn leash.

"Oh sweet Lord! I'm sorry, Olisa . . . but you know it's not your fault. It's an accident, okay? You couldn't help it if the leash broke." She hugged Olisa's stiff body as people gradually surrounded the dog's prone body.

"Mama, I promised Alton I'd watch his dog," she agonized.

Grace rubbed her shoulder. "Honey, there's nothing you or anyone else could have done any differently. The leash broke. You hear me?"

Grace received a barely perceptible nod.

"I'm going to walk out there with your Daddy. You stay here with Mama Willis and Noel, okay? Don't move. We'll be back."

She stood there motionless, head bowed.

Wilma was already out there, her arms wrapped around Alton who was beside himself in tears. I joined Harold who stood on the street staring disconsolately at Flash lying on his side.

"I'm sorry . . . so sorry. I didn't see him," cried out a man from inside his blue Cadillac. With great effort the heavyset man slowly climbed out of the car and came over next to us. He was clearly distressed by the whole incident. He had on his Sunday best: shirt and tie and a fedora he took off and nervously exchanged from one hand to the other as he sorrowfully stared at the dog.

"I didn't see him . . . He just ran in front of me. It was an accident. I didn't mean to hit him. I tried to steer my car out of the way."

"It's all right, mister. It's not your fault. We all saw what went down. No way you could have seen him in time," I uttered softly, looking at Flash's body on the street and feeling my throat tighten.

Mr. Willis kneeled down and examined him. Flash's breathing was ragged. Pools of blood swelled concentrically beneath his quivering body. Half of the leash remained attached to his collar. Mr. Willis' lips tightened when he gave me a sideways glance and shook his head. Katherine Willis had been talking emphatically behind us on her phone. She held the phone away and said, "The humane society is on their way." I waved at Wilma to continue to keep Alton away, but he struggled to break free of her arms.

He reached out with a trembling hand. "Flash? Please come to me. Please, Flash?" The expression on his face tore a hole in my heart. He shakily balanced himself on the curb while his mother gently wrestled him, tears spilling from both of their eyes.

"Come with me, Alton, honey . . . This is nothing for you to see. Flash is in God's hands now."

"No, he isn't!" he snapped back clapping his hands and whistling. He made kissing noises and begged earnestly for Flash to rise. Then he turned to Harold and pleaded, "Great Uncle Willis, please do something. Can you fix him? Can you? I've seen you fix everything, cars, TVs . . ."

"I'm sorry, nephew. Yeah, I'm real handy with my tools, but I ain't no veterinarian. You know if I could do something right now I wouldn't hesitate; you know that. But your mom's right. We can't help ol' Flash. He's . . ."

Alton bowed his head sobbing. "I don't care what anybody says! Flash is fine. He'll get up; you'll see." His body collapsed into Wilma's waiting arms. She fell back on the grass in her white dress, rocking him back and forth in her lap.

"Olisa, I thought I told you to stay on the porch?"

Still holding the leash, Olisa looked up at Grace with those melancholy eyes and said, "Can't we take him to a hospital?"

"No, Olisa. We might make it even worse if we try to pick him up. It's too late."

"But can't we make Flash better? He's hurt. I know we can help him."

Grace gently rubbed her shoulders and stroked her braids. "Honey, there's nothing we can do. Flash is on his way to a much better place where he will never ever feel pain again."

"But it was my fault. I have to fix it!"

That statement worried me. Olisa's face looked very strained to me as she rubbed her cheeks with her fingers and her body swayed from side to side. I really thought Grace should have taken her inside the house. Olisa's face was taut, and her eyes were disturbingly enormous. But then, abruptly, the tension in Olisa's face faded. She dropped the leash and walked over to Alton and rested her hand gently on his shoulder.

"Please don't cry any more, Alton. It's going to be all right. Watch. I'll make Flash feel better, okay? I promise. I can do magic. But you have to stop crying, okay? You must believe . . ." Her voice was eerily calm and reassuring. Its tone belied her age. She gazed deeply into his eyes.

A glimmer of hope dawned on his face, the kind that resides exclusively within children.

"Olisa, don't . . . You can't promise him something like that."

"Yes, I can."

Grace stopped short of saying another word when she caught sight of the intensity brewing in her eyes. What she saw in them was indescribable, something she had never seen before. What Olisa's eyes conveyed were as hugely unsettling as they were comforting. Olisa's eyes cast an opaque, misty otherworldly aura. Though her voice was that of a child's, its tenor registered an adult's resoluteness.

Grace was at a loss as to what to do.

Not Olisa.

Without any trepidation, Olisa knelt down next to Flash and stroked his body, gingerly touching him with her fingertips. Her eyes were riveted to the points she kneaded on his body like a surgeon as her fingers tiptoed delicately along the contours of Flash's body.

Grace walked over to me and said, "Joseph, remember the conversation we had not long ago about Olisa?"

"Conversation? Wait—oh, you mean . . ."

"Uh-huh. That talk. I believe it's happening."

Grace stoically posted herself behind Olisa like a sentry and crossed her arms tightly.

A small crowd of looky-loos wandered in like tumbleweed, many of their faces registering revulsion as they caught sight of Olisa with the dog. All I heard were voices coming from everywhere.

"What a horrible thing!"

"What kind of mother would let their child get that close to a dead animal, let alone touch the nasty thing?"

"Yeah, that's the most disgusting thing I've ever seen!"

"Nobody called the Humane Society to get this poor thing out of here? That's what they oughta be doing."

"The parents should be ashamed!"

Grace ignored the drone. The footguards at Buckingham Palace couldn't have been more impassive. Still, I feared a more direct confrontation as the anonymous grumblings grew louder.

Mr. Willis whispered in her ear, "Grace, don't let her do this. It's not good."

Grace placed her forefinger to her lips to shush him. But he couldn't hold back. He even more sternly whispered: "The dog is dying. Think about it. Both of these kids could be traumatized. Here, let me get her."

"Daddy, don't . . . touch . . . her! She knows what she's doing."

"But Grace . . ."

I felt sorry for Mr. Willis. I think he was shocked, exasperated, and a little hurt by Grace's cutting tone. Even so, it all washed away when I saw him mouth: "What the . . ."

The crowd gasped unanimously.

Flash's body rose and fell heavily. Beneath the fur, the skin undulated. It defied logic, but I realized that the bones were actually shifting, changing shapes, reforming. His skin rippled like snakes were crawling underneath it.

When it ended, Flash's eyes sprung open.

"Oh shit!" someone in the crowd gasped.

Flash struggled to his feet rising like a newborn colt. His eyes were glassy when he raised his head but became more animated as he looked around. He licked Olisa's hand as she helped him struggle to his feet like a newborn colt. Weakly, he braced on all fours. The stunned crowd was quiet as they uneasily ogled this ongoing phenomenon. Flash reticently tapped the pavement with his left front paw, testing for pain. The fur on his right side was matted with blood, but his body showed no signs of injury. Not one whine left his mouth.

The scream that shattered the silence was Alton's. Squealing with happiness, he broke out of his mother's arms and flew toward Flash.

"Alton, you be careful!" Wilma yelled, though her protective tone was overridden by the astounded expression on her face mirroring ours. She watched her son kiss and wrap his arms around Flash's body while the dog ecstatically licked his face.

"Mama, see? It's all right. Flash is alive. I told you. I told everyone he's not dead, but no one believed me!" he yelled triumphantly. "Only Oli did!"

Alton wasn't the most affectionate kid in the world, but I'll be damned if he didn't kiss a beaming Olisa on the cheek, making her blush. The two of them jubilantly jumped up and down. Soon other kids joined the celebration while the adults stood by speechless.

Sweating profusely, Cadillac Man stared at the bloody pool on the street. He gazed skyward, then closed his eyes and mouthed a silent prayer. He slapped his fedora back on and slowly drove away. He was lucky no police were around because he zoomed through the red light at the end of the block.

"Praise God almighty," Katherine murmured reverentially as she locked arms with Harold and Wilma in mutual awe.

I wrapped my arm around Grace's shoulder who shivered like she was standing in forty-degree weather instead of seventy-five. She sighed and slid her arm around my waist.

"How did you know?"

There was a long pause before Grace spoke. "I trusted what I saw in her eyes."

Flash was now totally revitalized. He raced around the children playfully growling and nipping at their heels like nothing ever happened. Except blood was still caked on his body. Flash darted in between people to retrieve the soft-ball he saw still lying against the curb. Some of the lingering adults fearfully backed away clearing a wide path for him. Flash trotted victoriously into the front yard with the ball in his mouth. Laughing, Alton and friends charged after him. The Doberman zigzagged past them and dashed into the backyard with the kids wildly in pursuit. Olisa was the last to follow. She waved at her parents before closing and locking the backyard fence.

The looky-loos slowly dispersed like rats in the glare of a flashlight. I heard two elderly women mumbling as they passed by us.

"Baby, that little girl put some hoodoo-voodoo on that animal to make it get up like that."

"Mavis, don't be ridiculous. That dog was probably just knocked out. Ain't nobody got power like that."

"Hmmph. The Devil do."

"Oh, please . . ."

"Girl, I knows what I seen. That child raised that dog from the dead with some of that evil stuff and got her mother standing right behind her whispering some kind of chant. You can bet all of them people is from Louisiana and they done brought that wicked stuff with them!"

"Oh, Mavis, how do you know where they're from? Have you ever talk to them?"

"Don't need to. I ain't never talked to Satan either, but I seen his work."

Wilma waited long enough for the women to pass out of ear hustling range. She gazed up at me. "Something was bound to happen, sooner or later, right?"

"Yes, but I never suspected she could do that!"

"I'm not even sure she knew she could until her emotions pushed her to."

"Well, I know this . . . What happened today needs to stay here in Oakwood."

"And how do you propose to keep all these people quiet, Joseph?"

"If there are no other public displays in the future, I'm betting people will start second-guessing what they actually saw. Hopefully, over time it'll turn into some kind of Venice Beach folklore."

"That's an awful lot of hoping."

"Uh-huh, with a little praying mixed in."

We all joined Mama Willis on the porch. Sitting and slowly rocking on the porch swing, she cradled Noel who slept through the entire event. She looked at Harold.

"So whatcha think, son?"

"Maybe the dog only had a concussion or something," Harold Willis replied weakly, staring at the shimmering blood still on the street.

"I think you know what you saw, Mr. Willis."

"Yep."

Wilma leaned against the porch railing, grass stains marring her white dress. "Hey, bro, sis, is there something y'all forgot to tell me?"

I grabbed her hand. "Wilma, if you've got a little time to spare, why don't we go inside and eat, and then we'll talk."

"Brother, I got all night."

"So yeah, Unc, just like what she did with Flash, Olisa was a study in determination. She was like a master musician. Her hands massaged this dude gently, rhythmically and deftly crisscrossed his stomach over and over. I watched her fingers tiptoe delicately along the contours of his upper body with a surgeon's precision.

"About that time two paramedics arrived. One of them walked up to her and got all condescending stating, 'Lady, whatever the hell you're doing, you need to stop *right now* before it gets worse. We got this! We're taking him to emergency. I'm sorry are you *listening* to me!'

"I wanted to knock him on his ass, but Olisa was so unbelievably calm I didn't move. She casually looked up at him. Her eyes exuded such intensity I almost felt sorry for my boy. He reflexively stepped back like she threw a punch at him.

"'It's over. There's no need for him to go,'" Olisa told him.

"'What? He's dead? Ma'am, we need you to please move out the way!'

"I helped Olisa up while the paramedics attended to the dude that got stabbed. The front of her flowered midi dress was soaked with blood. I asked her if she was okay, but she could barely talk; she seemed super tired and disoriented."

Of course, that I didn't like hearing.

"Meanwhile, I'm checking out the paramedics' faces and they look bewildered. One of them said to the other, 'I can't find a stab entry or wound.' The other paramedic says, 'What are you talking about? That can't be; there's blood everywhere!' His partner shook his head and said, 'If you don't believe me, check for yourself.' The other paramedic shakes his head while examining the victim's stomach and comments, 'This is crazy! It makes no sense.' 'I know . . . and his breathing is normal,' the other one replies. As serious as it is, I'm cracking up inside because both their eyes stray in disbelief to Olisa who I'm holding up because she can barely stand.

"The tatted-up gangbanger they've been working on abruptly opens his eyes and scared the bejesus out of everyone encircling them, including his boys. When the teenager bolted upright, the crowd let out a gasp that musta been heard around the world. Then he shoved one of the paramedics' hands away screaming, 'Get the fuck off me!'

"'Easy, man. Relax,' the paramedic remarked. 'We just wanted to check on you. You okay?'

"Dude snapped, 'I'm good! Why you ask me something like that?'

"'Because they say you got stabbed. There's blood everywhere, but we don't see any evidence of that except for that knife next to you.'

"When he saw the knife beside him, it was like he got hit with PTSD. He gripped his stomach like someone was stabbing him again. In his panic he frantically surveyed the people around him until his eyes fell upon Olisa. Nothing registered on his face at first, and then you could tell—he remembered. Waving the paramedics and even his boys away from him, he managed to stand up. He walked over to Olisa still trying to maintain a tough persona in front of everyone."

Gumbo smirked and shook his head. "Uncle Joe, do you know that bad-ass gangster trembled from the top of his head to the tip of his toes, then fell to his knees at Olisa's feet and wept like a baby? And he wasn't the only one messed up. Some pretty hardcore hombres were shaking, too, after witnessing what she had done."

"They weren't by themselves, Al. Everyone in the vicinity got quiet."

"Ain't that the truth, Lara? Even I forgot where I was until Lara pointed out that KLSC camera shooting away like crazy."

"Let me guess—Eva Sanchez and her cameraman 'Simply Red'?"

"You got it, Unc," Alton laughed, shoveling more popcorn into his mouth. "But we also saw a growing crowd moving in closer, many with their phones raised. That's when Lara told me, 'Alton, it's time to go!'"

"No doubt she was right. No one drove so it was time to step. Lara and I locked arms with Olisa and swiftly escorted her through the amassing crowd to Byron who had been crazily waving at us like he was doing semaphore. Lara and I ushered Olisa into the van, and we got the fuck outta there before anything could happen! 'Scuse me, Unc."

"That's all right. Who's Byron?"

"Byron's one of the regular sunglasses vendors on the boardwalk, a Japanese dude. He parks his van behind the booth. I think he and Olisa trade services all the time. You know, he gives her glasses, she gives him a twenty minute massage, stuff like that."

"Runs much deeper than that, Alton," added Lara. "Byron's wife suffered from cataracts and was waiting until she could scrounge up the finances to afford an operation. Olisa massaged her eyes, and now she sees with no problem. In fact, her vision is better than it ever was."

They waited for my reaction. I needed a moment to absorb everything. It was all so overwhelming. I had already developed a raging headache. Finally, I asked, "So how was Olisa through all of this?"

"Spacey."

"Uh, uh, not spacey, Al," Lara interjected. "Did you see her eyes? It was more like someone lit a candle in them. When I pulled her into Byron's van, her hands were practically burning. Can you imagine what effect this must have on her body to prevent someone from dying? She wasn't spacey; she was serene. We were the only ones freaking out."

"Yeah, you got that right, baby. I'm so glad you were there. When we got Olisa home, Lara cleaned her up, changed her clothes, and got her to lie down and chill out. Two minutes later, she cashed in her ticket to dreamland."

"Man, I owe you guys for taking care of my girl in a crisis."

"You don't owe us a thing, Uncle Joe." Lara put her arm around my shoulders. "You guys are my family. I'd do anything for you."

"Well, I appreciate it."

Grace burst through the kitchen door in her all-white nurses' outfit. "Who's eating nachos in here? I want some! I'm starving! You guys wouldn't believe what kind of day I had at the hospital."

"Sit down, Grace," I said. "Your day is just beginning."

Breaking News!

A Dramatic July the 4th at Venice Beach.

Gang Violence.

A Moment of Courage.

A Miracle? You Decide . . .

Up next on KLSC, the station that takes pride in giving you the full report. Join us tonight at 11:00!

This broadcast appeared during several commercial breaks during the television movie, which included a chyron during the show occasionally superimposed across the screen urging viewers to watch an incredible July the fourth event on KLSC at eleven. One commercial segment showed Black and Brown gangbangers throwing down, while in another, Olisa was clearly seen caressing the injured youth's stomach who was lying on his back in her lap.

Olisa was now awake, but other than asking her how she was feeling, we could tell she really didn't want to talk about what happened on the beach.

We'd save that conversation for another time. She also refused to watch the broadcast that would be on in about five minutes. She stood up ready to leave.

"Hey, cuz, you sure you don't want to watch this?" Alton inquired.

"For what?"

Alton shrugged his shoulders.

"So where are you going?"

"Out to my studio, Dad. Listen to some music, do a little reading."

"Just don't go anywhere else right now, okay?"

"I won't."

"Want a little company?" Lara asked.

Olisa grabbed her hand, and they left.

Even though my cell phone was on low it still startled me. "Hello? Hello? *Hello* . . . Papa Willis?"

"Hey, you watching?"

"Yeah."

"Huh?"

"I said yeah I'm watching!" I yelled, pissed that Harold had probably forgotten to turn his hearing aid up; plus his TV was loud.

We sat on the phone in silence as Papa Willis flipped to other TV channels. When it sounded like stereo in my ear, I knew he had returned back to KLSC. His voice sounded more gravelly than usual. "Saw the commercials; thought maybe some of the other stations might be carrying the report. Guess we knew it might happen someday," he sighed. "Damn!"

"Yep."

"Huh?"

"Yeah, I agree!"

"Give me a call after the news or tomorrow if you want. I'm sure you guys are probably going to want to talk."

"Okay, I will. Call you later."

"Yeah, it's gonna get better. Bye!"

"Unc, Aunt Grace, they're showing it now!" Alton turned up the sound.

The good news was, the Olisa story, thus far, failed to make national news. The bad news was, KLSC gave it a tremendous amount of coverage. Ms. Sanchez looked like a million bucks on screen. Her light-brown eyes exuded a glow of confidence, and her personable attitude made you feel like she was discussing the news with you in your living room. She rolled those Rs subtly enough to express her pride in her Latina heritage without alienating the local station's mainstream viewership.

"Good evening, Los Angeles! I'm Eva Sanchez, and tonight my story begins as another redundant chapter revolving around the recent gang violence that plagues our city. However, it ends as an essay on courage, humanity, and maybe . . . a miracle. Tonight you'll see for yourself what occurred this July fourth afternoon on the packed Venice Beach Boardwalk.

"Venice Beach is certainly no stranger to gang violence. Years ago, the war between Black and Latino youth claimed nineteen lives and sixty-seven injuries over a ten-month period, including many innocent people. Over time another truce was formed between the two groups, but that was all forgotten today. There are several rumors as to what initiated the conflict, like fighting over a woman; nonetheless, that's neither here nor there, because it escalated into some of the footage you are about to see. I warn you—many of the images you will see contain very graphic violence," she stated with a stern expression.

"There they go. Look at 'em, Uncle Joe," murmured Alton leaning over in his chair and attentively watching the screen.

The television displayed muddled scenes of kids duking it out. My eyes centered on the frightened faces in the crowd as open-mouthed people screamed and stampeded in all directions. The jumbled camera visuals made it hard to decipher what the hell was going on. Obviously, the cameraman got knocked down as sky and rooftops haphazardly came into focus. Yet, even that added to the drama.

"Courage is a quality not exclusive to gender, race, nationality, age, or economic status. Tonight you will see a woman that showed more bravery than many of us will see in a lifetime. They say our society is more apathetic than ever before. What you see tonight may skew all your perceptions."

Sometime later, I heard film sequences won some type of news award for their poignant imagery. They showed Olisa standing defiantly between the two gangs, unbraided hair fanning wildly behind her, arms spread out, a sorceress casting spells to keep the snarling wolves at bay.

"I apologize for the loss of sound. This woman who has placed her life in jeopardy is pleading for them to stop, begging them to respect the precious lives of the innocents as well as themselves. Unfortunately, we have no visual proof, except for eyewitnesses that the young man you see lying on the ground is mortally wounded. Even so, keep watching . . ."

I glanced at Alton. He somehow conveniently omitted that Olisa thrust herself into the middle of the dangerous fracas yelling at the opposing sides to stop and move back. He knew I was looking at him but smartly kept his eyes on the screen. I took a deep breath and returned to watching the newscast.

Olisa sat cross-legged on the ground huddled over him, his upper body hoisted onto her lap. Our vision was distorted by masses of hair draped protectively over him like a pulled curtain. All we could make out were her hands working steadily over his ululating belly. Each swipe of her hands became more crimson with his blood.

Through a shaky blue sky, we spotted police officers and paramedics in the upper realm of the camera barging through the multitudes. Zooming through a gap in the emerging crowd, we found a Latino youth in a blood-soaked t-shirt embracing Olisa like a lost child. Next, we glimpsed Alton's broad back as he quickly hustled Olisa out of the camera's eye view, followed by Laura looking warily behind her. They vanished, and we were left with the beachgoers hovering speechlessly around the boy who was stabbed.

"Hey, wait a minute! Where's my man?" quizzed Alton, frowning at the screen.

"Who are you talking about, Gumbo?" Grace inquired.

"The big fella! He shielded up when we ducked outta there. Ain't no way you can miss that big boy. That brotha had to be about seven feet tall, skin blacker than blue, and dazzling snow-white hair. Carried a mean bad-ass-looking gold trumpet with him. I figured he was one of the musicians that jammed from time to time with the other players on the beach."

"Did he say anything to you?" I asked.

"Never said a word. Brother man was all about action!"

I swallowed hard as I thought about the hulking figure I saw decades ago on the rooftop during the Los Angeles riots.

Focused back on TV, I saw the formerly stricken youth now standing up, ripping off his bloodied shirt, and triumphantly waving it like a flag.

"According to my sources, we found out the youth waving his shirt is the notorious gangbanger Ernesto Padilla, aka Chato! This same kid you see laughing and beating his stomach with no pain was critically injured only minutes ago. The witnesses we interviewed swear there's no doubt he was stabbed repeatedly. Is it possible this woman who intervened in the violence healed him. Have we witnessed a modern-day miracle? Or is this some kind of an elaborate hoax?"

"You go, girl . . . Milk it for everything you got!" I blurted out sarcastically, peeved and ready to throw up.

Chato jumped around playfully shadowboxing like he just won the featherweight championship. Throngs surrounded him, cheering and patting him heartily on the back. Hundreds of needlepoint hairs teamed to form a dark shadow on his closely shaved head. His thin muscular body boasted a gallery of tattoos. As Eva sidled up to him with her microphone, his eyes danced wildly; his breath came in spurts, and his feet shifted continuously as if searching for steady ground. He clutched his bloody shirt like it was a souvenir.

"With us we have Ernesto Padilla who amazingly has recovered allegedly from multiple stab wounds in the chest and stomach and—"

"*Allegedly?* What you talkin' about allegedly? Ain't nothing allegedly about it; shit was real!"

"Okay, got it. So, Ernesto, how do you feel? It's hard to believe you're the same person I saw minutes ago lying still on the ground."

"Yeah, he got me good, ya know what I'm sayin'! Peep this . . . this is where he stuck me. Man, I thought it was all over for my ass . . . know what I'm sayin' . . . All I remember is this Black mutha, dude sittin' on top of me and hammering my chest and stomach with a knife, ya know. I'm just happy to be still alive, know what I'm sayin?"

"I do. So what started the fight?"

"Oh, some stupid-ass"—*blip*—"over a woman or something, but it don't matter no more. We just needed an excuse to get busy. It's all good now, cuz I ain't into banging no more. Tossin' up fools is dead for me now, you feel me? God sent me a sign. He's telling me it's time to give it up before I get smoked. My homies will tell you I ain't never been afraid of dying . . . That comes with the territory . . . but something was different this time. I don't know. Maybe I'm tired of seeing *mi abuela* in tears. My grandmother must have felt something because she said to me this morning, 'You keep on doing these bad things and you gon die soon.' Told me she prays every day for the Lord to give me a sign before it's too late. I guess God sent me the message on a billboard today so me and everybody could see it!" he cackled.

"You called it a sign. You really believe this woman healed you?"

"You didn't see it? Hell yeah, she healed me. I ain't never been in that much pain in my life. Scared to breathe and stuff. I thought my guts was gonna fall out, ya hear me? Then she touched me . . . It was like someone giving you a warm bath, ya know what I'm sayin'?"

"Stop hittin' that crack, Chato!" yelled out one of his boys.

"See, my homies is laughing over there, but I'm serious. She saved me. I was in total darkness, couldn't see nuthin', until I saw this bright light, and it became super-hot. I open my eyes, and I see all this nasty-ass blood all over me, 'cept I'm feelin' *good*! Man, all this time I thought everything said about her was just talk, you know? But it's all true—she's got the power. Wouldn't surprise me if the Virgin of Guadalupe worked through her, know what I'm sayin'? Look at me; I am him! I'm the proof!"

He proudly pounded his chest, machismo oozing from him, along with a challenging stare daring anyone to dispute his claim. He delivered it with the same amount of gusto he'd used to protect his turf. "It's a trip, you know. She took care of me just like that," he declared, snapping his fingers.

"Did she say anything to you?"

"I don't remember all that much, you know . . . One thing is, I didn't know home girl spoke Spanish. That's what I'm saying, about the Virgin. I was so out of it, I thought I was a little boy again. It was like I was home in bed with my mother taking care of me or something, you feel me? What I remember is she kept saying, 'Believe and I will heal you.'"

"You said people said things about her. What does that mean? Who is she?"

"Aww, everybody that hangs out here knows her, ain't that right, *vato*?" He grabbed one of his buddies plastered beside him, mugging at the camera and playfully rubbing his bald head.

"Aww yeah, bro. All the locals knows her. *Mi abuela* says she is a *curandera*, someone who can heal people. I didn't really believe in the"—*blip*—"until now, ya know what I'm sayin'? Man, she has our total *respeto*, you know? We don't bother her or diss her cuz everyone knows what's up. If you got problems, drugs, health, they say you can go to her and she'll hook you up. They say she can tell the future too, man. You don't mess with people who talk to the *espiritus*, you feel me?"

"Do you plan to stop gangbanging too?" Eva asked with a slight smirk on her face.

Chato's homey held his head down for a second, smiling sheepishly. "Naw, I didn't say all that because that's family, ya dig? But we're gonna try real hard to keep the truce forever, you know?" He tapped fists with one of the Black gang members with a watch cap on his head standing nearby. "Look,

Chato's free to do what he wants cuz he's been *chosen*. Usually, you can't leave the family, but ain't nobody gonna"—*blip*—"with my boy now, *con respeto*."

Just in time, the camera cut back to the newsroom desk as gang signs were displayed, although it didn't drown out the crowd cheering enthusiastically behind them.

"And that's our extended story for this Sunday evening, Brevin."

"Wow! Fascinating, Eva," replied the handsome and eternally suntanned anchorman, Brevin Ireland, eyeing her appraisingly while importantly shuffling through a pile of who knows what papers. "What a way to wrap up a July the fourth weekend!" added Brevin, now showcasing a thoughtful expression on his face. "So what do we know about this woman I'd call the Good Witch of Venice?" he asked, cocking his head, squinting his blue eyes, and evidently delighted with his hastily conceived sobriquet.

"Not much, Brevin. All we know right now is that she's a regular on the Venice Beach Boardwalk scene giving massages, readings, and spiritual advice. However, the locals swear she's the real thing. I'm also told she is very humble and not one to seek publicity. I'm hoping she'll consent to do an interview. The public would love to learn more about this enigmatic hero."

"Well, Eva, I for one would love to hear more about this remarkable woman. It's an amazing story. Please follow up on this one for us."

"It will be my pleasure, Brevin."

Black matter exploded onto the screen as I disgustedly punched the remote but not quickly enough to escape the specter of Eva's ebullient face.

Afterwards, nothing was discussed. We shrugged our shoulders and called it a night as we all went our separate ways. Gumbo left with Laura after decimating our refrigerator and headed to their apartment in Mid City Los Angeles near the historic West Adams district. Grace retired to our bedroom. I chose to take a dip in our outdoor Jacuzzi. Nothing could beat soaking in the bubbling tub's soothing heat as I gazed at the blackened sky accosted by a sprinkling of slithering clouds.

Soon my solitude was interrupted by the sounds of police sirens whizzing down the street. Overhead a loud chomping "ghetto bird" passed by with its cyclopean eye flashing a wide swath of menacing light over Oakwood, as usual canvassing the area for the perpetrators of some crime. It was just another night in Venice.

The moist heat was the perfect tonic for all the stress that clung to my body. My fingers had turned into link sausages from all the soaking, but the weight of the world fell off my shoulders, at least for a little while. Slipping on my bathrobe, I peeked out the bedroom window at the attached studio. Grace was in bed propped up by two huge pillows and paging through a magazine.

"Olisa's light is still on, Grace."

Grace put the magazine down. "I'm sure she's sitting up reading."

"Why did she have to get involved? Why doesn't she just mind her own business?"

"You're upset because she helped somebody?"

"No, I'm upset because all hell's going to break loose. She helped some stupid shit that probably got what he deserved."

"Olisa can't choose who to help when someone's hurt. You know that."

"I know, I know . . . I just don't think being under a microscope is going to be a whole lot of fun for her."

"Maybe it won't be as bad as you think, Joseph."

"Grace, you saw the look in Eva what's-her-name's eyes. She's not about to let it rest!"

"Yes, but it was only one incident, and if Olisa doesn't do anything else, what further proof does she have?"

"In our dictionary *if* is a five-syllable word. You think you could ever convince Olisa to turn away an injured animal?"

"No, and I wouldn't want to."

"No argument here."

"Joseph, even though it's captured on film, it may not get picked up by the national media. They may just see it as a cute local feel-good story. Maybe it will just fade away after a while."

"Uh, uh, I want to believe that, but I don't think so. It's just a matter of time. It's always been a matter of time, hon," I remarked climbing into bed.

"I guess that's true, Joe. We tried for so long to protect her secret, didn't we? It's out of our hands now. Maybe this is what God wants. We'll just have to trust."

"Yeah, I guess . . ." I wrapped my arm around her and caressed her shoulder as she cuddled into me. "So what time do you think Noel's coming by tomorrow?"

Grace scooted up. "Noel never told me he was coming by."

"Grace, please, get real. We're talking about our son, the one we've known for twenty-eight years."

"Early, very early," she sighed as she laid her head down on the pillow. I squeezed her affectionately and turned off the night light.

No matter how hard I tried, I couldn't get myself to relax and fall asleep. It reminded me of the time I had insomnia a few months after Noel was born.

Counting sheep certainly didn't do the trick, so I decided to check on the kids. It was about 1:30 AM, and I figured the baby was on the verge of waking up as he usually did at that hour. He was sound asleep in his crib. I tiptoed into Olisa's bedroom, and she was on her knees at the head of her bed, intently peering through the parted curtains.

"Hey, what you doing up?" I whispered. "You see something outside?"

Not a muscle moved as she continued to gaze out the window. I heard soft sniffling.

"What's wrong, kid? You have a nightmare?"

"No, Daddy. The light next door woke me up. It's so hot and bright."

Her head turned, and tears streamed down her cheeks. Her hands were folded and pressing against her chest. She trembled slightly.

I immediately thought waking up unexpectedly and then seeing a light on next door must have frightened her. I peeked out her window through the parted curtains at the house. To me, the light wasn't bright at all; it glowed dimly behind the curtain as I watched a shadowy figure pacing back and forth. Ethan probably couldn't sleep, either. Gaping out the window made me feel like a voyeur, so I clapped the curtains closed.

"Daddy, can we help Mr. Robinson? He's very sick. If he dies, will he go to heaven?"

I sat down and embraced her. "Honey, what kind of questions are these? Did Mr. Robinson tell you that he's ill?"

"No."

"Then why are you talking like this?"

"When I held Mr. Robinson's hand today, it was really hot. His eyes were very red. He felt sick. We should wrap him in a blanket like you and Mommy do with me when I am sick, Dada. Let's go over there and take care of him, okay?"

"That's sweet, kid, but we don't want to disturb him by knocking on his door at this hour. I saw him yesterday morning, and we talked for a long time about the Dodgers baseball game the other night. Don't you worry your precious little heart about him. Ethan's fine. He may be eighty-six, but he will be around for twice as long. You can believe that!"

Ethan Robinson and his wife, Carla, lived next door and had been in the neighborhood for over fifty years. If you wanted to know how much Los Angeles had changed over the years, all you had to do was ask Ethan. He was one of the early Negro pioneers to settle here after World War II and very proud of it. He still had chickens, geese, pigs, cats, dogs, and even a peacock in his yard. He told me he had a pony until all the neighbors decided they'd grown tired of smelling horseshit.

Also, there was no better watchdog in the world than his black goose, Mr. Midnight, who honked a warning to all intruders. And you didn't dare provoke him. I'll never forget the newsboy who was feeling his oats and decided to challenge him like a matador to a bull. That goose charged him so fast that boy set an unrecorded high-jump record as he sailed over the fence.

Mr. Robinson was a character's character shining those pearly whites from wrinkled burnt-wood-colored face. He always joked that he had more lines on his face than a California road map. But he also claimed he earned it, and every line told a story. Even when Mrs. Robinson died in her sleep several years ago, he courageously maintained his sense of humor.

Olisa loved going over there. It was like being at the circus with all the animals he had there. "Whatchoo doing, girl?" he'd ask with his rapid-fire delivery. "You so cute I'm going to eat you up." Groups of kids hung out at Mr. Robinson's. He was the neighborhood griot sharing stories with the kids about his Mississippi upbringing and all the odd jobs he held, from tanning hides to hopping railroad cars.

My grandpa Henry was his closest friend. Those two old curmudgeons raised the art of debate to its highest plateau. Sitting around playing dominoes and checkers was their Friday night routine. I don't think a day passed that Mr. Robinson didn't share a tale with me about my grandpa Henry after he passed, wistfulness blanketing his face.

Ethan's hearing had been getting worse over the years. He didn't hear me when I yelled hello to him one Friday over the hedge. I figured he was just deep in conversation with a friend as I peeked over the bushes. He played checkers by himself, but not really; there was an empty seat on the other side of the board, and I heard him say, "That's right, Henry . . . Study long, study wrong. Don't blame me 'cause you getting your ass whooped!" Then he slapped his thigh with laughter and slowly eased back into his chair as puffs of smoke wafted from his pipe and dissipated into the night air.

Friday games were still on.

I was under the impression his health was excellent even though he was in his eighties. He regularly took early morning walks around 6:00 AM.

"I really think you had a nightmare, honey."

She looked at me as if she was really confused by what I said. Tears continued to roll down her cheeks.

"Aww, honey . . . Here, let me wipe those tears. I promise you it was just a bad dream. Lie down and get some sleep. You'll see. Tomorrow everything will be all right. We'll check on Ethan first thing in the morning, okay?"

"Okay, Daddy. I love you."

"Love you more, baby."

I gave her a peck on the forehead. She was already falling asleep. I stayed up with her until I heard that lovely tiny snore that always made me smile.

As I tiptoed into our bedroom, sidestepping the crib, there was a huge, startling boom that reverberated in the still night. Mr. Robinson's dogs were baying like crazy, and the goose was honking loudly.

Baby Noel started crying.

I heard a click, and the incandescent table lamp beamed like a spotlight as Grace hurriedly threw on her robe and lifted our crying baby out of his crib.

"What was that? It sounded like it came from Ethan's house next door!"

"I don't know." My stomach slowly curled into a tight fist.

"Are you going to check it out?"

"Yeah, I guess," I said, not moving.

"You don't think it was a prowler at Mr. Robinson's, do you? Joseph, what's going on? You look so pale. You're shaking. Is everything okay? Should I call the police?"

"I don't know, Grace, okay? I'll check in a minute. I'm just waiting to see if I hear anything else."

Noel's screams, the dog's hacking barks, and Mr. Midnight's train of honks rang in my ears.

Olisa squeezed past the open bedroom door and stood there in her lavender pajamas, rubbing her eyes. She toddled over and gripped my numbed legs in a bear hug.

It took a while for me to rid myself of the temporary paralysis that stalled my system. Prying Olisa's arms from my legs, I gathered her in my arms and took her to Grace and the baby. The dogs howled with the sounds of the approaching sirens.

Grace gave Noel his pacifier and rocked him in her arms. She peeped through the living room curtains. "Three police cars and now an ambulance pulled up in front of Ethan's. I've got a bad feeling, Joseph."

"Uh-huh, me too . . . Stay here."

I grabbed my robe and reticently headed out the door, thinking about the silhouetted figure pacing back and forth in front of the window. Squad car lights flashed across the lawn. Grave faces were planted at their windows. Police were milling about all over the front and back yard. Flashlights swept Ethan's front yard. Mr. Midnight, the goose, screamed and hissed relentlessly in the corner of the yard at each person that walked onto the property. The front door was wide open.

An officer blocked me from going in as I approached.

"Sorry, you can't come in."

"What's going on? Is Ethan okay?"

"You family?" she asked.

"Pretty much. My wife and I are next door. His wife of over fifty years died last year. Just tell me—is he okay?" She didn't have to say anything, I received my answer when I glimpsed over her shoulder. In the living room, Ethan slumped in a chair was being examined by a man with a glove. Through moistening eyes, I saw him removing a rifle from between Ethan's awkwardly splayed legs. There were huge blotches of red behind him on the wall. The officer's face softened when she saw my reaction.

"Sir, I'm so sorry. Can we talk to you?"

"Yes," I answered in a child's voice.

Mr. Robinson committed suicide. The police woman mentioned a scribbled note they found stating Ethan found out he had pancreatic cancer. It said how much he missed his wife and that he wasn't going to let strangers in a hospital see him through his last days. He asked for God's forgiveness and told Carla he'd meet her at "heaven's front gate" . . . and that was that.

Afterwards, I played repeatedly in my head what I would say to Olisa. "Sorry, everything was not okay as I promised. I was wrong; you were right. If I had listened to you and trusted you, maybe I could have saved his life." We lost a neighbor and a friend; and our daughter knew it could happen before anyone else.

Olisa knew.

I was talking with one of the mourners after the funeral as we walked away from the gravesite when Olisa grasped my hand. She beckoned for me to lean down and said, "Daddy, we don't have to be sad anymore; Mr. Robinson is happy now."

"Uh-huh. How do you know that, kid?"

"Cuz he just whispered it in my ear. His lips tickle," she giggled.

After her pronouncement, she skipped happily away to Grace up ahead pushing Noel in his stroller.

I heard her say, "Mommy, Mommy, guess what happened?"

After that, I never doubted Olisa's words again.

Never.

Chapter 3

After some time I fell asleep. My dreams were haunted by lurking shadowy monsters who followed me home as I cautiously wandered down the streets of my old neighborhood in Compton. Grotesque distorted figures hiding behind trees, peering over hedges, hunched upon walls, and stalking me wherever I went . . . No matter how fast I ran or where I hid, they always found me. Desperate to escape this mad world, I leaped into the air and flew over land and sea to areas I had never been but read about in travel magazines: warm, exotic, lush, and beautiful hideaways. The sensation of flying and traveling wherever I wanted to be made me feel in control. It brought me peace of mind. I was aware I was dreaming, so I tried to savor every precious moment. Of course my dreams were interrupted by a disconcerting bang.

"Sorry, honey, didn't mean to wake you. The cabinet drawer was stuck again." Grace's hair tickled my cheek as I smelled her perfume, followed by a warm wet kiss on my forehead. "Oh, by the way, your prediction was right—Noel's here. I'm going to say my hellos before I leave for General Hospital. I hear them talking in the kitchen. Oh, and please be nice."

"What are you talking about? I'm always nice to him."

"Uh-huh. I repeat, be nice."

A few blinks later, I parted company with my pillow. I splashed some ice-cold water on my face and guided myself through half-closed lids down the hallway to the promising smell of coffee.

"One of the Walking Dead appears! Morning, Dad."

"Morning, Noel." I plopped down in a chair. Olisa poured me a big mug of espresso.

"Dad, your red eyes match your robe. Sis, it might be better to hook him up intravenously."

"Noel's got jokes. Did anyone ever tell you comedy's not your calling?"

"Ha! Still a spark of life left in the old man," Noel laughed, clapping me on the shoulder as he scooted his chair next to mine. "So maybe now he'll seriously think about turning the Soul of Venice into a franchise."

I just shook my head and sipped on some more brew.

"Let's make it interesting. Suppose we play a game of Scrabble. If I win, we talk franchise."

"Son, you don't want no ass whooping this early in the morning. By the time I finish with you, I'll be wearing that Gucci warm-up suit you've got on and driving your Aston Martin! What's the score? I'm at least five games ahead."

"Only because you come up with all these crazy words you memorized from your little Scabble player's dictionary that no one would ever bother to use in this universe."

"Hey, whatever works. If you'd stop trying to hit all home runs with seven-letter words for the bonus points, you might be ahead."

"I'm a gambler, Pops, and gamblers take risks!"

"You guys kill me with your games," Olisa groaned. "Testosterone overload. And people wonder why we have wars! Men have to find someone they can physically dominate; it's in their DNA."

"Oh, I wouldn't go that far, Olisa. I think Pops and I are just frustrated nerds who deep down inside were wannabe athletes."

"Speak for yourself, junior flip. I was pretty good in track. Best high jumper in the high school conference."

"Come on, Dad; that's fine. But wouldn't you have liked to experience what if felt like to be a big-time superstar athlete? At least once, and all that goes with it: money, women, fame, and glory?"

"Man, I could care less."

"Is that right? So that's why you've rejected all my passionate entreaties to open up a major franchise of soul food restaurants and kill! Just imagine— the Soul of Manhattan, Soul of Seattle, Soul of Dallas, Atlanta, Chicago . . . doesn't that speak to you? All you've got to do is give me the green light, and I'll secure the funds."

"Already told you, too much work. I like our nice neat little business. Your aunt Wilma and I are in total control. We pay our bills and even make a little money now and then."

"Yeah, but I'm not talking a *little* money; I'm talking a lot of money. Dad, again, I'll do the legwork. All you and Aunt Wilma have to do is act as consultants, kick back, watch the money roll in, and enjoy life!"

I grunted and nodded my head as I sipped my hot brew. We'd been through this a hundred times.

"Little brother, you should know by now that Daddy doesn't want to franchise his restaurant. So give it a break and mind your own business."

"Yes, ma'am," Noel replied, grinning at his sister.

"Besides, he's not like you, Mr. Ambitious, Stanford MBA, and VP of talent and marketing at RPM Records." Olisa smiled admiringly as she stroked the smooth shiny waves in his short and fashionable haircut.

"I guess so . . . I'm just trying to look out for my pops. That's all."

"And I'm sure Daddy appreciates you," Olisa said rubbing my shoulders and adding an unnoticeable hard pinch.

"Yes," I muttered.

"Okay, I'll leave it alone, for now. Besides, the main reason I came by here is to toast Venice's newest celebrity!"

"Oh stop," Olisa laughed, quickly switching subjects. "I thought we were going to walk down to the beach and get some breakfast at the Fig Tree Café?"

"Let's do it," Noel replied, standing up and snatching his keys off the counter. "Dad, you coming?"

I gawked at them in disbelief. "Have y'all lost your damn mind? Has it dawned on you the effects of that broadcast last night? And now you want to casually head on down to the boardwalk like nothing happened?"

"Dad, hardly anyone will be at the beach this early on a Monday. Give it a few days and it will blow over. Watch."

"Yeah, and besides, she'll be with me."

"That's what I'm worried about."

"That's cold."

"Not trying to be, Noel. I just don't think it's a good idea. Things are too hot out there after yesterday."

"Dad, relax. Everything's cool. My guardian angel will take care of me." Her eyebrows lifted, and her eyes teasingly widened as she ominously surveyed the room. I wondered if she was half-serious. Olisa playfully pushed Noel out the kitchen door. On her way out she said, "Join us if you change your mind."

I took my shower, grabbed my bicycle out of the garage, and pedaled down to the boardwalk. The booths were being lackadaisically set up by low-lidded people sipping coffee. Cheap stuffed animals, incense stands, Rastafarian hats, and sunglasses were all being pulled out of cartons as vendors assembled their displays. A few derelicts stumbled by, muttering to themselves as I zigzagged between them. It was relatively quiet. My vision centered on a gathering of people in the distance ahead of me on the board-walk. I rode my bike straight toward the huddled figures. I knew what I'd find.

Olisa sat on a bench, ensconced in conversation with a blond dread-locked surfer covered in tattoos battling for space on his body. About ten people hung around, literally eavesdropping on their conversation. I was too far away to hear what was said as I leaned my bike against the railing encircling the Fig Tree's outdoor patio area. Occasionally, there were sporadic bursts of laughter as he peered sheepishly at the gathering crowd while Olisa held his hand, palm out, and continued to talk. A couple of times, his head jerked back dramatically, followed by intermittent giggles from the crowd. I wondered what startling revelation she just dropped on him.

"Why are you frowning, kid?" I asked as we drove home from the barbershop.

Her face was comically wrinkled up like a little prune. "Daddy, I thought we're not supposed to use bad words?"

"What word are you talking about, Oli?"

"I can't say it, Daddy."

"Go ahead; you can say it this once."

The word "nigger" jumped out of her mouth like it had been cooped up too long.

I stared straight ahead.

"Did you hear me, Daddy? You want me to say it again?"

"No, no. I heard you."

"That's a bad word, huh, Daddy? So why do all you guys in the barbershop say it over and over?"

"I don't know, honey. We're just joking. It's a way of letting off a little steam."

"But you told me if anybody called me that name, it was a bad thing."

That one caught me off-guard. "Yeah, I did, Olisa. But it's a little different in this case."

"Why?"

"We don't mean it. You know . . . it's just a way of kidding around, sometimes to make a point. You can't take it seriously. It's our way of defusing the term, you know keeping it from having any emotional strength. Look it's hard to explain."

The crease in her eyebrows tightened some more. *"If it's a joke, why do you feel bad whenever you say it?"*

"How do you know that?"

"I don't know." She frowned, kicking one leg. *"Because when I held your hand in the barbershop I felt a little pain every time you said it."*

We briefly sat in silence before I said, *"You're right. That's not a nice word, and we may not be able to keep the guys in the barbershop from using it, or in the streets, or in music, but you won't hear it coming out of my mouth anymore; deal?"*

"Deal, Daddy, 'cause we don't say bad words," she scolded with her forefinger in the air coupled with a goofy smile on her face. She grabbed my free hand and brushed it against her cheek, holding it there while my heart got soggy for the umpteenth time.

"Dad, Dad, we're over here!"

Noel waved at me from one of the patio tables. As I walked through the patio entrance, there was a twinge in the pit of my stomach the moment I spotted the back of a sharply dressed woman with short brown hair glistening from the touch of morning sunlight. Turning in her seat, Eva Sanchez flashed her bright white teeth in my direction.

Proudly, Noel announced, "Dad, this is—"

"Ms. Eva Sanchez."

"Please call me Eva, Mr. Timmerman." Her smile remained steadfastly in place as she ignored my icy demeanor.

"Just coffee, thank you," I told the waitress. I reluctantly sat down at their table.

"Noel and I have been having a wonderful chat. I didn't realize your son was so charming."

"Yeah, he's a chip off the old block, isn't he?"

She laughed politely. Noel narrowed his eyes at me.

"So what have y'all been talking about?" I asked, gravity tugging at the corners of my mouth.

"Oh you know me, Dad, I was talking her ear off about the recording industry." Noel rubbed his chin self-consciously after catching my why-are-you-consorting-with-the-enemy look.

"And it's been absolutely fascinating! I could listen to him all day long. One of these days I'm going to have to convince Noel to do an interview with me."

"Excellent idea. Noel would be a much better interview than Olisa; she's boring."

Eva chuckled; I didn't. I retained my scowl.

"Ms. Sanchez . . ."

"Eva."

"Fine, Eva. Just out of curiosity . . . do you usually come to this beach and this early?"

"No, Mr. Timmerman, rarely. I took a chance coming this morning. I heard Olisa often comes early, and I was hoping I'd find her here and be able to personally introduce myself to her and invite her to do an interview with me. But it looks like I'll have to wait in line."

The crowd had increased tremendously, to the extent two bicycle cops asked the crowd to clear the walkway. Olisa immediately stood up and greeted the officers warmly. She shepherded the crowd away from the café and further into the sand on the beach.

"Why are you doing this?" I asked. "Olisa doesn't need or want the publicity. She spent the last four years with the Peace Corps throughout Central America and Mexico. We have her safely back home now. Her life is good. We don't want to see her get hurt by this."

The perma-smile disappeared from her face as she empathetically touched my shoulder. "Mr. Timmerman, with all due respect . . . Can I call you Joseph?"

"Joe or Joseph is fine."

"Thank you. I understand your feelings. If I thought this was going to hurt her, I'd never attempt to secure an interview. I don't have to tell you your daughter is very special. And somebody like her needs to be praised and given accolades for who she is."

"And you might just receive a few accolades yourself, huh? Better ratings, higher salary, greater visibility for the station and yourself?"

"Guilty as charged, Joe. What else can I say? I'm a reporter, and that's what I do. And this is newsworthy. Olisa did something extraordinary. Not only did she prevent an escalation of gang violence on the beach but she also appears to have healed a critically injured youth on the spot. I just happened to be there to capture it on film—or maybe it was fated to be—whatever the case, the public wants and needs to know more."

"Get real, Ms. San—Eva. The truth is your viewers can only speculate as to whether she actually healed that kid. I don't remember your station making any definitive statements about her healing him. Why? Mainly because it would be embarrassing if it turned out to be a hoax! No station that lives and dies by the ratings is going to put themselves on the line without concrete proof. So why not let it die?"

Eva tapped her fingers on the wooden table like she was actually contemplating this. Meanwhile, we watched Olisa giving a reading to a sista who wore a burnt-orange Cleopatra wig, gold lame jumpsuit, and ton of gaudy jewelry that, when she moved, the dissonance of sounds would indicate her whereabouts if you were at the other end of the boardwalk!

"Joe, I can honestly sympathize with what you're asking, but . . ."

"But?"

"I'd be lying. I saw her heal him with my own eyes. If I hadn't seen it, I would have dropped it and chalked it up to being a fun story."

Clasping my hands behind my head, I watched two pigeons battle over a piece of breadcrust. "Eva, you're young, pretty, ambitious, and a complete professional. I believe you're approaching this with all the good intentions in the world, but your naiveté is going to destroy my daughter."

Pain rippled across her face like she'd been slapped. "Joe, I'm truly sorry you feel that way. You're certainly entitled to your feelings, but my story is going to make your daughter famous."

"She could give a shit about fame."

"The world does, Joe. People want to know about Olisa and her special gifts."

I didn't respond while I toyed with my wedding ring.

Eva went on. "Look at her. Within the short span of time I have been here, people are drawn to her like a magnet. Earlier this morning I watched a woman from El Salvador drag her two teenage boys here, literally by the scruff of their collars. When she stood them in front of your daughter, these *eses* were bug-eyed scared. Why? Because this was the woman who saved Ernesto 'Chato' Padilla, the 'mad dog,' *El Loco*! This woman rescued their idol. In their world, only a witch or the Holy Virgin Mother would demand such deference."

Nonchalantly, I folded my hands and rested them on the table. "So?"

"This woman stoically waited all morning hoping Olisa would show up. As soon as she arrived, she approached her, eyes bloodshot, and cried, 'Will you ask God to keep my boys from dying in the streets? Please, *señorita*,' she pleaded. 'No one can do what you do and not know God.'"

The waitress served a bowl of fruit salad with a scone on the side to Eva. She began brush stroking apple butter on the scone like she was sculpting clay. Munching away, she said, "At first I think Olisa was in a quandary about what to do. Then she did the unexpected, falling to her knees and clasping hands with the *señora*. The *señora* immediately fell to her knees, as well. The few restaurant customers and staff gaped in stunned silence, unsure of what to make of this."

Noel fidgeted with his fingers while listening to her story.

"Olisa warned them that God's love means absolutely nothing unless they are willing to accept it in their hearts. She asked them to hold hands with her in prayer. The boys kept standing, even though they visibly trembled.

Before long, they sank to their knees as if she had twisted their wrists in a deft martial arts maneuver. A short while later, they parted company so quietly I thought it turned out to be a big dud until I spotted the youngest rubbing his hand like he'd been stung by a bee. I ran up to them afterwards.

"'Señora, Señora, are you okay? What happened?' I asked. The *señora's* eyes were glazed. I wondered if she was even aware that I was walking alongside of her.

"'My boys are going to be fine. We are going to be fine. God is here,' she stated with such finality I glanced over my shoulder.

"*Yo no comprende, señora.* What do you mean?

"Eyes closed, the *señora's* fingers grazed along the sides of her face as if it had been transformed into gold. 'Her hands, God's hands . . .'

"What are you saying, *señora*? Are you saying you felt the power of God in her hands? Do you feel like *He* is working through her?

"A childlike giddy laughter erupted from her mouth as she grasped my hands. '*Señorita*, did you say *He*?'

"*Si.*

"All three of them laughed euphorically.

"'*Señorita*,' she remarked, with an elated expression, 'God is not a he, *He* is a *She!*'

"What?

"'*She* is God.'

"I stood there transfixed as I watched this person, who I pegged as a staunch old-world Catholic woman, dance down the boardwalk with her sons, spinning and weaving as if it were the *Yellow Brick Road*! So as you see, Mr. Joe Timmerman, I can't stop now. It's become more than just a news feature; it's personal. The best-kept secret in the world has been going on for quite a while in Venice Beach. Eventually my competitors will discover this story, too. News agencies are unsure if this is real or some kind of practical joke or stunt that might embarrass them if they report it as real news.

"Our video and amateur videos popping up online show Olisa's hands moving about his chest, but does that prove beyond the shadow of doubt that she healed him? And did we actually see who stabbed him? To date, there is no footage of that. Reporters are keeping it at a distance until they learn more. But I'm putting myself and my career on the line. Again, I saw her heal him. No way she concocted a scheme with a notorious gangbanger. For what purpose? Nevertheless, something else could happen in the near future, and then my competitors, who I believe are keeping a watchful eye on this, will jump all over this phenomenon. This is *my* story. I want and deserve the exclusive!"

"There it is! Despite all your stated sincerity, when all is said and done, this is nothing but a competition for you! It's not about Olisa's feelings or the impact it may have on her and our family."

"Sir, I promise you its more than just a competition for me. All I ask is that you work with me. I will handle this with as much sensitivity as I can, given the circumstances."

"Yeah, uh huh, I bet. Is that why I see your cameraman standing among the people around Olisa?" I snickered, while also grimacing as the crowd surrounding Olisa rapidly increased.

Noel tapped my elbow. "Dad, let's face it. Now that the story has broken, eventually they'll all be coming after Olisa. Why not cooperate with Eva? I mean what choice do we have?"

"We have choice of not doing a damn thing!"

Eva got up from the table. "I'm going to leave you gentlemen alone so you can talk privately."

While standing she was approached by a heavy yet athletic White man escorted by a contingent of people. Dressed in a suit and tie, his face looked familiar.

"Excuse me. You're that reporter, Maria, Ava . . ."

"Eva, Mr. Mayor. Eva Sanchez. What a pleasure seeing you here, sir. I'm flattered you recognized me."

"Pretty soon everyone in the country is going to recognize you, young lady, especially with stories like the one you covered last night. That was quite a report you presented regarding that Venice woman, the good witch, is it? Very impressive."

"Thank you. Actually, Mayor Halpern, this is Olisa's father Joe Timmerman and her brother Noel."

Noel leaped up from his seat, extending a hand as I begrudgingly offered mine.

"Gentlemen, it is indeed a great pleasure meeting you," he said with an expansive smile, readymade for those photographic moments that say, "I care." He coupled it with the patented campaigner handshake of grasping one hand warmly in both of his. Mayor Kenneth "Happy" Halpern, whose ambitions far exceeded his current position, was a consummate charmer and jokester, so much so that no one really remembered his platform as a mayoral candidate. People loved his "good ole boy" persona. Hap took full advantage of the notoriety accompanying his liberal rival Clarence Kimbrough's alleged action of picking up a fourteen-year-old minor and spending time with her in a North Hollywood motel about ten years ago. The young woman, apparently brighter and, some speculate, richer thanks to anonymous support, suddenly decided it was her manifest destiny to tell the public about her torrid one-night affair with Councilman Kimbrough who had been leading in projected votes during the hotly contested campaign.

"You must be quite proud of your courageous daughter," Halpern interjected, whacking me on the back.

"Yes, I am. Even before last night."

"Uh-huh . . . Ha! That's funny! Is that her over there in the crowd? I'd consider it an honor to meet such a fine woman," he said, grabbing my arm with a hand the size of a baseball mitt. There was still a solid grip in the pink knockwurst fingers of this former pro football player who starred at USC and became a backup right tackle in the late 90s and early 2000s with the Seahawks.

He ushered me forward like a hostage. His minions scurried close behind, steadily filming while the wide-bodied mayor threaded his way through the crowd like a running back while shaking hands in the process. A sprinkling of boos rifled through the populace, but it didn't faze his leathery hide one bit.

"*This* is your daughter, Joe? I can't believe this gorgeous gal took on the vermin of our city."

"I took on no one," Olisa retorted. "I helped a human being in need."

People cheered. Overlooking her response, Mayor Hap continued with, "What a pleasure to meet you, Olisa." He kissed her hand. "I'm Mayor Kenneth Halpern, Olisa. You can call me Hap or Happy like everyone else. When I noticed you over here, I had to ask your father to introduce me to his heroic daughter."

What introduction? He used me as his prop.

"Thank you, sir, but I'm certainly not heroic."

He was in his political mode, so, again, her response sailed right over his head.

"Dear, I hope you won't mind a few pictures?"

"Um . . . well . . . I don't know . . . I don't really like to . . ."

He masterfully slid next to her for a fusillade of photos taken by his staff. He prolonged the next handshake until he was sure the moment had been properly captured.

"Young lady, I've been talking with some of my associates about you, including the police chief. I'm pushing through a formal recommendation to issue you a special citation honoring the bravery you demonstrated last night. We'll have a special ceremony and reception to thank you the right way."

"Thank you, but it's really not necessary."

"Oh yes, it is! Ms. Olisa, you deserve a commendation for putting your life in jeopardy! I can't really comment on what they said about miracles and all that stuff they claimed happened after you held the youth, but the point is you tried to help."

A smirk played on Olisa's lips, but she followed my lead and nodded her head. She seemed a little dazed, though somewhat amused by all of this.

"Facing up to those hoodlums like you did was sensational!" he declared loudly enough to illicit applause and cheers from the gathering as he split time between eyeing Olisa, eyeing friendly faces, and eyeballing the camera. "The only reason I would have stood up to those criminals is because I'm too big to run and hide!" he joked. This loosed a bellicose guffaw that made his stomach roll like an avalanche. "Still, what in the world inspired you to put your life on the line like that?"

Olisa rocked back and forth on her sandals, arms folded, contemplating what had just been asked. It seemed like an eternity before she responded. When she spoke, her voice was soft yet resolute. Those gathered around them went completely silent, except for the mayor's labored breath.

"It's simple. Love . . ."

Ol' Hap got sideswiped by a left cross he wasn't expecting. His eyes darted around, but his head moved up and down like an automaton.

"A love for humanity. I love those people you referred to as vermin and hoodlums. I want to see them hugging instead of harming each other. I want them to go find an appreciation for life . . . to go and hug a child, an elderly person, even a tree. I want them to take that pain they won't admit out of pride, rotting their hearts, and dump it elsewhere. But they can't do it alone. Perhaps if we practiced loving them more than fearing them, we can help to put an end to the invisible war that rumbles inside of them and then spills into the streets. Don't be mistaken. I am not naïve. Sadly, some are lost to the ills of society, but they all don't have to be. Isn't that a great agenda for a party platform, mayor, to love them, not leave them?"

Two of the so-called hoodlums in the gathering mass tapped their fists as all eyes froze on Mayor Halpern.

"Oh yes, yes, absolutely! We're working on some programs right now," he accentuated, head still nodding mechanically, eyes glued on her. It amazed me how politicians like him could continue to smile despite hearing scattered boos.

"Wonderful, wonderful," Olisa chimed, clapping her hands and smiling broadly. "Mayor Halpern, it's great to be appreciated, and I certainly don't want to sound like some kind of ingrate, but I don't want an award or a pat on the back for doing something we should all be willing to do for our fellow human beings if they are in danger. My reward is knowing that I saved someone's life. That's it."

Those in the vicinity applauded wildly as if it were a political rally. The mayor looked a little disconcerted by this, especially since he didn't receive that type of ovation.

"But Ms. Olisa, people want to reward you, as you can hear, because this was something you don't see every day."

"Mayor, there are far more deserving people out there, street warriors, who work in the trenches daily to prevent the explosions you saw. They should be recognized. Give an award to Jorge Valdez and Silas Jenkins who are long-time gang prevention specialists. Reward Reverend April Cullender. She fights the good fight every single minute and hour in these streets from Culver City to Santa Monica, to Venice battling sex traffickers, making efforts to keep our young women involved in positive activities and steer them away from the seductive allure of the streets. While I'm at it, you can add Warner Hass to that list." Olisa pointed to a grizzled man in the crowd whose gray-white hair was super thin on top and the rest pulled back in a shoulder-length ponytail. At the mention of his name, his face got flushed, and he self-consciously waved.

"Warner is a gifted homeless artist with the thickest green thumb you've ever seen. He tries to beautify everything he touches in Venice by planting flowers and trees in vacant weed-infested lots. He's probably mad at me for even mentioning it, but I don't care. He doesn't do this work for publicity; he does it because he loves the community. And for a man without a home, this is his home."

You would have thought this was the ceremony the way the crowd applauded Warner. He modestly bowed, acknowledging the accolades. He blew Olisa a kiss, which she promptly returned.

"Sure, I'll keep them all in mind, but for now be sure to give your number to my assistant, Maude, over there so she can get in touch with you about the upcoming ceremony."

A prim yet attractive strawberry-blonde-haired woman who looked to be somewhere in her mid-thirties offered a brief smile while scrolling through her phone.

"So what exactly do you have going on here?" Halpern asked good-naturedly.

"Watch out now, Mr. Mayor!"

A Black woman wearing an orange Cleopatra wig, gold lame jumpsuit, clanking jewelry, and head bopping from side to side emerged from the crowd. She touched the mayor's arm with a little too much familiarity, encouraging a couple of bodyguards to edge in a little closer.

"Mr. Mayor, my name is Cleopatra Pickens, not to be confused with Cleopatra Jones, although people say I'm a dead ringer for her. Been calling myself Cleopatra for twenty years, ever since Wanda Ellis did me a numerology reading and said that I was Cleopatra reincarnated. Still lookin' for my Marc Anthony, baby, but I guess he ain't found the right body yet!" She snapped her fingers thrice and sashayed around the amused mayor, while people hooted and hollered.

"But, honey, let's not get into all that cuz I could go on and on. What I'm sayin' is I didn't think anyone could rock Cleo's world until my home girl here came along and gave me Excedrin headache #25! Ya know what I'm sayin'? Girlfriend told me so many things about myself, I swear . . . You listening? Better recognize, honey. I love my sista girl here, cuz she's keeping it real!"

She hugged Olisa and then did a little belly dance swirl and bowed. The crowd roared.

"Is that so? Sounds like a load of fun to me. Are you an astrologer, Olisa?" the mayor inquired, not waiting for an answer. "I always have fun reading my horoscope, even though I'm not one to go for that day-to-day malarkey. My wife tells me I'm a Taurus through and through: obstinate, stubborn, doing whatever I want to do. Is that true, Maude?"

"Not at all, Mr. Mayor." She flipped her hair back.

"Why don't you do a reading, mayor?" asked the blonde dreadlocked surfer Olisa read earlier.

The frown on Maude's face was barely perceptible, as well as the subtle head shake when she and the mayor exchanged eye contact. Her blue eyes were mashed against her squared lens glasses.

She announced, "Mayor Halpern, don't forget your busy schedule! You've got an appointment across town. Then we head to a luncheon with some of your constituents. We're already late as it is."

"Aww, come on, mayor, do a quick reading! It won't hurt!" a voice cajoled from the crowd.

Maude once again shook her head and vigorously pointed to her phone.

Meanwhile the crowd chanted, "Do it. Do it. Do it. *Do it . . .*"

The mayor's eyes danced as he surveyed the crowd, thrilled to hear the chanting crescendo.

"Aww, what the heck. Let's go for it. It can't hurt. This is all in fun."

Buoyed by the support, or more like baiting, Mayor Halpern carefully sat down in one of the beach chairs placed before him in the sand. Olisa sat across from him.

"Now you tell me what to do, as long as it doesn't involve telling me how to run the city," he chuckled, glancing reassuringly at Maude whose lips were pursed. She dropped her head and angrily scrolled through her phone. "Go ahead. The library is now open; read me like a book," he joked as his crew yucked it up. "So give me my forecast. What's in my future? Am I going to be elected for another term? And you'd better say yes!"

"Sir, I am not an astrologer. I don't do horoscopes."

"Okay, okay, no worries," he stated hurriedly. "Just do what you do. Should I hold your hand or something? You need to read my palms?"

The insides of my stomach burned as he held out his hand facetiously, hamming it up in front of the cameras like he was participating in a card trick at the Magic Castle.

Olisa was *not* smiling. "Mayor, perhaps it'd be better if we did this another day in a private session. Readings are very personal."

He pompously spread his arms out. "How personal can it be? I have nothing to hide among my friends here." He clapped his hands. "Now please, let's proceed. I'm running out of time, and Maude is about to skin me alive."

Olisa reluctantly folded her hands around his. A sneer lurked on the tattooed surfer's face as he edged in closer to listen. It wasn't difficult. It became unbelievably quiet. All you could hear was faintly scattered music coming from several vendor booths and the waves breaking along the shore.

Olisa's dark eyes gazed beseechingly into Mayor Halpern's. "Mr. Mayor, I'm really uncomfortable about this . . ."

"Why? Oh, I see . . . Is there a fee or donation or something? Is that it?" He quickly waved at Maude as she rolled her eyes and lethargically stepped forward.

"No, sir, money is not the issue."

He patted her hands encouragingly and whispered, "I may be the mayor of Los Angeles, but you can talk to Happy Halpern like you do anyone else. Let me tell you it's never held the press back!"

He winked at Eva. She politely smiled back, although her eyes were filled with anticipation, twice their normal size. She signaled to her cameraman to start filming.

"Come on now. Time is wasting. Let's hear it."

Olisa sighed resolutely. "Before I begin, I want you to understand something, mayor. This is not a game to me. When I talk to you about your life and who you are, I become a messenger relaying only what I see. Do you understand?"

He smirked and nodded his head, looking at his crew like "What the hell?" Except when his eyes connected with Olisa's, I think it finally hit him he just stumbled into quicksand. Now, it was too late. The cloud fell over her eyes. She was there.

"Mr. Mayor, you asked me if you were going to be elected for another term . . ." The natural warmth in her voice had been exiled from her throat and replaced by a halting, colorless, trance-like monotone.

A bemused grin spread across his mouth as he tried to play to a stone-faced audience. "What's ol' Hap got to do?" he asked, eyebrows tilted upwards.

"End the affair you are having with that woman on your staff."

I was always under the impression rigor mortis set in after death. Mayor Happy Halpern went so stiff he resembled an open-eyed corpse. All the color abandoned his face, and the patronizing little glint in his eyes flickered out. Maude pressed her phone protectively against her bosom, like her blouse had been stripped away.

"You wonder if your wife knows . . . She does. She's known for a long time. She's a smart woman, but old school. As long as it's not flagrant and is discreet, she tolerates it. She enjoys the lifestyle too much and isn't emotionally ready to rock the boat. Even so, that may change soon. You have a teenage son ready to graduate high school—"

"Anyone who reads the paper knows that," Halpern snorted flippantly.

Olisa ignored the tart comment. She was too far into her groove. "I sense your son is having a difficult journey through school . . . experiencing behavioral issues, acting out, talking abusively to his teachers, and skipping classes . . ."

Redness seeped into the mayor's face as the corners of his mouth twitched.

"You're aware of the problems, but you chalk it up to him being a rebellious teenager, except his drug use is worsening. It's okay to shake your head in disbelief; I understand. You must go home and see for yourself. When you do, examine his face; be aware of his extreme mood swings. Are his pupils dilated when he comes home late? When he's going, check out his room; in fact, ransack it if you want to save him. He's unabashedly left every kind of paraphernalia throughout it, practically in your face. He figures you're so wrapped up in your career, you won't notice or care.

"He never gets to see you unless you're surrounded by dozens of political constituents. He loathes what you do. He smiles to please you, yet his face darkens when you look away. He craves your attention but not through media shoots. His confusion is building, and he desperately needs help. He needs you. If someone doesn't get to him soon, he could overdose or maybe even commit suicide."

"Hey, I've been there. I could talk to him, mayor. I know how this stuff can work on you, man," blurted the surfer whose emotions metamorphosed from glee to sympathy.

"Oh come now; this is all getting a little ridiculous. I don't have to sit here and listen to this crap!" The mayor shifted in his seat but never stood up.

"As long as these distractions exist in your life, you'll never make it to a second term because they'll hit so fast you won't have time to recover. Your wife is in complete denial about the drugs, but should something go wrong, and it will, she will resent you. She's just not going to stand for it, nor the unbearable agony she's suffering to make your dreams come true, particularly if your son becomes the sacrificial lamb to your work and your indulgences. If so, she will seek a divorce and drag you through the mud. She knows your substantial worth . . ."

The mayor's foot tapped restlessly in the sand.

"Mayor, I feel it . . . You do love your wife, your family, and your reputation, so my guess is you will ultimately end the affair. The question is, will you end it in time? And if so, your next issue will be to find a way to establish a comfortable working relationship with your assistant or find her another job or form of compensation. She's ambitious, too, and sometimes we all serve a purpose for each other. If you fire her, she'll sue you for sexual harassment and/or race to the tabloids intent on destroying your future in politics."

Maude's glasses were replaced by shades as one finger dabbed at the corners of each eye.

"One last thing, mayor . . . *stop* drinking! Do you honestly believe that your son only learned the habit from school? There are people on your staff who know you're a drinker. They are considered your intimates, but how long do you think that will last? If a scandal begins, they'll realize you have no hope of being elected. The only thing they will think about is ensuring their own survival. If that means throwing you to the vultures, then so be it. That's politics; that's life. Like a flea, they'll find another dog to hop onto."

The mayor stared at the sand, shaking his head. She stroked his hand gingerly. "Mayor, right now you think I'm trying to hurt and embarrass you—not true. I'm only telling you the truth as the images appear in my mind's eye. View what I'm saying as an assist. You are a spiritual being like all of us with problems we can all relate to."

"Amen! That's right! Work it, girl!" screamed Cleopatra, jingling like a piggy bank as she clapped to the larger but small morning crowd assembled around them.

"Mayor, forego your ego, see the truth, accept what I am saying. I promise you it will save more than your career. Trust me. Any other questions, mayor? Mayor?"

An image that will forever haunt me was in a documentary I watched long ago. In it, Bushmen of the Kalahari Desert felled a giraffe. Although I understood its role as a part of the ecosystem, it was still incredibly painful to observe such a magnificent beast being leveled so humiliatingly from the skies and brought to its knees. Mayor Halpern was this beast, completely disoriented. His head whipped from side to side, anxiousness rising as he looked fearfully at the gaping audience.

Maude had already begun the trek back to the limo, leaving the mayor on his own. Olisa released the mayor's hand. It fell limply in her lap. Suddenly it withdrew like a snake sliding back into its hole as he self-consciously rubbed his wrist. His glassy-eyed expression only hinted at the wrestling match going on inside of him. He had the pallor of a man who had been sentenced to life in prison. Gradually, the murky film cleared from his zigzagging eyes, and a face full of pathos was beset by righteous indignation.

"H-H-How did you . . . That was cruel! Did you people enjoy that? What kind of reading . . ." He stumbled to his feet, swatting away the surfer's helping hand. "The fucking cameras are off, right?" he snapped, glaring angrily at the camera operators who were already packed and heading toward their van.

"Been off, sir," one responded.

"Oh yeah, yeah, that's right . . ." the mayor smiled crookedly. "So that's my reading, huh? You might want to try to make it a little more positive in the future. You know, a few jokes help."

Olisa stood up and reached to embrace him. "I'm truly sorry, Mr. Mayor. I don't know what else to say to you."

He coldly waved her off. "Oh, I think you've said more than enough; believe me." He looked around discombobulated, and then it abruptly vanished. It was like he suddenly recognized there had been an audience present the entire time. He struggled to regroup. He clasped his hands together in a half-hearted attempt to revive his joviality. It fluttered with a thud to a silent crowd. Even his cronies failed to laugh. He aged twenty years in a matter of minutes. The skin on his face sagged like the folds on a bulldog.

"All right everybody, let's go!" He awkwardly shook Olisa's hand, touching it as if it were a claw. Weakly, he raised his hand into the air, waving goodbye to the stunned, murmuring crowd. Walking unsteadily toward his vehicle, he halted in alarm when he saw Eva Sanchez and me standing in his path. He trudged toward her as if he were facing a firing squad, eyes hollow, pleading.

"So what did you think of that girl's reading?" he asked nonchalantly.

"Interesting . . . but meaningless unless it can be substantiated. Is what she said true, Mr. Mayor?"

"Absolutely not!"

"I see. Oh well, it would have made great copy, but since there's no truth in it, then there's nothing for me to report," Eva calmly remarked.

"Thank you, Eleanor, for not turning this nonsense into some sort of tabloid fodder. You know how people want to believe anything these days."

Eva smiled, not bothering to correct him on her name.

"Yeah, but all that matters is what you believe, Mayor Halpern. Right?" I interjected smugly, arms crossed.

He tried to play it off, but I knew he heard me. His quivering lips gave him away. A cameramen tapped him on the shoulder. "Sir, we really need to be on our way."

"Sure, sure . . . Nice meeting all of you." He spun around as the crew blanketed him and herded him toward his transportation. Before stepping inside, he glanced one final time at Olisa who was mobbed by people begging for readings. I was glad to see Noel standing protectively next to her. After an interminable amount of time, the mayor ducked his head and the chauffeur-driven sedan sped off.

"That was awfully nice of you," I said to Eva.

"What, not kicking the man while he was down? I didn't lie. I don't really have any facts to go on. That's an area for the gossip columnist to explore, not me."

"Do you believe my daughter told the truth?"

"Mr. Timmerman, you could read his face and tell it was the truth. No politician lets a perfect stranger detail why you're an adulterer, alcoholic, and a neglectful father before a voting audience without a challenge."

"Think he's going to follow her advice?"

"We'll know if he's elected."

"Hmmm."

"So Olisa is psychic too?"

"Can't say. She's never read me."

"Well, I hope Olisa doesn't have her heart set on receiving a plaque from the city."

"I hate to admit it: I couldn't stymie my laughter."

An African gentleman from Cameroon who was also a visiting professor teaching African Studies at UCLA used to periodically dine at the restaurant Wilma and I opened in Venice. He always asked to be called Chris, which was short for Christofere. Anyway, Olisa occasionally helped out at the restaurant. I will always remember Dr. Christofere Adama wiping his glasses and looking at me with a dumbfounded expression on his angular dark chocolate face, his cupped chin shadowed by a pencil line goatee.

"Joseph, is that lovely girl your daughter?"

"Yes," I answered apprehensively. "Why? What did she do? Drop food on you, spill water? Insult you? Do I need to pull out my wallet to compensate you?" I pulled up a chair and sat down at his table.

"No, no, Joseph, nothing like that," he replied laughingly with the accent of a man who spent a large part of his life educated in the British school system. He watched Olisa serving the other patrons. "How old is she?"

"She just turned thirteen this past month."

"What did you say? Thirteen? Unbelievable!" he slid his tinted glasses back on his face as if that would allow him a closer look at her.

"Why do you say that?"

"She asked me what type of work I did. I mentioned I was a professor of literature and linguistics and teaching African Studies at UCLA. Before long, we were engrossed in conversation about ancient African societies. Her knowledge of these civilizations and various cultures was amazing for a child her age. Has she ever been to Africa?"

"No. She's been no further east than Texas."

"Well, Mr. Timmerman, I am indeed impressed. You have to understand I don't always have long discourses with thirteen-year-old kids. I would have sworn this young lady had traveled all over the world. Her questions were more advanced than some of my graduate students'."

"She devours books, Chris. She's at the library so much I think they've reserved a spot with a nameplate for her bicycle."

"Incredible! You've got a winner there, Joseph. That child is going to go as far as she wants to. I'm sure you're enormously proud of her."

"I am. Thank you."

"What is her name?"

"Olisa."

"Pardon me? Did you say, Olisa?"

"Yes, sir. Why?"

He pushed his glasses down to the end of his greyhound nose, peering over them. He suddenly threw his head back laughing loudly.

I didn't know if I should laugh with him or throw him out of the restaurant.

"Oh, Joseph, please forgive me . . . I hope I haven't insulted you. I'm not laughing at her name. The humor comes from the irony of it all. Do you have any idea what the name Olisa means in regions of Africa?"

"No."

"Oh, you Americans. I swear . . . You name your children whatever sounds good to you as opposed to what it might mean."

"All right, Doc, so what are you telling me? That we named our kid after an African cockroach or something? My wife created her name from a combination of her grandparents' middle names. She said it came to her in a dream."

He chuckled again. "My friend, your wife is a powerful dreamer. Among the Ibo tribes in Nigeria, Olisa is a most esteemed name. It means God."

"God? You're kidding, professor."

"No, sir. I would never do so in a place that cooks such fine food. What's her middle name?"

"Nothing complicated there. She's named after my great-aunt Belle. Olisa Belle Timmerman."

He rubbed his shaven head, clearly bemused. "Either you are incredibly lucky, or the gods are having fun with you. Let's play a little."

"Hit me."

"By reversing the name and changing a letter, in the Ibo language it is not uncommon to see Belu Olisa."

"Meaning?"

"In English, it roughly translates to 'Nothing is impossible with God's help.'"

This time I rubbed my head. "Okay . . ."

"So with a name like your daughter's, she can't help but make an impact on this world, no matter what she does. I'm no shaman, but I'll predict her destiny is to do great things. The best part is, God will always be on her side. Isn't that funny?"

"Very," I answered softly, knowing the professor would miss the trace of sarcasm in my voice.

Chapter 4

The next time I saw Eva Sanchez was on the television screen.

"Hi. I'm Eva Sanchez, and for a third straight day, sweltering temperatures in the nineties sent a record-breaking number of Angelenos fleeing to the Southland beaches to seek relief from the oppressive heat. As you can see, this reporter has spent her day and afternoon at Venice Beach, enjoying the cool and refreshing ocean breeze and the carnival-like atmosphere that makes Venice one of the hippest and most popular party beaches in the world. As usual, there are hundreds of people milling about on the boardwalk watching the skate dancers, street performers, and musicians.

"Many of us have hung out on this particular beach today for another reason besides the heat. And that is to possibly catch a glimpse of the heroic woman who captured our hearts in last week's story. Everyone here is eager for the opportunity to meet this person who intervened in a gang war that in all probability might have escalated and potentially harmed innocent bystanders." A brief footage of the fighting was shown repeatedly.

"The dust seems to have settled, but no one has been able to stop talking about this woman who healed Ernesto 'Chato' Padilla with her own hands. This young man, our sources claim, was reputedly the leader of the most notorious gang on the Westside." More footage was shown as we once again saw Chato lying supine in Olisa's arms.

The camera zoomed in tightly on Eva's face.

"I became obsessed with finding a way to meet this superwoman who disappeared shortly after incident. Was it my imagination, or was it just wishful thinking?

"Like many of the eyewitnesses out there, I began to doubt what I had seen until I reviewed the video over and over. Unblinkingly, the truth kept staring at me. I had to seek her out and find out who she is and what would possess this woman to place her life on the line for an alleged gangbanger.

"I got lucky; some would say I was blessed. She's here with me today, the woman the locals have admiringly dubbed 'The Good Witch of Venice.' Nonetheless, her real name is Olisa Timmerman, and this humble woman with her amazing gifts is probably about as far removed from being a witch as the late Hugh Hefner from celibacy. Just so you know, I'm not the only one fascinated by her."

Eva plowed through the beach crowd, holding her microphone slightly aloft.

"As you can see, there are all types of people here, offering their thanks and showing their appreciation to Olisa. We've seen Hollywood celebrities, and even the mayor of Los Angeles stopped by last week for a chat."

Eva positioned herself next to Olisa as we saw a sycophantic circle of beachgoers standing and sitting around her. Her intricately braided hair was pulled back loosely into a ponytail. Her white flowing dress fluttered in the breeze, fanning across her bare feet as she warmly accepted hugs from several people who reverentially approached her on a one-by-one basis.

Her head involuntarily jerked back as Eva thrust the microphone into her face.

"Hi, Olisa. My name is Eva Sanchez of KLSC Evening News, the *Special Edition*. Please forgive the interruption. Would you mind speaking with us for just a few minutes?"

Olisa paused, eyeing her warily.

That's when I heard a *very* familiar voice off camera say, "Only a few, as discussed, Eva."

"Good enough. That's all I need. Thank you. That good with you, Olisa?"

"Um, sure . . . I guess so."

I could have killed Noel. *Now he's acting as her manager?*

"Well, it truly is an honor meeting you," Eva gushed, yet pointing the mike in Olisa's face as if she were a prisoner of war.

"You're too kind. Thank you."

Olisa seemed relieved to hug a small boy who suddenly was clinging to her legs.

"I think that little boy is symbolic of how this city feels about you."

There was a burst of applause from the onlookers as Olisa's face reddened along with the Venice sunset. Self-consciously lowering her eyes, she patted the little boy on the behind as he scooted back into the crowd.

"The question I think we've all been asking ourselves is why such a beautiful woman as yourself would get involved. Why not be like the rest of us and ignore it? Let the police handle it. That's what they're paid for."

"All I saw were members of my neighborhood family at war, my brothers. I know them, and I love them too much to see them hurt themselves or anyone else. This city has been bathed in too much unnecessary bloodshed. Please don't credit me. It was purely an emotional reaction. Something snapped inside of me, and I jumped from the backseat to the front seeing Ernesto lying bloody on the ground. I just wanted them to stop fighting."

Olisa glossed over the surface. She didn't mention what she confided in me days after the beach incident. All day long prior to the outbreak of violence, she had been troubled by flashing preternatural images. She didn't speak about the salvo of gunshots painfully ringing in her ears where none existed, or the bloodied people crying over unmoving bodies that were strewn around like it was a war zone, or the paramedics carrying away two small children with sheets over their faces who had accidentally been hit by the gunfire in retaliation for the stabbing.

No, this was never mentioned.

"I'd say you certainly achieved that goal. But you did more than that. You healed a young man with your hands. Many eyewitnesses swear on their Bibles that they saw you heal Ernesto 'Chato' Padilla, and I am one of them. This is known in my community as a *milagro* or miracle. And I say this with the risk that this telecast may end up being my farewell interview because everyone knows reporters are supposed to be objective, except in this case I know what I saw."

Eva paused, like a person standing on the gallows who'd been asked to say her last few words. Her face worked overtime to suppress all emotions. Finally, in an even voice she declared, "I'm choosing this moment to disclose that *this* reporter saw Ernesto being stabbed. I was close enough to see the flesh ripped from his body with each downward plunge of the knife. It was sickening. But I was helpless to do anything but my job and cover the story. I watched you kneel down and hold him so tenderly and lay your hands on his stomach. Those wounds should have been fatal. Then the bleeding stopped. My eyes didn't betray me. You healed him."

"No, I didn't."

"What do you mean you didn't?" Eva tried her best to appear detached, but her eyes gave her away. She realized she may have just committed career suicide.

"No. God did. I was simply the instrument through which God chose to act."

Eva's shoulders heaved and sagged in relief. "So you're saying God gave you the power to heal people?"

"No, I'm saying God *is* the power. I can feel the flow of energy coursing through my body."

"Really? Can you describe for us what that feels like?"

"I don't know . . . It's hard to explain. It's like a tidal wave of hot, prickly tiny needles and pins rushing through your body. The tingling sensation doesn't stop until the healing ends. Thereafter, I'm usually so drained I sometimes need to have someone explain to me what happened."

"I see ... and is it true that you are also psychic?"

"I'm not really sure what that means in the end-all. All I know is that God pulls back the curtain on someone, and I try to put meaning to the images I'm allowed to see. It does *not* mean I can see into the future." Olisa looked uncomfortable.

An arm scooped around her shoulders, and Noel's face eclipsed the screen. "Sorry, Eva, no more questions. My sister's tired, and we've got to go."

"Wait. I have just a couple more ... Olisa?"

Noel and Olisa merged into a sea of people.

Even with her body being jostled by overly enthusiastic onlookers, Eva's smile remained triumphantly planted on her face as she proceeded to offer closing statements.

Blip. The screen went dark.

My only sense of power lately was derived from pushing the Off button on the remote control, except the effects of the news report lingered like a sinus headache.

The landline phone rang. I heard Grace's voice in the kitchen.

"Hello? ... Yes, it is ... No, this is her mother. She's not available right now ... I'm sorry. Please hold. I've got another call on the line. Hello? ... No, I'm afraid she's not here. May I leave a message? ... You don't need to call back. She's not taking calls ... I don't know if she's doing private readings ... You can afford it; I'm sure you can ... She has her own phone ... No, I can't give you the number ... It's an emergency? Then call 911. I can't help you ... You're getting rude ... I'm going to have to hang up. Goodbye!"

And it rang again.

And again.

And again.

Soon it found camaraderie with the faint ring of Olisa's landline phone in the studio. We quickly muted the ringers, and the responsibility was delegated to voice mail. But our voice mails filled up as rapidly as we could blink, including our cell phones. Even with a change of numbers and phones, enterprising individuals seemed to find a way in.

To no one's surprise, I called for a family emergency meeting.

With the exception of my parents who retired to Las Vegas several years ago, all of the immediate family was present that evening: Grace, Noel, James and Katherine Willis, Junior, and Olisa.

"Turn her into a star? Are you kidding me, Noel? The purpose of this meeting was to defuse the crisis, not accelerate it."

"Agreed. But, Dad, I think we should take a look at this from all angles," Noel responded, leaning against the wall of the dining room. "I don't see it as a crisis. I view it as an opportunity. Olisa can use her gifts to help people on a grander scale. I'm sure my humble sister healed sick people during her stint with the Peace Corps."

"God, not me, Noel."

"Gotcha."

"Noel, there are no other angles except to protect your sister. She is not one of your damn hip-hop artists."

"Dad, you've got this skewed idea of what hip-hop and rappers are in today's world. She could be one of our motivational artists. I got a stable of people who can't sing a damn lick, but they sure can write their butts off. They put out lyrics that the kids can identify with, that tell stories."

"Oh, I get it now . . . You mean such profound Shakespearean-like prose such as, 'We be bitches and hos, and trying to make a score'?"

"Wow. All rap and hip-hop isn't that way, Dad. Yes, the music can be raw and often reflect the reality of the streets: drugs, gratuitous violence, abuse, and sexual braggadocio. But there are people out there talking about politics, inequality, police abuse to people of color and so much more . . . folks trying to do some positive things that don't get enough headlines. They're not all cop haters and booty mongers!"

"Oh, I'm sorry. My bad. So school me on the true integrity of this noble art."

"Okay, besides being a cultural phenomenon for so many years when people predicted it would die by now, it has bridged the racial divide. According to the recording industry over 70 percent of the rap/hip-hop consumers are White. The music is such a dominant force in the world it has raked in billions."

"Bravo! And your point in relation to Olisa?"

"Dad, come on . . . Right now I'm trying to get you to understand that the world is offering Olisa a forum which the world could benefit from. I'm envisioning a one-time local event. We'd call it 'Heal the World Day.' Give it the feeling of an old-school revival service. Olisa would give a short speech, and I'd pair her with musical and spoken word acts: gospel, hip-hop, jazz, R& B—you name it. She might even heal a few folks."

"Well, work's drying up on me right now, so if you're lookin' for some slammin' bass lines, who ya gonna call?"

"You, Uncle Junior!" Noel laughed, tapping fists with him. Junior wore his hair in tiny little dreads. He had a Fu Manchu beard and sported a sleeveless camouflage shirt alone with shorts and military boots.

"Hold up! What the *hell* is wrong with y'all?"

"Joseph, please. We want this meeting to be constructive," Grace admonished. She sat on our long L-shaped white couch with her parents. She gently grabbed my right wrist to stop me from my unabated pacing. She motioned for me to sit next to her on the couch. I stopped pacing, but there was no way I could sit down—too on edge.

"Look. We all swore if people found out about Olisa *en masse*, we'd do everything within our power to protect her. Now we're discussing the possibility of entering her into something like *Showtime at the Apollo*? Have we constructed a website or designed all the avenues for her in social media?"

"Working on it," Noel answered half serious.

Frustrated, I turned to my daughter. "Olisa, honey, you're the only one who can put a lid on all this bull! Your brother doesn't seem to realize your services aren't for sale. Go ahead; tell him. Let him know."

Olisa sat in a Praying Mantis position in the corner of the living room quietly absorbing it all. However, the look on her face was not what I anticipated.

"Dad, the way Noel presented it to me earlier was not quite as superficial as it may come off. Let's hear him out."

"Oh, I see, Noel, so you already started your campaign dribble to Olisa."

"See what I mean, Oli? He has never listened to me before; why start now?"

"Noel, that's uncalled for," Grace interjected.

"Mom, I'm sorry, but it's true. Nothing I say is relevant to him. I've had to deal with that my whole life."

"That's not true, Noel. I hear everything you're saying. It's just that I don't believe in exploiting family for profits."

"That's harsh! Y'all see what I'm saying now? I've been convicted and sentenced without even a trial!" With an air of defeat, Noel plopped down in an easy chair, mouth set in a tight smirk.

"Noel, I think having you as a son for thirty-two years entitles me to know a little bit about you," I said, finally sitting down next to Grace. "You're a businessman, and you see a way of making money in all this, aside from your newly professed altruism."

"That last statement is *so* wrong! That's okay; it's not unexpected. More importantly, let it be known I'm not hiding from who I am. *Yes*, I'm an entrepreneur but not at the cost of screwing my own sister over. I am so ridiculously proud of her. I believe in her, love her, and would never do *anything* to harm her." Noel warmly smiled at her as he clenched his fist and laid it on his chest where the heart is. Olisa reciprocated the same gesture.

Noel turned to me. "This thing is bigger than all of us, Dad. That's what you fail to see."

"Really? Then break it down for me."

Noel shook his head and huffed. "Can we at least agree on one thing? Olisa is an extraordinary human being."

Everyone in the room nodded, including me. How could I not? Noel let this thought sink in while his fingers intersected slowly together. He scooted up to the edge of his chair.

"This story will make money for the worldwide media before it ends."

"We're doing our darndest to curtail that, aren't we?" I retorted.

"Joseph, come on now. Let the boy speak his piece!" Harold Willis barked loudly, tapping his hearing aid as he sat on the edge of the couch. "You many not want to hear it, but I do!"

"Thanks, Papa. All I'm trying to say is once the national media picks this little story up—and they will—it's going to hit us like an AK-47. We won't have a choice. The media will make an ungodly profit out of this until the well runs dry. Having said that, why should Olisa run and hide? She certainly hasn't done anything wrong, and she has the opportunity to do so much with her gifts. We may not be able to control this phenomenon, but we can go with the flow."

"You can't control an ocean, Noel."

"You're right, Dad. However, you can sail on it."

My laugh sounded like a snort. He had all the answers.

"When I was there with her at the beach, I saw people looking at my sister with the same type of adulation and awe normally reserved for rock stars, celebrities, and internationally known dignitaries. Some of those folks looked like they'd be willing to walk into hell with a full tank of gasoline strapped to their backs if Olisa asked."

"Uh, uh . . . not Mayor Halpern," Papa Willis chuckled.

"Got that right, Papa Willis," Noel laughed. "I guess my point is, in this millennium, people are searching for peace of mind, and science and in some cases today's leading religious figures are not proving to be adequate enough. Belief over unbelief; faith over doubt."

Mr. Willis nodded approvingly, but I could tell he strained to hear as he closely watched Noel's lips. Except it was now a little harder as a reenergized Noel stood up and walked the room doing his pitch.

"Some of these characters belong in a *Looney Tunes* cartoon instead of a church. Look at all the money spent on con artists, cult leaders, born-again convicts, new-age shamans, mega-rich ministers, former pimps now posing as salesmen and marketing experts, and fake-ass politicians and presidential candidates supposedly running in the name of religion. And don't even get me to talk about televangelists. Go down to one of the religious network headquarters in Orange County. You'll see what that little picture tube can do to keep the faith! I was there with one of my clients who performed on one of their shows. I thought I had driven into Disneyland by mistake with how ostentatious their shows were. Billions of dollars are streaming into their operation. I'm constantly amazed at how televangelists convince folks to spend their hard-earned dollars and savings for an express box-office ticket to heaven."

"Talk that talk, grandson!" Harold shouted.

"God has made a comeback! Music, films, merchandising, and licensing is continually proving that. Religion in the United States is worth more than Google and Apple and others combined. The 'Faith' economy is over trillions a year and growing!"

"Damn. Mama told me to invest more in religion."

Katherine Willis playfully smacked him upside the head. "She meant *more* time in church!"

"Ow! Come on now, woman!" Harold cried out rubbing his head. I couldn't help but laugh with everyone else despite my irritation.

Junior chuckled as he blew out the open front door a thick cloud of vapor mist from his e-cigarette.

"How does Olisa fit into this equation, Noel?" Grace sternly asked, giving me hope that I was not alone on my quest.

"Mom, it's very simple. Olisa is a healer."

"Not me. God," Olisa corrected.

"No argument here, but accept the fact that you are blessed with God-given talents. You are the conduit, sis. As difficult as it may be, face it—you are one of the chosen. You don't have to utilize artificial devices like crystal balls or tarot cards. Look at these so-called prophets claiming they can heal any malady. They end up with mansions, fleets of luxury sedans, and build landing strips for their private jets and helicopters from all the money they receive. Imagine what people would give worldwide after seeing that Olisa's gifts are real."

"Be beatin' on her door with more funk than a James Brown drummer!" rattled Junior closing his eyes and rocking his head.

Olisa rubbed her neck uncomfortably as Noel and Junior grinned at each other.

Noel went on to say, "Olisa is not one of those psychic vampires sitting down at a table in Venice Beach offering a bunch of generalities in their readings and then waiting for you to help them fill in the blanks."

"I know some sincere people out there, too, Noel."

"I'm sure you do, Olisa. Nevertheless, they still lean on clues from us. I admit some of them are so good at analyzing body language, they'd put a psychologist to shame. Still, they're not even close to you! You're the real deal, sis; get used to it," he asserted, overlapping it with an affectionate smile.

Olisa's face offered no hint as to what she was thinking as she stretched her neck from side to side.

"The beauty of it is my big sister has always wanted to help people since we were little. Dad, you've always wanted Olisa to get a steady paycheck doing what she loves. Well, here it is, saving humanity."

I angrily raised my hands. "Noel, don't take my words out of context to make your point."

"Fine, whatever, but my point is the time is now!" Noel waved his arms expansively as he again walked the room. Every ounce the promoter, Noel was in his element, doing his pitch like he was in a boardroom filled with top executives.

"If we put Olisa at the helm as our spiritual leader, we can form an organization that uses its monies and profits to help people. And with this being the age of technology, Olisa could easily potentially benefit millions of people. Ironically, we'd use the media the same way they'll use Olisa. But our way we'll be for the greater good."

Where Olisa stood in all this continued to remain a question. I could read her face about as well as I could do Japanese arithmetic. Though her face was tranquil and her eyes closed, every word Noel uttered was under grueling scrutiny.

Frowning, Katherine commented, "Forgive me, but I still don't get it. What are you expecting my granddaughter to do?"

"Nothing except to be herself and just do Olisa, Grandmother. Any paperwork that needs to be done, I'll handle, including setting up a partnership or corporation. Olisa's only job is to help rescue this sorry-ass planet from itself. With Olisa as a spiritual leader, we'd form an organization utilizing its profits to truly benefit people. In this age of social media, Olisa could help countless people without performing an act. She wouldn't have to do much beyond an occasional public appearance. We'd film her from time to time healing people and make it available for millions to view."

"Basically, you want her to become a trained monkey performing tricks on cue."

"Joseph!" screamed a chorus of voices.

"That's all right. Let him get it out of his system. If that's how he sees it, he's wrong."

"Look, grandson, I know you're making a few pennies, judging by that fancy car, clothes, and five-star luxury condo you're living in on Wilshire, but this sounds like a pretty ambitious and expensive endeavor. Where you gonna get the kind of money to fund this?" Harold Willis asked, squinting his eyes.

"No worries, G-Man. I've got friends. I can get the money."

I couldn't hold back: "Good money or bad money?"

"Good or bad money . . . To my recollections, money is money. Dad, why do you keep hating?"

"Son, I'm not hating. It's not you I have a problem with. It's your carnivorous associates I don't trust."

"Is that why you've always refused to work with me?"

"No. But if I'm being perfectly honest, I think your whole idea is bullshit!"

"Hold down, fellas. My turn," Katherine Willis interrupted. "Noel, maybe we should slow our roll and look at this more closely. Are we tumbling into bed with the Devil? My feeling is to leave it in the Lord's hands; that's what Mama Willis would have said. From there, whatever happens will happen."

"Like Donny Hathaway sang, 'Everything is Everything,'" piped in Junior.

"Grandmother, Olisa is already a celebrity whether she wants to be or not. If we let the media go unchecked, I promise you she'll end up looking like the Antichrist. We must protect her and her image. In these days of so much interaction on the internet in the process, we'll be helping millions with positive and inspirational messages. This is what I do, promote my artists. This, however, will be a work of love. In my business, I've smoothed over some pretty hardcore images, and Olisa is hardly that. If you knew the real story behind some of these so-called musical geniuses, it'd make your skin crawl. They oughta be locked up in a jail cell, not a sound booth."

Noel stood in the middle of the living room and scanned all of our faces before saying, "Olisa is the balm we all need during these trying times. Narcissistic leaders have transformed lying into the new normal. Their agenda is masked as a cause in order to attain power and control. They ply folks with uplifting and regurgitated sayings that their constituents and followers want to hear to garner votes. Bottomline is, men have fucked it up for centuries with their testosterone-induced warring. Time's up! We need female energy. Society needs to be mothered, and Olisa is the chosen one."

"I'm all for female empowerment. But you're going to push Olisa out there as the sacrificial lamb? Let me ask you this: will *you* make any money from this venture?" I struggled to keep the cynicism out of my voice, but I'm sure it didn't work.

"Yes, and my services will be worth every single penny, Dad," Noel countered. "The majority of the money will be donated to charities of Olisa's choosing."

He circled the dining room table and defiantly walked over to me. I arose from the couch angrily chewing on my lower lip. The unflinching glare in his eye brought back memories of the indignant sixteen-year-old boy who threatened to run away after I grounded him for violating his weekend midnight curfew coming into the house hours later after partying with his boys. We had a stare down then too, which led to me saying, "Any time you think you're man enough to be on your own and pay your own bills, then get your ass out of here!" Seconds passed and he backed off, much to Grace's relief. This time, I knew I wouldn't be so lucky.

"So what do you suggest we do, Dad? Wrap her up in a cocoon? Put a bag over her head like the elephant man? Or better yet, ship her away for the rest of her life to some remote region so she can be tormented by her own innate gifts. That's a great life."

The explosion heard in the house was me losing it. "Don't you fucking get smart with me! I'm still your father no matter who you think you are!"

It seemed like we were the only two people in the living room as we stood there, nose to nose, loaded with old family war wounds. A disturbing new expression surfaced upon Noel's face.

"Let's cut all the bull, Dad. Just admit it."

"Admit what?"

"Admit you're jealous of me."

"Jealous? Gimme a fucking break."

Grace interrupted, "All right, you two, enough! We're getting way off the subject. This is not the time."

"No, Mom. We might as well go there. It's not like it's some big old secret. He knows I'm right."

"You've got to be kidding me," I huffed, shaking my head and moving away from Noel. I sat back down on the couch next to Grace again. She clamped a hand on my wrist like a handcuff.

"No, I'm not. You're jealous that I finished college, got my MBA, and ended up with a high six-figure salary, plus major benefits. Isn't that what you always wanted?" Noel asked derisively, jerking a finger at me. He addressed the rest of the family: "Look at him. He's got too much pride to ask me for help. He'd rather toll away at his own business and struggle than ask his son for a helping hand."

"Oh, get real. That's ridiculous! Ask your mother. Ask your aunt. The restaurant's doing fine. Sure, there was a drop-off; all businesses go through it, especially with all the issues revolving around the pandemic and economy, but we made the necessary alterations and it's picked up again."

His smug silence pissed me off. Finally he spoke. I guess this was his chance to get his issues about me off his chest. "Good. I'm glad. But one thing I'm sure of is that you focused most of your attention on Olisa while we were growing up. I guess because she had the gift, but did you ever notice me?"

"Now who sounds jealous?"

"Maybe so, as a youngster. Later, I understood why; sis possessed extraordinary talents. Thus, I made an effort to establish myself in this family. I earned all As, received numerous scholarships, academic awards, sat regularly on the dean's list, and was Phi Beta Kappa at Stanford. What's interesting is, I don't remember you offering me any accolades while I worked my ass during those academic years. Mom did, all the time. You? Nothing. Just dissertations on how to do better."

"That's right. I stayed on your ass . . . maybe too much. I wanted you to succeed beyond me. And you did. You achieved major success in the corporate world, but all the thanks I get is seeing a spoiled egotistical child who thinks he knows more than anybody else."

"What you really mean is more than you, Dad, right? That's why you're blocking me. Makes you crazy to think I may be able to do more for Daddy's little girl than you."

Enraged, I brushed Grace's hand away from my wrist and marched toward Noel. Harold and Junior immediately intercepted me. How much more this argument may have escalated I'll never know. Olisa's strangled cry sliced through the tension freezing all of us. She hunched over on her knees, scrunching her face in her hands.

"No more! Stop it! Both of you, *please* quit before you say things you can never take back!" She clamped her hands to her head. Tears fell as her voice settled to a whisper. "God, I wish I had never helped anyone, if this is what it comes down to . . . my family fighting over something I've done."

Tears ambled down her cheeks as Grace held her in a fierce embrace. The look my wife shot me made me feel so small. I should have known better than to get sucked into such an ignorant confrontation.

"I'm sorry, baby girl. We're all a little tense, and we took it too far. Listen; I'm just scared . . . scared of the predators out there who love to rip innocent people apart. And I'm an overprotective and sometimes obnoxious father who only wants the best for his daughter, and that includes keeping her safe and happy."

"We all do, Dad," Noel echoed softly. "We're just trying to find the best solution to this whole thing; you agree?"

I didn't say anything as I sidestepped Noel and meandered over to the front screen door like a dog with his tail between his legs. I stared out into the night. The house was uncomfortably quiet before Papa Willis asked, "Noel, what makes you think this will work out the way you envision?"

"The timing. It's perfect during this 'Me-Too' movement. If we're really honest with ourselves, doesn't society just want to be mothered? Our society runs contrary to our emotional makeup. We elect a male president to run the country, but even though we live in a society where the number of single mothers has increased, when the father does run a household, the mother still rules it emotionally. As kids, no matter how much we love our daddies, when we are sick, we high jump Daddy to get to Mommy. We want Mommy to give us chicken soup, wipe our foreheads, cuddle us, and read us stories. In these trying times, I'm not really sure it's male energy we're looking for. I think we secretly crave a woman's touch. Our society is begging for a goddess, and her name is Olisa."

"Noel, you can stop right there. I am no one's goddess."

"Maybe not, Olisa, but little was known about Jesus Christ performing miracles before men started embellishing his image in the Holy Book. If Jesus were here today, instead of disciples, he'd need a PR campaign using social media to spread his message worldwide."

The gasp heard around the world was Katherine Willis'. She was a devout churchgoer, organist, and choir director at Faith Baptist Church for over twenty-five years. She gawked at Noel as if he held a red trident and grew horns and a triangle-tipped tail.

"Okay, I may have overstepped on that one."

"That's putting it mildly," retorted Katherine.

"Sorry. Look; all I'm trying to say is when I saw Olisa interacting in that crowd with such unshakable energy and spirit, it convinced me she naturally has the power and charisma to take us by the hand through the twenty-first century. She's not posturing, and she's not fronting. I've watched complete strangers open up to her like they've known her all their lives. The challenge is finding a way to inspire and help millions with her gifts."

"So what you're saying is we may have the next Mahatma Ghandi on our hands," Harold Willis commented admiringly to his niece who now sat next to her mother on the couch. Olisa slightly smiled but shook her head like, "No way."

"Yeah, and we know what happened to him." I kept my back to them, hands pressed on the screen door like a cat with its claws stuck.

"Naw, Joe. She's gonna to be all right. That's cuz we got my niece's back. Hey, y'all know the deal with me . . . She helped me through all the stuff I been through. I still regularly attend rehab meetings, thanks to her. I would have died if Olisa hadn't been there to help me get that mess out of my system. I suppose the world should be given the same opportunity I had." Junior pointed at her, "Don't worry, Oli; I'm still working on that song for you. Just you wait and see. It's gonna be a scorcher, a real melter."

Olisa's eyes greeted him warmly.

"Okay . . . We know how Junior feels and my dad. What's everybody else's thoughts about what I'm proposing? Papa Willis?"

"Grandson, you know how I feel about you. You're as smart as they come, and I love to hear you talk that talk. Having said that, it hurts to say you don't know your ass from a hole in the ground on this one. Listen to your father. He's right. Don't let this girl get thrown out to those buzzards."

"But, G-Man, she can change so many lives. People love her!"

"That's where you're wrong, boy. Granted my granddaughter has out-of-this-world talents. Even so, initially, they'll sing her praises but never truly care about her. People are really only concerned about *numero uno*. If given the chance, they'll run over her and never look back if she is no longer useful to them."

"But, grandfather—"

"No, no . . . It's my turn. I just don't feel good about it. You get cynical when you get to be this old. I've seen too much bullshit in my lifetime. Like Joseph said, our job is to protect Olisa and keep the wolves away from her door."

Obviously disappointed, Noel turned to Katherine Willis.

"Don't waste your time, Noel. Harold spoke for me."

"Mom?"

Grace's drawn and red-rimmed eyes were awaiting mine as I slowly turned to face her. Her eyes never strayed from mine when she said, "Noel, you can end the survey here. We are not entitled to be a judge or jury on what Olisa should do. It's not up to us. And in terms of how I feel, I'm with your dad and grandfather. The thought of throwing her into the jaws of this wretched society frightens me. Perhaps I could be more objective if it wasn't my daughter, but that isn't the case. She is our flesh and blood. No matter what Olisa might mean to others, this is and will always be our big little girl." Grace paused before she rested her eyes upon Noel. "So you can't go by me. I admit I'm being selfish and self-serving, and possibly that's not right either. But however you look at it, you can't go by me or soliciting everyone's opinions. The decision is not ours to make. It can only be made by your sister."

"I wanted her to know how we felt," Noel uttered defensively.

"Bless your heart, Noel. I love you, and I truly believe you think you are doing the best thing for all concerned. However, the truth is you are just rallying support for your idea. Olisa already knows how we feel about her and all that's gone on. She is more than capable of making her own decisions. The right thing to do is don't ask us; ask her. You're discussing *her* life. Whatever conclusion she comes to, we will stand behind it." Grace's voice cracked, but her resoluteness was unwavering. All eyes drifted to Olisa.

Good, another person in my corner. Things were getting better . . . until I caught the look in Olisa's eyes.

Her eyes were closed meditatively. The second her eyes lifted, they immediately locked upon mine. Oh no! My heart fell. She made her decision. I didn't wait to hear her response as the screen door banged behind me when I ran outside.

Somebody shouted my name or maybe everyone did, but I kept running. My tennis shoes squished the pavement as I sprinted down Venice walk streets toward the beach. Houses on both sides seemed to cave in on me, so I ran faster.

I crossed Abbott Kinney Boulevard after coming off the walk streets and cut up to Venice Boulevard, heading west until I reached Dell Avenue. I abruptly turned left and ran up the small rolling hills to the canals. I looked around me at the radically changed landscape. Instead of streets, there were waterways intentionally built by Abbott Kinney like the canals of Venice, Italy, but on a much smaller scale. Pausing to catch my breath, I opened a gate to a place next to the canals that we called the "Duck Park." The sounds of quacking greeted me from the occupants as they paraded around. A couple of ducks evaded me and splashed into the water.

When Olisa was a little girl, I'd often take her to Duck Park so she could play on the swings and playground slide. Then we'd walk down the canals and feed the ducks.

Tonight the park was completely empty.

The humid air didn't help my wheezing as I sat down on one of the swings, struggling to regain my breath. My T-shirt was soaked with sticky perspiration. In the darkness, I watched the interplay of protean shapes and shadows created by the glimmering house lights bordering the park. Except one of the shadows rose up like a great leviathan. The immense shadowy figure stood ominously in the park on a small, raised bridge, looking down at the ducks that clustered around his feet. The man's face was smothered in darkness, but the top of his head glistened like a polar ice cap.

He held a goldenly long neck trumpet with a huge bell at the end of it. He raised the horn majestically to his lips. I almost fell out of the swing when the most beautiful and melodic music I had ever heard flowed out of his instrument. His body rhythmically swayed as he cultivated sounds from that trumpet like he was drilling for oil. Man, it was sweet . . . so sweet. His unique style defied categorization. I'm not exaggerating when I say I have never heard anyone play like that in my life.

He bent, shaped, and transformed the notes before they even came out of the trumpet's bell, which bloomed as bright as a giant sunflower. There was a special timbre in his playing that could be described at best as almost otherworldly. Every note from his horn proceeded to take on a life of its own, a living breathing wave of intense, steadfast emotions. What I experienced was the melisma of a virtuoso who breathed a lifetime into each musical note. The man rhythmically swayed while he played. It seemed like the music poured out of every fiber of his body.

Mesmerized, I got off the swing and sat down on a bench in the playground closer to him. He wore black shades, a black tie, and a dark single-breasted suit with a white collar that reminded me of one of those jazzy hipsters from the 1950s and 60s. He was an anachronism, his music timeless. I sat motionless on the bench, eyes closed and ears sopping up every bit of the music. The soothing ballad he played momentarily washed away my anxiety. I felt honored to be the only audience privy to this cat. By the time he finished his song, there were tears crowding my eyes.

"Hey, bro . . . that was just mad. Whatever it is, you've got *it*."

He tilted his head in my direction and seemed pleased with my assessment. He blew a few extra notes, and even those made my skin crawl. Every duck in the area seemed intent on cuddling around his feet. The ducks were incredibly calm, some even asleep. Oddly, he didn't have any shoes on. Maybe he took them off so he could sit down and dip his feet in the water below.

"So you liked my playing?" he intoned in a profound and mellifluous basso.

"Absolutely," I replied dreamily.

"Thank you. It was specifically for you."

"For me? Uh, yeah, okay . . . Thank you."

"Do you mind if I join you?" he politely asked.

"Oh no, not at all."

What else was I going to say? He walked down from the small bridge. The ducks lethargically parted just enough to allow space for him to walk through. The lone streetlight in the park wrapped its light around his body, forming a dark shadow whose outline radiated energy. I am 6´2˝, and he dwarfed me by about a foot. His massive shoulders stretched across his body like the topography of the Grand Canyon.

Yet, for a man with such an intimidating bulk, a gentleness resided in his body language taking precedence over his physical demeanor. As he approached me, I noticed he casually sized me up. There was an intensity behind those shades that made me appreciate his concealed eyes. He sat down on the bench next to me, and that's when I had a chance to truly study him even though I tried to discreetly do so. This might sound like a strange comment coming from a straight guy, but I'm being real. He was one of the most magnificent creatures I have ever seen, an artist's fantasy. His sculpted face looked like it had been constructed from the finest black marble: sharp angular cheek bones, high forehead, and a straight nose with wide nostrils flaring out in perfect symmetry. There was not one line, blemish, or wrinkle marring his face. It was so smooth and shiny that I imagined to touch it would be like grabbing a wet bar of soap. His closely cropped white hair literally glistened.

Self-consciously I asked, "So what are you doing out here? Practicing for a gig?"

A half smile parted his lips. "No. When I play my music, I am always searching . . . searching for the one note to transcend all others, a note that will be the epiphany for the greatest concert ever."

"Oh, that's cool," was my intellectual response.

"Let me elaborate," he added. "I just don't do what you refer to as 'gigs' anymore, though I still enjoy listening to the musicians of your time."

I thought, *My time*? After a while I said, "So what's a guy as smokin' as you are on the horn doing out here at night playing a trumpet for free? You ought to be in some nightclub, concert hall, or other venue ripping it up."

He fiddled around with his trumpet keys for a second, looking as if he were composing a song in his mind. "You're very kind, but I don't play for engagements. I play for God."

"I get it, and I'm sure you already know this because it's obvious you're a professional, but with your skills, you could cash it in big time."

"I appreciate your sentiments. As a humble servant of God, I play for the world with all that I can offer. The return is far greater than anything you could ever imagine."

I nodded, unsure of how to respond.

"Am I making any sense, or are my ramblings causing your eyelids to close?"

"Oh no, I hear you . . . It makes sense!" I uttered a little *too* exuberantly.

Brother man was different. Then again, so were most musicians. He enunciated each word as if it had to be factory tested before departing from his lips. His deep, rumbling bass had a pure and refined tone to it, slow, steady, thick, and just as powerful as molten lava, and possibly just as incinerating when angered. It was a worldly-wise voice. You would believe this was a man who could be equally comfortable sitting with a beggar or a king.

"I must tell you, my friend; tonight seemed more inspiring than others. I felt compelled to play a tune to ease the pain of one troubled soul. Would that be you?"

The question left me speechless. As he patiently waited for my answer, I had an uneasy feeling. When he turned my way his eyes were like burning coals behind those shades.

"Yeah, partner, I guess you can say that. I'll tell you, man, before you blew that horn, I didn't know if I was coming or going. Your music calmed me down. I no longer feel so out of it. I can think again."

"Good . . . That's what I want to hear." He seemed genuinely pleased. He cradled and stroked his trumpet like it was a baby. The conversation didn't end there. "Why were you so distressed?"

I studied the ground. The directness of his question caught me off guard. The evening's events hurdled the levee and rushed me like a flood.

Sensing my discomfort, the trumpeter leaned over and touched my shoulder with his hand. My skin instantly tingled. All at once, a most plea-surable warmth washed over my body making me feel inordinately relaxed and calm, so much so I bowed my head and almost fell asleep until someone playfully poked my shoulder. I lifted my head and was shocked to find my grandfather Henry standing over me, a big glowing smile on his face. He grabbed me in a hearty bearhug making me giggle like a little kid.

"Look out there, boy; what you doin' with that frown on your face? Tell Big Daddy what's wrong so we can fix you up."

I didn't hesitate. I trusted him more than anyone else in the world. He never laughed at me no matter how many outrageous things I told him. No one cried harder at his funeral than I did years ago.

"I'm worried about Olisa. You know how hard we tried to keep her secret. They know about her. I'm scared. I feel like something bad is going to happen to her."

Big Daddy placed his hands on my shoulder. "Son, you trust me, don't you?"

It was hard for me to see as tears welled up in my eyes fixed on his loving face.

"Boy, don't you worry about a thing. I promise it will all work out the way it's supposed to. You got me?"

"Yes. I miss you, Grandpa . . . I miss our talks."

"Grandson, I've never left you. Just know I'm always here. By the way, Ethan Robinson still can't beat me in checkers!" he laughed.

And with that, Grandpa Henry, his body still roly-poly, lumbered away until he disappeared into a mist, leaving me with an enormous grin on my face. I clung to my euphoria until the stranger dropped his hand from my shoulder. At that moment I shrank back into the real world, confronted by my own confused expression reflected in black sunglasses. Flabbergasted, I ascertained I just poured my heart out to a complete stranger. He held the horn to his lips, fingering the keys like he was playing a silent tune.

"What did you do to me?" I looked away, unable to stand viewing my confused face mirrored in his shades.

"Only what you needed, Joseph."

Once again, words escaped me as I rubbed my forehead.

"You are greatly anguished about your daughter's future. Why?"

"What do you mean 'why'? I'm her father. Shouldn't I be a part of my daughter's major decision making?"

"Your daughter is pursuing her life's calling, her destiny if you prefer. It is not your choice, Joseph. It's something she must do. Some call it fate."

Like a pouty kid, I kicked the sand below me with my foot. "Wait a minute—I never told you my name. Who are you?"

"I am a part of your past, present, and future. There are those who call me the 'Messenger'. Judging by your downcast expression, this explanation is unsatisfying."

My body involuntarily shook. It dawned on me who he was. He was the man on the rooftop over thirty years ago during the Los Angeles Riots. He was the man Gumbo and Laura spoke of who helped Olisa escape from the beach incident, and he was the presence I'd been feeling around me ever since Olisa was born.

"Are you an angel?"

The only response was the rustling of duck wings milling around his feet.

"Okay, let's say you are. Then what is our fate, angel? Are Grace and I just pawns in a much bigger game? We were just kids when Grace became pregnant the first time. We didn't know how to be parents, especially to such a gifted child. Nevertheless, we raised her in the best way we knew how. Now you're basically telling us to butt out?"

"No. I am encouraging you to be a part of her journey."

"Why were we the ones chosen?"

"Joseph, does human vanity lead you to believe you were chosen? Was the color of your skin chosen? Were you chosen to be born in this country? What is, has always been. Olisa found life through you. She could have been born in a Chinese village, but the essence of who she is would have still existed. Her birth is as much a part of your journey through life as it is part of her own path."

I was having a hard time listening as stinging tears blistered my eyes. I gripped the bridge of my nose with the tips of my forefinger and thumb. "I don't know . . . To be honest, I've always been in awe of Olisa. I've never felt worthy to have a child like her."

"Your worth is a value only you can determine, my brother. It has been an inner struggle for you and the source of many of your conflicts."

"You mean like with Noel?"

"Only you can answer that. We may not always understand what is occurring at a given moment, but eventually time reveals all truths. Your son is playing his part, too. He is doing what he must do on his journey. There are many paths but only one exit."

"Why are *you* here?"

"I am here, Joseph, because I have been called. And so has Olisa."

My body shivered, though hardly cold. "What do you mean by *called*?"

"Your daughter is the last hope for a world bent on self-destruction."

Not a muscle on my body moved.

"She's one person. You can't possibly expect . . . I mean what you're asking of her is impossible! How can she . . ."

He held a finger to his lips. "She's not alone in this. Your eyes widen with fear. Fear is your worst enemy, Joseph. Faith is your best friend. Just be there for her."

"My wife says the same thing."

"You married a very wise woman."

The comment brought a rare smile to my stricken face despite the foreboding words uttered earlier. We stood up and shook hands, his engulfing mine. Once again, I experienced that snugly warm sensation. I watched him slowly saunter away into the night. Before he was completely out of my sight, he turned. From that distance, the voice I heard should have been a yell, but it traveled to me as a whisper.

"Always remember, Joseph: nothing is impossible."

All I could see at that moment was a silhouette of him placing the trumpet to his lips. Shockingly, a street lamp's glass casing imploded, shattering into millions of pieces and flutteringly dreamlike to the ground. The isolated light bulb hovered unnaturally in the air like a tiny yellow moon. Then, slowly, effortlessly, I saw those same pieces ascend from the cement and reform anew enshrouding the glass bulb. It now shined with a light more brilliant than before. Afterwards, the horn player vanished. Did I truly witness what I just saw, or was my mind playing tricks on me?

I went back and rocked in the swing until my solitude was broken by the unexpected crunch of footsteps on gravel. It made me catapult from the swing. The ducks arose from their stupor, briskly flapping their wings and quacking incessantly as they scattered, hopped, and waddled toward the canals. Splash after splash filled the night air as battalions of ducks skittered across the water.

"Daddy?"

"Olisa, is that you?"

"It's me. You okay?"

"Yeah, kid, I'm fine."

"I had a feeling you might be here. This was our spot when I was a kid."

"Then get over here and give your pitiful old man a hug!"

The reflections from the house lights made the dark, murky waters of the canal sparkle as we strolled along the walkways hand in hand, just like the old days.

"I'm sorry, Daddy."

"Sorry? I'm the one that should be apologizing, not you."

"No, Daddy, this whole thing . . . Every time I try to do something like this, it falls apart. Just like with Grandma . . ."

"No, don't ever say that, baby. Mama Willis' death wasn't your fault."

We were at the Willises for a Sunday dinner. Four-something in the afternoon, Mama Willis complained that she needed to take a short nap. This wasn't an unusual request; she usually nodded off on the couch, Bible spread out on her lap, or she'd retire to her bedroom. A little later I noticed that Olisa wasn't

outside playing with the other kids. I figured she might have been in the room with Mama Willis, probably bugging her to read a story instead of letting her go to sleep. And, of course, her great-grandmother was only too delighted to do so.

I poked my head inside the partially open door and heard a tiny desperate voice pleading, "Please, Grandmama, please wake up. I want you to read to me, or I can read to you, Grandmama . . . but you have to get up first." Her voice crescendoed. "Please get up! I'm trying to help you. Why are you still sleeping? Wake up!"

With the building frustration in her voice, I realized something wasn't right. I rushed in and caught Olisa furiously massaging Mama Willis's chest, kneading it, and squeezing it just as she did with Flash. Marble-sized tears dropped from her eyes and hit Mama Willis' chest like a leaky faucet. Her heavy eyelids opened and closed with each effort. It was like she was trying to come back, but the ominous dark gray hues lined in her stiff visage where all of life had dissipated told a contrary story. Her left arm held her Bible fused in the crook of her elbow.

"Olisa, Mama Willis has made her transition." My voice was surprisingly controlled after my trembling hand touched her wrinkled brow. Seeing Olisa's agony made me delve for psychological resources I never knew existed. Teary-eyed myself, I gently pulled Olisa away as she crumbled into my arms crying uncontrollably. When I walked into the living room cradling Olisa in my arms, my drawn face clearly indicated the great tragedy that had befallen the family.

A couple of evenings later, still understandably depressed, Olisa sat alone in the corner of her bedroom in her red wooden rocking chair. She tensely rocked back and forth. I felt guilty encroaching upon the territory of this young but old soul who lived deeply in the sanctuary of her thoughts like no nine-year-old I'd ever seen.

"You all right, baby girl?"

"Daddy, how come I couldn't save her?" she asked like it was a human failing.

"Nothing you could do, Olisa. Your great-grandmother's heart just gave out."

"God blessed me with the magic. That's what you told me! Why didn't it work?" Tears invaded her crinkled eye. I saw the reflection of myself, the betrayer, in her pupils.

"I don't know what to say, sweetie . . . Yes, God certainly blessed you with the magic, but you've got to understand; it was time for Mama Willis to go to heaven. None of us have any control over that."

"Why not, Daddy?"

"Some people would say it was God's will."

Her lip poked out, and her feet hammered the floor like car pistons. She stopped rocking the chair. "Well, I don't like God anymore!"

I got down on one knee next to the rocking chair and got up in her face. "Don't . . . ever . . . say . . . anything . . . like . . . that again to me! You hear me!"

"Yes. Sorry, Daddy." I felt bad seeing her sobbing, but it had to be said. I followed it up by more gently saying, "Honey, remember what you said Mr. Robinson told you after he died?"

"Yes."

"Well, I guarantee you Mama Willis is happier now than she's ever been, too. Take a moment and think about that. When you're ready, come join us in the kitchen for some ice cream."

I gave her a big smack on the forehead. Before leaving her room, I looked back. She resembled a miniature version of Rodin's the Thinker as she sat in her red chair trying to sort it out.

For many nights thereafter, Olisa continued to wake up in a cold sweat, crying and pleading in her sleep, still trying desperately to save Mama Willis. For a while, she had been terrified to even go to sleep, fearful that God might snatch her overnight while she slept. Weeks passed before she slept deeply like a child again. It took an even longer time before she made her peace with God again.

We stopped in the middle of one of the bridges crossing the canal as Olisa gazed out over the water.

"Daddy, maybe I should have been more patient. The paramedics probably would have arrived in time to save Ernesto."

"No, baby girl. Don't start second-guessing yourself. Ernesto's wellness clock was ticking with the major loss of blood. You made the right decision."

"But, Daddy, look at the huge mess I created."

"The mess created itself. How would you have felt if you hadn't done anything? What if Chato had died? It would have tormented you forever."

"I guess . . . All the same, it didn't feel very good seeing my father and brother slugging it out over it, either."

"The problem is your father and brother are two ignoramuses who have their own stuff to work out. I guess I haven't been as great a father as I thought I was."

Olisa locked her arm affectionately around mine. "Now who's second-guessing? You've been a great father to both of us."

"Glad *you* think so."

"Noel does, too."

I shrugged. "Okay . . . I'll take your word for it. Aside from that, I just want you to know whatever decision you make, I'm behind you all the way, even if it drives me crazy, like you've been prone to do."

"Thanks, but I already made my mind up," she grinned, throwing her head back and absorbing the beauty of the night sky salted with twinkling stars.

I waited.

"I told my brother I couldn't do it."

"Why? I thought . . . Wait—you're not saying that because of me, are you?"

"Yes and no . . . more so because I just can't do it."

"Hmmm . . ."

"You asked me recently why I came back home."

"Yes, I did. I couldn't understand why you'd return home to a place where the water, heating, lighting, and toilets regularly worked, especially after the Peace Corps offered you such a luxurious existence in remote areas of West Africa and then Guatemala."

"Ha! You're being sarcastic. The real truth is I had no choice."

"Meaning?"

"The voices."

Ever since childhood, Olisa heard voices in her head: talking, laughing, whispering, and warning her. The kids thought she was a weird little girl, particularly when she spoke to the voices in her head out loud. The voices were, at times, as much a part of her as the air she breathed. She used to explain that they were like overhearing a multitude of conversations on a party line.

Olisa didn't learn to find peace of mind with them until she met with a Hopi Medicine Man, a friend of Little Oak's. He explained to her to never fear the voices she heard internally or fight to silence them. "Above all, do not shut them out . . . Listen and hear what they are saying," he advised. He'd expounded that they were the voices of dead spirits attempting to connect with her. She was the conduit to help them communicate with the material world. His advice worked. I never heard her complain again once she accepted the reality of it all. Once she reached that reckoning, she told me the voices were no longer muddled. They became clear and distinct, serving as guides for her in discerning feelings about people, good and bad, as well as a foreboding of things that may occur.

"So what did the voice say to you, kid?"

"To go home. You are needed there. They were so intense. I thought something happened to you or Mom. But now I understand. It was to save Ernesto's life. That's it. Now I feel like I can move on," she said, flipping her braids back over her shoulders.

This would have been a good time to tell her about my conversation with the angel. Anyone else would have laughed, not Olisa. She would have hung on my every word about him, but I couldn't . . . wouldn't.

"I'm glad you came to that conclusion on your own. I'd be fine either way," I lied.

"I really do love my brother. He is driven and rambunctious. I truly believe in his heart he feels he's trying to do a good thing."

"I've never been concerned about your brother's heart. It's the spirituality of his pocketbook that worries me. What did Noel say when you said no to him?"

"He was disappointed, said he understood. He suggested I go find you and let you know my decision."

"That was it?"

"That was it, except for adding I'm not being very realistic. He stressed I'm still going to have to deal with the fact that they will never leave me alone now that they know about me."

"Can't say he's wrong. We'll just have to tackle that monster one day at a time."

We walked home in silence, Olisa's arm interlocked with mine. I remembered how proud I was when we performed the father-daughter waltz during her debutante. She looked so beautiful, all dressed up in an elegant white gown, hair up in a chignon. Now her hair was in thick double braids, poking out of one of those floppy Chambers Brothers' hats with a retro sixties vest, bellbottoms, and sandals, and still beautiful.

The house was quiet as we entered the front door, except for ...

"Hey, Dad."

"Hey," I said, walking apprehensively into the brightly lit dining room as Noel pulled out a chair for me. He coolly strode to the other side of the table and sat down. Looking down at the table, I was accosted by a Scrabble board, a pile of neatly turned-over letter tiles waiting to be shuffled, and two Cuban cigars. Noel had a sly smile on his face as he held a pen and pad and motioned for me to sit down. Grace stood behind him, hands on his shoulders and grinning.

I tugged on my earlobe while studying the empty game board like I was appraising a classic piece of art.

Olisa strutted briskly past Noel, lightly cuffing him upside the head.

"Hey, keep your hands to yourself!"

She slid her arm through Grace's. "Mom, let's leave these two peacocks alone."

"Gladly." She was tickled to see the men in her life preparing to smoke the peace pipe.

"You are a masochist." I leaned over and lit his stogie as it kissed his lips. I rarely smoked except on special occasions. The first cigar I ever had was at Noel's birth.

"Must be, Dad . . . It hurts so much when I have to keep whooping you."

"Tell Scotty to beam you up 'cause you're living in a dream, boy."

"You gonna shuffle or do I have to do that for you, too!"

"Son?"

"Yeah, Pops."

I slowly shuffled the letters, carefully to not to turn them over. "You know your mother and I love you, right? We're very proud of you and all you've accomplished . . ."

"I know that, Dad."

"Good. I just wanted to make sure. Sometimes people say things in anger, but they don't mean it."

"I don't pay it no mind, Pops. We're all guilty of that."

"Uh-huh."

"Now that we've shoved the elephant out of the room, could you please stop shuffling those letters before I fall asleep?"

"Oh! That's how you gonna act? Now you forced me to put some stuff into the game like Edward G. Robinson did Steve McQueen at the poker table in the movie *The Cincinnati Kid*. You goin' down, baby!"

I whipped him by about a hundred points that night. Except it's not much fun beating a distracted player who makes amateurish mistakes. Oh, all the bluster was there, but the mental wheels gyrated in other directions. He occasionally stared deeply at the fireplace with those long curly eyelashes on that boyishly handsome face. No matter what had been said, the Olisa matter wasn't over yet.

Chapter 5

Timing is everything.

K. C. Richards, a record distributor and business associate of Noel's, desperately needed someone trustworthy to house-sit for two weeks while he and his family were away on vacation in Sydney, Australia. Richard's house was in the picturesque resort town of Santa Barbara, California, which is about one hundred miles north of Los Angeles. He also owned a coterie of animals that had to be fed: three dogs, a cat, an iguana, two hamsters, a rabbit, an ostrich, and a scarlet macaw.

Noel asked Olisa if she'd be willing to do it. She didn't hesitate to say yes. First of all, she loved animals and they loved her. Secondly, it offered her the opportunity to temporarily escape Venice Beach for a little while until things, hopefully, cooled out.

K. C. lived in a hill and ritzy area known as Hope Ranch. While there, Olisa discovered a desolate and magnificent stretch of beach. She had to clamber down a cliff to get to the sandy beach, but it was worth it. The privacy gave her peace of mind as she took daily strolls with her roommate, Freeloader.

Freeloader was Olisa's golden retriever. He was a three-month old pup whom she found barely alive in an alley several blocks away, frail, starved, emaciated, and dehydrated. Olisa triumphantly nursed him back to life.

Freeloader turned out to be a great companion: intelligent and fiercely loyal to his savior, Olisa.

The day Olisa returned home from Santa Barbara with Noel, something had changed about her, something in the eyes. They pulled into the garage, ignoring, as usual, the KLSC truck and other assorted vehicles camped out in the alley. Noel's tinted windows allowed no one to see inside the car. After so many false alarms, a blasé Eva Sanchez nonchalantly waved instead of engaging in her attention-getting semaphore routine.

Olisa and Noel quietly walked to Olisa's studio door. The perplexed expression on Noel's face totally contrasted with Olisa's placidity. He stood at the door with her for a few seconds, rattling his keys. Finally, he shook his head and muttered a quick goodbye as he marched into the garage. He angrily revved his car and screeched out the garage, almost hitting one of the vans stationed in the alley. Seemingly unperturbed, Olisa had a cursory discussion with Grace and me about her stay in Santa Barbara when we walked out into the backyard. Shortly afterwards, she headed into her studio.

I assumed Olisa and Noel had a spat. Naturally, I wanted to knock on Olisa's door and press her like a hot iron, but Grace tapped my shoulder. "Leave it alone. She'll come to us when she's ready."

Sure enough, just as we were settling for bed and I was about to flip off the switch on the table lamp, there was a soft tap on the back door. In a barely audible voice we heard, "Mom, Dad . . . are you up? Can I come in?"

"Of course, baby," Grace said opening the door and leading her into our bedroom.

"I'm sorry. I hope I'm not disturbing you guys."

"Don't worry about it, kid," I replied, patting the bed for her to sit down.

She lay down on her back along the foot of the bed crisscross from us with her hands behind her head.

"You want me to turn on the overhead light?"

"No, no, Mom . . . I like it better with just your lamp on."

I was proud of myself for exercising a little patience and not saying anything to fill in air space while Olisa juggled her thoughts.

"Dad, last night during my meditations on the beach, I thought about our conversation at the park, and thought, if I'm feeling this stressed out, what in the world will it feel like later? I even made plans to drive down to Ensenada and hide out among some friends until this whole thing blows over."

"Makes perfect sense to me. If you need some money, all you've got to do is ask. When did you want to go?"

Olisa folded her hands and lightly pounded them against her chin. Frowning, she stared deeply into the shadows against the wall.

"Everything changed last night."

Duck Park, here I come! Once again, I wanted to take off running, but this time I expected Grace to match me stride for stride.

"Last night I was walking on a deserted stretch of beach . . ."

She paused as if she wasn't sure whether to continue. "I am absolutely sure there were no other people in the vicinity," she blurted out defensively, not so much to us as to herself. "If there had been, I know Free would have at least given me a warning bark. Yet, I sensed this presence. It made my skin tingle. Free must have felt it, too, because his tail beat my leg mercilessly."

Olisa spoke like she was under a spell, trembling and twitching slightly. She continued to gaze into a universe we were not privy to. A whimsical smile spread across her lips as she abruptly sat up on the edge of the bed, her twinkling eyes ballooning.

"Did you see the full moon last night?" she asked, not really waiting for an answer. "The sky out there was midnight blue, and the moon had a supernatural glow. It looked so close, I felt like I could scoop it into my arms. The sky, it was so beautiful it was like seeing a living, breathing Van Gogh painting . . . and the sea . . . it truly glittered. I mean wow . . . the night was just magnificent. All of a sudden, I noticed a woman standing ankle deep in the ocean waters staring at me. Maybe she had been there and I just didn't see her at first because I was taking in the beauty of the evening. It was like a mermaid emerged from the sea. Except, the longer I gaped at her, the more it struck me that she wasn't standing *in* the water—she stood inches *above* it.

"I rubbed my eyes thinking it was just an illusion, a result from me fasting the day before. But I knew I was fooling myself. She was real."

I wiped my clammy hands against the covers as Grace leaned forward.

"I called out, 'Hello,' but she didn't answer. Oh, I wish you guys could have seen her. She looked like a shimmering porcelain doll in the moon's light. The vision of her floating just above the water was breathtaking."

Grace listened intently. She cupped her hands tightly together.

"She wore multiple layers of clothes that twisted and flapped in the breeze. Her olive-colored skin gleamed as if a fluorescent light burned beneath her skin. Her hair was loose, flowing, fanning the moon, so long that the tips danced against the edges of the water."

Grace turned toward me, her dark-brown eyes misting as she grabbed for my hand.

"Sounds like your lady," I whispered to her.

"Yes," Grace sighed nostalgically. "I told Olisa how she used to visit me on occasion during the night when I was pregnant with her." Grace's eyes grew heavy as I held her face in my hands and kissed her warm, full lips. I stroked the spongy salt and peppercorn rows that crowned her head while she snuggled into my arms.

"It was her, Mom," Olisa confirmed in an ethereal voice, her glazed eyes staring past us. "Sometimes I'd wake up when I was little, and there she would be standing in my room. I always thought it was just a reoccurring dream. As she faced me, I couldn't see her eyes, which appeared to be closed. In her presence, I felt as if every part of my body and mind was exposed. She never moved any closer than where she was, but when she finally spoke, I could hear her as clearly as if she were standing next to me. I can't say whether her mouth even moved."

"What did she say?" Grace asked softly in earnest.

"She began by asking a question. '*Why are you afraid, Olisa? You have nothing to fear. Not when God is by your side.*'

"Listening to her soothing voice was so ridiculously comforting and warm, it made me feel like I was soaking in a hot tub. I don't know if I spoke aloud or if it was in my head, but I answered, 'Because I am weak. I can't do this. For me, the blessing has been a curse. I am not the one you want. Let someone else who has more strength and more confidence be the bearer of God's great gift.'

"'*Olisa, God is all the strength you will ever need. Weakness and fear are frailties of being human. Do not lose faith in who you are, for your humanity is a vessel for the greatness that is God.*'

"'What does God want me to do?'

"'*To be a child again and open your heart to the world.*'

"'And how do I do that?'

"'*Be a world unto yourself.*'

"'I don't understand.'

"'*It is important for you to be open, to love freely, compassionately, and without restraint like you did as a child. Don't give fear refuge to be your judge and jury. You are here to help people as only you can.*'

"'I can't.'

"'*Yes, you can, baby.*'

"It was another woman's directly behind me, a voice that made my heart beat vigorously, one no longer straddled by age or pain."

Olisa's chest swelled as she paused to gather herself.

"I flinched more from surprise than fear when I unexpectedly felt arms close around me, arms that offered me so much comfort I wanted to remain in them forever. I recognized the hands, except they were completely smooth now, no longer callused or wrinkled; they were thick and strong welcoming hands, brimming with a new life.

"'Grandmama Willis?'

"'Yes, child, but don't turn around. I want you to feel how much you are loved.'"

Olisa had gotten up and crouched in the corner of the bedroom embracing herself. As much as both of us wanted to go to her, we didn't budge. She was reliving the moment. The last time we did that she became totally disoriented, later chastising us for disturbing her concentration.

"'Oh, Grandmama . . .' I cried as she caressed my quaking body. 'I miss you so much. Please don't leave me again. I need you more than ever now.'

"'Honey, I've never left you. Don't you realize that?'

"'Yes, no . . . I don't know . . . I just want you to stay with me.'

"'I can't, baby. I'm only here to tell you the universe has special plans for you. Don't be afraid to commit. Once you step into the light, you will understand the realities of your life.'

"As her hands and arms began to fade, the chill of the night air caused me to shudder tremendously. I cried out, 'You can't leave me now! There is so much more I need to learn, Grandma Willis.'

"'I'm here for you, baby . . . Just know you are loved more than you'll ever know.'

"Afterwards, I crumpled into the sand seized by a sudden panic. I thought I was having a full-blown heart attack. My breathing was exceedingly out of control as I scrambled and clawed madly at the ground like a burrowing sand crab. Grains of sand cut painfully into my eyes, and the precipitous savagery of salt water crashing against my body forced me to tumble over onto my backside. It dragged me into its maw like a piece of flotsam.

"I would have died last night, if not for the powerful hands that wrenched me from the riptides and pulled me ashore. As I lay in the sand, gasping for air and spitting out gallons of salt water, there was a sonic boom so deafening that my skin must have turned as white as these walls. A miniature tornado engulfed me with billions of fairy like particles of light swirling and dancing mischievously around my head."

Olisa's eyes blinked rapidly, and her head whipped back and forth.

"It was weird . . . My body became limp, and I began to levitate above the ground, rising as if I was being toted by a hot air balloon—all of this beyond my control. By and by it dawned on me that this is a test of faith."

She fixed her eyes on us.

"One of Grandmama's favorite sayings was, 'You must have faith in things not seen.' Somehow, I managed to open my mind and release my fear. Soon afterwards, an air of serenity settled upon me. I started to trust, and instead of fighting it, I surrendered to whatever fate had in store for me."

Olisa unconsciously straightened the covers at the foot of the bed contemplating all that internally transpired. Though she was only a few feet away from us, she sounded as if she were speaking from another room.

"A brilliant incandescent light fell from the sky and rapidly moved through me like a finger passing through my body. It filled me with so much joy that it caused spontaneous screams to leap from my mouth. I laughed loud and hard while floating through a velvety night sky. It didn't faze me when I began free-falling to the earth which received me like a fluffy pillow.

"When I awoke, at first I thought it was the warm surf splashing my face, but it was Freeloader licking me. I sat up shocked to find myself perched on top of a cliff. Below, a spectacular panorama of beach stretched out before me. Streaks of light rocketed from the ocean, followed by the tip of an orange-red sun lazily ascending above the water making the ocean sparkle like a million gems. It was the most awesome thing I have ever witnessed."

Olisa sat back on the edge of the bed, her fingers in a wrestling match with her hair. "Am I crazy or just being overly dramatic? Things like that don't ordinarily happen to people, right? Do you think it was just a silly old dream of mine?"

This would have been a good time for me to share my experience at the Duck Park, but I didn't . . . I guess I was still trying to come to terms with it. Instead, I replied, "Olisa, you don't just dream; you experience."

She cocked her head almost comically and, through the loose strands of rippling hair, produced a mischievous grin. "Is this what you'd call an epiphany, Dad?"

"For someone else, *yes*. For you, I would call it an affirmation. You have been subconsciously preparing for this moment your entire life. You are the host, not the guest to this party."

After a long silence she asked, "Will you guys be all right with my decision?" The question was directed more at Grace whose tears soaked through my pajama shirtsleeve.

"Yes, Olisa. It was only a matter of time. I just kept hoping it would never come."

"Time for what, Mom?"

"For you to fulfill your destiny."

It was on.

After hearing about Olisa's change of heart, Noel's grin was spread wider than Earvin "Magic" Johnson's when he signed his first Los Angeles Laker basketball contract. Noel was right about one thing—Olisa's decision, one way or another, would not affect the media machine, which had already whipped itself into a firestorm. A recent video turned in by beachside resident, Greg Hill, who shot another angle of the now-infamous gang battle, fueled the heightened activity. Though it was extremely amateurish, it gave an even better glimpse than KLSC of the stabbing. The new one showed the assailant's hand and knife working like a jackhammer on Ernesto's chest. For the hundredth time, we saw Olisa cradling Chato and kneading his bloodied stomach with her fingers.

Still, despite the most recent video, it was debatable as to whether Olisa actually healed the boy. The latest argued a pretty strong case for the latter although most reporters declined an opinion, leaving it to their audience to decide, with the exception of Eva Sanchez. Eva unflinchingly asserted that Olisa performed a miracle healing. Consequently, the station's ratings skyrocketed. In an era of superfluous reality shows and social media networking sites such as Facebook, Instagram, Twitter, and TikTok, the legend of this healer from Venice Beach didn't require the validation of the mainstream news media. It was blazing across social media circuits and turning into its own beast of a story, and Eva was riding the waves.

She wasn't alone. Given the green light, Noel took over handling everything that revolved around Olisa with an air of authority neither Grace nor I had ever seen in action. He feverishly worked at building a protective structure for Olisa and the family that would be prepared to deal with any fallout that might occur with all that was going on.

"Mom, Dad, I hope you don't mind. I called the phone companies on your behalf and had all the telephone numbers changed. I did the same for the rest of our immediate family. Please be selective about who you give your phone numbers to."

"Yes, sir," I said with a salute.

"In the meantime, anyone calling your former home phone number, including Olisa's phone, has been rerouted to a separate office phone for business. I've already got my executive assistant, Savannah, with an additional crew working remotely handling the phones and screening calls . . . Ooohh, is that the doorbell?"

Grace opened the door for a short squatty white man wearing a face mask and dressed in gray uniform overalls with a red Protect-A-Watch label on the breast pocket of his uniform.

"Over here, Jeff! Jeff's done a lot of work for me on other homes."

"Hey, hey, how you folks doin'?" he said in a thick Brooklyn accent. His eyes surveyed our house's interior like a guy casing a bank.

"This gentleman here is going to do a thorough inspection of the house and Olisa's studio and assess what kind of security system will work best. No offense, Pop, but it's time to trash that antiquated system you've been using and get a more sophisticated alarm," Noel quickly remarked, escorting Jeff past us.

"Whatever you say, Noel." I glanced at Grace who bemusedly shrugged her shoulders.

And that was the way it was for a couple of weeks: Noel ushering in a variety of technicians throughout the house. He footed the bills, though I suspect the record company reimbursed him since Olisa was listed as one of RPM's newest motivational artists.

In the beginning, Noel apprised Olisa of everything he was doing. There was a mutual show of respect and adulation between the two of them that was being nurtured. As much as I disagreed with what they were planning, the greatest enjoyment Grace and I received from this was watching our kids work together.

Nonetheless, business is business. Noel knew what he was doing way before I caught on, like a talented chess player ten steps ahead of the game. By keeping Olisa out of the public eye for several weeks, Noel sprinkled fertilizer on the public's curiosity about this miracle worker who was suddenly nowhere to be found.

Handmade signs cropped up on a daily basis on the Venice Beach Boardwalk.

Where are you, Olisa?

Olisa, SAVE US. We need your healing before we become normal Angelenos! We want the Big O!

Where is the Good Witch of Venice? Oz needs her!

Come on back, Mama Venice. Outsiders are trying to run the asylum.

Where's a good psychic when you need one?

KLSC continued to fire off clips from the same beach incident and interview periodically, but that was running thin. No other stations had anything else other than the same videos. Noel's efforts to keep her off the streets and out of the public eye worked successfully. The city had concocted a fever, and the time had arrived to treat it.

Noel made sure all calls from the media and interested parties were handled professionally and diplomatically. Callers were informed that Olisa was on a spiritual hiatus and needed time to recharge her energies. And yes, everything that was said about her ability to heal was true. Crank callers and racists screaming epithets certainly made their presence known, but they were soon blocked.

However, to my surprise, whatever Noel's timeline was, Olisa's was shorter.

One night Grace, Olisa, Noel, and I were chowing down on some take-out food from Akbar's Cuisine of India on Washington Boulevard in Venice. We were engaged in an animated discussion about the assassination conspiracies revolving around John and Robert Kennedy, Martin Luther King, Jr., and Malcolm X when Olisa sedately interrupted saying, "Noel, it's time."

I thought Noel was going to gag on his lamb biryani. "Time for what, Oli?"

She muttered, "I'm tired of sitting around indefinitely. I need to get out and talk to people before I go crazy. Whatever it is we're doing, let's do it!"

"Sis, relax. I hear everything you're saying. I got you!" Noel said reassuringly, hands in the air. "We're not just kicking back. We've been rehearsing for the big event, getting ready, more prepared, you know?"

The expression in her eyes said time had run out.

"I mean, you're right . . . It's time and you're ready now. You're ready . . . so, all right, here we go. Let me make a couple of calls, and I'll get something going. I was just kinda hoping you'd be a little more patient for—"

"No."

"Cool. No problem, sis. I love it. Let's do this. Don't worry; it *will* happen. I just need you to sit tight for a week more. and then we're there. That work for you?"

She nodded and resumed eating.

Solving the conspiracies would have to wait. Noel abruptly hopped out of his chair and headed to the den with his phone in one hand and a vegetable samosa in the other.

"Meet Noel Timmerman, one of the top executives of one of the fastest growing small independent record companies on the West Coast, RPM Enterprises. CEO Roberta P. McMillan has nothing but praise for this young man, crediting him as a significant factor in their continuing trajectory toward the top of the recording industry. We've asked him to join us this evening, not to talk about the success of RPM but to discuss a new venture he is starting with his sister, Olisa Timmerman. Timmerman, you'll remember, is a woman who is rapidly ascending her own ladder as a folk hero after her fearless stance during what the station fondly calls the 'Independence Day Resurrection.'

"Noel, thank you so much for joining us on the *Special Edition* section of our news program."

Eva casually brushed her long bangs with her fingertips even though her perfectly coiffed hair was in little danger of covering her eyes. A fast-rising celebrity in her own right, her new hairdo had been mentioned in fashion magazines, particularly because it was a bold and sexy cut for a newscaster. The public liked her willing-to-risk-it-all attitude, symbolic of her hairstyle. Many were touting her as the Latina version of Diane Sawyer, and of course, she ran with it.

"My first question is, how is Olisa? And where is she? I'm looking at my watch; there's still time for her to join us."

Noel chuckled as he adjusted his natty deep-green silk tie. "Eva, she would love to be here, but she is on a spiritual hiatus at this time. The events on July the Fourth caused her to reexamine her role in the world."

"Has she found it?"

"She has. She wants to use her talents to help people in the most effective ways possible."

"On that note, I'd say this is the perfect time to tell us about this exciting new organization the two of you have formed."

"My pleasure. We've created a company called OLISA, Inc. Naturally, my sister hates the idea of us using her name. Nonetheless, to me it signifies what she personifies. The acronym stands for 'Only Love can Inspire the Spirit to Awaken.'"

"Great title! So what is the purpose for your organization?"

"Simple. Our mission is to heal the world."

Eva teasingly smirked at the camera. "Gee, that's a novel idea." She turned back to Noel. "I don't mean to be facetious, but how do you propose to accomplish this?"

Noel displayed his most charming smile. "Drop by next Thursday evening for our concert, Ms. Sanchez, and you'll find out."

"Concert? I'll be there. Where is it being held?"

Noel faced the camera. "Thursday evening, starting at 6:00 PM, OLISA, Inc. is inviting all of you to attend the First Universal Concert for Spiritual Healing (UCSH) on the Santa Monica Pier. It's free to the public, no admissions fee, donations only. If you want more information, please call; I believe the number is on the screen . . ."

"It is."

"Great. It's on a first-come, first-served basis, and we are anticipating a high turnout. Only a limited number of people are allowed on the pier, so be there early!"

"What can we expect?"

"You can expect to have a great time! It's going to be the feel-good event of the summer! It will be well-organized, majorly secured, with loads of entertainment, motivational speakers, music, and bands including the renowned bassist, JJ Willis, who volunteered his services to act as a musical director. He has already assembled some of the hottest musicians in the area to perform. And there will be a couple of surprises if all goes as well as I anticipate."

"And what about Olisa? How does she fit into this?"

"Who do you think the headliner is?"

"Olisa?" Eva appeared genuinely nonplussed by Noel's calculated time bomb. "Doing what?"

"Doing what she does—*miracles*," Noel proclaimed.

"Excuse me?"

"You heard me right—miracles."

Eva waited for him to qualify his response. Noel only sat there with a complacent grin.

"Okay, we'll leave it at that, Mr. Noel Timmerman. I can't wait!"

"It will be worth it." Noel shook her extended hand, and then the camera cut to a closeup on Eva's face.

"There it is, folks. Maybe on Thursday some of the numerous questions in your texts, letters, faxes, and emails will, at long last, be answered. Was the healing of Ernesto 'Chato' Padilla a coincidence, hoax, or truly a miracle? We'll find out because I can assure you, KLSC will be there on the scene."

I wasn't sure what Olisa was thinking. Her face expressed indifference as she watched the telecast, but the light reflection from the television made her eyes glow like two copper pennies. I was only hoping no one heard my heart beating like dueling tap dancers. Once the interview ended, Olisa kissed Grace and me goodnight and headed into her studio with Free. Throughout the night, I periodically awoke to see her bed lamp burning behind her closed shutters.

As D-Day loomed closer, Noel moved into extra-high gear, diligently making sure everything was in place. He was the exact opposite of Olisa who was as mellow as Noel was super-hyped. If he slept over three consecutive hours leading up to the grand event, I would have been shocked.

"Son, you've got to slow down. If you keep going at this pace, you'll give yourself a heart attack. You look like you got weeks' worth of groceries in those bags under your eyes."

"Dad, we got one shot, just one, to make this thing happen, and I'm going to make the best of it. When we get past Thursday, then I promise I'll sleep for a week."

"Uh-huh . . . I'll hold you to that," I yelled to his backside as he walked quickly down the hall holding his phone (his third ear) and stuffing a Taco Bell burrito down his throat.

That's why I bugged him relentlessly to agree to go to lunch with me on Wednesday, the day before the concert, to relax and eat a good and healthy meal. Howbeit, some unexpected issues dethroned my good intentions. I knew trouble was brewing when I walked into his posh Century City office and found his lip stuck out so far you could have slipped a CD in it.

"All right, all right, stop pouting. Who took your ball this time? You tell those bad boys that your father—oops, sorry. I didn't realize you were on the phone." I tiptoed in and eased the door closed.

He dropped his finger from his lips and pointed to the chair on the other side of his desk. "Hey, Dad, have a seat. They've got me on hold . . . You won't believe it!" He held the phone to his ear like it was a lead weight.

The look on his face was so sour, I thought about running down to the lobby gift shop and buying him a pound of Rolaids.

"Yeah, Savannah . . . you got hold of her? . . . Good! Hold all the rest of my calls."

He rolled his eyes as he waited for the line to connect.

"Eva, Eva, Eva, how are you? . . . Tell me it isn't so . . . Wait. Hold on. My father's here. We're going to lunch after we finish talking . . . No, no, you don't need to hang up. I'm not about to let you go now that I've got you on the line. Do you mind if I put you on speakerphone? . . . Just a sec. Can you hear me?"

"Yes! Good afternoon, Joe. How are you?"

"Hanging in there, Ms. Sanchez. And you?"

"Very good, thank you, but please call me Eva. How's that amazing daughter of yours?"

"She's good."

"Wonderful! I'm looking *very* forward to seeing her tomorrow night. Venice Beach has the eighth wonder of the world living there. How could you have kept this secret for so long?"

"Just lucky, I guess."

"Well, Eva, let's get to the bottom line. My assistant tells me KLSC plans on keeping this secret a little longer. What the heck is going on?"

"I'm just trying to be upfront with you, Noel. Management has asked me to pull back on the story temporarily."

"I was under the impression your ratings vastly improved since you began covering the story."

"They did. But the word got handed down that the suits want me to focus on more real news instead of what they tagged as tabloid journalism. Look; they even cut my upcoming new special series report on the paranormal."

Noel planted his elbows soundly on his desk and rubbed his forehead. "Tabloid journalism—really? Come on, Eva. What you're really trying to tell me is management is afraid to bare their ass in public. They don't want to be the laughingstock of the networks if this turns out to be a hoax."

"More or less."

"Uh-huh . . . so let me get this straight. You coax me to be on your program. I announce our upcoming concert, which is tomorrow, and now you're telling me that the network is not going to cover it. That's not right, Eva."

"No, it's not. But it's not personal, Noel," she replied, lowering her voice surreptitiously. "I'll still be there."

"Yeah, but not in an official capacity, in other words, without the camera crew and the exposure."

It was quiet on the other end.

"So what am I supposed to do now, Eva?"

"I know you're a trouper. Go on with the show!"

"Without any publicity? You guys screwed me! I could have done other shows, but I made the mistake of trusting you."

"You still can. I'm sorry, Noel. I know you're upset, and I don't blame you. But I can tell you this: the other networks aren't going to touch it either, not until everything that occurred is substantiated."

"Substantiated?" Noel jumped up and stood spreadeagled over the speaker. "This is bullshit, Eva! You were there! You saw her heal Chato!"

"You're right. The problem is Chato refused all medical treatment. He never went to a doctor and disappeared a day later. No one can find him to do a follow-up. I don't doubt the authenticity, but to the big boys upstairs, it looks suspicious and they are sweating me about it."

"It's documented on film!"

In the midst of his annoyance, Noel offered me a cigar to which I shook my head. He slammed the cigar case and quickly lit one acting as if his mental equilibrium would be restored once it touched his lips.

"Some of it is documented. Even so, what certifies these images as being any more credible than the ones you've seen in a pitched tent at a good ol' country revival meeting?"

"Because she really did it!"

"Prove it. And again, this is not me talking."

Noel took an extra-long toke on his cigar as he slumped into his armchair that had enough leather to start a cattle stampede.

"Fine. I get the point. So now you think this is all a made-up fairy tale?"

"Never said that. Noel, you know how I personally feel about Olisa. Otherwise, I wouldn't have put my career on the line. There's not a lot of job security in this industry for a Latina reporter with all the overall competition out there. The only thing that saved my behind was how much the ratings increased. I can't afford to take that risk again. Everything must be corroborated. Eventually, I think I can pull enough information together to make this the greatest news story of the century. But that's going to take time. You understand?"

"Sure, as long as you understand that I can take Olisa's story elsewhere. The tabloids are making six-figure offers to us daily."

That's one I didn't know about. But typical of Noel to keep it tightly under wraps.

There was a long pause and a sigh over the speaker.

"That's certainly your option, but they're not going to offer you the legitimacy you seek. You want Olisa's story side by side with 'I met an alien with three heads in my backyard'?"

Noel sat back down. "Then I'll put together my own crew, and we'll make something happen."

"You have to make that call, Noel. I'm just asking you to be more patient."

The chair practically gasped as Noel propelled himself forward, trailed by a huge bloom of smoke. He paced back and forth.

"Mr. Timmerman, what about you? How do you feel about all of this?"

"Ms. Sanchez, this is Noel's show. You know where I stand. I hope the whole thing dies out with the eight-track tape."

"Eva, we're done. I've got to prepare for tomorrow."

"Well, no matter what you decide to do, I'll be at the show tomorrow no matter what. Okay?"

"Whoop-de-doo!"

"Duly noted. And I understand you're disappointed, and I'd be angry, too. Before you hang up, I just want to ask: I have been given a green light to do a show on paranormal phenomenon directly related to this. Do you think Olisa would consent to healing a person on our broadcast if we found someone with a certified medical ailment as part of a segment on healers and shaman?"

"Call me when you get it together, and then we'll talk. Goodbye," Noel remarked in a monotone masking the outrageous grin spreading on his face as he switched off the speakerphone.

"Pop, a change of plans. How's Italian food sound to you?"

"Boy, if you don't get that shit-eating grin off your face! Twenty minutes ago you looked like you lost your best friend. Ever since you got off the phone with Eva you've been smiling the entire drive to Horacio's in Brentwood. Big

Joe Turner would say you're like a one-eyed cat peeping through a seafood store. What are you so doggone happy about? I know you said Horacio's is one of your favorite Italian restaurants, but . . ."

"After today, Pops, Horacio's may be my favorite, period."

"That right? Then deal me in, 'cause I haven't got a clue to what's going on."

"First, have a taste of some of this prosciutto and cantaloupe I ordered for the table. It's kicking!" Glancing over his shoulder he whispered, "Lot of studio people hang out in here, you know."

I nodded as I stirred my salad.

"So what did you think of Eva's suggestion?"

"You mean about Olisa healing an individual on her show who has a medically proven illness? It's a little contrived, but it's a good idea if you're trying to get attention."

His grin spread even wider.

"No, not just a good idea. It's a great idea!" Noel closed his eyes and held his head back as he savored the taste of Merlot rolling around in his mouth. "Now think about this: what if this wasn't just your average everyday person but an internationally beloved film and theater superstar? What do you think would happen then?"

"The ratings on the show would blast through the roof. I can't even imagine . . ."

"Exactly. That's why I'm all smiles."

I still wasn't getting it.

Noel waved to the maître d, a tanned handsome young man who escorted two very attractive and voguish-dressed young women to a table. Once he departed from them, he headed our way. They giggled and appraised his backside as he confidently strolled toward us with a curved grin.

"It sure would be nice to have some decent service in this joint instead of watching the host flirt with all the pretty women!"

"Is that you, Mr. Noel? How did you slip past security again?"

"I told them I was here to kick your ass, and they immediately let me through."

"Ha! Can't trust nobody these days," he said as Noel stood up to embrace him.

"Danny, this is my father, Joseph."

"Pleasure to meet you, sir. For your sake, I pray you have other children?"

"Fortunately, yes."

"Dan's a real charmer, isn't he, Dad?"

"We always try to show our best face for the downtrodden, sir," he joked to me while rubbing Noel's shoulders. "So when are you going to sign me up, Noel?"

"Just hang in there, kid; your time will come. We just haven't found a spot yet for a rapper who sings Italian operas."

"Obviously, you're not trying hard enough, but how could you when you spend all your time in here."

"Caught," Noel chuckled, hugging his arm. "Hey, is the chief here tonight?"

"She is only available for our paying customers."

"Oh, it's like that? Okay, I've got some motivation for her. Let her know that her bastard son is sitting here with her Black lover and is about two seconds from doing a lap dance with one of her best paying customers . . . That should bring her out here."

"Why didn't you say that at first, *signore*? Let me see if I can find her. Again, nice meeting you, Father Timmerman." He warmly shook my hand. "Dinner is on me tonight, Noel, but only because your father's here."

"Great, then we'll be back tomorrow."

"Works for me. It's my night off." He squeezed Noel's shoulder. "See you later, buddy."

"Thanks, Daniele. We appreciate it."

"Hey, that was nice."

"Daniele is a really great kid and one hell of a tenor. If he becomes half as big in the world of operas as his father is to acting, then he's going to live a pretty nice life. And don't think those little honeys flirting with him aren't aware of that."

"Who is his father?"

"Ever hear of Nick Cavaliere?"

"Nick Cavaliere, *the* Nick Cavaliere?"

"*The.*"

"You mean the same Cavaliere who's practically won every stage and film acting award around?"

"That's the one."

"No kidding? Damn! That's my boy. He's the king!"

"Was."

The comment was so cold it made my blood freeze.

"Oh my God, Noel . . . You can't be thinking . . ."

"I am. He is one of the most revered actors on the entire planet."

"No doubt about that. Nicholas Cavaliere, who came from a dirt-poor Sicilian background, dug his way out of the trenches and fought and climbed his way to the top of the ladder. Over the past thirty years, he made so many career comebacks it became passé. Just two years ago, at the age of sixty, he was once again the top box-office draw, and his face was plastered on as many magazines covers as any young Hollywood gun. He was easily paired with leading ladies half his age because of his charm and still-outrageous good looks. He was one of those artists whose sophistication and manliness appealed to both men and women.

"Instead of riding peacefully toward the twilight of his career, Cavaliere stampeded to the apex, commanding mondo bucks per picture, that is until a falling scaffold on a movie set altered the course of his life by crashing into his spine and paralyzing him from the neck down. It was heartbreaking to think that someone who brought so much enjoyment to millions was struck down like that."

"And let me guess—you think you've got the cure for what ails him?"

"Only if you believe in miracles."

"Finally! He's here, my long-lost son. And who is this good-looking gentleman you have brought with you? Is he for me? You could have at least asked him to take off his wedding ring."

We both rose to greet an impeccably dressed woman in a dark suit with a purple orchid in her hair. Her hair was stretched tight into a bun with one thin white streak that flared boldly in the middle. She was a strikingly handsome woman with an elegance about her that lit up the room. From all the stories I had read about Cavaliere's impoverished beginnings, I couldn't believe this classy lady was ever from a poverty-stricken environment. But then again, I've always been a believer that true class can never be purchased. It's as much a part of you as the nose on your face. She gave Noel two wet smacks on each cheek, eventually fixing her emerald eyes on me.

"Mama Cavaliere, this is my father, Joseph."

"Wonderful! I have heard so much about you, Joseph. Welcome to our humble little eatery. Please, please sit down and eat before your food gets cold." Her flowery voice was strongly peppered by her Italian accent.

"Nice meeting you, Mrs. Cavaliere. Noel brags all the time that you have the best Italian food in the city."

"That's why we love having Noel here. He lays it on thicker than my special marinara sauce," she laughed. "But please call me Lena, Joseph. Your son raves all the time about your restaurant, too. Didn't I just read a review about it the other day in the 'Living' section of the *Los Angeles Times*?"

"Yes, we were happy about that."

"Good, good . . . I hope it brought you lots of business."

"Definitely. We're grateful for any boost we can get."

"I understand. The economy's been tough on all of us little guys in the restaurant business, especially with all the chains out there waiting to devour us as soon as they see us taking a nap. But we do our best to survive, yes?"

"Yes, ma'am. That's what it's all about."

"Well, you enjoy your food before it gets even colder. It loses its taste when you let it sit."

"Lena, you are invited to come down our way any time. We'll fill you up with so much soul food, you'll think you were born in the South!"

"I'm sure I'll love it, but I'm afraid my stomach and hips will be miserable. Having said that, life is too short, so I accept!" She laughed. "Now, you two enjoy the rest of your afternoon."

"Oh, Mama Cavaliere, before you leave there is something I would like to discuss with you," he interposed, whisking her hand into his.

"My goodness, Noel, don't look so serious. You're scaring me. Are you about to propose marriage again?" She tilted her head and looked querulously from him to me.

About this point I wanted to run and hide under the awning outside the building's entrance. I knew where Noel was going with this.

"No, Mrs. Cavaliere, not this time, although what I am proposing has everything to do with your husband."

"Nick?"

"Yes. How is he doing?"

"Fine," she replied with a polite smile. Her eyes started blinking rapidly.

"No, Mrs. Cavaliere, I mean how's he *really* doing?"

Her smile evaporated. "He's fine, Noel. Why do you ask?"

"I know someone who can heal him."

Initially I thought the din from the lunch crowd drowned out his words until I saw her jaw clenched so tightly it made a vein in her temple poke out like a broken bone. She paused and smiled at one of the customers passing by and then patted Noel's hand.

"I appreciate what you are doing, but let us continue to deal with this on our own. Thank God, Nicholas made a lot of money in his career. He's being treated by some of the world's finest doctors and specialists, but despite all the money we've shelled out, he's no better off than the day he suffered the accident."

"That's what I'm trying to tell you, Mrs. Cavaliere; you don't have to spend another dime. If you hear me out, Nicholas could be walking by tomorrow."

"We both know that would take a miracle."

"Now we're on the same page. The person I—"

"Stop, Noel." Lena's eyes glistened. "I'm sure you mean well, but what you suggest is impossible."

Noel wanted to say more, but she waved for him to be quiet.

"Nicholas wants to be remembered the way the public saw him two years ago: the confident and courageous man who was wheeled out before the cameras, smiling and promising he'd never give up the fight to walk and return to acting."

"Mrs. Cavaliere, you talk as if he'll never recover."

"At the time, I believed and had faith he would overcome this tragedy. But now I've come to accept his farewell performance occurred at that last press conference. He tried a few voice-overs for commercials and some cable documentaries, but when he realized that sound machines were required to enhance and manipulate his voice to make up for the loss of power and control, he took it as a slap in the face and gave up. Acting is Nicky's life, and it was all stripped away from him in an instant. Instead of rehearsing his lines anymore, he only speaks these days about dying. What hurts the most is knowing I'm not even a good-enough draw for him to want to live."

Her shoulders heaved as she put on her game face and smiled and waved at one of the patrons across the way.

"I'm sorry, Mrs. Cavaliere."

"Forget it. It's the life I chose."

"Well, I appreciate you sharing this with us, but—"

"Don't. I only told you this so you would honor my wishes and never bring it up again."

She lifted her eyes to the ceiling, battling against the legion of tears.

Noel quickly pulled a chair out. "Mrs. Cavaliere, you don't look so good. Why don't you sit down."

"Yes, I guess you're right. *Grazie*." She took a moment to regroup. "Don't you see? He's too fragile. My husband's ego has always been as massive as his insecurity, except his insecurity will no longer make room for the competition. How can I subject him to one more expert or one more letdown? All I want is my Nicky back again, positive and loving life. I can't bear to hear another doctor say, 'We're doing everything we can, Mrs. Cavaliere, but now we've got to leave it in God's hands.'"

"Listen to me, Mama C . . . My sister is not a doctor, but she has been blessed with extraordinary gifts. Olisa has been blessed with the power to heal people."

"Olisa . . . Olisa? Where have I heard that name before?" Lena looked perplexed as she continually tossed the name around in her head.

"You probably saw her on the news reports."

"I don't have time to watch TV, no . . . Ah-ha! I think I know where I've heard the name before. Do either of you know a woman named Cecilia Moss?"

Noel shrugged his shoulders. "No, never heard of her. You, Dad?"

"Hmmm . . . actually it sounds familiar. Who is she?"

"She is a very old friend of mine, and lately, she's bragged about receiving some amazing readings from this beautiful African American woman. She claims this woman is the best psychic she has ever been to, and that's high praise coming from Cecilia who has pretty much seen them all."

"That's got to be my sister."

"Lena, does Cecilia live in Malibu?"

"Yes, Joseph, so you know her?"

The Malibu Lady, I chuckled to myself. "Not exactly, but I think my daughter may have mentioned her name on a couple of occasions."

"Cecilia has been begging me to go see her even though she knows I'm not into that gypsy fortune-telling stuff. Now it's finally making sense."

"What is?" I asked.

"It was in early July . . . Cecilia left a somewhat disturbing message on my voice mail while I was out of town."

"What did she say?"

"Noel, I don't remember exactly. I was in Europe at the time, but she was breathing so hard she was practically hyperventilating. It was something like, 'Call me, no matter what time it is.' She said, 'Remember that woman psychic I told you about? She healed some gang kid on the Fourth of July, and it was all over the local news.' Then, she got the giggles and said she couldn't stop shaking because she was so excited. It sounded like she was on the verge of a nervous breakdown. Before the voice mail cut off, she said, 'Olisa can cure our Nicholas.'"

"She can," was Noel's assured reply. "I swear to you Cecilia is right. My sister can heal Nick."

Lena shook her head, pushing back a strand of disobedient hair. "I can't believe I'm still sitting here . . ."

"It's because deep down inside you wonder: is it true? can this woman heal my husband? do I dare to be wrong?"

Her eyes sought out mine, a parent-to-parent thing. "Is this the truth?"

I felt like a hostile witness subpoenaed to testify. "Yes."

Noel enclosed her hand inside his. "Will you at least talk to Nick?"

"No, you will. Finish your meal, and I'll drive you over there. We live only a few minutes away. I'll call him first and let him know we're coming. But don't expect a grand reception."

"Understood."

"I'm probably making the biggest mistake of my life."

"Only if you don't listen to me, Mama Cavaliere."

She walked away, still shaking her head. I kept expecting her to turn around and say, "Forget it!" But she didn't. She returned jingling her car keys.

The clink of Noel's fork startled me. His arms were crossed, and he was beaming. It had been a long time since I'd seen him look at me so proudly.

The home of the Cavalieres lay in a very affluent section of norther Santa Monica, toward the end of Ocean Avenue. The road curved upward into a residential area that sat on a cliff facing the hills of Pacific Palisades, which was littered with homes. We passed several joggers at the end of Fourth Street headed toward the famous step that all the trendites on the Westside regarded as a great cardiovascular workout. In fact, Noel bragged he ran the steps three to four times a week. Although I'd guess it was more like three to four times a year, judging by the emerging potbelly he steadily nurtured. People wearing earpods trudged up and down the steps, looking like ants spilling in and out of an anthill.

The car pulled into as an expansive two-story white Mediterranean-style house with a red-tiled roof. As we climbed out of her silver-blue Mercedes, I noticed a brown hand parting the curtains and then quickly closing them.

Seconds later, the front door swung open and a middle-aged heavyset Latina woman, huffing and puffing, hair askew on top of her head, smiled cheerily as she held the door open with one hand and fumbled with a pile of laundry in the other.

"Oh, hello, Estella. You didn't have to come down here and open the door. I know you're busy."

"*Esta bien, Señora* Cavaliere. Mr. Nick is waiting for you in the den."

"Thank you, Estella. This way, gentlemen." We nodded at Estella as we were escorted through a very ornate hallway with marbled floors and Romanesque columns leading to the stairwell. We entered a den that was twice as large as the living room and a library that contained so many books they looked like wallpaper. Behind a mammoth desk, a staid body sat up in a wheelchair facing us like he had been velcroed. The only sign of life was his eyes flickering open at our approach.

"Nicholas, these are the two gentlemen I told you about," she said, kissing him on the cheek and standing behind him.

The handsome face that ignited millions of hearts to flutter when it hit the big screen now resembled the Pillsbury Dough Boy. His greasy unwashed hair skittered to his shoulders, and a tangled full-length beard lay flat against his chest. His icy blue "dangerous" eyes were still captivating and sized us up like a leopard on the prowl. When he cleared his throat, it sounded like chalk scratching a blackboard.

"How ya doin'?" he said blandly. "Sit down. Don't let my presence disturb you. Just view me as one of those old Hollywood movie props they stick in a room." His familiar voice still projected but sounded like all the bass decibels were lowered.

"Nicholas, don't . . ."

"Forgive me, dear. I just thought the occasion deserved a dash of humor. I mean, after all, no offense guys, but obviously my loving wife is so frantic she's resorted to seeking witchcraft to cure my little ailment."

His hands were positioned to rest comfortably on his knees. It was hard not to feel something. I honestly could not look at him without picturing the vibrant actor held captive by his own body. It didn't help to see the plethora of awards behind him on the mantle, including his Oscars for best actor and best supporting actor. In every article I'd ever read about him, the words "masterful performance" were written so many times, he should have hyphenated it as a last name.

Lena ignored him and formally introduced us.

"Mr. Cavaliere, it is truly an honor to meet you. I have admired your career for a long time." Noel continued to baste on compliments with Nick flinging "thank yous" back at him. However, his eyes bounced like basketballs, so it was no surprise when he put an abrupt end to the pleasantries.

"My wife tells me you claim your sister can cure me. So tell me; who is this person planning to rub snake oil all over my body?"

Noel chuckled and, without skipping a beat, immediately launched into his pitch mode, pulling up a chair beside Nick's desk and bragging proudly about Olisa's accomplishments and all that happened recently, including informing him about the upcoming concert, OLISA, Inc., and anything else that came to mind. I found myself admiring him as I listened to him do this thing. He was articulate, personable, grounded, and absolutely fearless in his presentation. The kid talked to the superstar actor like they had been childhood friends.

Throughout the spiel, Nick's eyes were coldly analytical. Every time he swallowed, it made *my* throat hurt.

Finally, Noel looked him square in the eye and said, "Mr. Cavaliere, when you meet my sister, you'll see what I mean. Believe me."

Nick blinked hard, a sneer distorting his lips. "Believe? A few years ago, I believed I was invincible. Lena and I both come from a long line of Catholics. It's kind of an inherited thing, you know? We're so Catholic, at birth our umbilical card was a rosary. Now, my wife was never what I'd call a diehard Catholic, but have you missed one Sunday service since my accident, Lena?"

"No," she whispered as she continued to rub his neck.

"When I was paralyzed, I used to think God was finally punishing me for all the bullshit I did in my youth. But then it hit me—God doesn't really give a shit!"

He paused to swallow some water. Lena held the bottle for him as he sipped it through a straw.

"Millions of people are praying for me, and if I could get down on my knees, I'd join them. But with all these prayers, cards, letters, and good wishes from around the world, I'm still here. You could set my leg on fire, and I'd never feel a fucking thing. Everyone tells me, 'Nick, my boy, just have faith.' You know what faith got me? My own permanent theater seat."

His gagging laughter was the only sound in the room as I shifted uncomfortably in my chair.

"Even the local archdiocese trumpeted my cause, but here I am. So with all this heavenly blather racking up big fat zeros, how can your sister compete?"

His bitterness reminded me of the first time I saw him on stage. He gave a performance so powerful, I left the theater as if I'd been coldcocked.

"Ask me about that after you've completed your first marathon," Noel retorted.

"I don't get it," Cavaliere smirked, his blue eyes sizing Noel up. "You don't act like one of those wacko religious freaks, but I keep thinking they ought to put you away for what you're saying to me."

"They could put me away for a lot of things, but this is not one of them."

"I guess being stuck in front of a television set pays off sometimes. So that was your sister I saw being interviewed by what's her name . . . Sanchez?"

"Yes, sir."

"Mr. Timmerman, you must be pretty proud of your daughter for standing up to those delinquents like that."

"Pretty much."

"Okay . . . Being a father myself, at what point did you want to strangle her and send her to the most isolated region on the planet?"

"Oh, about two seconds after I heard the news."

"I understand, man . . . I truly understand," he said surprisingly, quietly laughing with me. "I've got two daughters and a son. The girls are modeling in Europe. If they ever did anything like that, I don't know . . ."

For the first time since we had been there, the stern countenance on his face softened as he smiled tenderly at Lena. She kissed him on the cheek.

"Still, I have tremendous admiration for your daughter. She's a courageous woman. It says something about you too."

"Thank you, but I'd be remiss if I didn't say my wife had a part in that as well."

"You're a smart man. But all this other stuff . . . healing this kid . . . I don't know. It defies all logic. Of course, I could be wrong. They say anything is possible. I've heard of stories about old women lifting cars off of loved ones when the adrenaline is flowing. Maybe I'm just too jaded. I know how far the press can run with half-truths."

Lena wiped the perspiration from his brow.

"So tell me; did she really heal him? And don't BS me!"

"Without question," Noel stated as he faced Nick's unyielding stare.

"Lena says she knows you guys and that you're sincere as all hell. I figured I'd at least listen to what you had to say. Hell, what choice do I have? I need people these days to blow my damn nose."

Lena massaged his temples and whispered softly in his ear as he visibly tried to slow down his breathing.

"Hypothetically, let's say she *did* heal the kids. Maybe this was a one-time deal. What guarantee do I have that your sister will be able to do her number on me?"

"A better guarantee than you starring in a one-hundred-million-dollar action flick."

I cringed feeling like we better get ready to call for an Uber.

Tears ran down Nick's cheeks, except he was laughing. Lena shot him a double take. Evidently, it had been a while since laughter eased into their home.

"Hey, man, I like you. You're all right. Plus, I hear you're a hell of a businessman. So what's the deal? What do you get out of this?"

"The deal, Mr. Cavaliere, is I want to see you mesmerizing us once again on the big screen."

"So would I, but there must be a catch. If you're so confident about her abilities, why didn't you just bring her here?"

"I want you to come to our concert tomorrow evening on the Santa Monica pier and let her heal you on stage."

The good feelings generated just exited the house.

"Whoa, you've got to be kidding! I've barely left my cocoon in two years, and you actually think I'm going to go out there and make a damn fool of myself in front of all those fucking people at some holy rollers revival service?"

Lena attempted to massage his temples. He shook his head angrily.

"Here's the deal. You bring her here, alone, and if she raises my body from the dead, I'll call a press conference and squawk like a parrot."

"Mr. Cavaliere, please . . . just this one time. We need you."

His head rolled back exasperatedly to the side, and the brief interest I saw in his eyes dissipated.

"No. You know what? Just forget the whole thing! I'm not going to be your fucking guinea pig! You think I want to listen to 'Sorry, Mr. Cavaliere, this has never happened before. I guess your faith wasn't strong enough'!"

"Oh no, that's not how it's going to be. Mr. Cavaliere, I—"

"We're done. My wife sincerely means well, but I should have listened to my instincts from the very beginning." He shot Lena an accusatory glance.

Noel pleaded, "Please, sir, just give Olisa a chance to show you what she can do."

"I'm sure Olisa is a remarkable person. And I wish her and both of you the very best. Thank you. Lena . . ."

Lena's purse was in her hands as she hurriedly shepherded us to the library door.

"Gentlemen, I'm sorry. Will you please wait in the living room? I just want to say goodbye to Nicholas. Then I'll drive you back to the restaurant."

Noel somberly turned and said, "If I have in any way offended you, I apologize, Mr. Cavaliere. That was certainly not my intention. All I can say is I really hope you will come or at least maybe we can set up a time for Olisa to come and visit you. We're talking about your life. I promise you won't regret it. At least, give it some thought."

No response was forthcoming. All we saw was Lena's trademark customer relations smile as she gently closed the double doors of the den in our face.

It was killing Noel not to be able to talk to Lena about what just happened as she drove us back to Horacio's. Thankfully, my son knew not to push it any further. On the way back to the restaurant, we babbled with Lena about all kinds of superficial things, like the meeting never occurred.

"I blew that one, didn't I, Pops?" Noel disconsolately asked later as we sat inside his Tesla outside the restaurant.

"No, not at all. You were upfront. It just wasn't meant to be."

"Hmmm . . ."

"What you've got to do now is get ready for the concert tomorrow."

"Yep, you're right."

"You gonna stop by the house for dinner tonight?"

"Yeah."

Noel sat for a second, then gunned the engine while reaching for his phone.

Chapter 6

I drove home cruising west on Palms Boulevard. It was a nice, peaceful drive. As I hit the crest going through Mar Vista Hills, a beautiful orange-red sunset greeted me. When I got to the house, it sounded like there was a party going on inside. Free cheerfully barked his way into the conversations. Jiggling animated heads were silhouetted in the kitchen window. I dramatically slammed the backdoor as I stepped into the kitchen.

"Uh-huh, caught ya. So this is what y'all been doing while I work my fingers to the bone day after day, night after night, huh?"

Grace laughed. "Took you long enough."

"Oh . . . my . . . God! There's a White man in my house with his arm wrapped around my daughter! What is the world coming to? Aren't people safe in their homes anymore?"

"Daddy's become quite the comedian since you left, Peter."

"Mr. T has always made me laugh, Olisa."

I held Peter by the shoulders appraisingly and gave him a bear hug. "You're looking good, Petey boy."

"You, too, Mr. Timmerman." His pale blue eyes were as warm as Caribbean waters, but dark circles bordered them.

"I'm doing all right, but man, look at you! All dressed up like you stepped off the cover of *GQ Magazine*. Is that how they're styling in the Big Apple these days?"

"Mr. T, in New York, I'm just a termite looking for a piece of wood. I can't compete. You know us native Californians; hand me a T-shirt and some jeans, and I am good. I don't think I'll ever fit in totally there. It's just not me."

"Just not me! The way I hear it, you fit in well enough for one of the top public relation firms in the nation to offer you shares in the company!"

"Yeah, but . . ."

"Doesn't my boy look great?" Grace remarked admiringly. "That cute little boy with the beach-ball eyes turned into quite a good-looking man. Still got all this curly hair too." Grace stood on her tiptoes and ruffled his hair.

"Yeah, buddy. I always used to wonder about you. For a blond-headed dude, you've always had a little color in that skin of yours!" I shot him the ol' fisheye. "Are you one of them Ethiopian Jews or one of the Jefferson-Hemmings castoffs?"

"Neither one, as far as I know," he grinned.

"Daddy, you done? I don't believe you sometimes."

"It's fine, Olisa. This is what I miss, being around my second family. Things wouldn't be right if Mr. T didn't pick on me."

"That's right! So mind your bidness, girl. Pete knows what's up. How's your parents doing, man? Still in Miami?"

"Still there, loving it, never coming back. They live in this retirement community that looks like something straight out of Disney World. Plus, now they have more time to trade guilt on whose fault it was for the way I turned out."

Grace wrapped her arm around him. "Oh, you know your parents love you."

"In their own way . . . I mean Mom is fine; my father is still wrestling with it. But before I forget, they send their best to everyone."

"Back at 'em!" I said, bumping Gumbo away from the kitchen island countertop so I could swipe some chips from the bowl he was hoarding. "Little Oak, you and I are there tonight. How did you know I had a taste for some of your special guacamole?"

"Because you asked me to make some, Uncle Joe."

"Anyway . . . what y'all doing back in Los Angeles, Pete? You here on vacation?"

His blue eyes deepened. "You don't know . . ."

Heads started dropping like autumn leaves.

"Don't know what? See, around here, sometimes they forget to deliver the mail in my hood."

"I'm staying in Los Angeles indefinitely. I took a leave of absence."

"What? Well, that's great! So there really is a cause for celebration. That means I'll finally get to meet your partner—Ryan, correct?"

Peter shuffled his feet, eyeing Olisa who offered him a sympathetic smile. "Ryan's gone, Mr. T. He died of a sudden brain aneurysm several months ago. That's why I needed to get out of New York for a while."

"Hey, I'm sorry, Pete. I didn't know . . ."

"It's okay, Mr. T. I really didn't say much to anyone about it, except for Olisa."

Olisa rubbed his arm reassuringly.

"Yeah, but are you okay, man?"

"I'm hanging in there . . . Just need some time away, to work on myself."

He looked so fragile and vulnerable, even with Grace and Olisa bolstering him up on each side like bookends. For a second, he looked like he wanted to slip between their fingers and collapse to the floor.

"You do whatcha gotta do, kid. And whatever I can do, please let me know."

"Just being here with family makes it a lot better."

"Peter, I only wish I had known . . . Maybe . . ."

"Don't, Olisa. You were out of the country at the time and in some remote area where I couldn't reach you by phone. There's nothing you could have done; it happened too fast. I just wish I could have told him how much I loved him before he died."

"He knew, big brother." Olisa hugged him and held on affectionately to his arm.

"Peter, this too shall pass, and it's going to work out fine even though it's hard for you to see now." Grace kissed him on the cheek.

Peter wrapped his arms around both women. "I love you guys."

Seeing Pete's face caused me to reflect on the little boy that used to follow Grace around like a puppy when she was pregnant with Olisa. He was so fascinated with the idea of a baby living in her stomach. I still see the awe in his eyes as he watched Grace cuddling Olisa as a newborn. Ever since she was born, Peter had always been a big brother to her. They managed to stay in contact even after his parents got the hell out of Mid-City Los Angeles and moved to the suburbs shortly after the riots. When he got old enough, he'd take the bus to our house.

As teenagers, a two-hour phone call between Olisa and Peter was a short conversation. Man, time passes fast. After all these years, the two remained friends. Olisa described Peter as "my friend for life."

"Pete, if you really want to take your mind off of things, why don't you join us at the concert tomorrow?"

Peter's face got flushed. "Man, Mr. T, now I'm really embarrassed."

I looked around, but everyone's eyes seemed to be looking elsewhere.

"Did I mention I've been living in the Dark Ages? So, Peter, enlighten me."

"Noel called me not long ago to seek my advice on doing press and additional PR for OLISA, Inc. I told him if he could be patient for a couple of weeks, I'd be out here and give him some free tips. Of course, Noel had already decided he wanted me to handle her PR program."

"What? Noel knows better than to be asking you to—"

"I really don't mind, Mr. T. It's a no-brainer and a good antidote for my depression. Plus, you know I'd do anything for Miss O." Olisa grinned from ear to ear.

Grabbing his arm, Grace inquired, "Peter, did you bring an appetite with you? I'm sure eating is far better than being interrogated by my husband."

"Yes, ma'am."

"Grace, I wasn't interrogating him. I—"

"Laura is cooking one of her special dinners tonight, so why don't we go into the dining room."

"Oh, you don't say? Little Oak is cooking tonight? Didn't you almost have to rush me to the ER at Santa Monica Hospital the last time she cooked?"

"Only because you ate too much, Uncle Joe," Laura sassed me as she peered into the oven and ladled sauce over the baking chicken. "Alton didn't seem to have suffered from my cooking."

"That because Gumbo eats alien hay in his bread. How can you go by him?"

"Bean sprouts, Unc."

"Whatever."

"Don't push it, Uncle Joe. You know Laura knows how to work with herbs."

"That's right, Uncle Joe. You don't want to find some rare seasoning in your food that doesn't sit real well in your stomach."

"I'm going to ignore that, because I can't believe my Little Oak would even think of ever doing something like that to her sweet uncle Joe."

Laura reached for a second dishtowel as she arched an eyebrow.

"Let me help you with that chicken, young lady. We don't want you to strain your back or anything. Right, Gumbo?"

"You're on your own, Unc. I ain't got nothing to do with it," chuckled Alton.

"Appreciate your support, Gumbo."

Alton shrugged as he recaptured the bowl of chips while I hauled the chicken out of the oven.

"Why thank you, Uncle Joe. Now I finally see what Aunt Grace sees in you," Laura remarked, winking at Grace.

"'Bout time."

"Aww, it's so great to be back home again," Peter smirked.

Noel dropped by midway through our meal with his newest "hottie" whose black miniskirt was practically sanded to her body. The muscles in her calves moved like harp strings as she nimbly stepped across the carpet in her red Louboutin heels. A sweet perfume wafted through the house assimilating with the spicy aromatic smell of Laura's chicken. She smiled like a beauty pageant contestant as she was introduced to the room.

"*Monsieur* Kaplan, did you have a good flight? Man, you don't know how happy I am to see you," he said genially as he and Peter embraced. "Welcome back, brother. Again, I'm so sorry about what happened. It's all going to work out."

"Hope so."

"Hey, looka here. I want you to meet La Tisha. She's a singer, and I'm working on securing a label contract for her. She's already shot a couple of videos for us. She's dope, isn't she?"

"Yes. Nice meeting you, La Tisha," Peter said, extending his hand.

"You too." She regally offered Peter a limp hand that somewhere in her mind she conjoined with class.

"Peter is the old friend I was telling you about. He's a brilliant public relations expert. Tish, when you hit it, this is the man you want to know."

"Ooooh," she cooed, wiggling her shoulders.

"Is someone out front?" Grace asked, peeping through the shutters near the front door.

I heard the front gate click shut.

"Oh, Mom, that's probably an associate of mine I asked to stop by. I hope you don't mind. Yeah, that's him. Come on in, man. Looka here, everyone. This is Logan Matthews."

"Oh, no, I'm just Logan, or Lo, or whatever you want to call me; it's cool." He ambled into the living room, hands stuffed inside his jean pockets.

Logan Matthews was one of the most laid-back dudes I'd ever met. I immediately took a liking to him. He merged into our midst as effortlessly as butter melting on a hot roll. Even Little Oak, who was leery of all strangers until she got to know them, sported a silly grin on her face. Logan's natural charms only enhanced his subtle good looks.

Grace put it best. "He's like punch that's been spiked. By the time you realize someone's slipped in the alcohol, you're already drunk. Slender with cinnamon-brown skin and glistening black hair with a low-cut fade and short dreads on top. Logan's droopy jaguar shaped eyes gave the appearance of nonchalance, but you could tell by the way he examined his surroundings when he entered the house that he didn't miss a thing."

"Where's my sister? I want her to meet Logan."

"At ease, Noel. Don't call the FBI. I'm here."

We were all gathered in the living room when Olisa casually sauntered in from the hallway.

"Olisa, this is—"

"Logan Matthews! What are *you* doing here?"

Those low-lidded eyes suddenly got very wide as Logan seemed just as taken aback as Olisa. He warmly clasped her hand. "I was about to ask you the same question. You . . . you're Noel's sister?"

"Most of my life."

"Wait a minute. You guys know each other?" Noel questioned.

Neither one answered right away. Logan broke the silence, "Well, kind of . . ."

"What does that mean? Like kinda pregnant? Either you do, or you don't."

The hint of irritation in Noel's voice surprised me.

"We met at a gallery in Santa Monica years ago, but she never told me her name."

"It wasn't just any gallery. It was the very prestigious R. D. Bowles Gallery in Santa Monica. They were hosting a photography exhibit honoring your work. We only talked a few minutes. There were so many people waiting to talk to you; I didn't want to take up all your time."

"There were other people there?"

"Yes." Olisa blushed.

I noticed the glances and subtle mischievous smiles exchanged between Grace and Laura.

"You know, after our conversation, I looked all around for you, but you were gone. I even searched for a glass slipper, but no such luck. Wow. I didn't think I'd ever see you again, and here you are. Ha . . . Noel's sister. Boy, what a small world."

"I guess it is," Olisa agreed.

Their hands gradually parted, but Logan's eyes still held hers.

"I'm trying to remember—did you even like my work? Be honest."

The burst of laughter from us startled him.

"It's obvious you really don't know Olisa," chimed Little Oak, laughing.

"Ignore them. I loved your work," Olisa answered quickly. "It's so passionate. Obviously, you love what you do because your photographs show an innate compassion and sensitivity for your subjects."

"Thank you."

"So tell us about your work, Logan," Grace cajoled.

"Okay, here you go. I love music, particularly jazz, so there are lots of photos of jazz musicians. Same thing with children. I have shots of children from places throughout the world such as Guatemala, Nicaragua, New Guinea, Rwanda, and Sarajevo."

"You're playing it down, Logan," interjected Olisa. "These aren't just your typical coffee-table photographs. You have managed to capture on an intimate level the quiet, innocent dignity, humanity, and even tragedy of these people. I feel like I know them. After leaving the show, your images found a home inside my brain for weeks."

"Meeting you did the same thing to me."

Whatever else Olisa planned on saying disappeared. Her face flushed.

"Noel never said your name, though he mentioned his sister traveled extensively, too."

"Yes."

"We'll have to get together one of these days and swap stories."

"I'd like that."

"Olisa, show our guest to a seat in the dining room so he can get something to eat," Grace insisted, filling in the awkward silence that transpired.

Once Olisa escorted Logan to a seat at the table, he exclaimed, "Ooooh, if this tastes as good as it looks, then I'm in deep, deep trouble."

"No, the only trouble you're in is if you get up from the table and go to the bathroom. Last time I did that, Gumbo cleaned my plate off."

"Aww, that ain't true, Unc. How you gon diss me in front of our guest like that?"

"Excuse me? Did you forget what happened on Labor Day, last year? Huh? Oh, you're quiet now? Uh-huh . . ."

"Unc, you still holding that against me? I swear I didn't know that food was yours. I thought Laura fixed another plate for me."

"Uh-huh, whatever. Just keep your eye on your food, Logan."

"I'll do that," Logan laughed.

He lied. The only thing he kept his eye on was Olisa. Even while he addressed me, his pupils mirrored Olisa's face.

"Logan, I'm dying to see your work after hearing Olisa describe it. Do you have any pictures with you?" Grace sweetly inquired.

"I'm afraid not, Grace. The only thing I brought with me is my best friend who is resting in the trunk of my car."

"Pardon?"

"My 35-mm camera."

"Ohhh."

"I don't believe you, man," Noel broke in. "Don't you know by now to carry your portfolio around with you?"

"You're right. I'm really bad about that. I just feel kinda funny doing that."

"La Tisha, you ought to see this man's work. You heard my sister. In my estimation, we're talking genius."

"Thanks, Noel, but let's not go that far. I'm just a photographer."

"Just? Give me a break. The way you manipulate the lighting in your work . . . What process do you use in your photographs?"

"Some photos I rework with oils, varnishes, crayons, and other mixed media. My objective is to explore the human condition, so I try to bring the truth of what I see to the surface."

"Outstanding! Man, your images are so arresting, you could get an orangutan a modeling contract. Hear me? I've worked with hundreds of photographers, and you are not only a photographer—you are an artist! Your photos are masterpieces!"

"Hey, man, I appreciate that. Thank you."

"You need to light a fire under your agent's behind. She's not selling your work the way she should."

"She's doing all right, Noel. A lot of it is on me. I'm probably not as cooperative and gung-ho to make all the public appearances she would like me to do."

"Typical artist. That's why I always say creative people should never handle business or finances."

"Logan, next time I hope to see your work," La Tisha commented, proud to contribute to the conversation as she robotically rubbed Noel's arm and glanced sideways at him like a child seeking approval.

"You may have already seen some of it, Lady T. Logan shot many videos for me including Mookie Moan's 'Tear Down the Roof' and Holy Cross's 'Gospel Strut.'"

She gasped as she picked at her food. "Wow! You did those videos? Those were so hot!" she exclaimed, jigging in her seat.

"Appreciate that. Most of it I shot with my eyes closed hoping for the best. I'm used to doing still photography, but it seems to have worked out."

"Yeah, Mr. Modesty, to the tune of several Grammy nominations and a couple of MTV awards on your first go-around! When he asked me how to go about filming this, I told him to give it the same feel as he did with his photography and women. That seemed to work!" Noel guffawed. "Oh, I'm sorry. I hope I'm not embarrassing you, Lo," Noel stated a little too innocently glancing sideways at his sister. "You know how it is when you get to talking shop."

Logan scratched the back of his neck and, for the first time, avoided eye contact with Olisa.

"Anyway, in a matter of days he shot the video like he'd been doing it his whole life. My boy's a natural!"

"Pardon the interruption, Logan. Would you like some more bread? I'm sure you don't need it buttered anymore."

The laughter lifted the tension as I passed him the bread basket. I could tell he was relieved to see the focus shift as we delved into politics and Washington scandals.

That didn't last too long. As soon as the first conversational break occurred, Noel asked, "So, Lo, what have you got next on the agenda?"

"Uh, nothing right now. I'm just waiting to see if a grant I applied for through the Ford Foundation gets accepted."

"Hey, that's perfect! I know it's last minute, but while you're on hold, you might want to consider this. I badly need someone to shoot photos of Olisa at our concert tomorrow. Overall, I need a photographer on an on-call basis. Now that I found out she loves your work as much as me, it could be a great marriage, if you're interested."

"Logan, please forgive my son. He knows better than to discuss business at the dinner table."

"Mom's right, Lo. My bad. You haven't even digested your food yet."

"I'll make it quick. I'm there. I'd love to do it," Logan said, genuinely excited.

"You sure?"

"Very."

"Cool. We'll discuss it in detail later."

"Hold on, hold on, Logan. Noel has no business putting you on the spot like that in front of us. You don't have to do this," Olisa asserted angrily.

"Olisa, I want to."

"Logan, he hasn't even told you what he's going to pay you."

"Olisa, it could be a freebie; I don't care. It would be an honor for me to photograph you under any occasion," he replied softly, causing Free to shuffle under the table. Please—I spotted Little Oak giving Grace a subtle elbow.

Tiny tics played at the corner of Olisa's mouth as she twisted the ends of her hair. "That's very nice of you to say, but you must have better things to do."

"Like what?"

"Like working on something that will further benefit your career."

"Shooting photos is my career, Olisa." He kept his eyes on her. "However, if, what you're really getting at is, you'd feel uncomfortable with me, a stranger, taking pictures of you, then I can respect that. I won't do it. Think about it and let Noel know."

Olisa dabbed at her food, her brown eyes gradually rising. "I'm fine as long as you are."

"You already know my answer."

"Well, all right!" Noel uttered, with a clap. "Lo, let's meet after dinner, and we'll discuss all the particulars."

"I can't wait to get started. Olisa, I just hope I don't get on your nerves."

"I wouldn't worry about that," Laura said nonchalantly as she collected the dinner plates. She made an extra effort to avoid the look Olisa shot her. "Dessert anyone?" Laura asked barely suppressing a smile, like Grace who quickly said, "Let me give you a hand." She followed Laura into the kitchen. Olisa quickly excused herself and trailed right behind them. Faint giggles emanated from the kitchen. When they came back out holding plates of chocolate raspberry cake, their faces, naturally, were passive.

"Hallelujah, I just have to say I think we've built ourselves one heck of a team," trumpeted Noel as he raised his glass for a group toast.

After the toast, Noel exchanged places with La Tisha and sat next to me. He whispered, "Great photography, cheap labor. Lo hasn't worked consistently in a year."

Noel planted a kiss on La Tisha's cheek as she blushed with appreciation. Once again, he raised his glass of Chardonnay. "Another toast—to Olisa and a great future!"

As the glasses clinked, I thought, *Noel may not be getting out of this as cheaply as he thinks.*

The concert was scheduled for 6:00 PM. By 5:00, the Santa Monica pier was jam-packed. The vendors were pleased because everyone was making money. The arcades, restaurants, old-fashioned merry-go-round, and pier entertainment rides, including the Ferris wheel and roller coaster, had extremely long lines. There were so many people, the spillage descended to the sand surrounding the pier and swarmed the volleyball pits.

It had been a hot day with the Los Angeles County temperatures in the low nineties, but we were graced by a refreshing ocean breeze. Judging by the excited chatter filling the air, there was an eagerness to get the festivities underway.

Except for me.

My fear was that a gigantic disaster loomed on the horizon, and my daughter was doomed to be the sacrificial lamb.

Rather than hang around in a backstage huge tent with family and friends, I elected to be in the audience. I don't know why, really. Most likely it was owing to being tired of listening to my stressed-out son marching around like a modern-day Napoleon, barking at the crew as they hustled to get the stage set up right according to Noel's specifications. If I hung out any longer, we'd just get into an argument. I was just as nervous as him but for different reasons. Olisa didn't need that. She needed support.

Conversely, being a part of the crowd was in itself a little scary.

Next to me was an elderly White man wearing a beaten-up old Vietnam War cap and veins crisscrossing his face like a Thomas Guide. He leaned against my shoulder, his toxic breath numbing me with its potent mixture of alcohol and tobacco. He took a long drag on a cigarette. After each nicotine hit, his face bunched up like a Shar Pei dog.

"Let me ask you something, fella. Whatcha think about all this?"

"I don't know . . . It's interesting."

"You can say that again, pal. I tell ya; the only reason I'm here is curiosity. A lot of these damn yo-yo's you see walking around here are looking for a religious cult they can join. Weirdos! If you ask me. There ain't nothing but a bunch of suckers in this goddamn audience waiting to be scalped!"

Little Oak would have had a field day with him.

"I've lived in Santa Monic for over fifty years, my friend . . . Native Californian, Los Angelean. There ain't many of us my age around. Went to Hollywood High School before it became Hollyweird. Ha! Ha! I've seen it all.

"I don't know where you're from, ace, but you should have seen what this beach was like during the sixties and seventies. Fucking hippies shoutin' all that peace and love stuff while the whole country was sliding down the crapper. All you need is love they was sayin' . . . That was just a big ol' corn-ball excuse to do drugs and fuck like dogs in the street. Look where it got 'em. People dying from diseases that knocked penicillin on its ass! Now all of them baby boomers are out there trying to make an honest buck instead of bucking the system. All that shit their mothers and fathers told them was right," he scoffed.

He flicked his cigarette to the ground, mashing it reflectively as he lit another one. He coughed as if he were gargling snot.

"Then there was a time all those crazy Jesus freaks were marching all over the place beating drums and chanting shit . . . crazy idiots! God bless California, though. This place is a grab bag for every kind of religion. People can't stop lookin' for Jim Jones and some of them even for political con artists. Hey, take a look at those young gals over there about four o'clock high . . ."

I saw three teenage girls dressed wildly. One had a combo platinum-blond and blue hair, shorn like it was cut in the midst of a major earthquake. Her black roots seeped out of her scalp like oil from the ground. All three displayed rings and tattoos on virtually every open area of the body, and I'm sure it didn't stop there.

"Ain't that something? What can you say about that shit? Look at 'em, sittin' there ready to light up some incense and top it off with some fentanyl or heroin later. How can any self-respecting parents let their daughters step out the house looking like that? Ain't they got mirrors! The morals of this nation lie in a politician's pants. Hmmph."

I crossed my arms and continued to nod politely.

"Buddy, I don't know how old you are, but you got to be much younger than me. I've been on this planet for almost seventy-seven odd years now," he proudly declared, his elbows smacking my ribcage. He cast a weary smile from his yellowed teeth. "There's always some new jerk trying to tear into someone's asshole. And tonight, we'll see it again. You'd think after watching all these cock-sucking preachers doing jail time after fucking high-class prostitutes with your money that they might learn something. Nope. People don't learn a goddamn thing!"

He spit out smoke with a sneer. "Man, I did some time in Nam and afterwards struggled through every kind of hell you can think of . . . Life ain't been real kind to me, but I'll tell you what! Ain't never going to let nobody dick me and then piss my money away! You got me?"

"Yeah."

"But some folks are just begging to part you from your money. Hell, you'd stand a better chance playing lotto," he hoarsely cackled. "The only good thing about this is I heard this gal is quite a looker . . ."

My subconscious willed his irritating voice to a muted drone as I spotted Alton, the newly designated chief security officer of OLISA, Inc. speaking into a walkie-talkie. As he spoke, I watched security, which included many of his bouncer buddies and fellow bodyguards, position themselves around the stage like a wagon train. Others assimilated into the crowd, but they were easy to spot since the majority possessed bull necks and horny toad stares. They weren't alone. The police presence in general was heavy-duty as two pairs of police officers clomped through on horseback.

"When's this doggone thing going to start? Hell, it's starting to get dark! Damn near seven. I thought they were supposed to start on time! Holy cow!"

As if on cue, Noel strolled onto the stage, charmingly addressing the crowd. "How's everybody this evening? We can't thank you enough for coming. Welcome to the First Annual Universal Concert for Spiritual Healing!" He paused for the modest cheers. "First, I must apologize. We ran into some technical difficulties, but it's all been worked out and we're ready to get it on!"

Those "technical difficulties" he referred to occurred because we couldn't find Olisa. We were supposed to meet at our house at four. No Olisa. At five thirty, still no Olisa. That's when the real panic set in. Poor Noel aged so fast he almost passed me.

We scoured the neighborhood in Noel's rented limousine. Thanks to Little Oak who knew Olisa's favorite walking routes, we finally found her seated on a decrepit milk cart in an alley near Palms and Abbott Kinney Boulevard, shooting the breeze with two homeless men. Ignoring a relieved but pissed-off Noel, she refused to get into the vehicle unless she could bring her friends.

I think Noel wished he could shoot her with a taser dart and drag his sister there, but time was running out. He closed his eyes and held his breath while her honored guests adjusted their tattered clothes and hustled into the limo. Logan couldn't stymie the fat grin on his face as he snapped their pictures with his camera. It didn't help Noel's nerves when Olisa debated him the entire ride to the pier about the makeup and attire he selected for her. Nor did he seem particularly amused by the malodorous air reeking from our unwashed guests as he thumped button after button until the electric windows sidled down.

Be that as it may, Noel on stage was the essence of cool and suave. He wore an elegant three-piece khaki-colored suit. He was very proud of his compromising back-to-earth look, particularly ever since Olisa informed him that the word khaki means earth-colored in Hindi and hailed from the days of the Raj. This was his semi-politically correct contribution to the occasion.

Amid the roar of the cascading roller coaster, he introduced the agenda for the evening and the artists planning to perform, saving Olisa for last. The applause was polite as a low buzz circulated throughout the audience.

"Now I've got to tell you; if you're here to have fun, then there is no excuse if you don't. If you feel like praying, then go ahead and pray. If you need love, then be ready to receive more love than you ever bargained for. Stevie Wonder's 'Love's in Need of Love Today' is the perfect theme for what we are seeking to accomplish this evening."

A smattering of applause rolled forth.

"And if you have been searching for some spiritual healing, get ready. It's here."

"Yeah, right," hissed Mr. Skeptical still standing beside me.

"No matter what you may be anticipating about tonight's event, I will guarantee you will *not* be the same person you were prior to coming here this evening. You are going to witness things you never imagined, things that aren't dependent on blind faith. Tonight you will leave here assured that miracles do exist."

"Listen to him! Who does this fancy-dressed hustler think he is, Rod Serling of *The Twilight Zone*?"

"If you think we're going to put the pinch on you for money or pass the plate around, forget it. We are not here to exploit you and ask for your life savings and then promise you riches beyond belief. *No*, it ain't that kind of show. We will be handing out pamphlets with our mailing address on them. If you enjoy the program, you can send donations and/or comments directly to the address listed at the bottom. This is not a church service or a fundraiser. It's purely a spiritual healing and celebration! If you feel inclined to give us a donation by the end of the evening because we've added some value to your lives, then that's your call. If not, hey, that's cool, too. No pressure here. You get enough of that in your daily life. Tonight's gathering is a plea for love and unity. But it's time for me to stop yakking, cuz you didn't come to see me. So without further ado, let's crank it up and hop on board the love train with JJ Willis and the Studio All Stars!"

Brother-in-law JJ and his ensemble of renowned studio musicians zapped us with some torrid jazz laced with a Latin sound as multicolored stage lights rapidly flashed about the band. JJ had rounded up the créme de la créme of musicians. They didn't have popular name recognition unless you read music liner notes. However, they were highly respected by everyone in the entertainment industry—Francisco Gomez on lead guitar, James "Deacon" Harris on keyboard, Melvin "Die Hard" Cooper on drums, Salvatore Blackshire on percussion, and of course, JJ on bass. All of them played at one time or the other with a who's-who lineup of musical superstars. The band wore contemporary brightly colored tie-dye shirts with "OLISA" in a hip-hop type of font across the front and "ONE LOVE" on the back. They burned up the stage with some hot bossa nova that got the crowd moving and grooving. Dancing broke out in random sections of the growing crowd. The sheer élan of the music made blood pressure and spirit rise simultaneously.

Performing next was one of the local high school choirs, offering a set of rollicking gospel numbers. They met with a rousing ovation from a like-minded crowd that unanimously decided, "If we get nothing else out of this, let's at least enjoy the music."

It turned out to be kind of a nice break when Ulysses Ferguson, an avant-garde literary poet widely heralded on the college circuit, read some inspirational poetry backed by Francisco on classical acoustic guitar.

The program flowed along nicely with a multitude that was into it on every level. Periodically, there were sporadic bursts of "We want Olisa!" Noel strolled out again amidst more thunderous "Olisa" screams. He gave the crowd a long teasing pause and a look like he was about to unveil the greatest secret in the world. Dramatically, he announced, "If you want her so bad, you got her!" A huge roar arose from the throngs. "But first . . ."

"*Awww . . .*" groaned the audience, cracking themselves up at their unified reaction.

Before Noel said another word, the band launched into a funky scathing rendition of James Brown's "Cold Sweat" and suddenly local-boy-turned-famous, Oakwood's pride and joy, hip-hop superstar and rapper Master Mookie X Moan (who by a remarkable coincidence happened to be on the RPM label) stormed out on the stage in a furious humping dance. Raising his fist, the band halted on cue as he faced the audience in a stare-down, spreading his legs wide in a sexually defiant stance, eyeing the audience through black geometric shades, mouth curled into a sensuous take-no-shit snarl, bald head glistening like a burnished light bulb.

The youngsters went stone stupid, hands rhythmically pushing toward the skies, mimicking him as he led them in this raucous gesture. In the world of hip-hop he was *the* man: hard, former OG, DM, dance master, and the wizard of rap. He faced them menacingly, sizing up the audience with a playful arrogance on his greyhound-shaped face. Mookie snatched the microphone, and the band kicked out more nasty "Cold Sweat" funk as his sandpapery voice sliced through the salty sea air, attacking the song with his virile staccato rapid-fire delivery that blazed wildly all over the song like a deranged Uzi come to life. The tone was set off in his usual braggadocio style, but the words paid homage to the creator and newfound messenger, Olisa. I vaguely remembered in a cover article in *Rolling Stone* magazine a brief blurb about how he found God—obviously, Noel remembered, too.

Before long the super-hyped-up audience got in on the action, voluntarily chiming in on each chorus, pumped up higher than a helium balloon as the band continued to deliver first-class funk. I loved JJ. He rarely made sense when he opened his mouth, but you understood what he was throwing down when he thumped, banged, and stroked the hell out of his bass. His dreads jumped around like Medusan snakes as his head pitched back and forth. Meanwhile, "Die Hard" beat the holy shit out of those drums like it was his last hurrah. Dancing spread through the crowd faster than the flu. They danced on the stage, on the pier, in the sand—wherever! Age didn't matter. Race was a non-issue. The beach rocked!

I had to give Noel his props. If his goal was to wake the crowd up and get them into it, he more than succeeded. They were pumped, revved up for a spiritual revival. The delayed start had long been forgotten.

When the band finished playing, the crowd begged for more. Mookie's gritty voice shouted, "Wass up, Westside! Wass up, Oakwood! Peeaace! Thanks for giving me some love, y'all. Thank ya, JJ; y'all is the bomb. They went nuclear at one point. Hear what I'm sayin'? Give 'em some love, people!"

A huge enthusiastic cheer went up.

He waited for the screams to subside then said, "Hey, we want to thank y'all for coming to the first Spiritual Healing Concert. Yeah, this is one of them old-school town hall meetings out here on the pier. Cuz we're here for a purpose: to celebrate God, and to celebrate life. Uh-huh . . . That's right. Give it up! We are also here for a woman who fought for love and peace with her life a month ago . . . Yeah, that's right. Go on and clap. Show her some love, cuz we as a people need to see that this peace and love can continue despite all the bullshit we got to deal with on a day-by-day basis!"

Screams of support zipped through the crowd.

He shook his head, talking to the crowd as if he were just hanging out in the streets. He sat down on the edge of the stage, arms encircling his bent knees as he held the mike up thoughtfully pausing and gazing at the masses. His voice dropped to a whisper. "Whew . . . the lady I'm about to introduce to you is going to rock you way harder than we did. She's going to drop some stuff on you that will last far beyond the music . . . You feel me?

"Any of you who've invested your time and money in the God cons and spiritual pimps of the universe can stitch up your wallets, cuz you're done with them. This is the real deal I'm talkin' about here. Ya know what I'm sayin'? Sista's all the way live. It's like dis: when Noel came up to me and said, 'Would you like to do something for this program?', ordinarily, I'm all about gettin' paid, know what I'm sayin'?"

"Heard that!" someone yelled.

"I did this concert for free, cuz it's more important for me to share with y'all about someone who can help you in your life, just like God did mine. I ain't layin' no born-again stuff on you or tellin' you how to be saved by going home and reading your Bible or Koran or whatever takes you on the path to salvation. Tonight I'm talkin' about someone who can help us right now!"

"Amen," was the chorus echoed from the attendees.

"Yeah, I was out there, just like some of you hardheads I see out there . . . bustin' ass, knockin' fools out, stealing money, sellin' drugs, doin' drugs, all that crazy stupid-ass shit! Until the day I met a gangsta badder than me. Same old story—y'all read it. Dude shot my ass five times over some fly lady I was layin' up with. The truth is I should have been one dead muthafucka, another one of those Black male statistics. I wasn't famous yet, so what the fuck difference would it have made to find another nigga dead? They'd say, 'He probably got what he deserved'!"

"That's right! That's the way shit goes down, homes!"

"Ain't it?" he said, pointing to someone in the crowd and nonchalantly flipping the mike in his hand. "I got news for ya—this nigga wasn't going nowhere! Your homeboy lived to see another morning!"

"Amen!"

"Why? Cuz God didn't punch in my time card. He gave me a second chance."

"Uh-huh! Tell it."

"So there was no way I was going to refuse to be a part of this landmark event! When Noel Timmerman asked for my services, I was honored . . . cuz I know this will provide anyone who needs it—a second chance."

He got up and started strutting as the stage persona returned.

"I opened my heart out to y'all, and now it's your turn by welcoming the real star of this show by showing some love from your heart! I want everybody that wants peace to clap your hands like you mean it. Don't hold back shit! If you ain't down with peace, then take your sorry butt on outta here! You feel me? Ain't no room at the inn. Let me hear y'all holler *peeaace*!"

"*Peeaace!*"

"Act like you're in church! Say it again: *peeeeaaaace!* Talk to me, Los Angeles. Say whaaat?"

"*Peeeaaace!*"

"It don't matter what color, religion, gender, how you look . . . *It don't matter*! All we need is . . ."

"*Peeeeaaaace!*"

"All right then! This wonderful lady wants peace, too . . . in this city, this nation, and in this world! Now, she ain't spoke in front of a crowd this large before, so she's feeling a little shy. I says to her, 'We ain't never experienced someone like you before, so we're even.' C'mon now and put your hands together for the flyest woman in the City of Angels! She don't care about mayoral awards, government citations, and all the shit! All she wants of you is your love."

The crowd stomped and applauded rhythmically as a sampler of the rock group Queen blared from the humongous speakers: "*We Will, We Will Rock You!*"

"Meet your one shining soul . . . *Olisa!*"

There was an enormous ovation followed by a chant, "Olisa, Olisa, Olisa," as Mookie conducted the cheers, waving his hands and swaying with the multitude.

How could she sustain this type of manic energy? The band had done a fantastic job of creating a celebratory urgency to the evening, but I feared the ending was going to be anticlimactic. I had only seen Olisa with small group interactions. I couldn't imagine her soft-spoken demeanor penetrating through to this revved-up gathering.

My worries suffered a quiet burial.

She stepped onto the stage barefoot, and a hush befell the expectant crowd. All you heard was the isolated rattle of the Santa Monica West Coaster Rollercoaster.

She paused on the corner of the stage, clearly overwhelmed by the large turnout, people ogling and aahing, fingers pointing toward her as if they were observing the landing of the mothership. For a second, I didn't think our star attraction was going to take another step forward as she surveyed the audience. At the opposite end of the stage, Noel applauded vigorously, smiling and bidding her to move forward. Only I noticed the nervous tics bouncing on his face piercing the calm veneer. Just when I thought he was about ready to lasso her, she languidly trekked forward, moving into an arena that offered no turning back. Logan swirled around her like a ballerina, his camera snapping like a teething puppy as he attempted to capture life's defining moments in that little box.

Demurely, she reached center stage, keeping her eyes almost entirely on the comforting presence of the band members who were playing a beautiful gospel-tinged musical interlude while deferentially bowing one by one as she passed by. Junior stepped forward and kissed his niece on the cheek.

She pressed her heart with both hands slowly and repeatedly like a mother receiving her favorite sons as thank yous were mouthed to the band members. The more humorous twist of the evening was seeing Mookie Moan, the stud prince of hip-hop, humbly addressing her like an acolyte to a priest as he handed her the microphone. Noticeably shaking, she set it down on a podium hastily set up by one of the stagehands and tenderly caressed the side of his face with one hand as she studied it like an aged map by firelight. I don't think he ever wanted to let go as he held her hand possessively to his face. Without warning, he crumbled into her arms like a deflated balloon as people gasped and some screamed. Several stagehands moved forward, but she waved them off, massaging the back of his head with her hand.

The musical superstar changed into a quivering young man, dark glasses askew, and rubbing his eyes with the back of his hands. She continued to hold him up, releasing him when his body straightened like a capsized surfboard. The shades fell back over his eyes, but he kept his head down as he inched back gesticulating toward the mike.

Olisa was genuinely surprised and touched by the whole affair. Even though the program was masterfully orchestrated by Noel, nothing could substitute for the heart and soul that went into it. As she stepped up to the podium, fixing her timid gaze upon us, she looked like the village girl who suddenly discovered, by some quirk of fate, she was the queen of the realm.

Looked the part, too, wearing a resplendent white gown and a high African gele headdress. Her shining high cheekbones endowed her with an air of nobility. She looked gorgeous, but I couldn't find my daughter within the mask. Noel's people had slathered on the makeup.

Although she tried to portray a good front, she was uncomfortable. Her confidence and decorum waned with the dying of applause. Her body continually shifted as she waded through an intimidating stack of notes perched on the podium. She stared at them in bewilderment like they had converted into mocking cartoon faces.

The first words mumbled from her mouth were, "Oh my God . . . the band, Mookie, all the performers . . . so incredible . . . What am I doing up here? I can't . . . I need a minute." She shuffled through the pile of formal notes glaring intimidatingly at her. Sadly, the honeymoon was over. The strain visibly seeped into her face. At the corner of the stage, Noel hunched like the ghost of Ed Sullivan.

It was awful watching Olisa's panic take shape. This was not at all what she had imagined for herself. I didn't know how she was going to handle this humiliating breakdown as the crowd's restless murmurings began to intensify. I blamed myself for not putting my foot down a little harder.

And I blamed Noel.

Why did he force her to take on something she wasn't suited for? It just wasn't Olisa. Didn't matter now. We needed to get her off that stage. Already Noel and Mookie were casually moving toward her like an emergency rescue crew but then froze when a cavernous bass voice thundered from the audience.

"Take your time, girl; no one's rushing you. We'll stay here as long as it takes, all night if we have to. Just say what you feel. It's all good. All we ask you to do is keep it real!"

A chorus of encouraging and supportive voices followed.

For the first time, a relaxed smile alighted on Olisa's face as she stared for a long time in the direction from where the voice emerged. I too tried to locate the speaker of those words, no such luck. Yet, no matter how much I tried to dismiss it, I knew whose familiar voice stated those words. Did Olisa? She leaned on the podium, her eyes suddenly animated. She eyed the audience mischievously. Carefully lifting the pile of papers like a ceremonial rite, she hurled them up into the air with such force that they swirled to the ground flapping like hundreds of butterflies around her as she raised her hands victoriously.

Meanwhile, Noel looked shellshocked until he heard the crowd roar like they were watching Pete Townsend smashing his guitar. His grimace coalesced into a grin.

"Would someone be kind enough to help me remove this podium?" Olisa asked. "We are not going to need it."

No more needed to be said. The winds had changed. Noel pounced on it. He clapped his hands and emphatically gestured for the stagehands to get it out of the way.

"Thank you very much. I don't need a prop . . . any more than I need a church to praise the Creator. God is everywhere. It brings to mind how a few years ago, one of my closest friends, Laura, who we call Little Oak, happens to be backstage, took me to see the Redwoods. When I entered that magnificent forest full of trees thousands of years old, I fell to my knees and cried like a baby. It was one of the most spiritual and humbling sights I have ever beheld. Nothing marred by man's hands. Once again it reaffirmed to me that no manmade cathedral could ever bring me to my knees faster than God's green earth!"

Her eyes were earnestly closed, face lifted toward the sky, arms outstretched, one hand gripping the mike, the other palm up, fingers slowly opening and closing.

"Can you feel it? Do you? Do you feel God's love? Ooohh, it feels so good, so wonderful to know we are blessed by God's presence," she cried out in ecstasy. "Smell it . . . feel it . . . the sweet smell of the sea air . . . the touch of a breeze on our faces . . . a warm yet cool night. Wait . . . Listen to the sound of the waves . . . Can you hear it? These miracles of life surround us each and every day. We just need to take the time to appreciate it."

A chorus of yeses met her. Even if you didn't feel it, her sincerity made up for it. You believed that she believed.

There was sustained applause as she bathed joyously in the crowd's adulation, hands clasped prayerfully against her breast. When she opened those unfathomable eyes, her gaze swept us and she said, "Thank you so much for letting me be a part of your gathering this evening. Sometimes that's all we really need, the knowledge that we're here for each other. This evening you've made me feel loved and welcomed. Your applause and giving spirit humble me. I am very grateful."

Who is this woman? Is it really my daughter? Her resonating voice was so powerful and engrossing that it sliced into our emotions yet, at the same, time held its intimacy and personalness.

"The last couple of weeks, I've been groomed and rehearsed in antic- ipation of meeting you. I've tried to be all the things I think you want me to be. Aren't you flattered?" she asked, raising her eyebrows coquettishly. As she spoke, she unwrapped her headdress while lithely walking back and forth across the stage.

"But what it really comes down to is being yourself, right?"

A resounding "*Yes*" punched the sky.

She pulled the last of the wrap, unfastened a hair clip, and, with a sharp shake, her hair tumbled down. Tropical vines of African braids fell into place around her shoulders like rank-and-file soldiers.

"Well, I can try to be myself, but in the end it won't be enough. Anything that happens tonight will be because of us, not me. You didn't think you were going to kick back while I did all the work, did you?"

Amazingly, she could make them laugh at their own high expectations.

"It's our faith that will make it possible. We are here to celebrate God, and life, and each other. We are here to build a united wall, a fortress of love that will not offer refuge to hatred or violence."

"No!"

"I am you, and you are me. We are flesh and blood. Our spirits are not grounded by such limitations. Ultimately, it is not our bodies we must nurture but our spirits. That is the only way we will be able to transcend the vulgarities and inanities of life."

"Tell it, girl!"

She stood tall on the edge of the stage with her hands clasped around the microphone, then turned and pointed at Noel. "That man over there is my little brother, Noel. I love him so much, but every once in a while, he has this habit of putting his foot in his mouth. *He* promised you miracles. I can't."

Again, the only sound heard was the rollercoaster.

Olisa paused weighting her words very carefully.

"Many of you saw or heard that I healed a young man this past summer. I didn't do it; God did. It all came from God. I was simply the vehicle. Miracles are not my promise to give. Only God can dictate that. And if the Creator grants it, then, yes, tonight we will be blessed with divine intervention."

"Yeah, right, here we go. Time for the big cop-out!" blasted the resurrected voice of my old Viet Nam friend.

Luckily, she couldn't hear him as she hunched down and studied the multitude of eager upturned faces.

"I am so happy to see so many of you here. Even those of you who are trying so hard to put on your Big Daddy Cool masks, except your eyes give you away. They tell the truth. They tell me you care. Look; I'm sure some of you only came out of curiosity. I don't blame you. Hearing all those bizarre rumors about some witch in Venice Beach would have gotten me to show up."

She waited until the nervous laughter abated.

"Or maybe I'm being vain and you didn't come to see me at all. Maybe you came to catch a glimpse of the lovely Eva Sanchez."

Olisa acknowledged Eva's presence in the audience with a wave. Eva was out of my vision, but it was easy to ascertain her vicinity by the way the crowd wadded up.

"Or maybe you came to view the tightrope act and see if I'd slip and fall on my bottom. It's possible. I'm not real agile. Whatever your reason may be, I do believe you care about the state of our world and want it to change for the better. What happened on July the Fourth was an act of spontaneity. It was not planned, despite what some of our friends in the media suggest." She chuckled. "At that moment, I found I cared more for those kids trying to hurt themselves than my own welfare. Why else would some skinny little black chick run out there and audition as a carving board for Thanksgiving?"

"Amen, sister."

"I didn't say that to seek pats on the back, because the next time something breaks out, I might be elbowing one of you to get by."

People laughed; many didn't, sincerely believing she'd never abandon anyone.

"That afternoon taught me something. I learned if we can find a way to put aside our own needs and learn to love, respect, and appreciate each other without expectation, miracles will happen. But it calls for self-sacrifice. I know it's not easy. It's the hardest thing in life to do. All we can do is try."

"That's why you won't see any miracles coming out of me, 'cause I love myself too much," joked someone from the audience.

Olisa smiled. "That's all right, my brother. You should love yourself; just try and ration a little bit for us too."

Grinning, he nodded and displayed the peace sign.

"I heard y'all joining in and singing 'One Love' earlier. It's not a cliché. One love *will* set us free. It can shape the future of things to come. You see love is the fulcrum for spontaneity. When we're in love, we don't stop to think; we react. If we can love and forgive each other without restraint, then we will wield true power and together create miracles that will shock the world.

"Tonight, I'm going to ask you to love me as I love you. And I ask that, for just one minute of your lives, you focus on loving the person next to you more than yourself. Don't freak out . . . Hold on . . . Give me a chance. Now, don't you guys cheat! Here we go. Repeat after me: 'I love you more than I love myself.' C'mon; look at each other when you say it. Don't stop. You'll see it feels good! *Say it!* I can't hear you!"

Hundreds chanted, "I love you more than I love myself."

"See? You don't want to stop, do you?" Olisa laughed, doing a seal clap with her hands. She still held the microphone in her hand. Each clap sounded like thunder. "I love it. You may not want to admit it, but I bet it not only makes you feel good, but it also makes you feel powerful, because you are in control of your emotions.

"This is what we are trying to bring to the formation of our new organization. We entitled it OLISA, Inc. mainly because we're not real creative," she stated humorously with a self-deprecating tone. No one would know that she fought tooth and nail not to have her name included in the title. But Noel finally convinced her branding her name was essential to making this effort successful.

"It means 'One Love Inspires Spiritual Awakening.'" She waved off the cheers. "The primary purpose of our organization is to prove that our love will not only heal the world but it will also be our salvation."

Her eyes swept the audience, and then she spoke for about twenty more arresting minutes, unlike any preacher I have ever heard.

She didn't rain fire and brimstone on us.

She didn't wage war upon our moral conscience and turpitude.

She didn't dig our graves and make us lie down in it for the shameless sinners we are.

Nor did she shovel heaps of guilt, fear, and self-worthlessness upon our psyches until we begged for forgiveness and redemption.

She only spoke of love, about how living a life guided by love and compassion is the way to uncomplicate our existence.

She even quoted Mother Theresa, "A life not lived for others is not a life."

Then she abruptly stopped and surveyed the masses of people gathered in the sand below the pier.

"This is not right, not right at all," she intonated. "I shouldn't be standing here above you. I should be among you."

To my great chagrin, she passed the mike to her befuddled brother, signaling for him to follow her. She strode down the stairsteps and into the arms of the crowd.

At the bottom of the stairs, she was quickly met by a concerned Alton who leaned over and whispered in her ear. Smiling, she stood up on her toes, kissed his cheek, and gently pushed him aside while Noel held the microphone aloft.

"We are all family tonight. I have nothing to fear from anyone out here, not when I walk with the Almighty."

Fervent applause and cheers filled the air as she waded into the masses of onlookers. It looked like a New Orleans parade with Noel on one side of her holding a microphone aloft like a candle and Alton on the other protectively escorting her. Logan sprinted back and forth holding his camera high and shooting away. A caravan of steely-countenanced bodyguards lumbered behind Olisa as she glided through the people.

"We aren't here to promote religion or declare that our belief is the only way to salvation. We are here to seek cooperation among all faiths and build a bridge of *change*. All we care about tonight is spreading love. Human beings aren't born violent. As babies, we want to be held, caressed, and loved, but wrongheaded people in our society have taught us how to hate, how to attack and prey upon others, and how to think irrationally and propagate distorted and manipulative ideologies. The negativity recycles itself, sprouting new arms and legs. Isn't it time to ask yourself how long do you want this vicious cycle to continue?"

Olisa stopped the caravan in front of a young teenage White girl with loping curls of chestnut hair whose hands were clamped to her elbows.

"When do you want it to end, girlfriend?"

The girl at first was flummoxed to find Olisa facing her and giving her direct eye contact. I think she shocked herself when she uncontrollably blurted out, "Right now! I just can't deal with it anymore! I want it to stop!"

"Good for you because you're right. *Now* is the time!" Olisa's eyes sparkled like hot flames. "And you and I will start it off with a hug."

"Okay," the girl agreed reluctantly, bowing her head. Her jaws tightened as she fought back tears.

Olisa reached out and gave her a prolonged hug. She pulled back, holding her by the shoulders and reading her face. "Look at that beautiful evening sky. Doesn't it feel magical?"

"Yes . . ."

"Do you know how vital it is for you to hold that feeling in your heart?" she asked gently massaging the girl's temples.

The girl nodded as the tears flowed freely.

"You are a very special person. Yet, he condemns you for not being good enough. You aren't listening to him, are you?"

The girl uncertainly shook her head no.

"You still wonder if he loves you enough. Move on with your life. Don't try to convince him or change him. If he truly loves you, he will figure it all out. As painful as it may be, you just have to stand your ground and no longer accept his mistreatment of you and taking you for granted. He may have to experience the pain of losing you before he realizes what he truly has."

"Uh, thanks . . . Wow," she said, smashing her curls with both hands and shaking her head. "Awesome, that's exactly what . . ."

Her sentence was lost to infinity. The caravan had moved on.

She stopped in front of a young Filipino male with bright orange hair and an open Hawaiian shirt, displaying his washboard stomach.

"I love you more than I love myself. Say it, even if you don't believe it, even if it feels funny. It gets easier with each repetition."

"Aww, I can't say all that, you know. That's not me. I don't love anyone more than I love me."

"Do you love your mother?"

"Of course, but that's family."

"Tonight, we're your family, too."

"Okay, I can roll with that. How about I just say I love the way you look better than me," he said, cutting his eyes flirtatiously at her.

"I'd say you're getting close, but you've got a little more work to do," she laughed, hugging him.

She then scanned the crowd, and her eyes fixed on my favorite person.

"We are not recruiting religions; we are recruiting soldiers who will help to create a better place for ourselves and our children—"

"Horseshit!"

Mr. Viet Nam pushed his way through, meeting Olisa face to face. Alton expanded as he slid in front of her.

"I think you've said enough, partner," Alton warned, flexing his dou-ble-barreled biceps.

"You don't scare me!"

"That's what makes my job more enjoyable."

Olisa put a hand on Alton's shoulder. "We don't need to go there. Let him express himself, Alton. What is it you want to say to me, sir?"

"Thank you. My name is Fred Plechas, ma'am, and I take major offense to people like yourself casually tossing about the word 'soldier.' You are talking about me and all my comrades, the *real* soldiers, alive or dead! I am a proud American citizen who fought in Viet Nam and would have gladly fought in any other war my country asked of me! You'd never find me hiding in some Canadian rathole like some of those draft dodgers and cowards roaming around in this nation who later traded in their yellow streaks for white collars."

A cascade of boos and heckles fell on him. He was unperturbed. "I've been around long enough to know when someone's playing peek-a-boo behind ten-dollar words!"

"Why do you say that, Mr. Plechas?" Olisa composedly asked, like they were having a Sunday morning tea.

"Because you're a fraud, miss! You don't have any special powers. You're like all the rest of them megawatt preachers, trying to steal us hardworking people's money. You're just prettier to look at. You think all this spiritual garbage and kissin' and huggin' is going to make us forget you're supposed to be some kind of miracle worker? I didn't forget! You can try to fool all these youngsters and naïve folks out here by disguising your failings with all this high-powered music, but it doesn't move me no way. Where are all the bullshit miracles, lady?"

I wanted to whoop his ass with that cane he was leaning on until I caught Olisa's eyes. They were as nebulous as desert sand. All of a sudden it was like they illuminated, coupled with an easy smile playing on her face.

"Some of us out here want a miracle so bad, we'll probably invent one in our tiny little heads and go screaming to the news media about it. Did you hire some out-of-work actors to pretend to be saved at the right moment? Is that what you did with that rapper up there on stage? Does Mr. Foul Mouth own a percentage in your new company?"

"No, Mr. Plechas."

"Doesn't matter. The bottom line is you're just as big a crook as all the rest of them greedy bastards out there!"

"Is that what you truly believe, Mr. Plechas?"

"Damn right! I call it as I see it. You can't snowball me. I've seen the best do their evil work, and it ain't gonna happen to me! Being a soldier in the greatest country in the world, the USA, is the most noble profession there is!"

"What the fuck . . . Read the paper, dude . . . sexual harassment, corrupt politicians, LGBTQ bashing, conspiracy fanatics . . . Just shut the fuck up!" yelled a man behind him with a beard twisted into two short pigtails and a long red pigtail, multiple facial piercings, and tattoo-covered ham-hock arms.

Plechas turned around and barked, "You shut the fuck up! You couldn't possibly know what being a true patriot is all about! Look at you, boy! You look like a beached whale! Ain't they told you the war is over? You don't have to piss behind Canadian trees anymore!"

"Fuck you, old man!"

He turned back to Olisa. "There you go, a prime example of what I'm talking about—ignorant liberal buffoons who are willing to accept anything. I only came here to see how you were going to con people into believing you're some kind of prophet or angel who can do miracles. But it's already the same old hype you're dishing out," he muttered with disdain.

The boo birds in the audience pounced on him, but he persevered, arms belligerently crossed as he glared at Olisa. She raised her hands patting the air like a quarterback trying to silence the home crowd.

"Why are you berating this man? He volunteered his opinion. Respect his right to communicate his feelings, whether you agree or disagree with him. You might be surprised—I partly agree with him."

The silence tumbled down like a broken stage curtain. Plechas eyed her suspiciously.

"Mr. Plechas," she continued, "I have been avoiding the part in the show where the woman performs a miracle. It's not for the reasons you think. I didn't want the real message to be overshadowed. My plan was to get people to perceive that we are all potentially capable of healing one another and performing miracles.

"Even so, it's never enough, is it? You saw through my act, Mr. Plechas. Maybe it's time and God is calling me through you."

She took a deep breath, her shoulders rising as she squeezed her hands together. Olisa stepped forward, and Plechas stepped backwards.

"So, Mr. Plechas, what do you want me to do?"

He was caught off guard. His eyes flitted nervously, mugged by the angry silence. He rubbed the elbow of the stiff arm that looked soldered to his eagle-headed cane. The knotted nose that had received its share of bar fisticuffs in its time faded in and out of its scarlet coloring as he habitually flicked his thumb and pulled on each nostril as if he were going to sneeze.

"Hey, wait a minute. I sure in the hell don't know. You're the so-called expert. Out of all the people here, there must be someone around here that needs your help. Just look around."

"No, I'm more interested in you, Mr. Plechas. How can I help *you*? Don't you need a miracle in your life?"

"Huh?"

"Move closer, Mr. Plechas. I really want to hug you."

"Say what? Oh no, I'm not into all that touchy-feely stuff... Pick someone else." He refused to budge, eyeing her warily.

"You're not afraid of me, are you?"

"Don't be ridiculous!"

"Then let me show you the innocence of a hug. I promise it won't hurt."

"Geez . . . All right then if that's what will make you happy . . . No big deal," he replied, lifting the lid of his cap to wipe the sweat off his brow. He stepped forward with his right leg rising and falling like an accordion. Plechas reached out to formally shake her hand. Unexpectedly, she pulled him inside her arms and held him tightly. Ordinarily, this would have made for a comical spectacle seeing this army veteran struggling to free himself from this petite woman's arms. Except things got really real, fast. A moment later, his arms dangled limply, helplessly, with only his fingers slightly wiggling.

"How long has your leg been injured?"

"Uh, uh . . . What did you do to me? I can barely move . . ."

"Relax, Mr. Plechas. Stop fighting me. The sensation you feel is God's love flowing through you," she whispered. Noel inched the microphone closer to their mouths.

"Um . . . it's been over fifty years since I took a couple of bullets on the battlefield in Nam," he shakily recounted.

"You must have received a purple heart."

"I did. Yes, ma'am."

"That's wonderful! You must be proud."

"Thank you, yes," he replied weakly.

"Mr. Fred Plechas, I can tell you have suffered deep hurt in your lifetime beyond just the injury. I wish I could have been there for you. You're a widower, aren't you?"

"Yeah, yeah . . ."

"You lost her several years ago, and you miss her like it was yesterday. I can feel your pain. It's been buried for a long time, huh?"

Plechas never answered. His eyes were closed like he was pleasantly sleeping. Conversely, Olisa's face was skewed in anguish.

"Though you've always been somewhat of a skeptic, your wife believed, didn't she? She never lost faith that a cure would be available for her one day. She saw doctors, priests, ministers, spiritualists, and psychics. You spent almost all your savings, but the cancer spread fast. She died, leaving you alone to pick up the pieces. I couldn't help you then, but God is here now. And I can say to you—your wife is better than she's ever been. She wants you to move on with your life, 'Cappy.'"

Bystanders shrieked as his body jerked spasmodically like he was being riddled with bullets from ferocious crossfire. Sweat glistened on his face as his hands feebly pushed against her chest. She let him go. He retreated, moving, stepping, feinting like a boxer, laboring to distance himself from her. Disorientation smothered his face. The scraggly chicken hairs sprouting from his head were no longer protected by the cap that flew off during the convulsions. I doubt if he heard Olisa's gentle entreaties as his eyes guardedly watched her. He tripped over someone's foot and plummeted to the ground like he'd been dropped from the sky.

Olisa bent down and picked up his cap, slipping it back over his head. She offered him a hand.

His hands scrambled over hers like crabs as he lowered his eyes deferentially. His lips remained unhinged. "She's the only one that ever called me Cappy, short for Captain America. How in the hell could you have known that?"

"I'm sorry I couldn't do anything for your leg, Mr. Plechas."

"Not God's will?" he uttered sarcastically, once again eyeing her suspiciously.

"I suppose not. It appears God found it more vital to rid you of the cancer wracking your own body."

At first I thought Plechas had fallen into some mud or beach tar as he vigorously wiped at the black substance layered on his arm, but it wasn't either mud or tar. It was some kind of black bile oozing from his mouth and settling on his shirt like an oil spill. When he grasped what was happening, his eyes were as wide as tea plates. Gurgling sounds emanated from his throat as the panic made him gag.

"This is not right! Get away from me! You really are some kind of witch! What did you do to me?"

"You've been given the chance to breathe again, Mr. Plechas. How does it feel?"

The compassion flowing in her eyes was so beautiful it pained me.

He groaned sickly as he slapped his hands to his chest. Something was going on inside of him. The look he gave her vacillated between praise and vilification. And then it all swiftly changed to one of pure joy.

"Oh my God. Oh my God," shouted Mr. Plechas giddily. "I . . . feel . . . great! Do you hear me? Great! I can feel it . . . The cancer is gone! I don't believe it . . . No pain! People will say how can you say that without a diagnosis—and I'll get one—but I just know my system has been cleansed. I feel like a newborn child! How in God's name did you do it?" he asked, grabbing her by the arm and then sheepishly releasing her as he was struck by the ignorance of his question. "Oh, what a big dumb fool I've been. I'm . . . Will you please forgive me for all that stuff I said?"

She laid her hand gently on his shoulder. "Mr. Plechas, enjoy your new life."

Crossing his arms and grabbing his shoulders, Plechas dropped to his knees, swaying autistically as several cigarettes from his breast pocket spilled lifelessly into the sand. The mixture of laughter and tears coming from him were as incongruent as a snow blizzard in July. A hairy arm plucked his cap, which had fallen to the ground again and torpedoed it through the air.

Olisa and I locked eyes for a second, but a mass of bodies sealed the gap. Raucous cheering, whistling, and Amens filled the night air. Cappy's hat flew through the air back and forth like a Frisbee. Someone invoked Olisa's name with the urgency of an ailing child.

To my relief, the next time I saw Olisa, Alton was hurriedly ushering her back up the stairs to the stage.

She announced, "I'm sorry to say that management has informed us that I need to stay up here or they will close the show earlier than expected."

The crowd groaned unanimously.

"I agree with you, but we don't want any accidents out here tonight. We are here to heal each other, not hurt each other. Okay?"

"Amen."

"So we're just going to have to bring some folks up here."

Before the evening ended, two more people were escorted up to the stage and successfully healed: a blind Pakistani ten-year-old boy and a Black woman with severe arthritis. Both were filled with such awe and gratitude that they refused to leave the stage until the show was over, as if their departure might break the spell of enchantment and they'd revert to their former selves.

Glancing at my watch, I was happy to see it was almost 9:00 PM. The City of Santa Monica required that all events on the pier must conclude by 10:00 PM. Olisa was showing signs of visible exhaustion, so I was happy to see it coasting to a close.

"We are all blessed with the ability to heal each other," Olisa declared. "It is not all physical. Sometimes it can be as simple as telling a friend how much you love them and assuring them you will always be there. Healing the spirit is the cure to all the world's ills."

Twenty minutes later, that message whizzed over the gathered masses standing on the pier and in the sand below faster than planes arriving and departing from LAX.

Olisa knelt down on one knee, cuddling the little boy Rusul whose effervescent smile was contagious. He constantly touched his eyelids to assure himself it wasn't a dream. He had regained the sight lost to him in a hit-and-run accident about two years ago when he was only five years old. This same accident took the life of his mother, his father tearfully informed us before Olisa laid her soothing hands over his eyes.

Kids don't prescribe to anybody's sense of time or diplomacy. As Olisa was concluding her speech, Rusul had been restlessly moving around in her arms to the point of distraction. No longer able to contain his excitement, he exclaimed: "Ms. Olisa, Ms. Olisa, look at that man! That's Merlin, the magician! He's sitting right over there. Will you ask him to come up here?"

Olisa's eyes skirted around, finally settling.

"I see who you are talking about, Rusul, though I don't think his real name is Merlin. We only have a little time left; perhaps we can induce the gentleman to come up here and join us. Sir, would you mind?"

Everyone turned their heads, searching for this Merlin character. It was then that I noticed a very large man in the audience with shoulders as wide as a landing strip. His short icy-white hair shimmered in the darkness. How could I have missed him? He towered head and shoulders over everyone else. My heart skyrocketed when he turned his head; even the dark shades couldn't conceal the fact that he saw me, too. He moved aside to let a woman pushing a man in a wheelchair emerge. They proceeded reticently up a ramp on the side of the stage. When they rolled toward centerstage, my heart leaped again.

Noel wasn't prepared for this either. He gawked like he had seen a ghost.

The woman was Lena Cavaliere.

And the Merlin look-alike was none other than Nick Cavaliere wearing horn-rimmed glasses and a black fedora. His dark hair streaked with swaths of gray trickled down to his shoulders, and his beard rested on his chest. I forgot that one of the last roles Nick played before the accident was Merlin in an epic remake of *The Sword and the Stone*. Rusul spotted him and made the association. No one else did. Nick hadn't been seen in about two years. Even the tabloids had only captured sketchy pictures of him during this period.

Glancing back over my shoulders, I wasn't surprised to see the big fella had vanished.

"Are you Merlin, sir?" Rusul asked innocently.

"I wish I was, son."

"You sure look like him."

I could understand where the child was coming from, but I don't think the movie Merlin ever matched the agony on this one's face.

"Why do you look so sad, Mr. Merlin? Don't you know that Ms. Olisa can help you too?"

"I certainly hope so, young man." His voice sounded like his throat was jammed by hundreds of cotton balls.

I don't think Olisa had any idea of who it was, not that it made a difference. She leaned over him, sandwiching is head in her hands. Her braids obscured her face.

"Do you believe in God, my friend?"

"I used to. I can't honestly say what I believe now."

"Do you believe you can be healed this evening?"

"I . . . I . . . I don't know . . . I hope so . . . Yes, I guess . . . What do you want me to say?"

"The Creator's love is so powerful that it doesn't really matter. Miracles happen whether you believe in them or not."

The crowd's silence was intense as she laid her head on his shoulder. She locked her arms around his body and pressed him tightly against hers in an almost sensual embrace.

"God loves you and wants you to know that your spirit is far more important than anything else the physical world can offer. You are ready to give up, but like your wife, I won't let you."

Tears rolled down Nick's cheeks, pooling in the creases of her elbow. Hearing his tormented cries made the palms of my hands moisten. His eyes were squeezed shut, cheeks puffing, and the veins in his temples protruded so far out I thought they were going to burst through his skin.

A barrage of unintelligible words streamed out of his mouth as if he were speaking in tongues. His eyes rolled into the back of his head, and he continued to babble, no longer caring about the onlookers. The air was hauntingly still.

His head fell back, and no other words came out of his mouth.

"Now you know the power of true love. There are no masks to hide behind here. You are free. You can stand up any time you are ready. Just let go of my arms first," Olisa wearily smiled.

His head sprung forward. Nick was unaware that he had been clutching her elbows. His euphoric howl glided through the air, louder than the seagulls.

"Lena!" he yelled. "Look at me, Lena! My hands . . . Oh sweet Lord. Can you believe it? Do you see what I'm doing?" He opened and closed his hands into fists.

"Yes! Yes! I see! I see!" Lena enthusiastically shouted back, her fingers fumbling to unhinge the belts that imprisoned him to the chair.

Gingerly, he rose from his wheelchair.

Lena's eyes were so big, I swear I could see the green in her irises from where I stood as she watched in stupefaction. The closer he came to standing completely upright, the more she hopped like a game show contestant.

Some people were ecstatically yelling, "Go, Merlin. Go, Merlin. Go, Merlin . . ."

Rusul held Nick by the waist as he giddily wrapped one arm around the kid. He looked like a first-time rollerblader trying to maintain his balance. Olisa snaked his other arm around Lena's trembling shoulders.

The stage looked like an outtake from a David Lynch film: a Merlin clone supported by a Black woman, a White woman, a Pakistani kid, surrounded by a bunch of wildly attired hip musicians, and Noel "Don King" Timmerman raising Nick's arms high in the air as if he'd just won the greatest title fight in history. And in a sense, he did.

But the Cadillac was just rounding the corner.

Nick Cavaliere wasn't the only one with a flair for drama. Noel slowly removed Nick's hat and glasses.

Still to this day, I get goose bumps from the screams that became the clarion call for the end of our privacy. I always joked it was Eva Sanchez who screamed the loudest because this had truly become the biggest story of the year, decade, maybe even century. The murmurs in the crowd swept through building from waves to a tsunami.

"Isn't that Nick Cavaliere?"

"Yes, yes, that's Nick Cavaliere!"

"No, it's not."

"Yes, it is! That's Nick Cavaliere!"

Those two words, "Nick Cavaliere," streaked through the crowd faster than email. After a while it turned into a chant. Heads bobbed up and down clamoring for a better view and jockeying around like hungry seals waiting for raw fish to be thrown.

Nick Cavaliere.

You couldn't have scripted a more perfect Hollywood ending as he fought to stay on his feet. I could just hear an epic John Williams score playing in the background as the credits rolled.

People randomly dropped to their hands and knees as if they had been smitten by a virulent plague. Others were huddled and wailing at the top of their lungs, faces heavenward as their hands fluttered above their heads. The newly sanctified made a trampoline out of the pier as they exuberantly bounced up and down proclaiming the appearance of the Holy Ghost. Those speaking in Spanish hailed it as the "*Espiritu Santo.*" Many individuals wore solemn expressions and clasped their hands tightly together as they recited the Lord's Prayer, their lips moving slowly and purposefully.

This was about as close to a preview of Judgment Day as I'd ever wanted to see.

The healing of Nick Cavaliere single-handedly legitimized to all present that this was no sleight-of-hand feat but an authentic honest-to-God miracle. Nick and his career were resurrected from the grave like a modern-day Lazarus.

It was mind-blowing to watch Nick standing up on his own, hands clasped shakily above his head. At the same time Olisa collapsed into Alton's rock-solid arms as he rushed her backstage.

I shoved my way through the throngs of people, ignoring the incoherent patter assaulting my ears. But I wasn't alone. A tidal wave of people, mostly teenagers, rushed the stage. My pronouncements about being Olisa's father and trying to get them to calm down was as impossible as trying to find a contact lens outside during a blizzard! Instead, I was met by reptilian stares and hands that smacked my chest and knocked me backwards as I collided into other flying bodies. While getting up, I dodged a person rolling past me like a bowling ball. He immediately jumped up and dissolved into the wall of humanity surging forward.

Mass hysteria.

The emotional decibels were turned up so high, the pent-up energy searched for some type of release. The bodyguards were affected by it, too. Their faces may have been carved in stone, but their eyes were overtaken by fear. Adrenaline rushed through them like rapids as they pushed and strong-armed folks around with far more brute force than necessary. They couldn't help themselves. They were fighting more than just the crowd. They were battling against what our primal ancestors have always feared, the unexplained forces of nature—magic, superstition, spirits, and God incarnate. It was the fight-or-flight syndrome. I think they wanted to run, run as far away as possible until they could sort it all out and place it in a nice, tidy compartment in the back of their minds, the same way I had been doing for so many years.

Eventually, the hyped-up crowd overwhelmed the meager number of security forces and hurdled on stage victoriously. They wanted the magic to last forever. They danced, gyrated, and lustily celebrated, grabbing whatever souvenirs they could get their hands on. Many tussled over the microphone, stand, podium, wheelchair, and notes, anything Olisa had touched. They ripped wood from the stage as if it had been anointed with holy water.

Soon an angry megaphone blasted orders for them to disperse, followed by an aggregation of helmeted riot police marching into the multitude, armed with incapacitants such as batons, pepper spray, tear gas, and rifles loaded with plastic bullets. Having been the recipient of a couple of errant batons in my youth, I didn't have any problem heeding their commands. Fortunately, Alton and his group had been able to get the performers offstage long before the celebrants had wrested control. I confidently assumed that my family knew better than to wait for me in the limousine. I'd get home fine since I was an unknown. I only prayed they would, too.

Meanwhile, police helicopters flashed their spotlight in a dizzying array of lights, transforming the night into artificial day, accompanied by network news copters just receiving word that a potentially full-scale riot was taking shape on the pier. I saw camera operators and reporters from all the major networks scurrying to the scene and interviewing everyone they could to get some sense of what was going on.

Luckily, things were already beginning to quiet down, and it didn't look like it would be as bad as I initially thought. Yes, a few rambunctious souls got roughed up and carted away, but there were no further skirmishes and the frenetic excitement fizzled out. No one really wanted any trouble. This was a riot fueled by people needing to burn off energy, not anger. For all the attendees, it was a great night beset by a celebration that got out of hand. Many people actually aided the officers in calming individuals down.

Irony of ironies as I headed toward the "blue" bus stop, I saw Mr. Plechas holding court in front of the merry-go-round with an assembly of reporters who poked microphones toward his throat while he spoke. He had acquired quite a few new friends since the last time I saw him. They patted him on the back while he talked energetically about the evening's experience.

Tell you the truth, I was more surprised to not see Eva Sanchez hustling about competing for interviews. Then again, she was most likely already at the news station.

"God bless you, brother."

"Yeah, you too," I replied layering my voice with a little more bass than usual. A burly White biker, clad in snatches of black leather, drunkenly stumbled into my path with his beefy hairy arm cupped around his Cruella De Ville-haired lady. He swigged beer from a can and haphazardly spilled a good portion of it on her bony shoulder. Nonetheless, this didn't even elicit a blink from her droopy eyes.

"Do you accept Jesus in your heart, brother?"

I nodded quickly and affirmatively hoping this would prevent a drunken discourse on how my soul would be stewed in the iron Dutch ovens of hell if I was a nonbeliever.

In those murky eyes sheltered under foliage of thick bushy eyebrows, he buckled a little as he sized me up. In another day and time, if he had been with his buds, he might have been more satisfied trying to kick my ass instead of instead of quoting scripture, but alas, this was a night reserved for miracles.

"Good," he said, finally successfully giving me a high five after a couple of intoxicated misses, "because the end is near. Only those who believe in Jesus, our Lord and Savior, will live in our Father's kingdom. You must beware of all false prophets—*Book of Revelations*, man."

"I hear you, man. I'm down with all that," I confirmed.

He reached out and squeezed my hand like it was a cow's udder, satisfied that we were on the same page. "We are blessed, dude, cuz we know what's up," he slurred, raising my hand in his greasy hand as he gave me a "We Are the World" look. His eyes fell back into his head as he abruptly and thankfully released my hand. He swerved clumsily toward a couple he spotted to victimize as he and his female appendage blocked their path.

I finally got home. However, home didn't turn out to be the treat I expected.

Chapter 7

Ordinarily, it would have taken around ten minutes. As a result of the evening's events, it took over an hour to get home by bus because of the traffic jam.

Noel greeted me at the backdoor, eyes glittering and chest puffed out. Behind him I caught sight of Eva Sanchez dashing down our hallway. Seeing me, she gleefully waved, then disappeared into our brightly lit living room pursued by her shadow.

"What is *she* doing here? What the hell is going on?"

Noel touched his forefinger to his lips and put his arm around my shoulders. He escorted me into the entrance of the living room and pointed.

While a camera crew adjusted the lighting, seated in the center of the living room on our couch were Eva Sanchez and Nick Cavaliere.

The beaming lights were nothing compared to Eva's grin before she tapered it down for the intimate interview. And why not? She possessed the scoop of the year. While all her rivals were at the pier eagerly picking up the scraps, she was meeting with the man himself. Nick Cavaliere rarely participated in interviews before the accident and at the height of his fame, so this was a real coup and Eva was taking full advantage.

It was even more amazing that he agreed to be interviewed so soon after being healed. I'm sure his PR people were against it and probably adamantly wanted him to go home and rest and take some time away for a viewer buildup, then do a later interview with a top broadcast journalist and television personality. There were millions of dollars to be made on an interview of this caliber. Yet, there he was, sitting in our living room and bristling with energy. His hair was pulled back in a ponytail, and his beard had been brushed out. His eyes may have been blood red, but his face was no longer gaunt. All the color had returned, and it was practically shimmering. His distinctive baritone had returned from its hiatus, though his tone was more humble than I remembered.

"Nick, you mentioned earlier that you almost didn't attend this concert. In light of all that has happened, I can't imagine that now."

"Thank God, neither can I."

"What finally convinced you?"

"My wife, Lena."

"What did she say?"

"Not a damn thing. Her eyes said it all. When the invitation was made to me to show up at this concert, I adamantly refused. Then I saw the look on her face . . . It was as if I'd betrayed all the trust and emotional equity in our marriage. I deserved it. We vowed to never stop fighting this thing and to always search for hope wherever we could find it. I gave up. Lena continued the battle against all the odds and naysayers. An hour before the concert, I told her to get her car keys."

"Did you ever think it would all end up like this?"

"No." He rubbed his legs, still in disbelief. "But that heaven-sent woman, asleep in her bedroom, changed all that . . . The accident was life altering and now, again . . . how do I even begin to thank her? With the Timmermans' blessings, I hope they will allow me to stay here until she awakens so that I have a chance to express my deepest gratitude to Olisa. I am eternally indebted to her. I owe her my life—everything."

A watery veil fell over his eyes as he motioned Lena to come and sit beside him. She snuggled into him, gazing at him like she had been reunited with a long-lost lover.

"And what about you, Lena? How do you feel tonight?"

"Truly and humbly blessed. It's all so utterly unbelievable. I haven't been able to absorb it all yet. It's like this great big, wonderful dream, and I'm hoping I'll never wake up. I just want to thank my adopted son, Noel Timmerman, for bringing us to his sister. Hopefully he's survived all the kisses I smothered him with."

Noel grinned like the little kid I knew as he placed his fist over his heart to acknowledge her sentiment. Despite all my disagreements about everything, I had to admit to myself this whole thing was worth it seeing the joy it brought to them as well as the other people who were healed.

"Nick, it may be a little difficult for our viewers to see, but we're showing the videotape of Olisa healing you. Can you tell us how you're feeling at that moment?" Eva asked, her gold eyes magnified.

"Out of control. Disoriented. Watching the video feels like an out-of-body experience . . . and maybe it was. I can barely remember anything. I just remember staring into big brown eyes you could swim in and feeling these prickly sensations competing inside my body. What I mean by that is it tickled, it hurt, and it was like tiny little hands moving things around. Until tonight I never would have believed something like this could have happened."

"You mean like a miracle?"

"Yes, a miracle. The fact that I'm sitting in this living room talking to you is a living testament to that. I'm exhausted, but it's like I was shot with some powerful stimulant. My wife tells me not to push it, go relax, but I don't want to fall asleep. I'm fearful it will all go away."

"How soon do you think you'll go back to working again?"

"You do realize that this all happened only a couple of hours ago, right?"

"I do . . . I'm just required to ask," Eva responded sheepishly.

"But I'll answer your question. Work, you ask? Like a child, I just want to play." He rocked Lena in his arms.

"I understand what you are saying. But speaking on behalf of all your loyal fans who will be watching this, now that we have you back, please don't deprive us of seeing you in the movies again."

"Thank you. That's very kind, but all I care about tonight is being with my wife, family, and new friends. Besides, maybe they've forgotten all about me. I might be lucky if I ever see another script again."

"Mr. Cavaliere, that's one worry I don't think you'll ever have to be concerned with. No one's ever going to forget about you after this night."

A hand grabbed my hand and led me into the hallway.

"Roberta, I told you we can't do this in the house. Sooner or later my wife is going to catch us."

"Shut up. Don't you know how worried I've been about you?" Warm and welcome lips pressed again mine.

Quietly we tiptoed out the backdoor.

"Oh, Joseph . . . Thank goodness you're okay. I don't know what I would have done if you had gotten hurt. Do you know how much I love you? I was so worried about you when all the commotion started."

Grace's head was in my chest as she squeezed me tightly. A breeze lifted the strands of her hair, tickling my nose.

"What are you talking about? I was the one who started it!"

"Just be quiet and hold me."

We stood in the middle of the courtyard clinging to each other.

"Nothing was going to happen to me, Grace. I'll always be around to make your life miserable."

"Promise?"

"Promise."

"Joseph, please don't laugh at me when I say I'm scared."

"Me too."

"You were right—we should have closed the door . . . Now it's too late."

"Sweetheart, the door opened when she was born. We could only avoid it for so long. If not today, then tomorrow. But you already know that."

"It doesn't make me feel any better."

"Grace, I can't believe I'm saying this, but it's all going to work out in the end."

I just wished I could have stated it with a little more conviction.

Shortly thereafter, Grace went back inside the house to check on things. I elected to stay outside. It was too claustrophobic in there. I had more than enough of my share of people, cameras, reporters, and bright lights. I parked myself on a lounge chair in the patio and took in the warm night air and silence.

"You mind if I join you?"

"Hey, Nick, of course not. Let me grab a chair for you."

"No, sir, let me!" he proclaimed proudly, hoisting one of the lounge chairs and sliding it next to me on the patio deck.

"Eva Sanchez still here?"

"No, she left a while ago, back to wherever reporters burrow."

"You're not real high on them either, huh?"

"No, except over my career, I've had to carve out a semi-peaceful coexistence with them, Joseph. However, I'm sure there are a few that aren't too enamored of actors, either," he laughed. "How's your daughter doing?"

"Still sound asleep. And at the rate she's going, she'll wake up sometime in the twenty-third century."

"That's good!"

"Where's Lena?"

"In the house, blabbing everyone's ears off. Can't you hear her? She's having the best time I've seen . . . ohhh, maybe in a couple of years I'd guess." He fell silent for a minute as he laid his head back. "Your family are good people. They've been great to us. Your wife insists that we spend the night. She's already preparing the guest room."

"Sounds like her."

"However, as tempting as it is, we'll probably leave. You folks, as well as Lena and I, probably need to take some quiet time before the circus festivities begin."

"Yeah, most likely . . . We'll give you a rain check."

"We'll take it, Mr. Timmerman. I just wish I could have been as hospitable to you and your son as your family has been toward me. I talked to Noel already, but I need you to know—I am very sorry. I—"

"Man, please . . . as much as you've gone through in your life? If it had been me, I might have taken a pistol and shot you in the ass on your way out the door!"

He laughed. "Still, I should have been a better man. Instead, I was a big stupid, egocentric jerk! You guys offered me help at the highest level, and I almost blew it."

"If it helps, Nick, it wasn't all the way like that. I came along for the ride. It was solely Noel's idea."

"So what you're saying is you didn't suffer any sleepless nights on my account."

"No, sir, not one."

"Thank you. *Now* I feel better."

We laughed.

"So is that why you look so glum on the happiest day of my life?"

"Not doing a good job of hiding it, am I?"

"Not at all, my friend, but I think I understand why." He leaned in closer to me, concern etched on his face as he thoughtfully tugged on his beard. "Don't forget I'm a father, too, and I've got a fairly good notion of how this type of mega press may impact you and your family. And there's a chance I'm significantly underestimating the potential effect. Nothing like *this* has *ever* been captured on film. And with the combo pack of our national press and insane social media consisting of amateur and self-made journalists, it can potentially be shown to millions of people, if it hasn't already."

"Exactly."

"Are you sure you're ready for this?"

"No."

"Even though I promised your son, if you'd like, I can kill the press conference tomorrow evening. I also have the right to kill the interview with Eva Sanchez. You just say the word."

"No, that's okay. I appreciate you, Nick, but the train was already set in motion back in July. We'll just ride it and see where it takes us."

"Joseph, I assume you're aware that reporters have been knocking at your door all evening? The big fella—I think he's your nephew? He's been chasing them away."

"Yeah, I know."

"That's nothing my friend, not even a fraction of what you are about to encounter. They will attach themselves to your family like leeches. And I'm not even including the public. If you ever need help, just ask. I know a lot of people. Okay?"

"Sure. Thanks."

"I mean it, Joe. I will never be able to do enough to reciprocate what your daughter has done for me, but I'll give you my best."

"Cool. Thank you, Nick."

Wilma stuck her head inside the door.

"Is it on?"

"Yeah, five o'clock on the nose. Come on in."

She slipped into the small back office of the restaurant and covertly closed the door as we sat on the edge of the desk while I channel surfed to see how many stations carried it. Damn near all the majors, plus. I turned up the sound so we could hear over the employees bustling around in the kitchen.

The press conference was held at the spot where it all happened: the Santa Monica Pier. I hadn't seen that much media in Santa Monica since the OJ trials. Nick Cavaliere sparkled like a million bucks. His wavy dark hair was neatly cut and graying in the temples like the edges of sea water caressing the shore. His former Rip Van Winkle beard was trimmed to a full beard framing his jawline and chin, highlighted by painterly strokes gray. The icy blue eyes that ignited thousands of bedroom fantasies exuded a quiet dignity as he smiled and graciously bowed in acknowledgment of the stupendous ovation he received by the members of the press and throngs of onlookers when he coolly walked on stage.

He wore a light-colored sport coat and brown cotton trousers that matched perfectly with the professorial tones he opened with to address the world press. He started out a little unsteady, but soon his natural grace and charm kicked in. His supple masculinity also returned, surrounding him like a halo as he patiently answered all the questions about his extraordinary recovery.

Nick was flanked by a legion of medical authorities who redundantly shook their heads as each one grabbed the mike and confirmed the unanimous diagnosis that this event was truly a medical phenomenon. Yet, many were reluctant to posit the word "miracle." The only one that seemed at ease with it as an explanation was Dr. Shimkin who was a noted homeopathic specialist.

One physician in particular, Dr. Michael P. Rosenthal, one of the top spinal injury experts in the world, made me want to administer the Heimlich maneuver on him because he appeared to choke every time he addressed Nick Cavaliere's miraculous healing. As might be expected, we were forced to endure all the rhetoric and warnings that the diagnoses might be a little premature.

Rosenthal also cautioned that we should be careful not to ascribe any divine powers so quickly to Ms. Timmerman without the sufficient amount of testing. "We still don't know the capacity and depth of the human mind and its ability to heal itself. It has been documented in medical literature that, in various societies, particularly ancient ones, that a strong belief in a shaman, witch doctor, or medicine man can sometimes lead the body to heal itself."

Nick's sniggering laugh halted the doctor's analysis.

"Doctor, ordinarily I'd defer to your authority because your credentials could fill a phone book, but this time you're way off base. Look at the film more closely. The truth is sitting there right before your eyes. Zoom in on my face if you must. That pathetic expression you will see hardly connotes undying faith. I was skeptical and simultaneously scared to death. The reason I went to the concert was out of desperation. I wanted to get the hell out of there as soon as I arrived. If not for my wife, I'd have left. You can present all the case studies you want. The woman you see in that videotape is the primary reason I am standing here before you."

"Mr. Cavaliere, I'm not intimating that what has happened to you is not astounding. It is! It's just that I don't want to mislead the public by saying I'm 100 percent confident that this woman actually cured you until we've had a chance to do further studies. I—"

"My being here is all the studying you need to do. This woman did what this fine team of experts failed to accomplish."

You'd think I'd be ecstatic that many of these authorities were afraid to step out there and say without hesitancy that Olisa healed Nick. And maybe that skepticism would quell the public's excitement and eventually we could all go on living a more normal life. But despite all my initial protests and longing for her to be an unknown in regard to her God-given abilities, the fact is I was still her father and so very proud of her and all that she is; it angered me to think *anybody* would question her proven abilities.

Nick took some more questions from the media as Dr. Rosenthal stepped back from the dais, frustrated and mumbling to himself. He had looked to his medical team for support. The majority averted their eyes.

"Thank you for asking . . . Yes, I will act again, thank God and thank Olisa, but . . ."

You could hear the whirring noise of the cameras, but no one said a word as Nick tried to compose his thoughts. "I really don't deserve to be standing here proclaiming how grand my life is. I'm a sniveling coward. Thoughts of suicide crossed my mind daily. I didn't fight the good fight as my PR would have you believe. All I cared about was whether I'd be quote, unquote, 'normal again.' Yet, there are courageous souls in this world suffering from paralysis who, unlike me, never cease fighting. They have made themselves a functioning part of our society. These are the ones who deserve to be healed, not me. I just got lucky.

"If I hadn't met with Olisa this morning, I don't think I would have returned to the film business. She's the one who encouraged me to do what I do best and act. She convinced me that, ultimately, I could do more good with my celebrity status than bowing out by helping people who are suffering from paralysis. Consequently, I have started the Nicholas & Lena Cavaliere Foundation to fund research for spinal injuries."

He waited for the applause to abate. "Thank you. I'll take two more questions."

"Theo Balanis, *New York Times*! Nick, congratulations! Glad to have you back!"

"Good to be back, Theo."

"I think Americans—correction, the world shares your enthusiasm. This is all so unbelievable! I'm sure I'm not alone by asking, when do we get the chance to meet this miracle worker? I have a list of questions longer than my arm. Why isn't she here? Is she hiding something or what?"

"I may have been gone for two years, but questions from investigative reporters never change. Theo, I thought you already received your degree from Pessimism U?"

"Still working on my thesis, Nick," he laughed heartily.

"All right, Theo, let me tell you this: the lady has nothing to hide. I invited her—no, begged her to stand and take her place here with me. She turned the offer down because she didn't think it would be appropriate."

"Appropriate? If all the scuttlebutt flying around are true, she'll be bigger than the pope! She heals one of the greatest actors of our time and she doesn't want to be a part of the celebration. She ought to be basking in the applause, not avoiding it."

"If she possessed the same ego as you and I, maybe so, Theo. But why celebrate what's second nature to you? She didn't know who I was. She treated me simply because she cared."

"Okay, so let's say I buy that, then why the big concert and everything?"

Nick paused to measure his words. "You still don't get it. Theo, that ingrained cynicism clouds your brain. She is one of the purest souls you'll find on this earth. You don't have to search for hidden messages with her. Olisa's only agenda is love. The concert was the first step toward unifying people. I don't think anyone here can take issue with that."

"You sound like her spokesperson, Nick."

"I'd be her footstool if she asked, Theo. I'm not exaggerating when I say she is the closest to God I'll ever get in this lifetime."

Wilma scooted off my desk and cracked the door open as a cacophony of loud laughter, frying chicken, and clattering silverware burst into the room. She leaned against the door with her back facing me.

"I guess I better go in and check on things. We're training a new cook this week."

"Great! We needed another one," I replied, examining the daily receipts on my desk.

Wilma turned and faced me. Obviously she was pondering something as she rubbed her hands together.

"What's up?" I asked.

"Got a feeling we'll be seeing a whole new crop of customers this week, so I want to get everybody in gear. We need to be prepared. What do you think?"

"I think that's an excellent idea."

"Yeah, me too. You gonna stay in here for a while?"

"Yeah, another thirty minutes to catch up on some stuff."

"Fine. Take your time. There's no rush."

"Thanks, sis."

She walked over to me and patted my shoulder. "Hey, did I ever tell you you're my favorite brother?"

"I'm your only brother and sibling."

"True, but you turned out to be a pretty good one." She leaned over and kissed me on the forehead.

"Whoa. What's that all about?"

"I don't know. Just felt like it."

"You didn't feel like that when you used to beat me up all the time as kids."

"Bored, I guess."

"Hmmm."

"Hey, seriously, if you ever need some time off, don't hesitate to take it. We'll make do here."

"Wilma, I appreciate it, but I can't let you handle the restaurant all by yourself. You need help."

"No. Your children are going to need you more than me. You must be accessible. Besides, we're better off without you. You've always been deadweight."

"Too late, Wilma. You already told me how wonderful I am."

"Damn. Oh well . . ."

"Thanks, sis. I appreciate you."

"You better!" She socked me in the shoulder.

"Ow!" I yelled, rubbing it. "Now that's the Wilma I'm used to."

I caught a smile on her face before the door clicked shut. The kitchen noise dulled, and the image of Nick Cavaliere continued to glow brightly on the TV screen.

"So what did you guys think of the First Universal Concert for Spiritual Healing?" Eva Sanchez asked.

All three girls giggled nervously among themselves. Finally the one with the purple and green hair and raccoon eye makeup spoke up. "It was the most awesome thing I have ever been to! One big party! It was soooo cool. Loved it."

"Yeah, it was dope!" another one added.

"What made it so great?"

"Oh . . . everything . . . the weather, the band, the people, and she, Olisa, was the bomb! By the time it was over, I felt like everyone there was part of one big family. It was so beautiful. My mother used to make me go to church every Sunday. I hated it. But I would have gone all the time if I felt as good as I did at the concert."

Eva slightly cocked her head. "But what about the riots afterwards?"

"Riots?" the girls guffawed. "That was sooo exaggerated! People were just having a good time and letting it all out! The only people who got out of hand were the security guys. A few people got super pumped up. That's all. It was a celebration, dude! God was watching over us last night and partying with us. I was one of the ones that jumped on stage and danced my ass off with everybody else! The bands and all that good music were to die for."

"And what about Olisa Timmerman? What do you think about her?"

"Oh . . . my . . . God! She is sooooo pretty! She's unreal, like a goddess," they sighed. "What we love is that she's just like real cool. We used to see her on the beach all the time, you know, but I don't think anybody knew she was all that. She make you feel totally comfortable, like you can just be yourself around her, and that's pretty fresh. She not fake like all those other preachers, you know? You feel like you can talk to her and don't have to feel guilty about anything you say, like she would never ignore you."

"Yeah, now if she had a church, I'd go every week and listen to what she had to say. She's not one of those church hypocrites. I wish she created a church; I'd finally have reason to go."

"Why is that?"

"Cuz she is someone we can relate to. She's one of us. She's the first one who ever really made me believe there is a God, know what I'm sayin'?"

"Y'all been creating quite a stir over there in California! Used to be a time I didn't see enough of my granddaughter. Now all I gotta do is turn on the television set or read the newspaper."

"Something, isn't it, Mama?" I said into my phone as I peeped through the kitchen curtain. There were about twenty paparazzi camped outside our fence on the walk street.

"Son, you're not kidding! This past week I think I've seen Olisa's face on practically every news program and magazine cover. Still, I'm worried . . . She looked tired the last time I saw her. How's she holding up?"

"You'd look tired, too, if every time you stepped out of the house your picture is taken."

"Lord . . ."

As if on cue, a reporter sitting on a tree branch snapped my picture. I quickly drew the curtains closed, then plopped down at the kitchen table. "Lord . . . Olisa is handling it better than me. I'm ready to bust somebody in the nose and stuff their camera down their throat when they get to bugging."

"That's my boy, just as ornery as his father," my mother laughed. I could hear her juggling the phone as the steam iron hissed away on the other end. "Sometimes Billy gives them a pretty good piece of his mind when they call. We even had a couple of reporters at our doorstep the other day asking questions about Olisa."

"They're showing up in Vegas?"

"Yep, but it don't bother us none. Believe it or not, it can get boring out here, so it makes life kind of interesting. Your father even fed a couple of them some smoked barbecue ribs he just made."

"Good. Did he poison them?"

"No, the ribs just expanded their waistlines a bit. He gave them a lot of nothing information to take back home with them. Told them the food had been blessed by Olisa and contained all kinds of healing nutrients inside."

"You guys are bad, and I love it! So now they believe that your ribs lower cholesterol level, huh?" That reminded me. I scrambled through the box of doughnuts left on the table and found the last jelly doughnut. Yes!

"Uh-huh. Seriously, son, I know I'm not telling you anything you don't already know, but you watch your back out there. Those tabloid fellas have been snooping around a lot. The offers they're putting out could pay off our mortgage."

"Now I know how you're going to pay for your next Caribbean vacation."

"Hush now. You're joking, but they actually came to our house and convinced our gardener that we hired them to do some interior design work on the house. They said they needed to get inside and do an inspection in order to give us a proper quote."

"What assholes!" I shook my head as I munched on my doughnut. Why didn't they get more jelly ones?

"Thank goodness, I forgot my purse and came back home just as they were strolling in. I had to threaten them with the police."

"How did they react?"

"Apologized, then slipped me their card and urged me to call if I wanted to make a financially lucrative deal."

"Man, those suckers don't give up! Mom, if you think it's bad there, imagine what it's like here. Our neighbors aren't exactly singing our praises with the way the press had invaded our quiet little walk street." I wiped my hands with a paper towel, then peeked out the window again.

"I bet."

I watched Alton and another security guard chase a reporter out of our front yard.

"Joseph, it's been over a month since that beach concert, and Olisa hasn't spoken to the public since then. Does she plan on doing an interview?"

"That's been the question of the year, Mama. She really doesn't have to say a word the way people have been coming out of the woodworks to talk about her. Olisa never knew she had so many friends."

"I can imagine . . . Bright lights bring out the idiots like cockroaches. Her healing that actor made everything crazy. Ain't nobody ever seen anything like that before, especially when it's captured on film. That little Mexican newscaster done made a career out of showing that footage. I see her all over the place nowadays."

"Not as much as me, now that she's taken KLSC to number one in the area." I shut the curtains again after seeing Jesus freaks marching down the sidewalk with a banner reading "Jesus is Lord, Not Olisa!"

While I was on the phone with my mother, the doorbell rang, and Grace received another flower arrangement for Olisa. She'd end up taking it to the hospital. Hundreds of flowers and all kinds of gifts were sent to Olisa, and she requested all of them be donated to hospitals and charities.

"To answer your question, Mama, Olisa will probably say something sooner or later. Dateline, CNN, MSNBC, 60 minutes, 20/20, and every news and talk program around have begged her to do an interview with them first. Limousine drivers drop by the house everyday offering to escort her to their studios. I can't believe how much money they spend to just court her. It's truly been an education."

"Lord have mercy. So why doesn't Olisa do a couple of interviews?"

"Same thing Noel keeps asking. Olisa doesn't see the point of rattling endlessly about herself on these shows. She'd rather do the concerts because she feels they are more productive. She finds interviews boring, egocentric, and a complete waste of time. To tell you the truth, she's very uncomfortable with the attention focused on her."

"How is my grandson? Is he still working at the record company, too?"

"He gave his notice the day after concert."

"He quit that great job? But that's so risky!"

"Mama, don't shed any tears for Noel; he's fine. The company doubled his salary, which was already pretty fat, just to stay on board as a consultant. Believe me. He's got a new office in Culver City, near the studios, hired a staff, and literally has expanded overnight. There, he fields requests and handles more mail than the White House. You ought to see the donations."

"Donations?"

"Money, Mama, raining into the company like a monsoon. It's absolutely incredible! Trust me; Noel is doing fine."

"All right, as long as he's doing okay. By the way, your father yelled you need to cut your grass. He saw your yard on TV."

"Ha! Ha! Tell him I'll take care of it."

She put my father on the phone, and we talked and joked for a while longer. I felt much better talking to my parents after getting off the phone. To say it had been hectic the month following the Santa Monica concert is the greatest understatement of all time. Every blurry footstep thereafter surged forward at warp speed. I get winded even thinking about it.

"Hey, Joseph!" Grace yelled from the living room.

"Yeah?"

"Come here."

I didn't like the sound of her voice. "What's wrong?"

"There's nothing wrong. I just thought you might want to see this. I put it in reverse and paused it at the beginning."

I rushed into the living room. "What?"

She patted the couch for me to sit next to her. I rolled my eyes as soon as I saw Eva Sanchez with that big cheese-eating smile on her face. Standing beside her was a heavyset Black woman who nervously shifted from side to side. Next to them was a sign that read, "Thomas Paine Middle School." Grace released the Pause and turned up the volume.

"With me today is Brenda Bennett, who attended the same private school as Olisa Timmerman. Brenda has worked as an administrative assistant at Thomas Paine for the past twenty years." Brenda nodded awkwardly at the camera. "Brenda, you were in seventh and eighth grade with Olisa, correct?"

"Yes, Ms. Sanchez."

"So, Brenda, why don't we go inside one of the classrooms and see what it was like for the two of you."

"Sure," Brenda replied, pulling keys out of her purse.

The camera cut to them sitting at desks in the classroom.

"So this is where Olisa sat?" Eva inquired, tapping the desk.

"Yes, sometimes." Brenda's eyes flitted around.

"Brenda, what was Olisa like? Any stories you can share with us?"

"Um, well, to be honest, I really didn't know her that well. She was quiet, stayed to herself a lot. Don't get me wrong; she wasn't snooty or anything, not really shy either . . . just different."

"Different? In what way?"

"Yeah. It's hard to explain . . . kinda spacey sometimes, like she wasn't always there. But if Mrs. Richard fired a question at her to see if she was paying attention, she'd give her about five times more than what she asked for. The teacher realized she was different, too. With other kids, Mrs. Richards would jump all over them if they looked like they were daydreaming. Olisa—she left alone. I used to sit across from her. Sometimes I could hear her talking to herself or rubbing her temples like she had a headache or something. One time she caught me staring at her. The look she gave me made me uneasy."

"Why?"

"It wasn't a mean look or anything. At first her eyes were kinda muddy looking, and her face was all pinched up. Wherever she was, it wasn't in the classroom. Then her eyes grew real large. I instantly felt this tingling sensation in my head, and every nerve in my body felt like it was on fire. As hard as I tried, I couldn't look away from her. Her eyes were real deep looking. I don't know . . . You may think this sounds weird . . ."

"Not at all." Eva touched her arm empathetically. "Please, continue."

Brenda self-consciously folded her arms and rocked unsteadily back and forth. "It's just . . . to this day, I swear she knew what I was thinking. It kind of made me mad. It was like my mind had been hijacked. I was feeling really vulnerable. She must have sensed it, because she started blinking a lot like she was struggling to wake up. After a little time, she appeared to recognize me. Her face became calm, even apologetic. I thought she was going to say something to me; instead, she smiled and resumed taking notes. It was very strange."

"I'm sure. Did you ever see her do anything unusual?"

"You mean like healing somebody? No, I didn't know she could do stuff like that until I saw her on your news program. But . . ."

"What? Tell me."

"I saw her hypnotize some classmates one night."

"Hypnotize? In eighth grade?" Eva gasped. She appeared sincerely taken aback.

"Oh, yeah!" Brenda piped up animatedly. "It was at a school retreat one weekend at Big Bear Lake. That Saturday night the counselors had a staff meeting, giving up free time to hang out in the recreational center. We were bored to death until this nerd named Natalie, who was one of Olisa's closest friends, mentioned Olisa knew how to hypnotize people. Of course, we jumped all over that. No one really believed she could do something like that. So we begged her to prove it. I could tell she was irritated with Natalie for telling us and claimed it was nothing, stuff she read about in a book. We didn't go for that and stayed on her.

"After a while I think she got sick of us bugging her, so she got up and asked for volunteers. That got us worked up, and we were ready for a big laugh. I hate to admit it now, but mostly at her expense. Behind her back, even then kids called her a witch, not because of what she could do. It was because her hair was always loose and wild looking." Brenda emphasized this by gesticulating with her hands. "I thought she was pretty, but never did anything special to herself. I don't think she cared too much about how she looked to people. She never talked about clothes or fashion, hair, makeup, boys, or any of the things girls talked about. It made her an easy target.

"So that evening, Olisa lowered all the lights and asked the volunteers to lie down on one of the mats in the center of the room. She rubbed their temples and spoke very softly, asking them to focus on her voice. Ten minutes later they fell into a trance."

Eva looked at her like, "You can't be serious."

"I swear I'm telling you the truth," Brenda laughed. "If you had been there, you would have seen people answering questions like robots. It was hysterical. She had kids singing, laughing, and flapping their arms like chickens, anything she wanted them to do. Everybody loved it. Olisa was the hit of the party. I think Olisa enjoyed herself, too. It was the first time I had ever seen her relaxed and not so uptight. When I look back, I think it was her way of fitting in. Usually she would go off by herself and draw or read a book. I saw a whole different side of her, and it was great to see her mixing it up with us.

"Even so, it all backfired when Freddie Banks asked for a turn. I remember him cracking jokes and winking to all his buddies. He was a little more of a challenge for her because he refused to take things seriously, acting as ignorant as possible. Olisa warned us it wouldn't work unless we all remained very quiet. And that was a difficult task considering there were thirty teenagers stuck in the same room with Freddie acting silly and making farting and burping noises."

Eva grinned knowingly.

"Despite all Freddie's antics, it didn't stop her though," Brenda continued. "She kept working on him. I think she was into taking on the challenge. She was down on her knees, steadily massaging his temples and whispering soothingly to him while he kept acting a fool and mocking her. The thing I remember most is the burning intensity in her eyes. I had never seen anything like it before.

"I wasn't alone. I think everybody noticed it, because after a while the laughter died down and Freddie's jokes abruptly stopped. We kept expecting him to suddenly burp or fart or do something silly like bounce up and start dancing, but his body was real still and his eyes closed. We gathered around them in awe, eyeing her with renewed respect. Olisa had taken down the class clown."

"'Is he really asleep?' someone asked.

"'He's in a trance,' she replied softly.

"'Can you ask him questions?'

"She nodded. 'What is your name?'

"'Frederick Douglas Banks,' he answered flatly.

"'Where do you live?'

"'Los Angeles.'

"'At what address?'

"'Uh, uh, on Chelsea Avenue.'

"'Forget all that,' someone shouted. 'Ask him who he wants to hit on.'

"'Is there someone you like in class?'

"He got this silly grin on his face. 'Yeah.'

"'Who?'

"'Kendra.'

"'Kendra hollered, 'Oh, no,' and we all fell out laughing. Olisa raised her hand for us to be quiet; otherwise he may come out of his hypnosis.

"'Do you want to kiss her?'

"He grinned. 'Yes.'

"'She's here right now. Show us what you want to do.'

"He wrapped his arms around his chest, and his tongue slipped out of his mouth like some nasty little serpent. Kendra ran out the room shrieking as we cracked up. We shut up the second Olisa's hand shot up. That's 'cause this was getting good.

"'Do you like music?'

"'Fo sure.'

"'Who is your favorite singer?'

"'Luther Vandross.'

"'Luther Vandross, huh? Let's hear you sing like him.'

"Sure enough, he did his best Luther Vandross impression. I think he sang 'Never Too Much' or something like that, snapping his fingers druggily along."

"C'mon," Eva interrupted. "Was he really hypnotized, or was he messing with you guys?"

"'Oh, no, Ms. Sanchez," Brenda replied resolutely. "He was hypnotized all right, and everybody was all over him. 'Look at that fool!' one of his boys said. 'Where the hell did Luther Vandross come from? I ain't got nothing against Lutha —he had a dope voice—but I ain't never heard Freddie singing old school stuff. Oh, man . . . ain't that a trip! Wait til this fool wakes up.'

"'Why do you like Luther Vandross?' Olisa asked.

"His eyelids fluttered and he told us, 'Cuz my parents loved him. He was their favorite singer.'

"'Oh? And what are your parents doing tonight?'

"Freddie frowned and shook his head from side to side; his lower lip loosened and started quivering. Olisa's face got tight."

And so did Brenda's as she conveyed the incident.

"'What's wrong, Freddie?' Olisa asked, suddenly cautious.

"'My parents are dead! They were killed in a store robbery when I was five . . . I miss my mommy and daddy. My aunt and uncle told me the news. They said you have to live with us now because your parents have gone to heaven. I told them I don't want to live with you! I want my parents to come back! I don't like being alone! I want my mommy and daddy! Mommy! Daddy!' he yelled in a five-year-old's voice, sniffling and wiping his forearm across his nose. His head rolled from side to side like he was having a seizure.

"Everybody in the center freaked out, including Olisa. I think even Freddie's closest friends thought that his aunt and uncle were his real parents. Everybody screamed at Olisa to wake him up. It stopped being funny when the shit got real! I'm sorry for cursing."

Eva smiled reassuringly and beckoned her to keep going.

"Olisa panicked at first, then took a deep breath and got really serene. Before bringing him back, she told Freddie he wouldn't remember anything except how good he felt. A couple of seconds after she snapped her finger, Freddie leaped up and broke into one of his happy feet dances. Immediately he started bragging that stupid stuff like hypnosis never works on him. He didn't even realize his cheeks were tearstained. He got a clue though when he observed how quiet it was and that some of the girls and boys were crying.

"Olisa was very disturbed by it all and walked back to her cot and started reading her book. A couple of times I woke up and saw her lying on her cot reading by flashlight."

Brenda stopped talking as she began wiping her tears. Eva handed her a handkerchief. Brenda heaved a sigh and went on.

"I've always felt kind of bad because no one said anything to Olisa afterwards. I wanted to tell her it wasn't her fault and that we were just stupid kids who got into something way over our heads. Instead, I just closed my eyes real tight and, like everyone else, tried to go to sleep."

"Brenda, from the little I know about Olisa, I can guarantee you she forgave all of you a long time ago. She hardly strikes me as the type to hold grudges."

"I hope so," Brenda sighed, burying her face into her handkerchief.

Eva smiled at her warmly and then asked, "Do you think any good came out of it?"

"Yeah. Freddie never cracked another joke about her again. Actually, he stayed as far away from her as possible."

Olisa's star blazed through the sky, overshadowing everything in its path. The public hungered for more information about her, and the mass media did its best to oblige. To date, she hadn't done one interview. It didn't matter. The media played off of her mystique. The public was intrigued by the unexpected emergence of this extraordinary person who crashed into their lives with the impact of a meteor. Who was she? Where did she come from? Anyone who had an interesting anecdote about Olisa suddenly found themselves on major talk shows and radio programs. They were fascinated by this woman who didn't fit the mold of what people had come to expect from their present-day religious icons, mostly men with designer suits, beatific smiles, and condemnatory glares.

Her enigma was further heightened by a timely music video filmed days before the concert, at least in the public's view. The real deal was it was shrewdly orchestrated by Noel. It was Mookie Moan's "Stairway to the Man," a rap narrative, borrowing musical licks from Led Zeppelin's "Stairway to Heaven." The song was about how a modern-day Job suffers through hell on earth facing drugs, poverty, violence, and racial hatred. Every time he found himself in deep despair, Olisa's image appeared. She was cast as an angel, splendiferously adorned in glistening white, with massive wings and mounds of hair add-ons billowing behind her from a heavenly studio breeze. Her ethereal image floated from scene to scene, always there to give the main character support as he encountered and conquered each obstacle.

The video concluded with Mookie as an old man escorted by other fashionable-looking angels into a brilliant white light. The video faded out, and we saw Olisa strumming an ornate African harp inside the slowly closing gates of heaven.

It cost a ton of money to achieve the surrealistic and stupendous special effect that imbued the video with its spiritual ambiance. Apparently, it was worth it. Subsequently, upon its release, the song zoomed to number one, toppling longstanding records for song, album, and video sales. Olisa informed me later she had a great deal of fun participating in it but was shocked by the results. Her presence overshadowed Mookie Moan's even though she was only a peripheral character. She received instant certification as the MTV darling of her time among the youth. Her celebrity grew bigger than any of the current crop of divas, all of this without playing an instrument or singing one note.

Even before she soared to fame, people swarmed around Olisa. However, it went way beyond that on a Sunday afternoon in late September.

"Hey, Mom, Pops!" Noel said opening the front door. "What's happening down at the beach this afternoon? I was driving down Abbott Kinney, and there were droves of people rushing down there. Is there some kind of special event today or something?"

"I don't know, son. When you find out let me know," I answered, barely looking up from my newspaper as he walked in and sat down on the couch next to Grace, plying her with a big smack on the cheek and happily cuddling her in his arms.

"When I see that grin on your face, I know you been up to no good."

"*Au contraire*, mother. It's all good. I've got some great news. Where's Olisa? I'm not saying another word until she's here with us."

"She's in her studio."

"No, she's not, Pops. I just got through banging on her door."

"Then where is she?"

"That's what I'm asking you."

"Uh, oh . . ." We all jumped up yelling her name and combing the house. "She's gone!"

I looked out the front window and noticed there were no photographers on the walk street. Usually their heads popped up like the villains in a video game. Damn! I should have known the peace and quiet was too good to be true.

About that point, I saw Alton and Laura waving as they ambled up the walk. Seeing the concern on our faces after they stepped inside the door, Alton said, "Please tell me Olisa's back."

Grace rushed up to him. "Alton, what does that mean? You knew she was gone?"

Alton made some sucking noises, and then his eyes slid to Laura's.

Meekly she reluctantly remarked, "She's going to kill me. I'm not supposed to say anything, but she promised me she'd be back by now. She called very early this morning and complained she was tired of being cooped up and had to go to the beach to see a sunset and have some breakfast."

"Do you guys think this is some kind of game? This isn't high school!"

Smirking, Laura refused to acknowledge Noel's outburst.

"Thank you, honey. You did the right thing in telling us," Grace interjected.

"Why did you wait until now to tell us?" Noel barked, angrily jingling his car keys.

"Because I made a promise! I thought she'd be back sooner," Laura shot back, blotches of red seeping into her face.

Defending Laura, Grace yelled, "Noel, get off her case! You know as well as I do that, when Olisa's in that frame of mind, nobody can stop her from doing what she wants. As least she told somebody. Now instead of going at Laura, let's go find your sister and make sure she's all right!"

"I told her not to go anywhere alone. She just doesn't listen!" I grumbled.

"She didn't go alone, Uncle Joe," Laura softly responded.

"Huh?"

"She went with Logan."

Noel jingled his keys again. "Shit!"

As we followed behind Noel to his car, I leaned over and whispered into Grace's ear. "All right, how long have I been in the Ice Age this time?"

"Probably about two weeks."

"So how did I miss this? Is something going on between them?"

"Most likely."

"How do you know that?"

"Didn't you notice the way they looked at each other when they first met at the house? Or should I say the second time?"

"No. Probably a father's denial. So what makes you so smart?"

"I'm a woman."

"That's kind of sexist, isn't it?"

"Yeah, maybe . . . Okay, because I'm me."

"That I can deal with."

Chapter 8

There are many ways to God.

—Arapaho proverb

E ven though the beach was only a few blocks away from our house, we had no idea how far we might have to go to find her. Noel had his Range Rover this time, so we all hopped in. As it turned out, we only had to drive a few blocks before we figured out her whereabouts. All we had to do was follow the stampede barreling down Windward Avenue toward the beach.

As soon as we fortunately found a parking spot and got out the car, we heard, "She's over there, where the roller skaters are! That's her!" kids shouted, some running and others skateboarding past us into a swelling mass of bodies covering the hill where the former Venice Pavilion stood like ivy on a rampage. At the heart of it all, standing center at the highest point of the incline, was Olisa. The Pied Piper of Venice was surrounded by people who literally gathered at her feet, some sitting cross-legged. It was unbelievably quiet for such a large group of people. They were consumed by every word she uttered. Logan's camera dangled from his neck as he clandestinely moved through the sea of bodies like a sniper, interweaving between the trees, searching for the best possible angle to shoot from. Peppered throughout the crowd like metal flowers were news cameras. Helicopters roared overhead, whirring like gigantic dragonflies.

A police officer behind me spoke breathlessly into his walkie-talkie for backup. Olisa seemed completely unfazed. She just kind of organically went with the flow. She genuinely loved being outdoors, interacting with people rather than being stuck inside a cramped house. Ironically, a biblical passage written in graffiti on a side wall near her read: "Whoever drinks the water I give him will never thirst. Jesus."

Although I could not speak for Noel, I got past my irritation with Olisa. I found myself entranced watching her standing regally at the top of the slope, her hair covered by a scarf, talking, counseling, and preaching to a rapt audience. Logan was only a few feet away from her snapping pictures like it was an automatic weapon.

Observing the people making up the Venice Beach circus who were in awe of Olisa was a sight all by itself. They were all there: urban gypsies, Rastafarians, psychics, folk singers, Michael Jackson derivations in sparkly coats and gloves, men and women dressed like Prince, body builders, spray-painted people in multitudes of colors, Ecuadorian musicians, an Iranian harpist, an aboriginal string quartet, flamenco guitarists, basketballers, rollerbladers, surfers, conga players and percussionists, addicts, prostitutes, homeless people, and more. All of them surrounded her in a proprietary and reverential manner. She was Venice's own "Mother Spiritual," the guru supreme of this assortment of colorful and eclectic personalities who made up the "real" showtime of Venice Beach. A writer for *Vanity Fair* wasn't too far off when he dubbed her the "High Priestess of Venice."

Alton managed to get us closer to the front, flashing his security badge and intimidating physique. The closer we got, the more congested it became, so we halted our trek after a point to prevent any further tension from developing.

"We tried, didn't we, Joseph?" Grace waxed nostalgically. "But we can't hold her back."

"No, we can't, Grace." I stroked her neck. "As Grandfather Henry used to say, 'You can build a basement, but you can't stop a tornado.'"

Seeing all the people gathered around Olisa caused me to reflect on the church we used to attend in Los Angeles when Olisa and Noel were kids. All the elders used to sit around Olisa and play a game with her in which they would call out a book of the Bible and a random verse number, such as Proverbs 16:16. She had to recite the passage verbatim that corresponded with that numbered verse. They rarely stumped her. It still makes me chuckle thinking about how they'd shake their heads in amazement as she quoted the text while they scrambled through their Bibles to find it.

My mind segued to an interview Eva Sanchez did on television the other day with Betty Stanford. That was a name I hadn't heard in a long time. They had to do serious research to find her. As it turned out, they found her living in a nursing home in Kansas City, Missouri. They conducted the interview in a park not far from the home.

"Olisa Timmerman? She was such a sweet girl," Betty stated, shielding the sun from her even though she wore dark shades when she looked at Eva. They sat on a park bench. Betty's jaws habitually moved in a chewing motion as she scratched her jet-black wig, which became slightly askew. White hairs peeked out from underneath.

"The person I wish you could have asked about Olisa was my husband, Karris . . . God rest his soul. He made his transition almost . . . let me see . . . about ten years ago now. It's funny to talk about the past to you because my husband and I didn't talk about her for twenty-something years until he was lying on his deathbed. All the chemotherapy and drugs had him lapsing in and out of consciousness when he asked one night, 'Betty, do you think she's okay? Do you think God ever forgave me for turning her away?'

"I wasn't sure who he was talking about until he said, 'You know . . . little Olisa.' And even though I didn't know how she was doing, I comforted

him saying, 'Yes, honey, I'm sure she's doing fine, just fine.' After hearing those words, he fell back to sleep with a smile. He never asked again after that. He died the next day."

"That must have been pretty tough on you, Betty."

"Oh, it was, but at least Karris's demons had finally been quieted. Praise God he didn't take that turmoil to his grave with him," she added, crossing her heart with her right hand and then signifying by raising it to the skies. "My only regret is that he is not here to see how his child prodigy turned out. But then again, he just might be . . . Well, never mind."

Eva rubbed her chin thoughtfully. "Betty, do you think he knew about Olisa, what she was really capable of?"

"Of course, child. He knew way back then how blessed she was. God had enriched his life with someone more precious than he had ever encountered before. That's why for years he was tortured by the thought in turning her away; he had also rejected God.

"Having your people track me down has brought all of that to the forefront again. When I saw Olisa on the news and realized who it was, I had to grab a chair and sit down afore I fainted. And then, sweetheart, I cried like a baby. Don't misunderstand; it was a good thing, because I knew, at last, my husband's tormented soul had finally made peace with his maker."

"Tell me about their relationship," Eva said, leaning into her.

Betty's chewing motions began again. "The Willises had been members of our Los Angeles church for as long as I can remember. Stay with me . . . I'm going back over sixty years. James and Katherine Willis were married by my husband when he was a young man and had just taken over the church after the prior minister died. Karris baptized both of their children: Grace and James, Jr. He presided over the funeral of Grandmother Willis.

"But nothing prepared Karris for that amazingly sweet child of Grace's that landed in his Bible study class." Betty leaned back against the bench smiling and clapping her hands in delight. "Oh, we heard she was smart, but they never mentioned the rest. We never thought anything when she was the loudest kid's voice in the choir as she sang every song with a child's innocent gusto. One of those exuberant singers always passed through. At the age of six, while older "A" students struggled with two to three lines of a Bible passage, Olisa smoothly recited word for word, not just lines, but pages of the Bible. Karris had seen some pretty bright and precocious children in his time, but none were like Olisa. When he asked Grace and her husband—uh, I forget his name . . ."

Later, Grace never stopped teasing me about that. "She forgot your name? Ha! Ha!"

"You're speaking of Joseph?"

"Oh yeah, that's it. Thank you, Ms. Eva. So when my husband asked Grace and Joseph if they realized what an incredible child they had, he'd quietly say thank you and no more than that. It wasn't so much he was being modest; he seemed to take it for granted in an odd way. Their son was bright, too, but Olisa was on another plane.

"Initially, Karris was beside himself with joy at having the opportunity to mentor this gifted child. God had blessed him and dropped the child right in his lap. He truly believed God meant for Olisa to be a part of his life. She made it incredibly hard for him to avoid favoritism. Still, who could blame him? Olisa gobbled up all he laid out to her with an eagerness that was unimaginable coming from a youngster. Her passion for learning was so intense and deep that Karris often came home from an educational session bone tired. He didn't even come close to satisfying her insatiable appetite. He didn't mind; he loved it! Her questions were more profound than some of Karris' theology students."

"That must have been a very rewarding experience for a minister."

"It certainly was. Some nights, Karris couldn't sleep without thinking about his beloved scholar. He'd be all smiles discovering her sitting at the feet of the deacons and church elders, absorbed in their conversations instead of being outside on the playgrounds with the other children. 'Betty, in my lifetime, I have never seen anything like this child. She's one of a kind,' he'd constantly say to me. 'I look into her eyes and she understands, Betty. She really understands!'"

During Betty's narration, a photo was shown of Olisa standing at the pulpit in a choir robe, her hair parted into two long pigtails. What stood out were her eyes. Even a black-and-white photograph couldn't mask the wide-eyed enthusiasm.

"Olisa was so remarkable at the age of ten, my husband occasionally allowed her to take the pulpit and preach the Sunday sermon. Now that was something to see. At first you'd see smiles exchanged among congregants; 'Isn't she cute?' And then the eye contact would convert to astonishment. This little girl preached the gospel like an old soul. The smiles would wither because suddenly she was no longer viewed as just a child but a messenger of the Lord.

"Naturally, there were times my husband had to coach her, because she'd get a little too flashy and delight in her own brilliance whereby she got carried away, but that was rare. Olisa genuinely believed God was her inspiration. She transfixed the congregation with her sincerity, emoting as if she knew God personally, something that takes many a clergyman years to accomplish as public speakers. I have to repeat—it was truly unusual to see so much ardor in one so young."

Another photo showed Olisa sitting with the Reverend Stanford at his desk next to a huge open Bible. He had his arm around her, and they both broadcast smiles on their faces as she playfully tugged on his goatee.

"We were raising three wonderful boys. Olisa became the daughter Karris never had. Having said that, the problem with a child so gifted is, over time, Olisa began to question everything she had been taught. That girl must have asked a thousand questions a day and no longer accepted patented answers. Many of the elders began to get a little uncomfortable with her line of question-ing. From what I recollect, she wasn't trying to be belligerent or arrogant, but she would challenge their answers with a child's curiosity and a scholar's logic. This just didn't happen with children. Many of the elders viewed her challenging their biblical knowledge and faith as disrespectful. Granted, much of it had to do with the fact they didn't have answers, but they chose to believe she was just turning into a spoiled little brat. None of the men wanted to admit that she intimidated them with her proficiency."

"Did she exhibit any odd behaviors?"

Betty's jaws moved, as she mulled it over. "Definitely. There was some idle gossip floating around that this child had the sight. At church functions and picnics, they said she would walk up to people and embarrass them on the spot. She innocently told them things about their life that no one could possibly have known. It was hard to get on a little kid about such presumptuousness, so they started scolding her parents, blaming them for spreading vicious rumors that were causing problems in the church. Consequently, they also failed to own up that all those things turned out to be true. Nevertheless, they needed scapegoats, so if you can't blame the child, then blame the parents.

"Now, on the other hand, some of our congregants weren't put off by this at all. They sought Olisa out, beseeching her to tell them about their lives and future. They would pull her aside at a church event, acting as if they were marveling over how big she had grown while at the same time interrogating her for as much information as they could gain. Sometimes they went way overboard with the questions, and her parents would politely intercede and whisk her away or push her to go play with the other children. It got ridiculous at times. Some folks couldn't stop themselves . . ."

Betty shook her head at the memory. "They pressed that poor girl repeatedly, and in some cases with little diplomacy, especially after things she predicted started coming true in their lives. It got a little scary. I didn't want to believe it, but there it was—this child had the ability to see into the future. She told it as she saw it. Eventually, this created all kinds of rifts in the church."

Another picture highlighted Olisa lighting a candle at the altar with the Reverend Karris and Betty Stanford watching.

"My husband tried his best to protect Olisa as much as possible. Regardless of his efforts, the straw that broke the camel's back was when all the testimonials poured in from the congregation claiming the girl possessed some kind of healing power. Mrs. Rice was the first one, talking about how Olisa laid a hand on her elbow one day and cured her bursitis. Before you knew it, others began making similar assertions about her healing abilities.

"It was getting beyond control. C'mon now, a child who had the audacity to challenge church authorities, tell fortunes, and heal people?"

Betty and Eva were now shown standing at the rim of a lake in the park. Ducks dipped their heads in the water searching for fish. Occasionally people propelled through the water in paddleboats.

"You have to understand . . . We were basically a very conservative church and not into the shenanigans of the evangelicals or Pentecostal folks. We didn't do all that stomping around hollering or speaking in tongues." Betty stated it like it was an accusation. "We housed a strong middle-class constituent and were dependent on their money to keep operating. Olisa had unintentionally offended a few of the old money bags, giving them information about themselves that they weren't too happy to hear. It didn't matter that it was probably true. People don't want to hear the truth unless it's good. The child wasn't a psychologist; she was just honest."

"That hasn't changed," Eva added.

The thought of Mayor Happy Halverson briefly crossed my mind. I had heard recently he unexpectedly announced he was not going to run for another term. Apparently, the reason was he wanted to spend more time with his family.

"I'm sure it hasn't. And I haven't even talked about the sermons in which she discussed the visions that came to her in the night and hearing other-worldly voices in her sleep. Needless to say, this was just a little too much for the long-standing church members. She became a divisive force instead of a unifying one. The worst part is that some felt she was spouting things contrary to the traditional Word of God, challenging steadfast church traditions and conventions, testifying that God spoke to her personally every day. Though most of the ministers in the United States claimed the same thing, this was somehow different. Long-standing church members were ill at ease with a child voicing such controversial things."

The next photo showed an image of Olisa reading to kids not much younger than her in the church's Sunday School.

"Members, and that included some of our largest contributors, started demanding action be taken before this turned into one of those carnival churches. Before you knew it, Karris' ear was bent and twisted every which way like some kind of Gumby doll. There were also veiled threats to Karris' own job security and some not quite so subtle. Everyone was aware she was his little prodigy.

"Karris wrestled with his own internal devils. You see, he found out later he was not her sole mentor. He heard that her parents took her to other church denominations, synagogues, temples, Islamic centers, Pentecostal, Holly Roller storefronts, and so forth, and it was because of Olisa's request, not her parents'. She wanted to explore how other people worshipped. It hurt Karris' feeling that he wasn't her only mentor. I loved my husband and miss him so much. I'll admit Karris' ego didn't know small, but he managed to keep it grounded. Maintaining that balance made him such an effective speaker. Even so, he succumbed to the sins of jealousy. His possessiveness with Olisa led him to turn his back on her and cave into the pressures battering him from all sides. Don't get me wrong; Karris was not one to back down from a fight or to let anyone influence him beyond God. But he allowed his personal needs to get in the way this time."

In the next shot, Betty and Eva sat on a park bench, this time in a garden populated by roses.

"He didn't sleep at all the night before he talked to the Timmermans. He informed them that he felt Olisa was creating too many problems in the church. He was aware that his words were euphemisms when he was actually asking for her to be exiled from the church. He didn't know how to say it. I think you would have preferred it if the Timmermans would have cursed him out. Instead, they handled it with so much class it baffled him. Olisa's parents seemed resigned, as if expecting it. They even switched roles; it was the Timmermans comforting Karris and assuring him everything was going to work out the way it should. After their discussion, they asked him to stay for dinner like he had never expressed a word."

"How did Karris handle it?" Eva caringly queried.

"I found Karris in his study the next morning head down on his desk, an empty bottle of bourbon next to him and his hand still curled around the glass. He kept his back to me when I walked in. He turned to face me. His face sagged, and it was heartbreakingly apparent he had been crying.

"Karris was a very proud man. He always tried to be strong and projected oftentimes an impregnable demeanor, but this devastated him. He began to question his true loyalties. Was it to God or to those who financed his ministry? Or was he jealous of his authority being usurped by a child who possessed more God-given talent than he'd ever have? Are any or all of those reasons why he failed to stand up during this crisis?

"You know what really tore him up the most?"

"Please tell me."

"It was seeing Olisa's face peering from her bedroom window when he left her house that night. She mouthed the words 'I love you' to him. It ate him up."

Hearing this was tough. Grace was crying, and I was close to it. Even Eva appeared to be on the verge of tears. Betty unearthed memories that we didn't realize how deeply we buried.

"It was more than just the words, Eva. It was the look in her eyes—she knew, knew that everything between them had changed and they would never see each other again. Yet, in just a look, he beheld nothing but love flowing from her face. Her expression 'all was fine and don't worry' . . . She understood why he did what he did. What chilled me more than anything was gazing into those bloodshot eyes and hearing him say in a garbled voice, 'Betty, all my life I've been taught to say, "Get thee behind me, Satan!" Except, this time it is Judas standing behind me. I sold her out, Betty.'

"I jumped all over him for saying such absurd things. It did little because his manic laughter drowned me out. I grabbed him and held him as tightly as I could until the laughter subsided of its own accord. I can't tell you how relieved I was to hear the welcome sounds of snoring.

The Timmerman family never came back to the church. They moved not too long thereafter to Venice Beach. Karris never saw Olisa again."

"So, what happened to you guys after that?"

"Us?" Betty took a moment to compose herself as she removed her glasses and wiped her eyes. She slipped her glasses back on. "We were lucky to make it through the rest of the year. Karris was not the same man after that. He could barely preside over the congregation anymore or minister to anyone. He hustled up numerous guest speakers to compensate for his inadequacies. It wasn't long before he suffered a nervous breakdown. The police brought him home one night because he had been walking down the street stripping off his clothes while reciting the Lord's Prayer and blessing cars and people as they passed by. Eventually, we left and moved back to our hometown in Kansas City where we still owned a home so Karris could take time off to heal."

"Did he ever return to the ministry?"

"No. Karris retired. He continued to work with kids and young adults, becoming a director of a program that helped troubled youth find the right path to leading a productive life. He was sensational! I can't begin to tell you how many kids benefited from his guidance during the ensuing years. He enthusiastically took on each as an exciting challenge. I believe in my heart in each one he saw Olisa. As a result, no one was ever turned away from him, trying to help them. Olisa's name was never mentioned again in our household, but it was never forgotten either.

"All those years we waited silently for a sign she was okay. It didn't really hit me until I saw her face on TV how much it meant to me. Praise God Almighty, she's all right!" Betty gestured triumphantly, raising both fists in the air. "My impression those early years is that her parents really didn't want people to know about Olisa, but I'm ecstatic the world will now know how special she is. Karris knew then. Now his soul can finally be at rest. Praise God."

Grace, sighing, crashed into my subconscious like shattered glass.

"What's wrong, Grace?

"Guess who?"

The crowd parted to let Evan Sanchez through. She boldly strode up to Olisa, hugged her, and then wagged a microphone in front of her face like she was bribing her with a lollipop.

"Olisa, how are you? Hello, everybody! Do we love her?" Eva asked, goading the crowd and pointing at Olisa as they lustily responded in affirmation. With every bit of media savvy she could muster, she had bogarted her way through and managed to take control of this impromptu gathering.

"Look how much they love you, Olisa!" Eva wiggled her fingers in greeting to people she knew in the growing crowd. "We rarely get the chance to see you. I got so excited, I had to come up here and at least say hello! Everyone in the world is trying to get in touch with you, and here you are, just hanging out with the good citizens of Venice Beach. I think it's wonderful!"

There was an abundance of popcorn explosions, signaling the arrival of more paparazzi.

"People, I must ask you to forgive the intrusion. We, and by that I mean the media, have competed to get an interview with this amazing woman. I guess we just don't have your clout."

The crowd roared their approval.

"Olisa, it is so beautiful to see the rapport between you and this wonderful community. I suppose we can all learn a lesson from this. This is what it's all about, being with the people. I hope no one minds me saying this, but to be honest, I'm feeling a little selfish. I don't want to leave because I want to be a part of this good feeling, too. Is that all right with you?"

The sustained applause confirmed her support.

It was a brash move and might have brought the boo birds out if it had been anyone else crashing the party. But this was Eva Sanchez—the people's reporter. As competitors double-parked on Windward Avenue, heedless of the printed tow truck warnings and toted their equipment onto the beach to position themselves as close to Olisa as possible, with one slap, Eva had put her rivals in check. No other media darlings would dare step forward at this stage of the game. Some of the paparazzi got put in place real fast when they tried to jostle the wrong people. But no one messed with Eva Sanchez. They loved and trusted her. Moreover, her popularity had grown exponentially with Olisa's.

The Latino population had more than doubled in the last twenty years, and they had the LA home girl's back. Over the last year coupled with Sanchez's daring reportage of Olisa, KLSC was solidly number one in Southern California. Eva's involvement in their prime-time programming rocketed KLSC skyward. She single-handedly drew more Latino households than anyone across the country, even outpacing the Spanish-language stations, which was a major accomplishment.

Eva was a fighter and a hands-on kind of person. She didn't mind getting her hands dirty and did all the reportorial grunt work, covering stories in some of the seediest and most ostracized parts of town. She had provided the station a gritty, hip-hop homegrown street flavor that would have been a liability not long ago but now uniquely made her "a keeping it real" kind of gal, and the public recognized and appreciated it. She was a community advocate, frequently trumpeting causes such as exposing avaricious slumlords or greed-stricken retailers who charged insane prices to inner-city residents, exceeding the prices of the same products in such affluent areas as Beverly Hills. It was Eva you saw, not Brevin Hightower, working the weekend shifts talking to drug-addicted mothers, teenage runaways, trafficked children, reformed gangbangers, and illegal aliens. Criminal suspects who were Latino often phoned the station promising to turn themselves in to the police if Eva Sanchez escorted them to the station. It didn't hurt that such support was derived from a city boasting the most diverse number of religions in the United States, including a strong Roman Catholic constituent, which coincidentally was the predominate faith in the Hispanic community, the country's fastest growing ethnic minority.

"Since so many of us are dying to speak with you, Olisa, do you mind if I take my microphone around and let people informally ask questions, then even more of us could hear you? I might even ask a couple myself."

Olisa gave a bemused smile. "That's fine."

Sure enough, Eva improvised faster than a jazz musician, setting it up as a special forum in which people asked Olisa anything they wanted with the added draw of appearing on television, too. It had a nostalgic feel, reminding me of the old days of rallies and protests in front of the Venice Pavilion before the legendary landmark was torn down by yuppie developers. She had turned from being an intruder to a host of this event. I hated to admit it, but damn, it was absolutely brilliant. I could hear peers collectively sighing.

"Since I have the microphone, may I ask you the first couple of questions, Olisa?"

Olisa nodded, a tranquil grin on her face as she folded her hands in front of her. Someone offered her a chair, but she refused it.

"The archdiocese and the most respected physicians in the world are investigating all the particulars surrounding the Nick Cavaliere episode to officially declare if this is truly a miracle—"

"We don't need no stinking official word!" someone heckled. "We know what's up!"

"Understandably, the court of public opinion has already spoken. But does it frustrate you to know that, even though the evidence is on film, medical specialists are still cautioning that before we get hysterical and jump the gun, we need to explore the circumstance more closely? The inference is that this might be a sophisticated scam of some type. Do you think it is a power play by some?"

"I don't really care. Miracles occur every day, and they have nothing to do with me," Olisa replied.

"Yes, but shouldn't you defend yourself against all the doubting Thomases out there who still question your abilities?"

"No," countered Olisa firmly. "People have a right to their opinions."

Thunderous applause followed coupled with shouts of, "We believe in you, Olisa!"

Olisa immediately corrected them, "I am not the one you should believe in. God is."

"What's your question?" Eva asked a kid holding a basketball in one arm, baggy pants hanging past his knees.

"Dude, I just want you to know you're the bomb, you know . . . I just want to know how it feels, you feel me? Does it hurt or anything?"

"'How does it feel?'" Olisa pondered. "It's hard to explain . . . It's a loving spiritual energy that is so expansive, it fills every fiber of your body. It can make you so physically tense, you want to explode. When someone is healed, I can feel the energy draining from my body. It is such a relief when it ends that I just want to sleep for an eternity. Does that make any sense to you?"

"Oh yeah, I hear you. I get feelings like that now and then, too, but it ain't because I healed someone." He grinned sheepishly as his tanned face reddened while he self-consciously rubbed his shaved head.

Everyone, including Olisa, laughed heartily.

"I'm not sure if that one will make the news," Eva chuckled. "Olisa, I have to ask you another question."

"Yes?"

"I noticed that you walked on stage barefoot, and I see the same thing today. One email that came into the station wondered if this was your way of demonstrating solidarity with the hungry and poor people of the world."

"I wish it was that well thought out, Eva. I just don't like wearing shoes. I like the feel of the ground beneath my feet. It's a habit I picked up when I visited Cape Verde. Everyone walks around without shoes there."

"Okay, next. What would you like to ask?" Eva held the microphone up to a woman with metallic blue hair who giggled nervously.

"When I look at you, I see someone so special and beautiful. How do you see yourself?"

"I see myself as God's servant. But thank you for the complement."

"Like a modern-day Jesus?"

"Oh, no, Eva! No! I would never even think about such a comparison."

"Well, others do. I can't tell you how many people call, write, fax, and email the station swearing you are the second coming of Christ in a woman's body. Wouldn't you agree you exhibit all the same qualities? For example, Jesus healed the sick, Jesus was a preacher, Jesus claimed to be the Son of God sent down to earth to help the needy, Jesus was a prophet and a spiritual seer who could see into the future . . ."

"Don't do that. I am not Jesus." The harshness in Olisa's voice let Eva know she needed to veer off that road.

"Noted. You do have the gift to see into the future, correct?"

"I get lucky. Although I consider myself more psycho than psychic."

"Hardly . . . There are quite a few people out there who would beg to differ."

Olisa brushed back several strands of hair from underneath her scarf but gave no response.

Meanwhile, I noticed that, in the midst of all this, Noel made his way to the top of the hill. He stood next to Logan, and they were engaged in a very intense discussion. Noel was doing most of the talking. It was more than evident the conversation was not good. Logan began to abdicate from any further discussion as he turned away, but Noel grabbed his arm and uttered something rapidly in his ear. Logan yanked his arm away and moved to the other side of Olisa. The enthusiasm he exhibited earlier while shooting photos had significantly dwindled. Noel continued to stand there, arms crossed imperiously, a half-smile on his face.

"You seem to be getting a good laugh out of this, sir."

Eva spoke to a small, diminutive Caucasian man, wearing a very dapper suit and time. He glaringly stood out among the scantily clad beachgoers.

I spied him earlier, furiously jotting down notes on a pad along with occasional spurts of scathing laughter. The sun bore down on his shiny bald spot that served as an island for his muddy reef of hair.

"If I'm being completely honest, I find the fascination with this young woman by the media and all these people out here both amusing and disgusting, Ms. Sanchez. It's not necessarily her fault. I just worry about the numbers of people being led into a one-way tunnel of darkness."

"Why do you say that?"

"The fact that you have to ask tells me all I need to know about you, ma'am. Nonetheless, I would like to ask Ms. Timmerman a question, if I might."

Olisa acknowledged him with a nod and an intrigued expression.

"Young lady, it's really not my business, but I'm curious. What is your religion? Are you Christian, Catholic, Lutheran, Muslim, Buddhist, Zoroastrian—what exactly?"

His tone was pleasant, but it leaked with condescension. His beady eyes were plastered against his wire-rimmed glasses. He wore a smug, knowing smile on his face that indicated his mind was already made up, regardless of her answer.

"I am none of them, yet all of them."

That wasn't quite the answer he anticipated. One eyebrow partially lifted as he waited patiently for her to finish.

"My God is your God. To me, it doesn't matter if you are a follower of Jesus, Buddha, Muhammad, Yahweh, the Great Spirit, Krishna, Or Baha'u'llah. In loving God, we are all one."

The man's arm stiffly flew out, grabbing the microphone. "Pardon me, Ms. Sanchez, I certainly don't want to exceed my quota for questions. Nevertheless, I must ask you one more thing, Ms. Timmerman. But before I do that, I commend you for tolerating such a foolhardy question, surprisingly from Ms. Sanchez, comparing you to Jesus Christ. However, again, forgive me, but I want clarification: do you believe in our Lord and Savior,

Jesus Christ, the Redeemer, who will one day come back to earth to seek judgment on the sins of mankind?" A self-righteous smirk barged its way into his staid smile.

"Careful, Olisa," I whispered to myself as Grace's body stiffened.

The loaded question fueled the intensity in Olisa's eyes. "We don't have time to wait for Christ's return to earth."

The man mockingly cupped his hand to his ear. "Excuse me, ma'am? I don't believe I heard you correctly."

"The world we live in is on a course toward self-destruction. Unless we move together as one, we may not be here for judgment. One push of a button can set the stage for annihilation of the human race. Jesus said, 'Love thy neighbor as thy self,' yet was put to death because of who he was, his passions, and his efforts to promote love and peace throughout the world. Those who coveted power feared him. His message of love was delivered long ago. We can't just sit back and wait; we must act now. Today is the time to promote global unity. This marks the new age for humanity to begin an era of transformation. We must obliterate all corrupt and harmful political, social, and interpersonal obstacles that prevent us from being free to enjoy our lives to the maximum degree. We cannot wait for spiritual liberation; we must do it ourselves."

The resounding applause did nothing to soften the disdain orbiting in his eyes. He trashed the fake smile as he sardonically remarked, "Well, I do hope, your highness, you will find it within yourself to one day forgive our dear Lord for moving at such a slow pace. I pray he will make time to schedule an appointment with you to help him choose the Day of Reckoning," he sniggered with overwrought self-importance. "Hopefully, those lost souls who are willing to follow you into the quagmires of hell will make a special note of that," he propounded, surveying the audience pitiably.

"I'm not searching for followers. I'm looking for people who are willing to be at war for the hearts and souls of humankind and who will join me in bringing about peace in our homes and streets."

He stopped his jittery writing as his eyes fluttered. "Well spoken. You have a very persuasive style about you, Ms. Timmerman. You are astute at saying the type of things servile people want to hear."

"Similar to the man you are associated with?"

The statement buckled his cool. He pretended to ignore it, but the sudden vein jabbing his neck gave him away. "Satan is also a good speaker," he pronounced in a voice that sounded like metal grinding together. "Although I am certainly not trying to infer anything."

"Of course you are not," was Olisa's cutting rejoinder. It was evident she was uncharacteristically annoyed.

"It's just that the Bible clearly warns that we ought to beware of false prophets. And it sounds to me, with all your preaching, you're a proponent of some new kind of cult religion or something."

"I am not a prophet, nor do I have any aspirations to be one. I am also not pontificating for any specific denomination or religion. The only platitudes I am exhorting are peace and love, bromides which appear to be foreign concepts to you."

The man patiently waited for the applause and screams of support to die down. "Touché, Ms. Timmerman. As I mentioned earlier, you truly are a persuasive, articulate, and eloquent speaker, among the other controversial gifts you are being hailed for. Having said all that, I'm still waiting for you to put me at ease by answering whether you believe in the Holy Bible as the only *true* Word of God."

"There are many truths to be found in many holy books."

"Ma'am, the Holy Bible is the *only* book. It tells me all I need to know. You don't believe that?" It was more of an accusation than a question.

"I believe denominations, religions, and books have been ways to imprison God in tight and neat boxes that allow us to make sense of it all. It lends power to an ordered script we can follow and a rulebook that we can always have at hand to reference. But is man so arrogant as to assume he can truly interpret the Almighty? For centuries, who God is has been developed and sold by men as the *true* religion to billions of people through *divinely* inspired writings. We fight wars due to the varying and contradictory nature of these interpretations, vehemently arguing text and then killing and maiming in *the name of God* because the other guy didn't follow the prescribed rules and regulations. The question then becomes, *who* is really seeking to be all-powerful, God or us?

"Instead of us being created in God's image, we have vainly created God in ours, specifically to service our needs and to massage our vainglorious egos. We have created a God reflecting all of our insecurities. We contend if you don't show God respect, if you don't praise and worship Him, His rage will strike you down in a heartbeat. God is not a dictator or an imperialist. God doesn't exist to enslave you. God is simply and purely love. Therefore, I believe it is in acts of love, acts of compassion, and in acts of valuing yourself and the world that you will discover and embrace the true nature of our Creator. I don't need anyone to find God for me; God is in the very nature of our existence. God has always been present with us. Our failure is in *not* seeing it and acting accordingly once you accept that awareness."

The man gruelingly smiled through his clenched teeth as he notably endured this salvo of words streaming from a woman whose eyes were lit up like Olympic torches. The insipid little grin he tried to maintain began to look more and more like crumpled paper. It bothered me when he once again pulled out his tiny notepad and scribbled on it as if he were about to issue a parking citation.

Grace leaned into me. "Joseph, who is this man? He looks familiar to me, but I can't place his face."

"Yeah, me too. It's driving me crazy."

Olisa wasn't finished. "We praise God's infinite wisdom, yet we turn a blind eye to the possibility that maybe this Supreme Being appeared to us in countless ways and guises throughout the history of our world. Ask yourself: is it conceivable that this might explain the diverse writings and interpretations? We do the lip service and say God is everywhere, yet we denounce any religion outside of our own that claims a vision of God."

Eva was about to say something, but a voice from the crowd rang out: "Olisa, then what is right? Teach us how to discover the truth!"

"My friend, I can't do that. What I will say is the truth lies somewhere within you. Don't be afraid to question what you have been taught. God is not going to harm you for asking questions and seeking answers. During my travels, a shaman once told me: 'Olisa, all religions point the way to salvation. God, not man, is the source from which all religions flow. And if they are truly about God, they all share one universal truth—to love ourselves and one another.'"

Seconds passed before the man's jarring intrusion jerked me away from the seductiveness of my daughter's mellifluous voice.

"You act as if you know God personally."

Olisa stepped up to him and gazed unflinchingly into his indignant eyes. Swirls of botchy red floated to the surface of his doughy face as he attempted unsuccessfully to reciprocate her stare.

"I do know God, just like anyone here can know and speak to God. We don't need an intermediary to speak for us. God resides within you and me. We are all God's children."

It took him by surprise when she reached out and embraced his thorny little body. The biscuit-headed man tolerated her hug for about an eighth of a second before edgily backing away. He jammed the pen and pad into the inside pocket of his suitcoat, snorting as if he had been waterboarded.

"God bless you," she said to his vanishing backside as he knifed through the mass of people, coughing spasmodically.

An errant voice shouted, "Hey, man, don't go away mad! Just go away!"

A stray elbow tagged the man. He fell to one knee briefly, picked himself back up, and took off running again like the hounds of hell were chasing him.

"No, no, that's not the way!" Olisa scolded. "We don't treat anyone like that no matter how much we disagree with them. Violence is not the solution. We can still love even though we may differ."

Fortunately, sanity was restored. If Olisa had not spoken out at that moment, Biscuit Head might not have made it out of there in one piece.

"I may not have convinced that gentleman of our birthright as God's descendants, but how about the rest of you? It doesn't have to be so complex. It's very simple. We don't have to wallow in a lifetime of scholarly research to discover the Creator. God is available to us the minute we accept the reality of life. That's what makes it so beautiful!

"How often do we take the time out of each day to see the world around us? How often do we observe the skies, the trees, the flowers, inhale the perfume of blooming jasmines, lister to the pure laughter of little kids, wrap yourself in the emotion of a gospel song, feel the touch of a baby's hand, hear the rhythms of the ocean waves, or meditate in the still of a country night? God is in all those places. Divine inspiration lies in our own backyards. Do you hear me? Do you understand? We don't have to be told; it's ours to uncover."

"Amen!"

"The true battleground is not about whose religion is better. It's whether we can one day learn to love, respect, and accept our differences. Again, so simple, yet for centuries we have made it one of life's greatest puzzles."

"Can't we all just get along?" Eva joked, but Olisa didn't bite.

"Uh-huh—a desperate, innocently coined plea that a cynical society attacked and tucked away as fodder for late-night talk shows, hip comedians, and bullying editorialists spewing elitist values and refusing to see anything valid in such an odd Pollyannaish concept as love. Nevertheless, it's the crux to our survival as a civilization."

Eva warmly acknowledged a woman in the audience who was about six feet tall. Her prematurely white hair belied her pretty face. She wore a loose T-shirt and sweat pants. Her face was youthful, expressive, and full of vibrancy as she leaned into the mike. "Hi, Olisa. My name is Beverly Fairchild, and I am the executive director of WIN, Women's International Network. We work on behalf of women's rights and causes throughout the world tackling such issues as physical and sexual abuse, genital mutilation practices, incest, and discrimination."

"Ms. Fairchild, no introduction needed. I know exactly who you are. It's a pleasure to meet you. I consistently read your magazine and admire your organization."

"Thank you so much! I am flattered to hear that, especially since we are so impressed with you and your accomplishments. Since you are so difficult to catch up with, right here and now I'd love to extend an invitation for you to meet with our group sometime soon!"

"Invitation accepted."

"Wonderful! I will contact your office. Um, while I've the opportunity, I'm curious—how do you view the role of women in the church?"

"It's tough to answer that. There are so many kinds of churches. I find it appalling to still hear that so many church leaders continue to struggle with the issue of women taking a prominent position in the church. Lately, I've noticed some churches are slowly changing the old rules to accommodate the contemporary woman's desire to seek a more empowered role in the church hierarchy.

"Still, I'm not surprised when conflicts occur, particularly when you are speaking about the archaic rules established by men of long ago that are steadfastly maintained by men of today to keep women in their place. Compare the numbers of female and male rabbis, ministers, pastors, etc., and you will see what I mean. How truly egalitarian is it? Can't women be as inspirational as the men? Churches need civil rights movements within their own institutions. That's one of the reasons why I decided I don't need an intermediary, man, woman, or church to discover my place with God."

"Beautiful, simply beautiful," Beverly cheered, clapping supportively. "I knew you were the one. The movement greatly needs someone like you. You should start your own church!"

Olisa bowed her head modestly. "No, no, as I said, I don't want to be a part of a structure, only a part of the action."

"My name is Jamal Harris, and we need you, too, sister," declared a light-complexioned Black man with a firm and possessive articulation on the latter word. He wore an African cap over his bald head and an open mud cloth vest revealing his bare chest. "Our African American brothers and sisters in the United States are still subjected to the oppressive system of western apartheid fueled by racial hatred and bigotry with a police force that continues to make unwarranted attacks on our people. We are recurrently denounced by a systemic White power structure that spouts racist ideologies and methodically tries to bury us alive in the graveyards of the economy. Where are our reparations? Where are our forty acres and a mule? They may grin in our face and pat us on our backs, but they refuse to recognize the 'original' man, we who proudly hail from the cradle of civilization and whose ancestral makeup reflects the kings and queens of the continent of Africa.

"I say this with all due respect, Ms. Timmerman . . . You are the queen of all queens, my beautiful sista. The organization I represent would *also* love to have a word with you," he articulated with a pronounced smile, swiveling his head competitively toward Beverly Fairchild. "And, I am sure, like me, you too are tired of the ongoing discrimination that African American people are forced to confront every day of our lives. We are not taken in by their plastic smiles and artificial hugs!"

Olisa took a beat before she replied. "Yes, I am very exhausted with the prejudice and systemic discrimination we frequently confront, but my mission in this is to battle all bias and narrow-mindedness."

"I hear what you're saying, sista, but we need to take care of ourselves first before we can help anyone else. We need to stay woke."

There was scattered applause.

"Yes, I feel you. We must help ourselves, and I'm with you all the way. However, we also must keep in mind we cannot build a fortress whose walls cast a shadow over our neighbor's land. In essence, we are *all* responsible for each other, and we must *all* accept the blame if we intend to survive as a human race. We share a symbiotic relationship as human beings. Indeed, the parts do equal the whole. You can't put a Band-Aid over a bullet hole and expect the bleeding to end. You've got to get to the source first. No one gets shot if the gun is not available. Likewise, no one gets killed if enmity is not in our hearts. There can be no vacancy for hatred in the human heart. It must be vanquished, regardless of race or gender. The pot of gold lies at the end of the entire rainbow, not at the end of a single color."

Brotha Man nodded, but I doubt he was listening. Didn't matter. The crowd's ovation would have drowned out any rebuttal he might have made. Before Eva could say another word into her mike, a figure splintered from the wall of people and plunged at Olisa's feet attaching himself to her ankles.

"Please help me. I want to hear. I want to know what the world really sounds like. I want to hear your voice, the voice of God," he pleaded in the shortened trombone-like phrasing of the deaf.

Olisa knelt down, cupping both his ears and prayed over him. A few minutes passed before she firmly shouted, "Stand up!" At first there was no reaction except for him wincing as if he were in severe pain.

She lifted his head up so he could see her lips and again commanded him to rise.

"Yes . . . yes . . . yes," he exclaimed repeatedly. "You said stand up! I can read your lips and I hear noise, so much noise, but you mean for me to stand. Yes? Yes! Say it again. Please say it again! Yes, yes, yes, yes. Oh sweet lady, it sounds so lovely to me," he wept joyfully in her arms, hugging her with all his might. "Oh my God, thank you! Thank you, oh my God!"

The elation only lasted seconds more before I saw lines riddling Alton's forehead as he bulled his way through the crowd to get to Olisa, primarily because there was a frenzied mass of people barreling straight at her.

The man's outburst and the subsequent healing triggered something. Some of the people looked like the *Walking Dead* billowing toward Olisa, wailing and crying out her name. I saw a man knock a woman over in a wheelchair without even checking to see if she was okay. Someone screamed, "Get the fuck out of my way, asshole. I'm next!" Two elderly women beat the tar out of each other with their purses to get to Olisa first. All were anxious to be cured of whatever affliction troubled them. Many had been waiting patiently for the right time to approach her and try their luck. Panic ensured at the thought they may not get that opportunity.

Matters became even more confusing as the police who were standing by aggressively entered the fray. Eva looked terrified initially until she realized she wasn't the target as the crowd literally surged past her in their effort to get near Olisa. No one gave a shit about the other. They climbed over each other's backs like crabs in a barrel, hands sticking out, grabbing and ripping Olisa's clothes. The next miracle would be to get Olisa out of there unharmed. My heart was palpitating. I was helpless to do anything. Grace and I were squeezed so tightly into the logjam of people, all we could do was watch and pray.

Thankfully, Gumbo was there.

He cleared a path like a tight end for a running back in football, flinging people out of his way. Logan wrapped his body around Olisa, and Noel was right behind them as they made a beeline past us, accompanied by a host of what I found out later were undercover officers who, gratefully, were friends of Gumbo's. Somehow, we managed to follow closely behind them amid anguished cries and pleas for her to stay and help them. Gumbo looked like the Incredible Hulk as clothes were shredded from his body by hands that sought to find a way to get to Olisa. It was one of the hairiest situations I had ever encountered. We all got out of there unharmed as we were steered into an unmarked police van.

We watched behind us as the overly enthusiastic adulators grew smaller and smaller chasing us with outstretched hands. Moreover, we saw a police cruiser besieged by rocks and bottles. A block away, a news van was being vandalized by gangs of youth. Thankfully, Gumbo's buddies on the police force gave us a ride home; otherwise we would have had about a thousand uninvited guests following us home for supper. As it was, helicopters buzzed overhead.

Olisa, adrenaline still flowing, sat upfront, busily chatting with a female officer. Noel sat in the back with Grace and me staring out the window. The last time I saw him sulking like that, he had barely been passed over for a Rhodes scholarship. Occasionally under his breath I heard, "Stupid! So stupid . . ."

Grace snapped her fingers. "I just figured out who that man is."

"What man?"

"You know, Joseph, the one taking all those notes and interrogating Olisa."

"Gotcha. The little hall monitor."

"I don't know his name, but I've seen him on TV seated behind his boss."

"Uh, oh. That doesn't sound good. Who's his boss?"

"Walter Pocock."

"Walter Pocock . . . Pocock . . . Wait! You mean Mr. Televangelist himself? Are you sure?"

"I should be. He almost knocked me over trying to get by. That's when I noticed he had one of those dumb-looking Pocock family crest insignias on his lapel."

Noel suddenly got interested. "That dumb-looking emblem stands for one of the biggest multimillionaires around," he interjected. "He just built that mega-sized church skyscraper in Orange County on all those acres. He describes his citadel as being 'only a fingertip away from heaven.'"

"So, Grace, you think that little weasel is reporting to him, huh?" I asked.

"I'd bet on it."

"But why?"

"Because in his eyes, Olisa's the competition," Noel spat.

Chapter 9

E va's smiling face loomed on the screen. "Thanks for joining us in our search to find out more about the enigma that is Olisa Timmerman. Today we are at McCabe's Guitar Shop with Kevin Lipsyte, a folk musician from up north in Santa Cruz, California." The camera panned back to show them on a small stage sitting on stools. Kevin let his strawberry-blonde hair drop down to his shoulders as he adjusted his San Francisco Giants baseball cap. He also held an acoustic guitar in his lap.

"Now, Kevin, I wasn't wrong in describing you as a folk musician, was I?"

"No, that's me. I mean we do all kinds of music, ranging from country to blues." Kevin picked a couple of blues notes on his guitar to accent his point.

"All right! Sounds good. I might have to come by here tonight and listen to you guys play. Do you play any boleros? That's the music from my homeland."

Kevin laughed. "If that's what it will take to get you here tonight, we'll add it to our repertoire."

"Then you may see me tonight," Eva responded in kind. "Okay, Kevin, so tell me what you know about Olisa Timmerman. You guys met in Santa Cruz, right?"

"Olisa? Yeah, we met there. She is one of the most out-of-sight women I have ever met in my life, always courteous, always nice. And those eyes . . . Oh man . . . deep, perilously so. When she looks at you, you feel like you've been stripped down to your underwear. You're laughing, but I'm serious."

Eva still chuckling said, "I can see that you are."

"Oh yeah. She used to frequent George's Coffeehouse and Café, usually on Friday nights. The owner, George, was Hungarian, a true jazz aficionado. He offered live music every Friday evening. It wasn't only jazz; he presented folk, country, classical—you name it. Sometimes he even featured poetry readings. George's was the best. It was the finest place to hang out and unwind. I played acoustic guitar, and George invited my band to play so many times we became the unofficial house band."

"So, how did you meet Olisa?"

"At George's. If I ever needed a smile, man, all I had to do was look hard enough into the audience. I'd easily spot her face in the midst of the patrons. Whenever I did, she never failed to give me that life. Afterwards, she hung around and had something nice to say to us following every show, even if we sounded like falling horse turds."

He played a flat note on the guitar to accent his statement, which tickled him as he shook his head. "She'd discuss the songs we performed and give us feedback on it, how it affected her, and what lyrics had more special meaning in her opinion. Dude, she was a bitching gal. We missed the hell out of her when she graduated.

"Forgive me for rambling; I took a detour. Let me get back on track. You asked me if I could tell you something special about her. I guess you mean like magical, spiritual, or something in that arena, the kind of stuff the press is reporting these days, right?"

"That would be good," Eva replied.

"Funny I didn't think about her that way then, but then again, we were always high. Olisa—she was on a high naturally, without the drugs. Me? I was living in a drug-induced fog in those days before I spent some time in rehab, you know?

"I recall one time after a show we were invited to an after-party at George's new pad tucked away high up in the hills. When I showed up, Olisa and one of her close BFF's an Indian chick with hair down to her ankles, were already there. I think her buddy's name was Lana or something like that. She used to dress kind of militant: feathers, earrings, beads, the works, including yards of attitude. If I even looked at her cross-eyed, you could feel the arrow in your back. She had a way of making you feel like you were the reincarnation of General Custer without saying a word. Hey, but you know what? That didn't bother me at all. I understood where she was coming from. The White man literally decimated the Native American population and culture, man. I got all that from her. Once I got to know her and she began to trust me, she taught me a lot of things. I was kinda naïve about people of different cultures. Shit, I was a White boy from Los Gatos; the only thing ethnic I was in contact with in my family was usually the cover of National Geographic."

Eva grinned as she nodded for him to continue.

"That night it started raining hard, so we all agreed to turn this puppy into a slumber party and crash at George's pad. So, here we are, kicking it, philosophizing, drinking, getting high, just partying. Now this is where things get a little sketchy for me. Out of nowhere, someone suggested we ought to do a séance. George grabbed some of the lighted candles in the house and placed them on the center of the coffee table in the living room as we all sat cross-legged in a circle holding hands. The Indian woman even did this little ceremonial chant, although I was too busy staring at her to remember what she was saying. You know how it is . . . getting high, horny . . ."

Eva gave him a blank look and shrugged.

"Oh, okay . . . so in the séance you're supposed to be calling up the dead and all that stuff. About now, I was floating nicely and feeling like one of the dead until the Indian babe started getting really serious, telling everybody that, if we really wanted to be in touch with the spirits, we needed to stop bullshitting around and concentrate. She swore Olisa could actually talk to the dead. All I cared about was getting a hit on whatever pipe she was smoking. I think I even cracked a joke about that, and she cussed me out. Man, she ticked me off, and it was affecting my high. Made me want to smoke some more reefer, but I didn't want to be the one to break the chain of hands so I rolled with the program.

"In my drugged state, I thought Olisa must really be high if she really believed she could converse with spirits and all that. Except I only saw her sip a little wine."

"Tell us what happened next."

"We all started reminiscing about all the legendary sixties musicians who died young, you know like Janis Joplin, Brian Jones, Otis Redding, Jimi Hendrix, Jim Morrison, Sam Cooke, Tammi Terrell, and so on."

"Some of my favorites."

"For sure. Well, this is about the point where things got even more interesting. We finally agreed on one name from the group to call on: Jimi Hendrix. Dude was the man! I feel like every guitar player needs to bow down and give my boy his due."

Eva rotated her hand for him to move the conversation along faster.

"Okay, so the Indian chick—"

"Laura, you mean?"

"Yeah, Laura. So Laura, the Indian chick—she tells us to say Jimi's name over and over to help Olisa focus. Well, the more we chanted Hendrix's name, the more intense it got."

"Intense in what way?"

"I'm talking super intense. You know when you hear about the air particles getting thick in some of your horror books? That shit is real."

Kevin lifted his baseball cap and swept his hand through his hair. He was beginning to perspire heavily like he was reliving that moment.

"It started getting real icky. I almost couldn't breathe. At first, I thought maybe I had got a hold of some bad stuff, 'cause I was feeling all tight and queasy. At that same time, I noticed Olisa was swaying from side to side and seemed to be in some kind of trance. Her voice was building in this strange way, and she kept reciting: 'Jimi, if you are in the room with us, please let us know. Show your presence. Communicate with us in whatever way you choose. Don't be afraid; we are here only for you . . . Give us a sign.'

"And thereafter, things got weird. All of a sudden, the flames in the fireplace started popping like gunshots. Just as abruptly, everything stilled. It even stopped raining. The candles in the room flickered like go-go dancers. Was it just me witnessing all this? I began to think someone slipped some acid or peyote in my drink because candles don't make shapes like that. The more I stared at the flames, the more they resembled human shapes. It was tripping me out. That wasn't the only thing . . . It was like we were heading into the Ice Age again. It got as cold as shit in the house, even with the fireplace going."

"Ooooooh!" Eva gasped, her eyes wide like she was listening to a story around the campfire.

"Olisa was into a groove, man. She chanted Jimi's name faster and faster. Then the landline rang. I swear we all jumped as if we'd been goosed. For Christ's sake . . . You know we were on edge reacting that way to a phone ringing. Everybody laughed nervously, except for George. His already pale face looked bleached.

"The deal with George is he had only moved into the house a couple of days ago, so this was supposed to be a housewarming party too. He hadn't even placed an order for the phone to be connected yet. Earlier, he had a big laugh watching me, high as a kite, trying to call my girlfriend on a disconnected phone. He let me spend about five minutes dicking around with it—oops, sorry about that. Anyway, he was in hysterics before showing me I was trying to use a phone that had been ripped from the wall by a prior tenant.

"George wasn't laughing anymore as the phone rang and rang and rang. Neither was anyone else. Each ring kept building up like gathering storm clouds. The rings were starting to get so insistently loud I wanted to crap in my pants. The only one that didn't seem shaken by it all was Olisa. She got up to anchor it, but George blocked her path. I had never seen him like that, all bent out of shape and screaming irrationally at her not to touch the fucking phone. To this day, I don't know what he would have done if she had taken another step forward. This was not like him. George was the most easygoing guy I ever met. Not then. He had a wild petrified look in his eyes. He kept gaping at the phone as if it was some kind of hideous monstrosity. Dude's face was so constricted I thought he suffered a stroke."

"That didn't sound good. What more can you tell us about George?"

Kevin paused while he played a few notes on his guitar before responding. "George was not exactly a young man. He was somewhere in his late fifties. He'd lived a life. George was a world traveler and faced all kinds of dangers in his lifetime. His family fled from Hungary during all the war and bloodshed. During a safari, George even survived a mauling by a lion in East Africa. George wasn't one to be easily frightened. But that night, he was terrified as the resurrected telephone kept ringing. Olisa smiled warmly at him and sat back down on the floor. She didn't take offense to George's aggression. She understood."

"Sounds like our girl."

"I swear that phone rang about ten minutes before finally giving up. Almost immediately the room filled with heat, and I heard the rain slapping the windows again. I looked around, and the most comforting thing was that everyone else there looked scared shitless, too, except for Olisa and her Indian girlfriend. The Indian chick, uh, Laura, grumbled to Olisa sarcastically about the courage of the White man and how he continues to be the burden of native people. I also heard her complain, 'I warned them not to mess around with spirits unless they meant it—so typical!' Periodic chills swept through my body, which shook me involuntarily. Didn't bother me. What bothered me more was the nice little high I nurtured was gone!"

He hesitated, expecting a reaction from Eva. Nothing there. She possessed a reporter's detachment, although I got the feeling she would have loved to have made a crack about his last statement.

"Afterwards, we all just sacked out in the living room, excluding George. He retired to his bedroom without saying goodnight to anyone or making a move on a single woman. Everybody who knows George knows that such odd *behavior is contradictory to George's ordinary temperament. George turns everything into an epic event.*

"One night, months later, George and I were having a drink and I brought it up during a discussion. His eyes instantly got that funny look in them, and I dropped the subject. I've never brought it up again since then.

"Still, I will always wonder who was on the other end of that phone. After that incident, the song 'Purple Haze' took on a whole new meaning to me . . ."

The televised KLSC interview ended with Kevin playing a few acoustical guitar licks from "Purple Haze" during the credits.

On the way home from the beach, we were trailed by a phalanx of reporters, paparazzi, curiosity seekers, and fans in cars. The police and security were already positioned there, clearing an opening through the alley so we could drive through.

Safely tucked inside our house, it was a relief to see Laura, Gumbo, and Logan clanging the gate shut and trudging up the walkway as I got up from my window seat to open the front door.

"Everybody good?" Though I tried, I couldn't get the shakiness out of my voice.

"Yeah, Unc, we're fine," Gumbo wearily answered smothering me in a generous hug. "How 'bout y'all? Where's Olisa?"

"Upstairs in our bed. She—"

I didn't have a chance to finish before Grace cried, "Noel, *stop!*"

Noel rushed Logan as soon as he stepped inside the house. Laura had to jump out of the way.

"Hey!" Logan didn't know what hit him as he yelled defenselessly. I saw two pair of feet sink over the couch. Noel's hands were fastened around his neck. Gumbo was on top of it, prying Noel's fingers loose and yanking him off Logan. Bewildered, Logan gradually sat up, vigorously rubbing his neck and accepting my outstretched hand as he warily rose to his feet.

"What the fuck was that all about, man?" Logan asked, never dropping his eyes from Noel's as he brushed his clothes and bent down to pick up his camera and black Kangol hat. He swiftly inspected the camera; the only thing broken was the strap.

Olisa once told me that Logan was sent to take photos of the killings and casualties that occurred as a result of Boko Haram terrorism in Nigeria leading to hundreds of thousands of displaced people. It would take far more than something like this to fluster him.

I wish I could have said the same thing about my son who grunted and cursed as he futilely did pull-ups on Gumbo's locked forearms trying to get to Logan. "Let me go, Alton. I ain't playin'. I'm serious, man . . ."

"Soon as you cool down, cuz."

"All right, all right . . . I'm cool." Noel lifted his hands up in the air. Gumbo's arms stayed wrapped around his chest.

The second Gumbo relaxed, Noel slipped out of his arms and charged Logan and once again found himself sandwiched in Gumbo's brawny arms.

"We can dance all night, cuz. Ain't you tired yet? I know I sure am."

"Okay, Gumbo," he said huffing and puffing, chest still stuck out. "I'm not lying. This time I'm definitely fine. You can let go. I'm through with his punk ass."

Gumbo cautiously unfolded his arms as Noel still held his arms straight up as if to assure him he was under control before letting them dissolve to his sides.

"You guys chill out! Olisa is trying to sleep up there," Laura pointed to our bedroom. "You guys didn't get the memo? Fighting is not going to resolve anything. We're all about family here. Find a way to work it out," Laura admonished.

"Tell him to work it out, Laura. This is not on me! Noel's got the problem."

"Want to know my problem, Lo? My problem is you! That's what the fuck my issue is!"

Gumbo gave Noel a reminder tap on the arm as Noel inched closer to Logan.

"Noel, I'm telling you. Don't walk up on me anymore," Logan warned as Gumbo hastily stepped between them. "I took it the first time, but I'm not your whipping boy. Out of respect for your family, I'm going to leave." He nodded at Grace and me standing side by side in shock. "So, you don't have to worry about me. Just don't come at me again; we cool?"

Noel shook his finger at Logan. "Nigga, don't tell me what I *can* and *cannot* do! Come on, Gumbo, back off me. I'm done!" he barked shoving Gumbo's hands.

"Just get to stepping, Lo, and take all your shit with you. It's over! Understand? Send me your bill. I'll pay whatever I owe you, plus. Shit . . . I probably got enough money on me to cover your ass right now!" Noel uttered condescendingly, fumbling inside his jacket and drawing out a huge wad of Ben Franklin's. "Here you go! Take what I got. I'm sure this is more than enough to cover your expenses!" He flung the money at Logan.

Logan swatted the bundle away. "No! Keep your damn money, man! I told you before; it's not about the money!"

"Then what's it about, getting my sister killed or trying to fuck her?"

The expression on Logan's face was more leveled by that comment than Noel's necktie tackle. "Man, I'm not even dignifying that last question with a response. I tried to protect Olisa."

"Don't let me have to ask you again: did you do something with my sister?"

Logan waved him off and turned and walked toward the front door.

"Don't turn your back on me, Lo! Look at me when I'm talking to you!"

"Ok, Noel, that's enough," Grace asserted, closing her eyes briefly. "You've stated your piece. I can't even believe your father and I allowed it to go on this long. No guest has *ever* been treated like this in our home." She grabbed Logan by the elbow before he was able to walk out the door. "I am so sorry, Logan. Please forgive us."

"Mrs. Timmerman, it's okay—"

"Guest? Mom, he's not a guest. He's not even a friend. He's an employee. I hired him to do a job! You don't need to apologize to him! He almost got Olisa killed! He had absolutely no right sneaking her out to the boardwalk behind our backs. Who the hell does he think he is? He knows what kind of security risk it is; we all talked about it!"

"You got it all wrong, Noel. I swear I didn't—"

"I don't want to hear it, Lo!"

Noel glared out the window. When he turned back to face him, a different expression was on his face. "You know what, dude? Mom's right. I apologize for losing my cool. My bad. Situations, sometimes, don't always work out the way you want. Ya know what I'm sayin'? That doesn't prevent us from acting like professionals, right?" Noel walked around the living room and bent over to pick up the loose bills strewn about the floor. He gathered the bills and neatly folded them, placing them back in his jacket pocket. "Seriously, bro, send me your invoice. You put too much time and energy into this. We'll chalk it up to a bad day. You feel me? I still want to work with you. I'm still a consultant at RPM. We have another video coming up, and I'll tell you what—the job is yours! I may get stupid now and then, but I'm no fool. I meant it when I said you're a great photographer. I'll give you a call in about a week, okay?"

"No, *not* okay."

Uh-oh.

Olisa emerged from our bedroom upstairs down to the living room, eyes hard. "What exactly is going on here?" She walked up to Noel, arms tightly folded. "Why are you going off on Logan?"

"Going off on Logan?' Noel asked incredulously, his arms outstretched. "I know I didn't hear you right. This is the guy that damn near got you killed, and you think I'm going off on him? Am I missing something? There was a mob scene out there today, Olisa. Many people potentially may have gotten hurt. *You* could have been hurt," he contended, pointing his forefinger at her.

"We had no way of preparing for something like that on such short notice. We're lucky we made it home in one piece."

"But we did, Noel."

Noel rolled his eyes in frustration. "Oli, those people were ready to tear you into souvenir pieces."

"They wouldn't have harmed me."

"You don't know that, Oli. Some of these folks aren't thinking with clear heads. They are stoked by emotions. In the future, don't even think about going out there without notifying one of us first! Logan had no business bringing you to the beach without sufficient planning and the necessary protection. Do you think all the alarms and all the security we've got around her is just for décor? All I'm saying is he should have talked to me beforehand." Point made, he stepped back from Olisa and planted himself against the living room wall.

"Is that what this is all about, Noel, talking to you first?"

"Olisa, please. You make it sound like I'm wrong to try and protect my big sister when I see her life may be in jeopardy. We are family and a team. That's my responsibility. Get real! In my business I've seen what can happen to—"

Olisa gestured for him to stop. She marched up to him. "Noel, you are my brother and I love you, but this is my life. I don't have to talk or explain anything to you first."

He refrained from saying anything. Instead, he crossed his arms in a snit and looked away from her. Olisa grabbed him by the shoulders and tried to make contact with his restlessly roving eyes. Eventually, he looked her solidly in the eyes and said, "Olisa, I get what you're saying, but you can't run around doing impromptu interviews. You're tossing all our work down the drain. I had you set up with Susan Blair on Channel 7 for an exclusive one-on-one interview."

"Who is Susan Blair?" she asked, releasing him from her grip. He looked relieved.

"Only the superstar diva of all the major networks, that's all. Put it this way: it doesn't get any better than Susan Blair. The leader of the Free World is on a waiting list to meet with her. She is the number one news anchor. What do you think her reaction is going to be when she finds out that a wannabe like Eva Sanchez got you there first? I'll be lucky if her people even take my call."

"Oh, they'll take it."

"Is that right, Logan?" Noel was again intercepted before he could get even halfway to Logan by Gumbo. Noel comically stood on tiptoes peering over Gumbo's mountainous shoulder to argue his point to Logan. "'Scuse the hell out of me!" Noel shouted. "Now you profess to know what Susan Blair's gonna do! When did you become the network president?"

Olisa sighed in exasperation. "Noel, stop . . . Please."

"It's okay, Olisa. Yes, I do know, Noel. Susan Blair has a reputation for acting huffy, but she's still a hustler and she's not about to risk losing an interview on one of the hottest news stories to date, especially with the opportunity to upstage rising star Eva Sanchez. I guarantee you she'll do the interview."

"Oh, well now that you've given us your guarantee, I guess I can get some sleep tonight!" Noel threw his hands up. "So, almighty Kreskin, did you happen to peek into your crystal ball before we got mobbed today?"

"Can't say I did. Ironically, Susan is a big fan and has purchased quite a few pieces of my work. She's already made it clear to my agent she wants to do a story on me soon. She given me her personal number to keep her abreast of any upcoming material. I could call her for you if things don't work out?"

Noel rolled his eyes, but it shut him up. I think Logan immensely enjoyed his little jab about knowing Blair. Admittedly, I certainly did.

By this time Gumbo had moved away, and Olisa was back in Noel's face.

"Noel, let me get another thing straight: it wasn't Logan's idea. *I'm* the one who called and begged him to watch the sunrise with me. He argued with me to stay home or at least let someone know where we are. So I called Laura. I told Logan I was going to the beach whether he joined me or not.

Don't blame him! Blame me," she punctuated by tapping her finger to his chest. "I'm the one who misread the situation. Thank God he was there when things got out of hand."

Noel self-consciously rubbed the back of his neck as he released a heavy sigh. He turned to Logan. "Hey, man, I'm sorry . . . I don't know what else to say . . . I—"

"Don't sweat it, Noel. I understand. If it was my sister, I might have reacted the same way."

The tension was further broken up when Peter blew in through the front door, satchel in hand and tie flapping over his shoulder. "Hey, everybody! You guys all right? Olisa, I was worried . . ."

"I'm fine, Peter," she assured him as they embraced.

"Good. I had to park five blocks away from here. It's a zoo out there! The traffic is bumper to bumper going down Lincoln Boulevard. I'd have gotten here faster if I had gotten out of my car and walked. The adventures of our gal Olisa are all over the tube and social media with aerial shots of where you live. The neighbors must love you guys."

"What? So that's why they haven't spoken to us for the past couple of weeks? What happened to all the love?" I remarked sarcastically.

"Glad I could provide you with the answer, Mr. T. When security let me pass, one of your neighbors emphatically asked me to be sure to pass along a sexually explicit two-word phrase that shows how deeply he feels for you."

"Don't bother telling me. I can feel the love."

"That's what I'm talking about! On another note, get the champagne glasses out, people! Noel doesn't even know about this. You mind?"

"No, it's on you," Noel said tiredly, massaging his forehead with one hand.

Peter clapped his hands excitedly. "Okay, first, I want everyone to take a seat at the dining room table so I can properly make the announcement!"

"Peter, just tell us. I've got a major headache. I'm not into games right now."

"Noel, give me a minute and I'll get rid of that headache real quick. C'mon, everybody; just humor me," Peter cajoled.

We all reluctantly sat at the table.

"Olisa, your friend, Ms. Moss, called today."

"Cecilia Moss?" she exclaimed. "How is she? Is she ready for another reading?"

"Forgive me I forgot to ask," Peter laughed loudly. "Just out of curiosity, Oli are you aware of how much your friend is worth, monetarily speaking?"

"No. We never talk about stuff like that. I don't care. I never charge her."

"Of course you don't," Peter chuckled. "But do you have *any* idea?"

"I vaguely remember her late husband did well in retail or something like that."

"Yeah, he did pretty well . . . Ryan Moss initially made a fortune in California real estate during the sixties. He then parlayed some of that money into a virgin idea that led to him owning the world's oldest, largest, and fastest growing health food store chain, along with Moss' airport gift shops, RM's exquisite mail order catalog, and all its subsidiaries. Oh, and a few five-star hotels along the way. They had no children, so widow Moss was the sole inheritor of her husband's estate. She is the major stockholder in Moss Enterprises."

"Basically what you're telling us, my dear Peter, is that Malibu Lady is loaded," I deadpanned.

"Indeed, Sir Timmerman. She notified our office this morning that it's her seventy-fifth birthday, and she's decided to be a philanthropist and be involved in some good works before she takes leave of this planet one day. She stated she can't think of a better thing to do on her first order of business than donating $25 million to the growth of OLISA, Inc."

Peter said more, but I couldn't hear a thing after the chairs screeched loudly on the dining room's hardwood floor with everyone jumping around screaming. Even Olisa bounced up and down, clapping her hands.

"Petey boy, you didn't lie; you just turned my headache into a footnote!" Noel lifted Peter off his feet with a bear hug. Gumbo lifted them both with his hug.

"She donated $25 million?" I reiterated, still unable to grasp that figure.

Peter pointed at me. "I repeat, for the hard of hearing, 25 million dollarinos! She defined that the money is to be distributed in whatever way Olisa sees fit, including building a center for the company. That's not all. She plans to campaign on our behalf to some of her rich society gal pals to get them to contribute as well. She insisted that I tell Olisa how much she loves her and that she has complete faith in what she's doing and will donate even more if necessary! Her only request is that Olisa give her a reading."

"Mercy me," Grace gasped.

"I don't believe it . . . That is so beautiful of her. I'm calling her tonight."

"Yeah, you do that, Oli." Noel beamed while he was dancing around the room. "People believe in you, girl. They are sending whatever they can, a quarter, a dollar, cookies in foil, whatever they can contribute. In so many ways, it's improbable. It's beyond the scope I imagined . . . and this is just the beginning! Tonight the OLISA, Inc. has officially become a multimillion-dollar company. Wow!"

"Which means we can start allocating funds to organizations that greatly need a boost right away as we agreed, yes?" Olisa was fired up.

"Of course, Olisa. Let's make sure, though, we have all our bricks in place, first. We need to meet and review and sort through all the information pouring in, and then we'll get to do the fun and rewarding part and make decisions on where the initial monies should be allocated." Noel's eyes practically glowed and his energy flooded back. He was all business again.

"Do you see what I've been trying to tell you? You see what's happening, Olisa? I know how you love hanging out with your friends at the beach, but things have changed. You have more worlds to conquer than being on display at the boardwalk. Just like we talked about, you are going to help millions of people in your life before we're through. Wait until you see what happens when we set you up all over social media. It's going to blow your mind, baby! Are you listening to your little brother? I keep telling you. Let me take care of things. Let me take care of you. All I ask is that you stay focused on our mission. We cannot let anything or anybody ruin things for us. We have responsibilities to others now."

Noel kept his eyes trained on Olisa even though it was fairly obvious through his peripheral vision whom he was referring to in regard to letting "anybody ruin things for us now." Apparently, Logan got the meaning, too. "Congratulations, Olisa." Logan pecked her on the cheek. "*Ciao*, all."

Olisa stepped in front of him, reaching for his hand before he got to the door. "Wait, Logan. Why are you leaving? You're a part of this celebration, too. Is it because of what Noel said? I'm sure he didn't mean it the way it sounded."

"No, Olisa, I think that's exactly the way he meant it. Ask him."

She glanced sideways, but Noel averted his eyes.

"See? It's okay, Olisa. This goes back . . . It isn't the first time your brother and I have had *discussions*."

The glare from Noel's eyes could have lit the logs in the fireplace.

"I'm not sure what you're intimating, and I don't really care. If Noel's forcing you to go—"

"No, that's not it at all, Olisa," Logan interjected as he played with her fingers.

Noel thoughtfully rubbed his thumb back and forth across his bottom lip.

"Then why?"

"It's because of you."

"Me? What did I do?"

Logan gazed into her unyielding eyes. Nervously, he clasped her hands. "Can we talk somewhere else?"

"No. Say what you have to say here. We've come this far."

We should have given them privacy and left the room. No one moved.

Logan sighed. "I'm all messed up over you. There it is. It's even deeper than that . . ."

"I'm still listening."

"I don't fit into the game plan. You don't need distractions or conflicts in your life at this stage. The public is making enough demands on you as it is. You need to be clearheaded so you can concentrate on your future endeavors."

"Is that you talking or my brother?"

"Does it really matter? What matters more importantly is you helping others."

"And what do you need, Logan? The least you can do is give me the courtesy of an answer before you take off, or should I wait until you consult with Noel first?"

Despite the chill in her voice, her rapidly pooling eyes betrayed her.

"No, I can speak for myself, Olisa," he defended. His fingers wrestled with her more rigid ones and then interlocked. "I need you, simple as that."

Olisa chewed on her bottom lip. She tried to look away, but Logan wouldn't let her. He gently lifted her chin so he could hold her eyes in his.

"When that crowd started coming at you, I didn't know if they wanted to hug you, kidnap you, or kiss you to death. All I knew was I didn't want anyone near you. For one of the few times in my self-centered life, I didn't care what happened to me as long as you were safe. Unless you truly know me, you'll never understand how significant that is."

"Does anyone really know you?"

"I think you do."

He caressed her face as a tear rolled down his thumb and slashed across his wrist.

About this point, I was wishing I could fade into the walls and get out of their way. I'm sure my fellow spectators felt the same way. Nonetheless, we continued to stand there like backdrop. No one dared to move or even cough. It was like to do so would break the spell that somehow involved us all.

"Olisa, I'm not used to this. Feel kind of funny, ya know . . . all mush mouth."

"Good. I love it."

He smiled. "Do you? I'm glad, but it doesn't work for a photojournalist. I'm not supposed to let my emotions stand in the way of a job. I've been to places where I've shared a cup of coffee with the devil. You do your job regardless of the circumstances. You live and die for the big-prize-winning shots. Nothing held priority over my craft until I met you. The first time I laid eyes on you at my opening, I was undone. It's an understatement now because the world has seen it. I knew you were something special. Not the God person, I'm talking about the woman. In you, I saw *my* miracle."

She wouldn't—*couldn't* look at him as he held her hands against his chest.

"Like I told you, it's never been about the money; it's about you. Maybe I'm being presumptuous . . . All I want is to be close to you tonight, tomorrow, and every day thereafter. Now do you see why I must go? Emotionally, it's impossible for me to just be your photographer. I want more. Yes. I'm being selfish. My timing has never been great. I guess I picked the wrong person and the worst time to find fall in love . . ."

Olisa turned away from him, folding her arms protectively. He moved behind her and endearingly embraced her. "I'm sorry, Olisa. I probably shouldn't have said all that. I didn't mean to embarrass you in front of everyone."

"Oh, don't worry about us. We—" I clamped my hand over Grace's mouth.

Logan never blinked when he said, "I've never felt this way before about any woman."

"And what way is that?" she asked softly, turning into him.

"How can you ask when you already know?"

"My emotions are in the way. I can't tell if it's something I'm feeling or something I want. Sometimes a girl just needs to hear the words for herself."

We didn't get to hear any further words. Olisa touched his lips with her finger and led him past us through the kitchen and out into the courtyard. It seemed like the air got sucked out of the living room. Suddenly it felt very cold and empty after Grace closed the door behind them.

They say, "The hits just keep on coming . . ." and so did the guests on the new *Eva's Special Edition* who claimed to know Olisa. The worst part was there I was again, sitting in the den and watching this piece of flotsam they called a TV news show. Although, I had to admit, "ole boy" was dressed to the nines in his tailored Italian suit. He looked familiar.

"Our studio guest this evening is, Donald Hulen, a financial analyst and CPA out of Hancock Park." They sat on plush sofas facing the camera as she leaned over and shook his hand. "Welcome to our show, Don."

"Thank you for having me, Eva," he grunted importantly as he adjusted his glasses.

"So are you handling Olisa's finances, sir?"

He chuckled. "I wish, judging from the rumors I heard recently."

"We spoke earlier. I want you to be brutally honest and tell the viewing audience what you told me about your past relationship with Olisa."

He rubbed his hands together and grunted again. "My pleasure. I didn't really know Olisa, personally. If I'm being honest, she wasn't part of our crowd. She did go out with my partner, though. One date, and it changed his whole life."

"Just his?"

"Truthfully? No. Mine too. I often think about it, and that was like fifteen years ago. Bruce Walker and I were high school running buddies. Let me tell you: we partied hard . . . until he met Olisa."

"Go on."

"It all happened because he lost a bet with some of the fellas. Been so long I can't remember how he lost. All I remember is afterwards we railroaded him into asking Olisa Timmerman to be his homecoming date. Since he lost the bet, the rule was he had to accept the dare. Let me tell you, back in those days, Bruce was the man. Every girl's breath contained the words 'Bruce Walker': 'Oh girl, he is a hunk,' 'He is super fine!' When I ran with him, his leftovers were other guy's trophies."

Eva sat back. "So now I'm curious. Tell me more about Bruce Walker."

"He was a pretty boy: honey complexion, green eyes, curly brown hair . . . upper middle class, bourgeoisie. His father owned a very successful dental practice and was president of the Black Dental Association. Bruce's mother was a gorgeous high-class fashion designer and owned two boutiques. One was located in Leimert Park and the other in Century City. Bruce was one of the few African Americans that came from an old-money background, aristocrats, where politeness was a state of being."

"Same for you?"

"Uh, uh. Not me. My father had nothing. Started out as a very ambitious janitor working his behind off. He eventually secured his wealth from all the maintenance services he owned and operated. We were a family of 'bean counters.' Our money could disappear tomorrow. We weren't old hands at living the lifestyle, and I guess as a result I tried harder to be a part of the bourgeoisie crowd, acting out how I thought rich kids act, which meant basically my head had a habit of being up my ass. I can say that, right?" He covered his hands over his mouth.

Eva patted his arm. "You're good. I've heard far worse. Tell us more."

He adjusted his glasses, which kept sliding down the bridge of his nose. "I loved being one of the chosen few. Didn't hang out with anyone who wasn't in the best social clubs." He jokingly wiggled his head in a haughty gesture. "We considered ourselves the 'webes, not wannabes,' the 'style makers,' not 'fashion violators.' In a nutshell, we fancied ourselves the 'I' in 'it'! I'm not proud to admit I was pretty superficial.

"Bruce did have a conscience. I felt kinda bad that we forced him to play this game with Olisa . . . Nevertheless, a dare was a dare; you couldn't turn it down."

Eva crossed her legs and folded her hands on her knee. "Why did you pick Olisa?"

"I don't know . . . Ignorance, I guess," Donald replied, pulling on his earlobe. "Nothing to analyze. Typical high school jive. I did a lot of things I am embarrassed about in high school. Hey, it's part of growing up, right? We were immature. So? 'Get over it' was the way I tried to justify it later in life. Anyway, at the time, the drums said she was a space cadet. She had a pretty face, but her hair floated all over her head, no style to it. She wore these passe flowerchild, beatnik outfits straight outta the sixties. We used to call her 'time traveler' because of all the bizarre outfits she'd come up with, mixed-up, dated stuff. In retrospect, she was probably ahead of her time. She was doing retro sixties' stuff before it came back in vogue. Plus, she hung out with the outcasts . . . low-class 'po' folks, political groups waving signs about nothing. Word was she was either a 'Jesus freak' or 'voodoo child.' People said they often saw her talking to herself and wandering around in a daze as if she were on another planet. I pegged her as a druggie."

"Guess it's true—you can't judge a book by its cover."

"For real," he said, shaking his head. "You know what the real trip was? She didn't get it when Bruce hit her up. Most babes had a cardiac arrest if Bruce even glanced in their direction. My partners and I sat there nudging each other, figuring she'd either stumble all over herself or take off running when Bruce strolled over and sat next to her, rubbing shoulders during lunch. Man, we were in for a big shock. She greeted him like he was anybody else on campus. Tripped us out as we watched. Smiling and talking with him, not because of who he was but like it was nice to have company during lunch. I'm thinking, *This girl has definitely lost touch with reality. Girl, don't you know? That's Bruce Walker!*"

"Shame on her," Eva grinned sarcastically.

"Bruce comes back about a half hour later, looking all hang dog like he just lost a tennis match. I ask what's wrong, and he says, 'Donnie, she turned me down. Says it isn't really her kind of thing, but thank you so much!' He's got this pitiful look on his face, and we're cracking up, figuring he's messing with us and would crack up laughing any second, except it didn't go down that way. He was dead serious." Donald cocked his head and demonstrated how Bruce looked at him.

"I panicked for a second and told him to shine it. He's officially off the hook and something to the effect this chick lives somewhere in fantasyland, so, let's move on. I changed the subject and asked who does he now seriously think about taking to homecoming. He gets quiet, sulky, and looks me dead in the eyes and says, 'Her.' I say, 'Who her?' He says, 'Olisa.' He sees I'm about to shit on myself and walks away, leaving me hanging. I hollered something obnoxious like, 'What she do, put a mojo on your ass?' He ignored me.

"Before the week was out, Bruce was laying down a heavy-duty rap on Olisa, trying to get next to her every chance he got, sitting with her and her friends during lunch, walking her to class, meeting her after school. Her friends seemed as blown out as we were. My first thought was, *'Oh, this is an ego thing. Bruce has never been turned down before, especially from someone like Olisa. He's just trying to prove a point.* Except deep down inside, I knew that wasn't Bruce's style. When all was said and done, he was a gentleman. It was rare, but he'd been rejected before. He'd move on. This time though, it was serious. To me, it was getting ridiculous—to the point of obsession."

"What made you think Bruce was obsessed with her?"

Donald held his glasses to his nose and thought about it. "On the QT, he took me aside and told me she was really a trip to talk to and he enjoyed their conversations. He tried to convince me I'd be surprised if I took the time to get to know her. Said he'd never shared so much about himself with anyone in his life before as he did with her. He professed that looking into her eyes was like being in a land of enchantment. He actually stated he'd never known beauty like hers."

"Wow. Nice."

"Maybe to you. Remember—we're young and stupid. I'm gaping at him like, 'Bro, you all right? You get hit in the head? Did she cut one of the hairs on your head or steal an article of clothing behind your back for her voodoo doll? What's up, homey? What kind of spell did she whup on you?' He laughed and looked at me like *I* was the one lost. The more he kept talking about her, the more it got under my skin. All in all, I ended up gaining a new respect for her. I said to him, 'No, Bruce, my man. We all underestimated her. She's smarter than you think, bro. She did what all the other honeys couldn't do to you. She's playing you!'"

"You didn't."

"I did. And Bruce went off on me, telling me I was close-minded. Bruce had never shot me down like that. We were boys, partners . . . Olisa changed all that. I began to really believe she had put a hex on him or something. My boy was going through some major changes right in front of my eyes, turning more quiet and introspective. Even worse, I kept getting the impression I was the one being measured under a microscope, that he was assessing me and all his other friends.

"Well, his wish, or curse as I called it, eventually came through. A couple of weeks later, she accepted his invitation to go to homecoming with him. Can't tell you how irritating it was to see him acting all humble and grateful after she said yes."

Sanchez eyed him quizzically. "You really had a problem with this."

Donald returned her stare. "I did. No matter how disgusting I found it, Bruce was still my boy. I apologized to him for my attitude. He appreciated it. Plus, I made an extra effort not to say how I really felt about her in front of him anymore. Homecoming night we double-dated. Hey, I must admit Olisa looked pretty damn good that night. Don't get me wrong; she still wore her typical odd ensemble, but on her it worked: long flowing gold chiffon gown, cape, scarf, kind of a gypsy look, loose frizzy hair flowing from underneath the cap, but somehow sister girl managed to pull it off. This may sound stupid, 'cause I'm definitely not a poet, but in hindsight I'd even describe her as being exotically radiant. That's another thing—I never realized how flawless her skin was. I'd never been that physically close to her before, either, as we sat in Bruce's Mercedes."

Homecoming night . . . After he described the way Olisa looked, it all came roaring back to me. I always wondered about that night, because this guy, Bruce, didn't seem like the type of dude to date her even though he was very much a gentleman. Naturally, Olisa didn't tell me anything about how the night went. This was getting even more interesting. I turned up the volume.

"Bruce told me when he went to pick her up. Her parents were very cool and about as down to earth as you could get, despite her father giving him the eagle eye. The flip side of the coin was her mother seemed delighted with the prospect of her going out."

Eva leaned toward Donald with her elbows on her bent knees and hands folded under her chin. "This should be good. Tell us what it was like to be out on a double date with Olisa." An anticipatory grin creased her lips.

"Don't really know what I was expecting of Olisa. She certainly poked a hole in all my theories. I assumed she'd be real quiet, shy, withdrawn, maybe even a little intimidated to be hanging out with us."

"Yeah?"

"Uh, uh . . . You couldn't shut her up. I don't mean that in a derogatory way because she was very gregarious. She was giddily excited, asking millions of questions, giggling and laughing, including some sisterly bonding with my date. Not reserved but open with her emotions. Bruce and even my damn date loved it. Me, on the other hand, was sickened by it. If anything, I'm the one who came off introverted that night.'

"Why so?"

"'Cause I was in shock that's why. Usually we all had our noses in the air and pictured ourselves as pseudo intellectuals. That night I distinctly became aware that I didn't know what the word truly represented. Anyway . . . Bruce was definitely right about one thing. Olisa's eyes are her most striking feature: deep, dreamy, mesmerizing. A couple of times when she looked my way, I started feeling a little uncomfortable. It's as if she knew what you were thinking, like she could get inside your head any time she wanted to. It was kind of creepy or maybe just my overactive imagination inspired by the flask of wine I had brought along for the ride."

Eva playfully slapped his shoulder. "So she finally won you over, right?"

"Not at all. Having said all that, I remained fiercely and stupidly defiant and determined to make her realize how lucky she was to be associated with us instead of vice versa, kind of like a person obstinately pursuing a meaningless argument. I wish someone had lynched my ego Homecoming night."

Eva eyed the camera directly and shook her head. "Men."

Donald shrugged. "I guess. What can I say? Whenever she was separated from Bruce, I made a supreme effort to whisper in her ear, like a megaphone, how much of a privilege it was for her to be with us. I'd say stuff like, 'Don't you know how popular my boy is? See all these women checking him out? You do know you're not really his type?'"

Eva gasped. "I can't believe you said that!"

Donald shrugged his shoulders again. "Yep. Like I told you, I'm not proud of it. She took it, too, everything I dished out at her. She never seemed affected by my big mouth or string of cruel remarks, so of course, I couldn't rein it in until I could see some pain in her eyes. To this day, I don't understand why she made me so angry or why I wanted to hurt her. I was acting like a parasite trying to tear her insides apart. Her calm demeanor screamed at me and made me want to bully her more. While Bruce and my date were on the dance floor, for some ignorant inconceivable reason, I wanted to break her. The more alcohol I drank, the nastier I got, finally playing my trump card and exposing our horrid little secret, supposedly under the auspices that it was for her own good. I let her know that Bruce only asked her out because he lost a bet."

"That must have crushed her. How did she react?"

"Instead of seeing the anticipated pain on her face, I received only a pathetic smile. She said, 'Thank you, Donnie. I know.'

"'Huh? How did you find out? Didn't that piss you off?'"

"'No. He told me the truth a long time ago. Once he was honest with me about it, we became friends and I accepted his invitation to go out.'

"I was speechless. I backed off after that. She beat me at my own game. Here's the irony. She held my arm and said, 'How about you? All the things you've shared with me about your life are nice sketches, but they're superficial. The only way to create a true painting of your life, one that has color and vibrancy, is to open up your heart.'"

"Ho, ho . . . how did you react?"

"Dumbfounded. I angrily asked what she meant by that comment. She scrutinized my face, probing my eyes. She didn't hesitate either. She said, 'I look at you and see you have everything you want . . . except what really matters. You're a good-looking guy, great athlete, have many friends and admirers . . . I see all that, except for happiness.'

"So now I'm irate. 'Yeah. Okay . . . you tell me what would make me happy.'

"'I'd guess you want your father to be a little less busy, be around a little more to appreciate what you've accomplished in school instead of expecting it. That might help.'"

"Uh, oh," inserted Eva.

"Uh, huh. Tell me about it. That shit . . . screwed me up. Even though she said she was guessing, she knew she was right. My only question was how she could have known? I didn't even discuss these types of things with Bruce. It was all part of the façade."

"Why do you say that?"

"My father was never around, always on the road. When I told him about my grades and victories, they were never enough. His story was always better, his life was always tougher, and he assumed I'd always do well, constantly reminding me how he made everything easier for me. So how did she know? Ultimately, it wasn't important. I was already upside down for the rest of the night."

"Wow." Eva eased back in her chair as Donald stared at the floor. "So, Mr. Hulen, you told us how you felt that night. How did it affect the rest of your life?"

Donald cupped the back of his neck with his hands as he stared at the ceiling. "I guess in retrospect, that night permanently changed me. I finally got it. I understood where Bruce was coming from. I knew why he was so attracted to her. I understood why he thought he was in love with her. In fact, before the night was over, I was jealous of Bruce and wished I had met her first. I wanted to know more about her and scoop her up like a ball with jumping jacks.

"As it turned out, there was no love connection between them. Bruce did ask her out again. She turned him down, telling him she wasn't ready for a relationship right now. They ended up good friends. Due to her, Bruce gained a whole new perspective about life, probably much better than what he would have gotten out of most relationships. He changed, too, or the person he truly was finally arrived. He distanced himself from the old cliques and made a point of meeting a greater diversity of people."

"Do you ever see Bruce anymore?"

"We still keep in touch from time to time. He's married now, got two boys. He's a chiropractor with his own practice in Seattle."

"Interesting."

"Turns out Olisa was good for me too. And I say this with all due respect to my wife and family. I love them, but in one night, Olisa helped me to become a better man. Perhaps if I had been more courageous, something might have happened between us, but I was too in awe of her after that. I'm not even sure if she would have had me. She was one of the best things that happened to me. I'm really glad I got the chance to know her."

"We're getting a chance to know her, too. Donald, thank you so much for your honesty. We're pleased that you shared your Olisa story with us this evening." Eva gave him a hug and smiled broadly at the camera.

Chapter 10

"This is just infatuation, right? She can't really be in love with him."

"Sure she can," Grace replied matter-of-factly as she carefully laid her head against the rapidly vibrating car window.

"Man, I just can't believe it," Noel stated from the back seats. "Why now?"

"Why not now? Name me a better time, son." I swerved my car to the right and drove up the steep dirt road, idling the SUV until Gumbo's red van popped into the corner of my rear mirror. The sun's blinding glare obscured the already indecipherable letters on the sign.

"You know what I mean . . . Things are finally coming together big time, and now we've got a distraction we don't need."

"Correction—*you* don't need it. Olisa is elated about it."

"Yeah, I know, Dad. That's what I'm talking about. How's she going to find the time to have a relationship with all that's going on?"

"Noel, let it go. Let your sister be happy."

"Sorry, Mom. It just . . . baffles me. We're just getting things underway."

"Love has a way of finding time whether you're ready or not," Grace pronounced, frowning at the window. "All the women you've dated, you've never fallen in love?"

Noel gave it two seconds of reflection. "No, not really . . . Okay, maybe once. I thought I was in love when I was in college. She dropped me for a football jock. That cut me to the bone. After that, I promised myself I'd never be anybody's plaything again. It's definitely not fun letting somebody jack up your feelings that way."

"That's your experience, Noel. Not everyone acts or thinks that way. Considering the success you've had, I don't think you have to worry about being dropped for a jock anymore. So don't give up on love. The bug might hit you one day when you least expect it. I might even see some grandkids instead of staring at your baby pictures."

"Not in my playbook right now, Mom. My baby is business. My career is priority. Who knows? One day you might see those grandchilluns you're looking for."

I couldn't let it go at that. "I don't get it, Noel. You're the one that hired Logan. So relax. Let it be. Your sister's a big girl; she can handle it."

"I didn't know they had met before! I brought him in to be her photographer, not her lover. No doubt the guy is super talented, but aside from business, I don't know him that well. He comes in and out of town. When he calls looking for work, I hire him. For all I know, he could be a serial rapist or a killer."

"You been watching too much TV."

"What I'm trying to say is one thing I do know—Logan's a player. Don't think this is the first woman he's been with that he photographed. He's a dog."

"You should know," I chuckled.

"Now you get it."

"Whatever. They're adults. If it's meant to be, it will be. Like I said, Olisa's grown; she can handle herself. She's well-traveled, too. Currently, there are worse things to worry about, like am I headed in the right direction? No street signs, and my GPS seems all out of whack," I grumbled.

"Joseph, you need to wash these windows," Grace fussed. She briskly brushed the inside window with her hand to no avail. The dust was thickly caking on the outside.

"What difference does it make, Grace? We're in the mountains, driving on an unknown dirt road, and you're worried about whether the windows are clean?"

The windows were dirty but not so messed up it prevented me from glimpsing a huge shadowy character bounding and weaving his way through the trees. And it wasn't Sasquatch!

"Whatever."

"Honey, I know what's really going on inside your head. Just keep in mind it ain't the first time she's been gone. At least she'll be here in a place where we can drive up and see her any time, instead of some remote area in another country."

"You're right. You're right," she admitted resignedly. "I should be more grateful. This *is* the best thing for her. I'm just being a mom."

"And one of the best," I added.

"It's just . . . I'm afraid, Joseph. I can't shake this feeling of dread, like last night might be the last time we'll see her at home. Am I making sense?"

"Of course you are," I said, drumming the steering wheel. I glanced at my set of directions, which seemed in direct opposition to the street sign suddenly appearing. I might as well have asked the coyote I saw sprinting through the shrubbery for directions. "It's going to be all right," I muttered to myself unconvincingly.

The last few days had been excruciating. How often does a parent hustle their daughter out of their home because it's no longer safe for them?

The last couple of weeks, invaders from all over Los Angeles County besieged our little walk street, some from as far away as "Merry Ole England," begging for a peek at the "Good Witch of Venice." I felt like we had been conquered by a foreign country the way complete strangers settled into our community, hung out in the streets, camped out in yards, passed in herds down the street, hassling the neighbors with question after question.

After all was said and done, the police offered little assistance in the way of advice except for us to get her out of here so they could maintain better control and ease the neighborhood congestion. Local crowds and a steady stream of visitors and transients who now stretched the path of the Venice Boardwalk to our house overburdened them.

It was building too fast for comfort. Police authorities stated they didn't want to assume responsibility for whatever might transpire in an emergency situation. They didn't have the personnel to constantly parole and monitor the vicinity and could be outmanned if something broke out quickly. They contended that the officers couldn't stop and ID every single person who passed through, especially on a walk street, as a potential suspect without turning it into a police state. Junior, who was visiting on that particular day, snidely remarked: "It already is; what about racial profiling?"

Still, we listened to them. Without further ado, I concluded I didn't want my family tested any further on their ability to protect us, mainly Olisa, even though we had Gumbo and his crew providing private security on a 24/7 basis. It was too dangerous to take chances. There were hardly any moments in the day we didn't hear the crunch of footsteps, the snap of a camera, the whirring of a video, or an obscure voice shouting Olisa's name. These sounds had become as much a part of our ecological habitat as the birds in the trees and the police helicopters in the sky.

Fortunately, Nick Cavaliere phoned expressing concern over the impact of the latest developments. He vehemently urged us to get Olisa out of here and, I think, feeling a little guilty that he may have been the prime motivator for this havoc. He called upon a few friends and found the perfect hideaway for Olisa on the southernmost slopes of the Santa Monica Mountains, off Pacific Coast Highway, near Will Rogers Park, a retreat that was very difficult for just anybody to get to without being seen, perfect for screening intruders. It was one of several houses owned by an immensely wealthy real estate developer currently in Saudi Arabia. Malmud welcomed Olisa to stay there, rent free, for as long as she liked, although we had previously agreed that she was never to stay in any one place for too long.

The house had been vacant for over a year after Malmud chased away the former tenants who claimed to be import/exporters but turned out to be major drug dealers. He hadn't planned to sell the house for a while anyway. Nick cautioned that it might be run down since no one had inhabited it for months.

I wish our house were that run down.

The house sat in the uppermost section of the mountains and was camouflaged by the nestling trees. It took a few seconds for me to register we were parked in front of the entrance. It was a gorgeous Spanish hacienda-style ranch house with a low, red-tiled roof made of stone and concrete. The walls encircling it were around eight feet high. True, it was a little worn and run down, begging for a paint job, and about an acre of ground that hadn't been taken care of, but it still was a great deal; that was for sure! The only access to the house was to drive in from the road, so it was fairly easy to secure, and that was exactly what we needed. Nick knew that, having been one to have experienced the stifling glow of fame before and dealing with it now due to his own resurgence with career offers tumbling in by the pounds.

As we stepped out of the car, Gumbo's van slipped in behind us.

"Where's Olisa?" Noel worriedly asked Gumbo after noticing only Laura and Logan climbed out of the van.

"You know, Oli—a sunny day, a fall breeze, a chance for some space and solitude. She made us stop the van so she could get out and walk the rest of the way."

"By herself?"

"She's got Free with her."

Irritated, Noel tried to spot Olisa from the crest of the hill.

Meanwhile, the front door was locked, so we paraded around the walls toward the back of the house.

Behind the house, actively working on the hillside alongside his crew was Nick Cavaliere. I noticed people working inside the house, cleaning, gardening, painting—the works. Nick absorbed all the costs, having already refused our offers to recompense him. As he put it, it was something he had to do.

He looked even better than the last time I saw him. Tanned, trimmed, and shaved, his cleft chin stood out in his structured face like a beacon. He was vibrant and full of energy as he labored with the crew, pulling up weeds. His ebullient spirit was contagious as he laughed and cracked jokes. It was obvious this man luxuriated in his second chance.

The Latino workers were in awe of him, in a way that transcended his stardom. They knew his history and rebirth, like most of us knew, but this was different.

"Hey, what are you guys doing standing there? Come on over!" Nick got off his knees and wiped his hands on his pants as he greeted us with hugs and handshakes. "It's so noisy out here I can't hear a thing. How are you? Where's Olisa?"

I told him Olisa was out hiking with Free. I couldn't help but observe that every movement in his body, every muscle, sinew, appeared manufactured to provide him with the greatest pleasure.

He patted my shoulder. "Good, good. I'm sure she needs it."

"You guys are hard at it."

"You better know it. Got the best crew in the world working here, most of whom are friends and relatives of my housekeeper Estella. The majority of people you see are from El Salvador, although we have a few Guatemalans in the mix. I love them, man. They are the best. See the older man over there painting the wood trim? That's Oscar. He was a doctor in El Salvador before he fled here during the revolution. Guy over there owned a couple of stores in El Salvador before they were burned to the ground. It's sad, but it didn't stop them from pushing forward. It's amazing how resourceful people can be when their backs are pushed against the wall. Changing subjects, what do you guys think about this place?"

"It's beautiful, Nick." The black cloud finally lifted from Grace's voice.

"Let me show you around," he said, escorting her by the arm as we followed.

"This house was built at the turn of the century, reminiscent of Spanish colonial revival. Did you see the stone tower in front? The building was formerly a hunting lodge before Malmud renovated it. Right now, he's visiting family in Iran and doesn't plan on being back for a while. As you can see, the house is made almost entirely of stone, indigenous stone. They actually blasted the mountain to get the rocks and carted them here on horse-drawn wagons."

"I love it! What ingenuity!" Noel exclaimed, marveling at the large U-shaped courtyard as we passed through.

"The walls have a natural finish exterior, and over there is an atrium, garden room, pond, outdoor and indoor fireplace, hardwood floors, and skylight on the stone stairwells. Give us a couple of more days, and we'll have it up to par. I think Olisa will be mightily pleased with the place, however long she decides to stay. As you see, access is not easy. And we're in position to see anyone that comes up this way. She's in good shape."

"I'll let her know. But do you mind if Grace and I move in with her?" I joked.

"Seriously, you're welcome to. There's space enough with four bedrooms and three bathrooms."

"Shoot, I wish. Unfortunately, we've got to stay at the pad, just to make sure we don't get any uninvited roommates. Luckily, my nephew and his wife along with additional security have consented to stay here, which allows us to breathe a little easier."

"Very good, but you're welcome any time to stay as long as you want."

"You are appreciated," I remarked, embracing him.

"Please . . . I'm the one who is deep in gratitude," he remarked as we retraced our steps back to the hillside behind the house.

Noel pointed toward the trees. "I see Free. It's about time they got here."

Free popped into view, dashing around the side of the building, tail whipping as he crazily sprinted in circles, barking excitedly. All of a sudden, his fur bristled. He bared his teeth and slowly backed up with a low warning growl.

"What's wrong, boy? Where's Olisa?" Free was relieved to see me as he darted to my side, bumping against my leg and leaning against me protectively. "Why are you panting so hard?" His only response was the warm pee I felt on my leg as he relieved himself. "Free, what the hell is wrong with you? You've got hundreds of trees out here and you choose my leg? He's never done that before, Grace. Can you believe this?"

Free looked at me like, "I'm sorry. I don't know what got into me."

"There's your answer, Joseph," Grace said softly pointing toward the trees.

I looked up, and there stood Olisa in the distance, her back facing us. Her hands shielded her eyes from the glare of the sun. Five feet to her right was the reason for Free's anxiety. It was in front of me the whole time, playing tricks on my eyes with the suns' assistance. Camouflaged against the trees was a huge buck deer. Magnificent. His antlers endowed him with the grace of royalty. He stood rigidly attentive, deliberating his next move. Olisa made no furtive move as she calmly watched him.

He reluctantly took a couple of steps toward her, body shaking, prickling with nervousness. Calmly, Olisa reached out and caressed his stiff upright head, which gradually lowered as he moved in even closer to her.

"Whoa, careful, Olisa," Noel whispered aloud.

"Too late now," I whispered out the side of my mouth.

It was one of the most awe-inspiring visions I have ever been blessed to see. A wild creature like that compelled to trust her despite all the potential harm human beings hold for it. She wasn't inducing him with food either. It looked like something from a fairy-tale illustration as we watched holding our collective breath while Olisa tenderly stroked his muscular physique. He didn't bolt until he heard the jarring click of Logan's camera. With a leap and a kick, he disappeared into the trees as we all exhaled.

"Apparently all of God's creatures find it easy to share a kinship with you, Ms. Olisa," Nick teasingly yelled as the two approached each other and embraced.

A curt scream made us all jump. It was emitted from an elderly woman who sank to her knees clutching her chest. I thought the poor woman was having a heart attack. She murmured incoherently in Spanish, or at least incoherent to me. It commenced a chain reaction, and other men and women were soon to follow, displaying the sign of the cross against their chest.

People recognized Olisa. Slowly, they moved forward, abandoning their rakes, shovels, and paint brushes, greeting her one by one with hugs, handshakes, and praises. It was an unexpected reception. Olisa was totally unprepared for the show of adoration. They gathered at her feet as she sat down on the grass. Moments later, she was conversating with them in Spanish.

With the exception of a young man who worked feverishly on the hillside, as if his life depended on it . . . He tore at the weeds as if he were ensconced in battle, gathering the piles and throwing them into trash bags purposefully. His wiry brown muscles glistened in the sun. He shook his head like a wet dog, beads of perspiration flying everywhere. Unlike his workmates, he exhibited little interest in what was currently going on. Occasionally, he glanced at the circle of figures but proceeded to work more determinedly than before. I wondered if he was an ex-con or somebody who wanted to make a good impression with his work ethic or just a person who was desperate to receive his full wages. The kid had a tough street-hewn look to him, so I doubted he was a brown noser.

Nick walked over to him. He reassuringly placed his arm around him and gestured to the gathering, but it seemed to have no effect. The young man politely declined to join them and kept working.

I found myself caught up in watching him. I noticed his rapidly moving lips indicated he was talking to himself. So my boy was just crazy, that's all.

Yet, he looked familiar to me. Maybe he was one of the homeless youngsters that sometimes came around the restaurant soliciting food. Oftentimes, we'd fix up a plate for them of whatever excess food we had left over, instead of dumping it after the restaurant closed.

Shortly, an elderly woman departed from the circle, an irritated expression on her face. She stomped up to this heavily scarred young man. I couldn't hear what she was saying, but it was evident, judging by her gesticulations, that she was scolding him. Now and then, she whipped her finger in his face and then pointed at Olisa. His stared at the ground, intermittently nodding, his face stoic. Frustrated, she waved him off in frustration and returned to the group clustered around Olisa. We stood not far from them.

"I told Maria Elena not to bring him," I overheard a Latino man with a broad-brim rancher's hat say cynically to another guy wearing a Dodger cap. His skin was as brown as mine, and his face looked as if it had weathered many storms, physically and emotionally. He had just left one of the portable outhouses as he adjusted his belt buckle and glared at the lone worker.

"Yeah?"

"She never listens to me. She don't listen to no one. She's bullheaded."

"Just like you! Why don't you want him to come? He don't talk to nobody. So what? He's a hard worker."

"Yeah, but he's not Salvadoran, like us. He's Mexican, you know . . . They're different from us," he commented, saying the word "Mexican" like it was a curse word explaining all anyone needed to know. "I can look at him and tell he's no good. That guy—he's a gangbanger. My sister—she don't care. She always finds a way to see something no one else can see in somebody. I guess that's good, but still . . . I can tell this guy is a troublemaker. Oh, but Maria Elena felt so sorry for him. She says to me, 'Miguel, that boy needs help. Look at his face; he doesn't know whether it's day or night. We must help him.' She don't listen to me. Next thing I know, she went right over to him hanging out by trash cans and brings him inside our house, this stranger. She sees a homeless boy who needs help, a stray cat. Me? I saw a wounded mountain lion. When he gets better, look out!

"She gave him food, and now he stays in our house! We don't know nothing about him. Maria Elena—she's a good person. Him? He can't be trusted. I just know one day he's gonna steal us blind. He never talks about himself or where he came from. I don't want him around! Maybe now she will see what I've been saying." He pulled the lip of his hat tightly down over his forehead.

He wasn't finished yet. The rant continued.

"Look at how he acts, *señor*. He's in the presence of a holy woman and the very famous man she healed, a man who was kind enough to let us work here. He shows none of them manner or *respeto*. And he's the one that opened his mouth and begged to come along when he heard we were gonna do some work for *Señor* Cavaliere. It's the first time I saw some kind of life in him. After all that, he refuses to come over and show his respect? He might as well have spit in God's eye."

The man's sister emerged from the circle of people on the grass. She reached out for Olisa's hand and led her toward the lone youth. Everyone else excitedly followed closely behind them. This was going to be interesting. But that's when recognition hit me like an errant fastball. I couldn't believe it took me so long.

"Hello, Ernesto."

His hands froze, and his body straightened as if he had been identified in a police lineup. Tears chased the dirt down the sides of his cheeks. Besides being out of context, I failed to recognize Chato because his tattoos had been obliterated. Despite that, the bruises and scars remained the holdovers, the final remnants of his past as one of the most terrifying gangbangers around. The facial arrogance that formerly commanded fear had been transformed into a haunted and contrite expression that seemed unable to deal with this developing scenario.

"My dear Ernesto, why are you over here by yourself? Why didn't you come over and say hi? After all, you and I share a special bond."

His eyes blinked rapidly.

Maria Elena's brother took advantage of this opportunity to chastise Chato. He got up in his face and yelled. "Because he's crazy, *Señorita* Olisa! Look at him. He shows you no gratitude or appreciation. You should be ashamed, boy. Have you no honor?"

Olisa gently waved for him to move back. "No, *por favor, señor,* no criticisms, no put-downs. This is what's he's encountered his entire life. He cannot help what's going on in his head. He's confused enough already."

Chato's head stayed rigid as he bent over, mechanically pulling weeds. His eyes—even though they remained steadfastly straightforward—projected a bottomless sadness.

"Won't you look at me?" Olisa asked tenderly.

"I can't."

"Why?"

"Like they all think, I don't deserve to," he lamented, his body trembling.

"That is *so* not true. Why would you say something like that, Ernesto?"

Hearing his given name constantly repeated triggered something inside of him. His eyes, albeit reluctantly, met Olisa's. His face revealed so much inner turmoil, it made me cringe.

He struggled to speak. A spillage of words turned into a flood he could not contain.

"The day you saved me should have been the happiest day of my life, you know what I'm sayin'? For about a day it was, you know. I thought I would end up being one of those Jesus dudes happily running all crazy down the streets preaching the gospel, the Word, or something. But as soon as those lights, cameras, and all the people were gone, I scooted into a corner scared to death. I changed. My head was all weird . . . different. I didn't want no muthafuckas around me! I'm sorry, ma'am. That's how I speak most times, you know? When all this happened, I didn't know what I was supposed to do next. I was scared and confused.

"Ha! I tried to be like one of those kids on the Brady Bunch, you know, all goody two-shoes and shit, but that wasn't working. It's like I kept hearing this voice yelling in my ear: 'That ain't you, *vato!*' The only friends and family I know is my homies, and they avoided me, cuz they didn't know how to act around me anymore, and I didn't know how to act around them, either.

Everything changed on July the Fourth. My grandmother was happier than I had seen her in years. All she talked about to me, friends, and family was how the healing *saved* me. Now I could leave the bad life and move on. Move on to what? I didn't belong nowhere. Instead of being happy, I swung the other way and hated myself. I figured if I went ahead and got rid of all these tattoos, things might get better. So I headed down to Mexico and paid to laser off all the tattoos with what I had left of what my mother called the 'Devil's paycheck.' Nothing changed. It didn't laser away all the stuff rotting in my head. All the shit I done did. Couldn't change that even though you gave me a new life. I even thought about going back and banging and shit . . . I missed my old posse, but they wouldn't let me be a part of the 'family' no more, told me this was no life for a person touched by *Espíritu*. They called me an *intocable*, an untouchable. I didn't want to go home. I was all confused and started trippin' and wandering around the city until *Señorita* Rivera took me in . . . I guess that's why I'm here."

He knelt down and weakly pulled at some more weeds. Olisa got down on her hands and knees and joined him in pulling weeds while she talked.

"Ernesto, you are trying so hard in your head to be good, you're already there. Your prior state of mind was hurting others. Now you are reckoning with the God of Love that exists within you. It's a foreign emotion for you to deal with, one that requires you to accept the evil ruling your past is gone. Today is about loving Ernesto, not Chato."

"Yeah, but 'Chato' did some hardcore, bad stuff during those times, the kind of things that would make you and all the people here want nothing to do with me."

"We're not here to judge you, honey. Don't beat yourself up renouncing past things. Can't change what's done. You must remember the past to avoid making the same mistakes again. You must let the knowledge you gained enable you to harvest your future. I don't love you for what you were. I love you for what you are now and can be."

She cupped his face in her hands, and he fell into her embrace, his shoulders heaving, his sobs muffled. Signings of the cross swept through the workers as she declared, "Ernesto, you can change your life. There is a famous quote by St. Augustine that goes like this: 'The key to immortality is living a life worth remembering.'"

Ernesto withdrew his arms from her. "How do I do that?"

"Haven't you figured it out? That's why you are here: to be with my family and friends, to work with us, and to help us achieve our goals." She held him by his shoulders. "Ernesto Padilla, you and I are connected. You are not going anywhere. You are staying right here. We've got work to do."

"You serious?"

Just as serious as the pained expression on my son's face—Noel looked like he was in the middle of a strained bowel movement. I knew it was killing him to refrain from saying anything. When Olisa spoke with this type of conviction, forget it.

"Of course I am. This is not a coincidence. You are here for a purpose. Your destiny awaits you. You are family."

Ernesto grinned like a little boy that just got a shiny new bike for Christmas.

So caught up was he in the moment, he failed to notice the new level of respect accorded to him by people who moments ago were ready to give him the same goodbye party as Joan of Arc.

Chapter 11

"You want the door closed, little brother?"

"Even though I live for the sound of a bustling restaurant, it might be a good idea, Wilma. Thanks." I resumed clearing paper off my desk to provide space for Peter and Noel to sit their plates of food.

"Thanks for hooking us up with some lunch, Aunt Wilma! Yum!" Noel joyfully rubbed his hands together in anticipation of the good food awaiting him.

"This looks awesome!" added Peter. "I miss your cooking, Auntie Wil."

Wilma smiled. "Anything for my growing boys. Enjoy!" She closed the door to my office. Finally we could speak without yelling.

"Noel, I haven't seen figure skaters perform faster turnarounds than you with Ernesto," I teased while adding hot sauce on my short ribs.

"Okay, okay, I admit it—the kid is great! He works his butt off. He's been with us—what, a month? Sometimes I do have to tell him to slow down and take a break. I've never seen someone so happy to get a second chance. Living in the house with Olisa has been the best thing in the world for him. I guess considering where he's coming from, it makes sense."

"The best part was watching him come into his own at the Greek Theatre," Peter ruminated as he scooped up a huge forkful of jambalaya.

"Did you see the expression on Ernesto's face after he was given a standing ovation?"

"Like he had died and found himself in heaven," I recounted.

"Hey, not too bad for a guy who was supposed to be helping out with security. Of course, my sister could have told me she was going to introduce him to the audience."

"It's called spontaneity, Noel."

"I guess so, Dad. What shocked me is Ernesto walking up and handling the microphone like a champ."

Peter nodded in agreement.

"His impromptu speech was so impassioned . . . the way he reached out to the audience and asked them to be his friends and support now that his life had diverged from where the path he was on. Anybody with half a heart could relate to his sincerity."

"Well, the *Los Angeles Times* certainly did. Check this out." Noel began reading the newspaper to us:

> *PRODIGAL SON RETURNS! Notorious former gangbanger Ernesto "Chato" Padilla, who dozens of eyewitnesses claim was healed by Olisa Timmerman, surprised everyone when he appeared at the standing-room-only crowd at the Greek Theatre featuring another Universal Concert for Spiritual Healing sponsored by OLISA, Inc. Padilla, who vanished after the alleged healing, has been sought after by the police, press, and medical community for months. His reemergence completely shatters the rumors that he died shortly after the stabbing that some blatantly declared a deliberately planned hoax. They pointed to his sudden disappearance as clear proof of it. Padilla described the incident in detail and his life thereafter for the first time since the July Fourth weekend to ardent, primarily young, and supportive attendees that were there to see the touted miracle worker, Olisa Timmerman. Timmerman, among other alleged acts*

of healing, has been largely recognized for healing acclaimed actor Nicholas Cavaliere.

In a moving speech, Ernesto spoke earnestly to the audience about the adversity he faced in his life. Born in a very poor section of East Los Angeles, Padilla was a victim of domestic violence by an alcoholic father who worked as an itinerant laborer. His father continually walked in and out of their life, stranding his mother with three children to raise. One night Padilla's father returned in a drunken rage shooting and killing his mother, two siblings, and then finally himself. Ernesto escaped death because he had snuck out the window earlier that evening to play with his friends. He ended up living with his grandmother in the Venice/Oakwood area.

Padilla, who was especially close to his mother, couldn't deal with it and found himself drawn to trouble like ugly to a blowfish. He talked about being kicked out of schools, gang life, drug dealing, attempted suicide, and the rebirth that came from "God's saving hands through Olisa." Padilla concluded his speech by making a passionate plea for a major truce among all the gangs in the city. His heartfelt story and request for peace brought down the house with the force of a spiritual axe as the audience rewarded him with a rousing ovation.

Noel slapped the newspaper down on the table. "Not bad, huh?"

"Not bad at all, Noel," I echoed. "And the best part is Olisa didn't even have to perform a miracle last night."

"Who needs to when you have a living miracle standing in front of you?" Peter commented, in between sips of lemonade.

"Yet and still, they don't want to give her any credit. C'mon, 'alleged acts of healing'? They are still looking for loopholes. Kills me."

"So what, son? She doesn't need the press to validate her as long as her mission is to help people in whatever ways possible, right? The people know what's going on."

"Your dad's right, Noel. You hired me to do public relations for you, but my impact, comparatively speaking, hardly matters. Word of mouth, videos, and the healing of Nick Cavaliere has provided the kind of publicity money can't buy. I've been more caught up in control issues and handling the tremendous number of requests than a direct PR push. The upcoming concert at Cyrpto.com Arena was sold out the second the tickets were posted. They camped out in sleeping bags to buy tickets. The arena is begging us to commit to some more nights. The truth is we need to search for larger venues. Right now, the Rose Bowl is on the table, but believe it or not, it's starting to look small in relation to the demands."

Noel cupped his hands behind his head as he took in what Peter was saying.

"Remember, Noel, when you had to scramble for musical groups outside of your label? You'll never have to worry about that again. We're getting calls worldwide from entertainment agents pleading to get some of their clients booked on any future concerts we orchestrate. Working in association with Olisa and her cause is some of the best exposure they can obtain. I'm talking A-list musicians, celebrities, actors, comedians, and politicians who have committed to giving proceeds to OLISA, Inc. Everyone wants to be a part of the UCSH revue."

"Incredible!" is all I could offer as I reread sections of the *Times* article while eating. "I guess it makes sense. Ever since the word got out that Olisa's family owns the Soul of Venice, we could put together a waiting list for the next two years. Our lines are longer than the ones on Black Friday sales before the stores open. We've had to hire extra personnel just to turn people away. Seriously, when they do get in, they either hope to catch a glimpse of Olisa, want to know if I have her same abilities to heal people, or want to verify if there are healing ingredients in the food."

WAYNE L. WILSON   *e*   295

"What do you tell them, Pops?"

"I joke it's a trade secret and leave it at that."

"Dad, you act like getting rich is some kind of social disease or something."

"I lack your talent for pushing the envelope. Seeing money pour into the restaurant because of my daughter's spiritual finesse wasn't exactly how I envisioned it."

"Dad, money is money! This would be the perfect time to open up that franchise."

"Uh, uh. You know where I stand on that."

"On another note, gentlemen, Olisa asked I bring something up to you, Noel."

"She couldn't do it herself, Peter?"

"She figured you'd handle it better if it came from me."

"Uh-huh."

"Well, first of all, she greatly appreciates all the protection you've given her and she loves her mountain retreat. She can hike, enjoy the solitude, meditate—"

"Peter, cut the icing. Bottomline—what's up?" Noel anxiously tapped his glass of lemonade with a knife.

Peter rubbed his chin nervously. "All right . . . The isolation is driving her crazy. She wants to be more involved. The way things are going is not what she expected. She's starved to get out, socialize, be more active, and get back to communing with folks."

"Is that all, Peter? You know as well as I do that we're going national with concert dates booked across the country. She's about to get stupid busy! She'll be begging to hole back up in the mountains. Not to mention, I could schedule her enough interviews per day to last into another millennium. Done deal. Tell her to relax."

Peter chomped down on a spicy andouille sausage. He downed his lemonade. Peter wiped his forehead. "Whew . . . That was good!" He paused to gather his thoughts. "She also wanted me to mention she's willing to do the scheduled interview with Susan Blair, but after that, she emphasizes no more. She finds interviews a complete waste of time and doesn't want the spotlight focused on her like that."

"She should have thought about that before she jumped out there and healed Chato. Oops, sorry, he's Ernesto now!" He tapped his glass again with the knife.

"Noel, you know that's not right."

"Thanks for raising my consciousness about it, Dad."

"You don't have to be nasty about it."

"Sorry, Pops. It's just—when is my sister going to realize she lost her privacy on Independence Day? The public owns it now. Part of my job is to keep this from being a paparazzi hoe-down. Why is everyone shitting on me?"

"C'mon, Noel, we all appreciate the effort you put into this."

"I hope so. Cuz I've got a pretty good idea of how hard it is to be under the spotlight after working with celebrities in the music biz."

"No one's challenging your expertise, Noel," Peter assured him.

"Then what's really making her so antsy? Am I moving too slowly for her on the donations? Is that it? We can start donating major monies to whatever institutions or charities she selects right now if she wants, Peter. It's fine with me. I've tried to do everything I could as her liaison and controller so she can do what she does and not all the financial concerns."

"She knows that, Noel."

"Then what the hell is it, Peter? She confides in you. What's going on?" Noel tapped even faster on the glass of lemonade.

"To reiterate, Noel, she wants more active involvement in the direction the company is going. Certainly, she would love to get those donations out faster to people and nonprofit organizations that are seeking to do good in society. I'm preaching to the choir by saying Olisa's primary motive in putting herself out to the public is to help people. She's very aware she can't physically heal every person in the world that wants and needs it. To do that on a daily basis, even if it was just one person, sooner or later she'd become so exhausted she'd self-immolate. Performing miracles can only occur occasionally. And it's contingent upon her being able to summon the Creator's help. Thus, she wants the donations to perform acts of miracles for thousands of people throughout the planet as opposed to her performing individual miracles which clearly will not encompass the numbers of people that can be helped. All in all, Olisa doesn't want her efforts to be regaled as a bunch of superficial celebrity-sanctioned pabulum."

"I get it now. She read Theo Balanis' editorial in the *New York Times*." Peter nodded with a smirk.

"Tell her don't pay Theo Balanis and his editorial diatribe any mind. Balanis makes love to cobra pussy, so, excuse me, who gives a fuck what he thinks? Obviously, he's going to be skeptical because he has not eye witnessed any of the events. He disrespectfully calls her 'the preacher's answer to David Copperfield.' To hell with Balanis. He just wants another Pulitzer Prize on his mantle."

"Tell us how you *really* feel, Noel. Olisa knows what Balanis' agenda is, bro. She just wants to stay as far away from the trappings of show biz as possible. The concerts are okay for now, but we all know they are only spokes in the wheel. The long and short of it is, she believes her true interacting directly with people certainly has impact, but for it to become more effective and help more people with its healing blanket, it must coincide with the incredible amount of monies raised."

I grabbed Noel's hand. "Noel, you're about to shatter your glass of lemonade if you don't stop banging that knife against it."

"Yeah, you're right." He halted clanking the glass for a few seconds, then resumed, this time adding a fork to the drum roll. "So, Dad, what's your hit on this?"

"Why do you even bother asking me? I wanted to ship her away to Siberia a long time ago. Olisa knows what she wants. Trust her. In light of our discussion, her instincts are usually on the money."

"Uh-huh. So, Peter, apparently my wealth of knowledge and business experience doesn't hold any weight. Does my sister have a specific idea of what she wants to do?"

"Funny you should ask. That's what she wants to run by you."

"I'm honored. And what would that be?"

"It's an idea that Ernesto came up with."

"Ernesto? One speech and now he's Neil deGrasse Tyson? What pearls of wisdom did Mr. Padilla drop on us? All about gangbanging you were afraid to ask?"

"Noel, do you really need to go there?"

"Actually, he's close, Mr. T. From the mouth of babes . . ."

The camera shot a close-up on Eva's face and then pulled away to show her seated in the studio in a very chic business suit. Success looked good on her as she flashed that award-winning toothpaste smile.

"Good evening and happy holidays! I'm Eva Sanchez, and this is *Special Edition*, December 1. The holidays arrived early this year." Every time the camera captured her from another angle, she smoothly transitioned to face it, never missing a beat during her narration. Now the polished professional, fluidity was her middle name. She emoted sincerity as she went on to say, "Usually, when the word 'drive-by' is brought up, you think of gunfire. Sadly you think of the innocent lives stolen away simply because they happened to be in the wrong place. You think of the sickening turf battles that occur as routinely as the seasons. You think of the aftermath of bloodied bodies in the streets.

"This evening I'm relieved to say that the word 'drive-by' can also connote something positive. Tonight, we are going to investigate the flurry of drive-bys starting to appear with some frequency in the City of Angels. It's the type that is quickly finding favor in other metropolitan areas as well and growing in popularity as rapidly as a hit record that soared to the top. This kind of drive-by doesn't leave a trail of tears or heartbreaking statistics. Tonight, we will explore one of the most outstanding, innovative, and successful programs I have *ever* served the pleasure of reporting.

"This holiday season there is an excitement, intensity, and spirit in the city that is thrilling! Olisa Timmerman's brother, Noel, was the first to forewarn us on *Special Edition* last month to get ready for the drive-bys, and it's hit like El Niño!"

A photo of Olisa and Noel flashed on the screen as she continued with her report.

"'Drive-by Blessings'—packages containing generous amounts of food, books, and sometimes cash bundles have been left in impoverished areas of the city, on the doorsteps of churches, school, rehabilitation centers, skid row, housing projects, women's shelters, clinics, and homes to the joy of its recipients. Sometimes at the risk of their own lives, these individuals have dropped off this material before quickly disappearing. Let's hear what Eunice Carter had to say about this phenomenon."

My immediate thought seeing Ms. Carter appear on screen was, *Sista, couldn't you have at least fixed yourself up a little bit before you let the cameras catch you?* Eunice was cloaked in a tattered beige robe and wearing a scarf that ballooned out like a covered wagon due to the curlers inside. Only half her yellowed teeth showed. I shook my head, embarrassed, yet happy for her as well while I listened to what she had to say:

"Hey, at first, I didn't know what to think. I was getting' myself a drink of water around three in the morning when I sees carloads of people stop in front of my house in the middle of the night. So I get my equalizer and yell out the window, "Y'all bout to get some bullet up your, you know what, if y'all don't get away from here. I ain't playin'!" They yell back, 'God bless you, Ms. Carter!' I'm like what the hell . . . By this time my two youngest boys nine and eleven are up. We look out the window and see three people lining up boxes on the porch and then they jump into this red van and speed off.

"I'm scared it might be a bomb or something. My youngest boys had already run out the house like damn fools, ignoring all my screaming and ripping open the boxes like they got no sense. Praise the Lord! There was enough food in those boxes to feed everybody in Carson, plus gift certificates to a grocery store and a clothing store! I found a note that said, 'One Love inspires the Spirit to Awaken. We love you! Middle of the morning and tears are raining from my eyes. To receive something like this . . . after all I've been through . . . it just made me feel *so* good! God bless you and yours, Olisa!'"

"Ms. Carter, you remember, lost her son, Aaron, a football star at Carson High School to a drive-by last year." Aaron Carter's picture popped up on the screen. He was suited in his football uniform holding his football helmet in the crook of his arm and a charming smile. "Aaron received a full-ride football scholarship to the University of Notre Dame before he was viciously gunned down by an unconscionable gangbanger because his ex-girlfriend started dating Aaron. After all the Carter family has gone through losing a son and brother, we certainly wish them the very best."

The camera cut to Eva's smiling visage at the studio desk. "And I'm receiving daily reports that hundreds of gifts like these are being dropped off throughout LA County. Moreover, it's been reported these drive-by blessings are beginning to circulate in other cities in our nation as well. No one knows when the next one will occur or where, but the anticipation is very high and this has become the talk of the town. Maybe, for the first time this reporter is aware, the City of Angels is finally living up to its name. It's so refreshing to broadcast such a positive phenomenon during this telecast. As Noel Timmerman said, the focus of the Olisa Group is 'Don't wait for government intervention when you can create your own miracles!' Here are some more interviews we've gathered from some of the people hit by these rewarding drive-bys."

I didn't have to hear anymore, particularly since I knew every location that was targeted. It certainly didn't stop there. In the coming days, Olisa was seen in dungarees accompanied by taggers and gang members, cleaning graffiti off the walls throughout the city. It was something she used to do prior to becoming famous, but now it was an event, shadowed by the camera, and she hated it. Noel insisted it was for the greater good.

Ernesto, who had risen to legendary fame, recruited many gang members who oftentimes were formerly rivals in the worst sense. Considered an "untouchable," Ernesto could pretty much approach any group because of how he came to his notoriety. Once they realized it was the former banger "Chato" they were dealing with, they found a way to work together and honored the truce. No matter what you thought of these little hoodlums, interestingly, spiritual things awed many of them.

For instance, working with Olisa, it blew me out to observe how many Latino gang members wore crucifixes and rosaries around their necks. This included religious icons like the face of Christ ringed with a crown of thorns on a medallion, the Christ figure nailed to the cross, Virgin of Guadalupe, or the Madonna with baby tattooed on their arms. Ernesto told me these all served as a form of protection and comfort. It was ironic how strongly religion played a role in their lives, albeit in contrast to living a peaceful life.

The more I thought about it, the more I realized it wasn't that different from the mainstream. After all, isn't God's name invoked in a huddle when we ask for strength to go out and kick our opponent's ass? Somehow, the gap between a supposedly civil culture in which we played healthy sports such as football, soccer, basketball, and boxing and indulged in religious wars in which we prayed for God's strength suddenly lessened the gap between gangs and us.

Noel got what he wanted, powerful visuals: a lovely, vulnerable woman, working with some of the most fearsome looking cats in the city. The same dudes who'd have shot you for looking at them cross-eyed scrubbed walls like it was a prized Rolls Royce. The powerful images not only motivated you to go out and find a wall with graffiti on it, but it made you want to go find you a gang member to help clean it!

Olisa was nowhere to be found publicly, yet seen everywhere, thanks to Logan's photographs. Moreover, Noel supplied the prized visuals to the press who gobbled them up. There were shots of Olisa talking to junkies on the street, homeless vets, teenage runaways, youth groups, and so forth. Once the word spread that there was an Olisa sighting, people came in droves, and we had to get her out of there as quickly as possible.

The money continued to pour in from all over the world. The daily cash amounts were so overwhelming, it made me shudder. Not to mention, the maelstrom of attention Olisa was receiving was far scarier. Noel had done his job too well. I urged him to pull back. A nerve had been touched in the public's psyche. He had hot-wired an engine that we knew nothing about. Olisa couldn't step out in the public without creating chaos. Everyone wanted to get next to the healer and be healed of their afflictions.

Olisa watched a woman named Sonia meticulously paint her hands with henna on a tabletop in the large courtyard in her mountain retreat. The ancient style of Indian adornment known as *mehndi* was popular with Olisa ages before Hollywood celebs became smitten with it. Her feet were stained with a striking henna tattoo.

Before the fame, Olisa would have driven down to Little India in Artesia on Pioneer Boulevard and hung out in Sonia's shop, doing lunch, buying music, shopping for spices, and art.

But that was then.

Since it was next to impossible for her to spontaneously leave her mountain home for fear of the crowds, Noel indulged Olisa's whim by generously flying Sonia up by helicopter to the Canyon retreat. Olisa was ecstatic. She loved socializing with Sonia and found the application of *mehndi* art on her body meditative.

Meditation was certainly not on Noel's mind as Grace and I angrily watched him pace around in the courtyard from our lounge chairs. Gumbo and Laura were also there. Laura sat next to Olisa and fiddled with a crossword puzzle. Gumbo sat point at the end of the long rectangular tabletop, rummaging through a bowl of mixed raw vegetables.

"Ouch!" Noel cried, after accidentally kicking over a planter of orchids. At least, I assumed it was an accident. "Olisa, you absolutely cannot do it! I mean come on; you're not really serious, are you?" Noel lowered his voice in an attempt to sound reasonable.

"I am very serious, Noel. I want to do this. I'm going to accept Walter Pocock's invitation to attend his church service and meet with him."

"Oli, this guy doesn't want to make friends; he wants to castigate you in front of his congregation in the worst possible way. You've been getting too much press for who you are. Believe me he's not very happy about that. He doesn't just want to cripple you; he wants to do a takedown on you. He's the 'Crusader for God's Law.' You've seen his television show and heard his radio program. You know the hype."

"Yes, but something inside of me is compelling me to go."

Noel squatted down next to Olisa, urgency in his voice. "Olisa, ordinarily I'd understand, but this is Pocock, a sanctimonious piece of vulture feces. He cannot be trusted. I can't even believe you're considering it."

"Noel, what can he do to me?"

"I don't know. That's what worries me the most. He's got something up. I just know it! It has all the makings of a modern-day ambush."

"God will protect me."

"Olisa, I'm not even sure God would venture there without his toughest angel bodyguards."

"I'll be fine." Olisa raised her henna-painted hand admiringly while Sonia worked on the other.

Noel stood back up. He gazed at the sky in exasperation. He looked back at Olisa. "Olisa, don't you get what I'm saying? That man wants a piece of you. You don't need him or his funky validation. We don't need him. Besides,

I thought you made it a policy not to affiliate too closely with any single group or denomination?"

"Noel, I can't explain it . . . Somehow this is different."

"Oli, the man hates you. Do you think you're going to win him over? You can't convert someone like him. That's like asking the Devil to trade in his horns for a halo."

"Hmmm," was Olisa's only response as she watched Sonia.

Sonia didn't appear to be bothered by any of this. She continued to paint decorative birds on Olisa's hand.

Noel took a quick breath and prepared for round two with Olisa. "He hasn't come out and said it yet, but he's about two broadcasts away from naming you the Antichrist on his radio show."

"I've heard."

"Then why are you determined to go into the enemy's camp?"

"We are not at war."

"Tell him that."

"This may rank as a historical moment, but I agree with Noel," I chipped in.

Olisa glanced at Grace who solemnly nodded in agreement.

"Cousin O, just keep in mind, security's gonna be difficult once we're inside his fortress, you know?" Alton munched on carrots plastered with so much dip they looked like ice cream cones.

"Give it up, guys."

"Give up what, Laura?" Noel didn't mask his irritation.

"Can't you see that she's going to see Pocock no matter what you say?"

"How do you figure?"

"Look at her—she's already splashing on the war paint," Laura half joked. "She's getting ready to do battle."

Noel's shoulders dropped. "Is that true?"

"I'm not the one preparing for battle," she stated matter-of-factly as she continued to admire Sonia's handiwork.

I handed Noel a portion of the newspaper in my lap and leaned back in my lounge chair while I checked out the latest football scores. Eventually, I heard a sigh as he retreated into his chair and immersed himself in the newspaper.

Anaheim.

Knotts Berry Farm.

Disneyland.

The Glass Cathedral.

The Glass Cathedral, bastion of Walter Pocock and associates, was as notable and as entertaining as all the others located in its home base in Anaheim. I didn't even want to guess how many millions it took to build this fairy-tale castle. I kept expecting to see a miniature golf course surrounding it. Still, the physical makeup of the church was both awe-inspiring and imposing, much like its maker. We were allowed in by church people who greeted us as if they were used car salespeople ready to make a deal and just as ready to spit on our backs if we walked away without closure.

"Good morning, Mr. and Mrs. Timmerman. Right this way, Mr. Logan Matthews, Alton Lee. And hello, Ms. Laura Nelson. How are you today?"

They knew who we were. They had done their research. Each staff member politely greeted us by name and discussed pleasantries with each one of us like we were reunited high school friends. Ordinarily, I would have been flattered.

Instead, I was scared shitless.

We were the visitors on their home court. I imagined them studying our bios and reviewing videotapes of us during their church management meetings until it was emblazoned in their brains. They had to know everything about us before they could do battle. And they expected to win, but I couldn't figure out their game plan.

I couldn't perceive Pocock outright verbally attacking Olisa at a church service he invited her to; that wouldn't look right in front of his congregation and television audience. It could prove disastrous. So what was he planning? We agreed to take a wait-and-see attitude until he played his hand.

Meanwhile, the crowds outside the gates were building and waiting eagerly to enter the church as if it were Judgment Day. Apparently the word had intentionally been leaked to his faithful as well as the press. We were quiet on our end and told no one about our invite to attend the service. Pocock's ubiquitous legions proudly displayed the Ps on their lapels as they finally opened the church doors and ushered people to their seats. There were so many rows in the church, it looked like an indoor coliseum. However, there weren't enough to seat the hundreds of dejected people forced to remain outside. Before the church doors quickly closed, I heard people chanting Olisa's name.

A conservatively dressed sycophant whose offset smile never disappeared gave us the grand tour of the institution. Her effusive hospitality was overcompensation for the patronizing expression in her eyes that said, "I was like you once, adrift in a secular wilderness until I found my salvation in Walter Pocock and the Glass Cathedral."

Soon we were escorted to an executive boardroom so gigantic you expected Jesus Christ to show up and take a meeting.

It wasn't hard to spot the impeccably dressed Reverend Walter Pocock among the elders with his helmet of shocking white hair. Right there beside him was old Biscuit Head whose eyes targeted us like a sniper. He whispered something in Pocock's ear, and Pocock responded by gesturing in broad sweeping motions for us to join him inside.

Pocock was slight of build and far more low-key than the magnanimous figure that filled the television screen. He shook each of our hands, clasping them long enough to give you the impression he was trying to suck the energy from your body. When he got to Olisa's, he held on to her hands as he sustained eye contact with her. The way he subtly sized her up was more like a snow leopard than the kind and wise grandfatherly image he conveyed on TV.

"Olisa, what a pleasure. I am so delighted you decided to honor us with your presence. I gather you've already met my trusted associate, Arthur Furhman?"

Furhman, known to us as Biscuit Head, nodded affirmatively as he struggled to maintain his smile. I noticed he didn't offer to shake her hand. I guess that last episode made him aware he was allergic to her touch.

"I trust we have treated you and your family well, thus far?" Pocock asked.

"Yes. Everyone has been very kind, Reverend. Thank you for inviting us."

"No, thank you. It's not every day we get such an esteemed celebrity to grace us in our worship of Christ, our Lord," he posited with a tinge of possessiveness. "I pray we don't disappoint you."

"I'm sure you won't."

"Praise God!" he emoted with a paternal stroke of her arm. "And here I had this impression you felt uncomfortable worshipping inside a Christian church."

"You can worship God anywhere as long as your heart is true. I love the church and all it represents. It's those who defile the purity of God's love that I am opposed to."

"Amen," Pocock shouted out, followed by a carnivorous grin as he continued his unabashed study of her. "I would love to continue this discussion, but I must attend to the good work of saving souls. Perhaps, if you are willing, you might spend more time with us after the service."

I hated the way he phrased that.

"We shall see."

I suspect Olisa didn't fail to hear the caustic remark layered under his honey-toned voice as he scurried away with his entourage. Old Biscuit Head couldn't resist turning around and shooting us the same look a black widow spider gives her mate before the final kiss.

Next, we were escorted to seats near the front of the stage as phantom whispers accosted our movement through the congregation. The stage looked like an island as it loomed among the sea of onlookers. Consequently, for something that supposedly was not publicly announced, I was stunned at the number of media present. Pocock was known for eschewing any media not closely identified with his controlled environment, particularly since the press had not always smiled upon his many extravagances. Eva Sanchez, Theo Balanis, and many other media elites attended.

No doubt this was an ambush. Pocock's true intentions, I'm sure, bore no goodwill toward Olisa. The climate had been set for her downfall. Furthermore, the press recognized a potential skirmish. They were equally surprised Olisa chose to visit the lair of the same person that lustily denounced her over the airwaves. The old fox wasn't about to surrender his crown or his money to some pretentious godchild.

The little ditty I used to read to Olisa when she was a child rang in my head: "Run, run, as fast as you can, you can't catch me I'm the gingerbread man." According to the fable, the nice and encouraging old fox swallowed him up in one gulp.

"The Lord is my delight and my salvation; whom shall I fear?" bellowed Pocock, addressing his predominantly White conservative congregation with the fervor of a coach at a pep rally. "The Lord is the strength of my life; whom shall I be afraid? Though a host should encamp against me, my heart shall not fear. Though war should rise against me, in this will I be confident—the Lord is my strength and my shield!" The recitation was from Psalms excoriating the enemies of the church and railing against those who defied the true Word of God.

The demure man offstage had transformed into a fiery crusader extolling the virtues of all those who fought the good fight for God, emphasizing "we against them, righteousness against evil, and believers against nonbelievers." A hailstorm of amens zinged the atmosphere.

I was aware of Pocock's enormous popularity and following, but I usually only allowed him about thirty seconds of channel-surfing time. This was the first time I listened to an entire sermon. Had to give him his props—he truly was an amazing speaker and perfectly suited for television where the attention span can sometimes be less than a commercial break. Under ordinary circumstances, I might have even found the sermon inspiring if he wasn't spewing all his underlying vitriol at my daughter.

"Who is this King of Glory? The Lord God almighty. He is the only King of Glory!" And with a grand flourish, Pocock raised his hand dramatically toward the church ceiling as the congregants did, likewise, uplifting their faces heavenwards. I also looked upwards, except my vision of heaven was intercepted by the letter "P" floating blatantly among the painted clouds in the ceiling.

Pausing, he surveyed the audience as he wiped the perspiration from his face with his silk handkerchief. "My friends, we have come a long way, haven't we? However, we have so much further to go. It won't be long. We have God on our side as long as we believe and continue to do his good works. And that, my brothers and sisters, will happen as long as we give to this ministry our time and our resources to help the unenlightened escape from perverse darkness to divine light!

"In this evil society of ours, we are easy prey to all those new-age books and gurus who talk like they know God. Friends and family, they've even convinced some of you to trace their footsteps all the way into the ungodly fires of hell. Friends, what you need to do is follow the pathway to the Bible. Its message has remained unchanged for centuries and is far more relevant than today's gurus, shamans, and swamis who might not be here tomorrow. When Jesus Christ reappears in all His glory, He is going to run these heretics out of town like a pack of wayward mongrels! The Bible states, 'Beware of false prophets!' You better pay attention, people. If you want redemption and you want salvation, then look no further than right here in this holy book! *This* is where it begins, and *this* is where it will end. Thank you, Jesus!"

He smugly grinned as his devotees leaped to their feet rabidly yelling. It was no coincidence after the applause died that he chose to bestow his attention upon us.

"Brothers and sisters, I have been informed that God has sent us some new friends here today to sit among our family. I ask you to please welcome our visitors with open arms."

You've been informed? You *invited us!*

"One of our guests has been all over the news of late. They've been calling her names like the High Priestess and Good Witch of Venice, which I personally think is unflattering for such a lovely lady. Her name is Olisa Timmerman. Ms. Timmerman, would you please honor me by joining me on stage for the benediction?"

His hands were outstretched, his smile as inviting as a piranha's.

Olisa took a moment to gather her strength before slowly rising and proceeding up to the stage. I had to dig deeply to keep from yanking her back as she scooted past me. She grabbed my hand and Grace's, squeezing them reassuringly like, "I got this!" I held my breath as she sauntered up the steps. She looked absolutely radiant with her thick mane of rippling hair flowing defiantly behind her. Wearing sandals, she sported her henna-stained hands, along with her brightly colored sari adorned with jewelry. Most likely Pocock likened her to a savage walking amid his "civilized" minions. Probably didn't help much when Little Oak, dressed in a conglomeration of Native American regalia, stood up to hug before Olisa walked up the ornate staircase.

Pocock extended a hand to assist her on to the stage. Instead of giving her a good old-fashioned fellowship hug, he held her hand and petted it. Old Biscuit Head must have forewarned him about the deleterious effects of one of those hugs.

"Olisa, thank you for coming. We are glad to have you with us, particularly in light of all the controversy you've had to endure."

Controversy?

"Despite that, we accept all of God's children here."

How generous of you!

"The one thing that can never be debated is your depth of courage, seeing you stand up to those misdirected souls. Praise be. That's something not even the liberal leftist media moguls can fake!"

Implying what? Anger coursed through my body.

Before Olisa was given an opportunity to speak, we heard, "Reverend Pocock! Reverend Pocock! Help!" wheezed an anxious voice from the congregation.

"Forgive me, Olisa. I must attend to this. I'm sure you understand."

Pocock bounded down the ornate staircase in the direction of the unseen plea. As he stood in the middle of the congregation, he cocked his head with his face contorting empathetically as he spoke to an individual consumed by church members. The person wasn't visible on the gigantic video monitors sprinkled throughout the church like scoreboards at a Lakers game. We could only hear them talking on microphones.

"What can I do for you, young man?"

"I need healing, Reverend P."

"Son, that's something only God can grant."

"I don't doubt it, sir, but they say she can heal people, Reverend. I mean I'm not trying to be disrespectful, but that's why I came here today."

Pocock released a heavy sigh. "I suppose we should be grateful for whatever reason brings God's children our way. What's your name, young man?"

"Rodney, sir. Rodney Isaac."

"Rodney, I don't think anyone here disagrees with you that Olisa Timmerman is, indeed, an extraordinary person . . . but aren't we asking a little much of her?"

Olisa appeared surprisingly unaffected as she stood on stage and listened.

"Reverend Pocock, I saw her on television healing that gangbanger and actor. She's the answer to my prayers."

Pocock looked at the congregation like he was severely beset with tribulation as a result of this statement.

"Rodney, it would be truly serendipitous if Olisa were able to heal whatever ails you today. I don't want to be a doubting Thomas, but you know television does not always reflect reality."

"Yes, sir, can't we at least give it a try? They say she has the gift."

"Rodney, far be it from me to dissuade someone with so much faith that a miracle can't happen here today. The Bible tells us that miracles have existed for centuries. I would be remiss if I didn't caution you there are no guarantees Ms. Timmerman can heal your ailment as the media's greatest cheerleader, Eva Sanchez, tells us." He turned and looked at Olisa. "Am I right, Ms. Timmerman?"

"Yes, Reverend Pocock. No guarantees."

Pocock turned back to the congregation exhibiting a complacent smile. "There you go. I *can* promise you one thing . . . As long as you place your faith in Jesus Christ, your reward will be eternal happiness."

The congregation punctuated it with an "Amen!"

"All right, son," Pocock sighed wearily. "If Olisa is willing, I will back away."

Olisa met Pocock's subtly challenging eye contact with, "I am."

"Then come on up, son. Ushers, please lend this young man a helping hand."

As ushers converged on him, I spied a towering being standing unobtrusively against the wall beside a stained-glass window left of the stage. He intensely observed the proceedings from the abyss of his black shades. The sunlight streaking through the stained-glass windows made his already obscured physique fade in and out.

After an interminable amount of time, Rodney Isaac made it on the stage. He was a young African American man in his early twenties: gaunt, crippled, and aided by a walker. He agonizingly clanked across the stage escorted by a solemn Walter Pocock.

Isaac ended his trek standing unsteadily in front of Olisa.

"Olisa, please help me," he pleaded, his eyes lowered deferentially.

"Only the Creator can, Rodney." She reached out and lovingly cradled his face in her hands as they stood silently in meditation. All the while his legs markedly trembled.

Then something happened so jarring the entire church gasped in one breath.

It wasn't a miracle.

Olisa forcefully shoved him away, screaming disdainfully, "What is this? How dare you make a mockery of the church! Don't you have any respect for God or the people here or *yourself*? You are despicable! What you are attempting is abominable!"

Isaac tumbled painfully to the ground, trailed by his walker crashing loudly against his prostrate body. The amplified stage made it sound even more godawful. Terrified and disoriented, he lay passively on his back as Olisa glared down at him.

Secretly, I always feared another Mama Willis disaster might occur again. As it stood, the nightmare finally arrived. Olisa was unraveling.

Walter Pocock was as shocked as all of us, maybe more so. Yet and still, I glimpsed a faint smile escape his lips and reappear in his eyes. He looked like he wanted to burst into a Riverdance but restrained himself as he kneeled down beside Rodney. He wound his arms protectively around him. An usher holding a handheld camera moved in closer as Pocock eyed Olisa like the Devil clawed his way onto the stage from the bowels of hell. A minute later, his expression calculatedly evolved into one of pity.

"My God! Don't take your frustrations out on this poor young man, Olisa! You can't blame him for not being able to change his woeful condition. You did what you could with the best of intentions," he uttered condescendingly. "Even so, the truth is, Brother Rodney Isaac placed his faith in you on hearsay. Dear congregation, once again we are minded—*only* God is omnipotent."

He dropped down on his knees and closed his eyes to take in the tremendous applause and plethora of "Amens." Pocock clumsily flicked his hands out for both Olisa and Rodney to grab to serve as a symbolic bridge— one of the only times I saw Olisa refuse to take a hand offered to her. She ignored a cascade of boos and remained standing. Pocock dramatically left his offered hand out there for her to look bad. He prayed, "Dear God, let this good woman join me someday in helping to guide *all* those strays back to the path of righteousness..."

Once Pocock finished his prayer, Olisa continued to glare at Rodney who was still on the floor clutching the Reverend Pocock's hand.

"I'm still waiting for the truth, Rodney!"

Isaac had been avoiding eye contact with her. He hesitantly raised his eyes and gazed into hers.

Pocock's tone changed rapidly as his eyes flipped open. He patted Rodney's hand before standing up to face Olisa.

"Ms. Timmerman, don't do this to yourself. You're being viewed in a live broadcast that is being captured worldwide!"

Ignoring him, she repeated, "Rodney..."

I thought it was only fear I saw in Isaac's eyes. There was more to it than that. His expression reminded me of a John who realized he propositioned an undercover officer.

At Pocock's signal, a couple of ushers started to grab Rodney by his elbows to help him up. Another went for his walker.

"*No!* Do *not* help him! Move away!"

Not expecting to hear the resounding authoritativeness in Olisa's voice, the ushers stepped back and then looked to Pocock seeking his guidance.

"Get up, Rodney. You don't need any help! Do you hear me? I said *get up!*"

"Enough, Olisa. I remind you that you are in the House of the Lord! I will not allow this man to suffer any further degradation."

Rodney was already on his feet, still shaking, but *not* because he needed a walker.

Pocock's face became ashen.

Shouts of "It's a miracle!" peppered the air.

"*No!*" Olisa quickly doused the budding adulation. "This is not God's work!"

Her crossness yielded to compassion as she reached out for his hand. "Why, Rodney? Why come her and ridicule God and deceive those welcoming you in their embrace? The real truth is you're not disabled; you're an addict!"

"My God, woman, have you no shame?" Pocock locked his arms around Isaac. "First you present this man with false hope, then knock him to the ground and chastise him? In the history of our Lord's church I've never felt the need to ask someone to leave . . . Today, I'm afraid I must—"

"No, Reverend!" Isaac blurted out as he wrestled away from Pocock and crumpled to the ground on his knees clasping Olisa's hand. Tears fell steadily from his eyes as he struggled to get his words out. "I'm sorry. I can't lie to you . . ."

He clutched both her hands like a man afraid of drowning if he let go. "You know. It's in your eyes. You know I ain't nothing more than a broke-down smack user."

"You've been crying for help for a long time, haven't you, Rodney?"

"Wait—what is going on here?" Pocock demanded.

"They told me Olisa was a fake! Not true. Oh my God, no it's not!"

"They who?" Pocock asked defensively, his eyes morphing into granite.

"They said God would reward me in heaven if I exposed her inside your church for being a fraud. They claimed I was doing a good thing."

"*Who* told you?" Pocock grilled again.

"All they said is they were friends of yours."

Pocock huffed, "Come now. That's ludicrous!"

"That's what they told me, Reverend. I was just standing outside the market begging for change when two guys showed up in this big stretch limousine, decked out and flashing a wad of hundred-dollar bills at me. They slapped down five $100 bills in my hand and promised me $1000 more if I acted crippled. They convinced me Olisa was a witch and that she and the media were in bed with the Devil. They said I was chosen by God, and this was my final chance in life to be a hero by helping them put an end to this dreadful evil. They gave me the walker to use in my act. What was I supposed to do? I caved in. I ain't no rich man. I live in a halfway house, so I jumped all over it!"

"*Hey*, turn those cameras off!" Pocock commanded, his eyes darting from camera to camera. "This is reprehensible!" he exclaimed self-righteously. "No viewer should be subjected to this atrocity in a church of mine! You get out of here! Ushers!"

"I will. First, I want to apologize to Olisa and the congregation and to God for doing wrong. Please have mercy on me." He bowed his head to Olisa, much to the obvious chagrin of Pocock.

"We all forgive you and love you," Olisa said tenderly as she pulled him to his feet.

"Amens" once again undulated throughout the congregation, freezing the ushers who were about to escort him out.

"You really do have the gift, don't you?" he asked admiringly.

He closed his eyes and hugged Olisa with great élan. An undercurrent of murmuring immediately ensued throughout the congregation. Pocock's eyes volleyed to ol' Biscuit Head who quietly scampered off stage. Turbulence erupted as Pocock's flunkies seeped in, confiscating cameras and hustling a recalcitrant press out of the church.

It was far too late for all that. His staff couldn't impede the dozens of people who had already run up on stage nor the ones that formed a line that spilled from the top of the stage to the bottom of the auditorium. A tone had been set by Isaac's embrace of Olisa. They all wanted to touch her, hug her, and have their spiritual moment with her. It didn't matter how long it would take; they weren't going to leave until they felt her caress.

Olisa obliged them. She enfolded them in her arms, mothered them, and cradled adults like children. Olisa remained on stage for almost two hours, giving and receiving love without any strain showing on her face. The filmmakers and photographers who escaped the disconcerted ushers broadcast these moments on networks around the world.

Eva Sanchez interviewed many of the recipients of Olisa's embrace outside of the church. One said, "I believe she was sent here on a mission from God. I've never been around anyone who has exuded so much love. It was like looking into God's eyes."

I didn't feel even a tinge of sympathy for Walter Pocock who stood forlornly on the corner of the stage groping for words. He tried to improvise, tried to muster a high-minded smile, but he had lost control. The pouty expression he cast made you think God punished him and sent him to his room.

After the service, an impossibly more dour Furhman escorted us to the exit where a huge crowd assembled at the gates roared for Olisa. We strained to hear what the vermin had to say.

"Reverend Pocock asked me to extend his apologies to you. He planned to spend more time with you but unfortunately fell ill after the service ended."

How shocking!

"Oh, I'm sorry to hear that. Is there anything I can do?" Olisa asked.

"No, no, I'm sure he'll be fine. He just needs a little rest. He's been keeping a pretty hectic schedule, plus experiencing that disturbing scenario in which that poor misguided man desperately concocted a horrible scheme due to his drug addiction."

Yeah, that poor misguided man. I'm pretty certain it wasn't him who concocted that scheme.

"God bless him, though. He'll be in our prayers tonight, as will you and your family," Furhman pronounced in a hollow tone.

What, as hostages?

He signaled for security to escort us to our limousine. He bid us a pleasant goodbye, but his eyes tracked us like a California condor.

Chapter 12

Ha! Surprisingly, Olisa never received another invitation from the Glass Cathedral. The Reverend Pocock's image and credibility suffered a public flogging as he continued to deny to the media any association with the mystery men who tried to frame Olisa at the Glass Cathedral. Pocock's foiled plan and nationwide humiliation consumed him and transformed him into a character as obsessive and pathetic as Captain Ahab. He excoriated Olisa every chance he got in his weekly radio and television broadcasts.

"I truly hate to think like this, but sometimes, my friends, you must in the perilous and never-ending battle for men's souls. Has it ever occurred to you that in all the recent and embittered attacks on my character by the liberal media that no one has brought up the possibility that maybe, just maybe, some of Olisa's more radical devotees, in collusion with my enemies in the press, might have corruptly set this whole thing up to make me, of all people, look bad? Why is it that no one's ever discussed this issue?

"Please understand I'm not saying Olisa Timmerman is not a good person; I think she means well. The truth of the matter is those people around her, her entourage, the ones the press refers to as her disciples, are certainly not the kind of disciples I'm familiar with. Those folks scare me. They're a little unsavory and potentially dangerous. I would even go so far as to liken them to what is known as 'lizard people' who live to impose the end of our holy biblical times on our civilization.

"Do you hear what I'm saying, people? Are you listening? One of her followers has a criminal record as long as a yardstick. I'm not exaggerating. Look it up! He is a notorious criminal, gangbanger, whatever detritus you want to call him, is noted for his reign of terror in the Venice and Mar Vista areas. The head of her organization, Mr. Noel Timmerman, and his music business cronies have shoveled more filth, depravity, and violent thoughts into our young people's minds than can ever be accounted for. They have Satanically and unscrupulously promoted some of the most debase artists and entertainers in contemporary times, whose sexually explicit and angry lyrics continue to corrupt our innocent youth. Many of these purveyors of the evil running rampant in our modern society have unabashedly brought their perverse declamations to their inappropriately named Universal Concert for Spiritual Healing shows. They talk out the corner of their mouths about God and then go out and make millions for the Prince of Darkness while herding thousands of people away from Jesus!

"One of her best friends is a man who loves his own gender a little too much, if you know what I'm saying. Apparently, he planned on marrying one of his boyfriends until he died of a brain aneurysm. It's always sad to hear about anyone dying in such a horrible way, but in the Bible God condemned homosexuality. In my humble opinion, this is our Lord's way of meting out punishment to all who defy His laws.

"I don't think anyone can fault the Indians—oh I'm sorry, Native Americans, for being so angry after suffering some abuse in the history of our great nation, but it's over now. According to history, there were wrongs and broken promises committed on both sides. We can't and are not going to pay for what our ancestors did for all eternity! And I'm not ashamed to say I still herald President Andrew Jackson as a hero and great statesman regardless of what the Indian leftists think. It's time to move forward. Hey, you know I've got ongoing issues with some of those folks in Washington, but they have at least tried to correct those wrongs. The Indians now own land, oil wells, and casinos! They've got the equal opportunity to gamble and make money just like any sinner.

"Be that as it may, Olisa's other best friend apparently hasn't heard that the Indian Wars with the States are over. She speaks on college campuses and reservations lambasting Christianity while turning right around and indulging in pagan rituals. It's kind of hard to fit into society when you're going into those sweat lodges doing God knows what, isn't it? Correct me if I'm wrong, but I've got a feeling they ain't singing Jesus' praises in there.

"Let me tell you, brothers and sisters: this person they've been calling a holy woman, Olisa Timmerman, has sometimes been seen in those pagan centers too. Ms. Timmerman informs us she doesn't like to be confined to worshipping within a church structure. Howbeit, she can spend time sitting cross-legged against those musty walls of the sweat lodges . . . Hmmm . . . kind of interesting, don't you think?

"Furthermore, they've got this lewd photographer boyfriend out there shooting propaganda for them. His supposedly renowned photographic retrospective of children around the world lashed out and blamed our beloved United States for not helping these malnourished children. America has done more to help more people than any country I know. We're at the height of patriotism, yet this person dares to insult the greatest country in the world!

"I'm asking again: do you hear me, America? These people say they're trying to unite us in some kind of ambiguous cause. I've got a different take on this. It seems to me they're hell-bent on tearing this country apart. We're supposed to laud a photographer who tried to shame our country the same way they've tried to humiliate me when their sect burst into our church. The same man whose tribute to women of Third World hellholes was really nothing but a porno exhibit showcasing naked breasts. Of course, if you were aware of his lifestyle over the years, you wouldn't be too surprised.

"You see, friends, I've been doing a little research. Maybe I sound like a foolish old man spouting things off the wall . . . I don't care because I'm proud to say at least I'm a fool for Christ! Their whole deal is to try to pass this woman, Olisa Timmerman, off as some kind of miracle worker. There may be some truth to that; even so, be forewarned at your own risk. If you read your Bible carefully, you'll see that Revelations tell us that one day the Antichrist will appear in the guise of someone very powerful, a person we'd never suspect. Moreover, I may not be quoting the holy book verbatim, but I can tell you this much—I've never heard any tales about Jesus Christ returning as a woman. Have you? So who, really, is Olisa Timmerman?

"They talk about her in all these saintly terms. However, correct me if I'm wrong. Wasn't she once referred to as a witch? Seems like a lot of us forgot about that with all this stuff they've been force-feeding us. I didn't forget, brothers and sisters, because I've dedicated my life to rooting out Lucifer. The Devil was once an angel, too, before he was cast down from heaven. His knowledge of the Scriptures is second to none. He knows God. You can bet he uses that to his advantage when he builds detours to turn us away from the righteous path. Satan can also perform miracles. Never forget—when the Rapture, the Tribulation, the Second Coming of Christ in Judgment is here, only those who accept Jesus as their Savior will find a seat in His heavenly palace."

I'd had enough of Pocock's tirades masked as sermons. I switched the radio station to the soothing sounds of jazz. Too bad Pocock's personal vendetta could have ended just as easily with the flip of a channel. In the weeks to come, he campaigned for support from some of the most powerful churches in the country, including several prominent Black church leaders. Some didn't mind going to bed with the same man who initially abstained from participating with other White churches in offering an apology to the Black descendants of slaves for many of the injustices incurred for centuries and ignored by the Christian Church.

In spite of that, now they were willing to unite in one unholy alliance: to circumvent Olisa's movement. The real truth was Olisa had not only upstaged them but she had also unintentionally usurped their power, prestige, and influence in the community. The alliance was intent on stopping her before being completely shorn of their sanctimonious authority.

Despicably, they refused to see that, by attacking Olisa, these institutions were laying down paint on the wrong canvas. The person they perceived as a detriment to their aims and advancement was the same person whose sole purpose in life was to weave a spiritual quilt among all people in an effort to eliminate racism, sexism, and any other obstacles that got in love's way. I gathered it was difficult for these entitled groundskeepers of glory to focus upon a concept so simple and pure.

"Once you commit to ridding yourself of all self-absorption and hatred, then you begin to discover how much easier it is to feel compassionate toward others. That's how I feel toward the Reverend Pocock despite his opinion," Olisa was quoted as saying in a *New York Times* interview with Theo Balanis in response to the vicious and personal attacks mounted by Walter Pocock.

"But, Olisa, some of the Reverend Pocock rants are libelous, scathing, and defamatory attacks on your character," Balanis stated, bewildered she was not angered and perturbed by Pocock's vitriol.

"It doesn't bother me. I know who I am. Does he truly know himself?"

That was what I loved about my girl. She could be more diplomatic than a politician. The difference was, in her, it all came from the heart. It would take more than rabid statements from Pocock to rock Olisa's equilibrium. Nonetheless, Grace and I remained worried about her. No matter how eloquent her statements could be to the press, the pressure and the strain taxed her. And with the upcoming tour Noel planned for her, when she was alone with us, she was edgy and irritable, which was very uncharacteristic of Olisa. At times, she would just withdraw inside herself and speak to no one for days.

The one person able to bring her out of those moods was Logan. He was a truly comforting presence to her, mainly because he paid more attention to the woman in her, not the goddess. It made her happy and took her mind off the pressures and bludgeoning she endured by assholes like Pocock and people in the media.

Noel tolerated their relationship but viewed Logan as a wandering Lothario who would one day get bored and walk out of her life or ghost her in the quest for a new creative high. I didn't really care about Noel's complaints about Logan. Both Grace and I shared good feelings about him and were grateful he was in Olisa's life during these trying times. Grace often smiled when she'd watch the two taking long walks through the woods, hand in hand. I think it brought back romantic memories for her of *us* in *them*.

Grace and I were also simpatico that this tour thing was no good. Grace spoke constantly of having premonitions about it. It was already overwhelming dealing with the enormous attention at home, let alone confronting potential road issues. A torrent of emotions existed out there and not all good. Olisa was loved and revered, and she built a bridge between the haves and have-nots. Still and all, there was a freaky amount of hate, suspicion, and skepticism out there, much of it fueled by Pocock and his cohorts.

Admittedly, we were at fault, too. We took the ball and ran with it under the auspices that our mission was to change the world. In retrospect, I wonder if things might have gone differently if we'd tried harder to downplay Olisa's gifts. Unfortunately, we'll never know. Fate has a funny way of intruding upon your life when least expected.

The first time Olisa indicated she was burned out and disenchanted with the whole process happened while the two of us sat on the couch watching a heated debate on *The Susan Blair Hour*. It consisted of an in-studio televised panel hosted by the number-one news anchor, Susan Blair. The discussion involved noted personalities: Beverly Fairchild, founder and president of WIN seated in the center, Hakeem Woodson, activist and poet, seated to the left of Fairchild, and to her right, Richard K. Marin, author of *God and the South Will Rise Again*.

The discussion was already underway by the time we tuned in. Susan Blair was a real-life *Murphy Brown* in terms of attitude and looks. She was in her mid-forties, shoulder-length blonde hair, elegant in style, and could exhibit as gruff a demeanor as one that was charming. Rumor had it that she was really ticked off she was given an interview with Olisa after the little upstart, Eva Sanchez. Nevertheless, Olisa was what the public craved and Noel promised her a one-hour interview with Olisa in her home. The interview was scheduled a month away, so in the meantime, Blair decided to conduct a panel discussion revolving around the Olisa Timmerman phenomenon.

"You really believe that God has blond hair and blue eyes?" Susan asked smirking as she leaned forward on the long table facing the panel.

"Well, ma'am," the White elderly man drawled, "I grew up seeing pictures of Christ, not only in my Bible, but in the stained-glass windows of my church in Arkansas. That's all I've ever known. I believe that God inspired the artist who created His portrait. Yes indeed, I mean maybe his eyes were brown or black instead of blue . . . Whatever the case, there is no doubt in my mind that he must have been a Caucasian-looking man."

"Okay, so let's hypothesize for a minute. What if he wasn't a Caucasian man? Would you still cling to your belief that Jesus is Lord?" Susan clasped her hands together and waited for his response. Her coolly analytical blue eyes gave no indication of what she was really thinking.

Martin adjusted his suit and tie. "I can't really answer that, Ms. Blair."

"Why not?"

"That's because he doesn't have an answer, Susan!" snapped Hakeem Woodson.

"I'm not answering that question, sir, because it's a fantasy question. I'm talking about reality."

"Then you better reread your Bible, Mr. Martin. Nowhere in the Bible states Jesus was fair skinned with blond or light-brown hair and blue eyes. Jesus Christ was described as having dark olive skin and hair like lamb's wool. Explain that!"

"I don't choose to, Mr. Woodson, because that's what you and all those other history revisionists say."

Incensed, the Black man shook his head. "No, the only revisionists I've seen regarding history, sir, are White authors like yourself who persist in reinventing your own kind of storytelling by making all gods and heroes in your own image. It's manifest destiny; except in this case, instead of leg irons, we are enslaved by psychological chains! We're expected to pray to a Christ who is the same color as the slave master. But what do you expect? It took two hundred years and DNA to prove to White folks that 'your' great President, Thomas Jefferson, was responsible for all those mulatto babies running around the plantation hollering, 'Where's my daddy?'"

"Sir, I think you're not only digressing but being overly emotional." His eyes blinked rapidly as a thin smile pierced his lips.

"Yeah, well, you know how we are. Thank God we are so damn emotional. It motivated us to fight for our inherent rights and to search for the truth instead of accepting myths like a blue-eyed Jesus with blond hair!"

Martin's smile disappeared as fast as his blinking eyes. "I'm not going to respond any further to that, Mr. Woodson. The truth speaks for itself," Martin stated patronizingly.

"Let's talk about the truth, Mr. Martin. Both Joseph and Mary had Hamitic ancestors, meaning they were of African descent, which also means they were Black, not White. My advice to you is to read books like *What Color was Jesus?* by William Mosley or *The Black Lineage of the Christ, Jesus and The Black Presence in the Bible* by Walter McCray and—"

"The only thing I need to read is the good old fashioned King James Bible, not some radical leftist fairy tales written yesterday!" He pulled out his pocket Bible and placed it authoritatively on the table.

Susan quickly intervened. "Gentlemen, I think Beverly has something to contribute to this conversation."

With a stern countenance Beverly Fairchild jumped in, "I sure do. And I think both of you have narrowed this discussion of 'Religion's Place in Our Society Today' to competing male egos on western Christianity."

"Beverly, I'm not a Christian. I'm just trying to point out to this man the hypocrisy of his beliefs and how self-serving they really are. Personally, I'm a Muslim."

"Oh Lord," Martin spit out, rolling his eyes. "So you're one of those terrorist folks that wants to kill all the White Devils. Say no more. Now I get it."

Hakeem pounded his fist on the table. "Once again, Mr. Martin, your ignorance stands out more markedly than that Confederate flag on your lapel. First, let's get something straight—I'm an orthodox practitioner. I'm not of the nation. Secondly, if you knew anything about the Koran, you'd realize that color has no bearing on those who are the true followers of the Islamic faith. We are all equals in Allah's eyes."

Marin leaned forward on the table and glared at Hakeem. "That's good to know why y'all will follow him to hell! It says in Psalms 2:12: 'Blessed are all those that put their trust in Him!'" he shouted, accidently spitting on Beverly's hand in the process.

Beverly wiped her hand with a Kleenex she yanked out of her purse in disgust. "And it's the emphasis on Him that is the crux of your problem, gentlemen." She flipped her hair defiantly.

"Excuse me, young lady?"

"What that means, Mr. Martin, is that God is a great deal younger in age than the Goddess."

Both men stared at her as if she had grown a third eye.

"You might want to explain that, Beverly." Susan looked amused.

"Before there was Christianity, before we evolved into a patriarchal society, many of the ancient religions were matriarchies and worshipped the Goddess. It wasn't until centuries later that western civilization took over with its male-dominated societies and started devouring all the scriptures concerning the Goddess and revising their sacred histories. Libraries were set on fire and record-keeping priestesses were slaughtered. God was made in the image of man, and women were tossed aside."

"My goodness, if this isn't about the biggest bunch of I don't know what—"

"If you don't mind, I'd like to finish, Mr. Martin," Beverly flatly stated.

"Sure. Whatever . . ."

"Look at Eve. She was considered inferior, unclean, and couldn't exist without Adam's rib. Western religion validated women's persecution. Goddess worship was soon belittled as a cult of people who practiced black magic."

"Ain't it?" Marin grumbled.

Fairchild gritted her teeth. "A woman's position in western religion is one that is inherently devalued. The patriarchal emphasis in western religion is the main reason why our society is so screwed up. And if my memory serves me correct, it took til the year 2000 for the AME church to elect the first female bishop in the denomination's history, who happened to be African American. It was gender, not race that was at issue here."

Hakeem shifted in his seat as Martin shot him a self-satisfied glance. Fairchild rapidly deflected it.

"We need to shift gears and begin to focus on a matriarchy again, a system that encompasses tolerance, sympathy, and love. When a child is ill, it searches for its mother. Our society needs to be mothered. I see us emerging toward a Goddess movement out of necessity. People like Olisa Timmerman are accelerating it. She is not only the most amazing person I've ever seen in my lifetime but the embodiment of the earth mother."

"Who I might add is African American," cut in Hakeem.

"And who they also call a witch," bit back Richard Martin.

"This is a prime example of man's way of discrediting her, because if she had been a man, she would have been called a prophet!"

"Oh, that's hogwash, woman!"

Susan Blair attempted to regain order as the argument continued to spiral, although she didn't look unhappy. It made for great TV.

I turned to Olisa and said, "I may not have your psychic abilities, but can feel you thinking. Talk to me."

Olisa laid her head on my shoulder. "Dad, now I know what Gandhi meant."

"About what?"

"He said, 'Everyone is eager to garland my photos and statues, but nobody wants to follow my advice.'"

"No truer statement than that."

"Why don't people get it, Dad? Why are they wasting time arguing over color, over gender, over politics, and over religion? They're focusing on everything but finding ways to love each other. Is it me? Have I been sending out the wrong message?"

"No, daughter. It's certainly not you. You're about as right as rain. Look; no one said it would be easy. People don't share the same prescription lenses. They see everything from their own eye view." I wrapped my arm around her and playfully wiped the frown off her face just like I used to do when she was just a youngster.

"Daddy, can I just disappear for a while? Do you think that would be okay?"

"Honey, I think you can stop this bus and get off any time you want. And I'll do whatever you need me to do to help."

She sighed and laid her head on my shoulder. We fell into a comforting silence watching the low flames dancing in the fireplace. What I said was bullshit, but it sure sounded good. She wasn't on a bus; she was on a jet plane, and that's not as easy to stop.

I didn't realize how serious she was until the next day. Grace, Olisa, and I were sitting outside in the patio having breakfast Sunday morning when we heard Noel pull up in his car. Five minutes later, he traipsed into the patio with a little hitch in his stride.

"Hey, family. Is it a beautiful day or what?"

He rubbed his hands and gave Grace and Olisa a wet one on the cheek. "I might have to join you for your walk today, Olisa. I need to get rid of some of this fat. Look at this!" He lifted his T-shirt and clasped the fleshy handles of his stomach.

Olisa idly stirred her fruit salad.

"So what's on the menu?" he asked, serving himself some bacon, eggs, and pancakes from various platters. "Oh, man, see? This is exactly why I get fat."

"How was the drive?" Grace asked handing him the syrup.

"Too nice to be working, Mom. At least I didn't have to deal with traffic driving up here."

"That's good."

"After we finish eating, Olisa, let's meet. Or since we'll be taking a long drive, we can talk in the car tomorrow if you prefer. I've got some great stuff I want you to see. Our new staff can't wait to meet you before we hit the road on the tour."

"Noel . . . I can't do it anymore."

"Can't do . . . what?"

"Shows. After the Shrine Auditorium, no more," Olisa stated delicately.

Like a *Twilight Zone* episode, Noel instantly aged from thirty-three years to seventy-three years old. "No more? I need some clarification. What are you saying?"

"Noel, I'm wiped out. I just can't do it anymore. I told you when we first discussed the idea that I might feel like this one day."

"Yeah, I understand . . . Look; we'll just say you're super sick and the concerts will have to be moved back for a few days. That will give you some time. Olisa, we're just getting going. Saving the world takes a lot more work. I know I'm being facetious, but people are depending on you."

"No, Noel. The organization can continue forward without my active participation. I can work behind the scenes. It's not working out anymore."

"Not working out anymore? It's working beyond our wildest expectations! We're making so much money for the organization, Bill Gates is looking over his shoulder. *Not working out?* We're building you a headquarters in Malibu, Olisa! That proves it's working—superbly, I might add. You're doing exactly what you always wanted to do: making an impact on the world by helping millions of people!"

"And we can continue to do that. We can take that money and do the things we're supposed to with it. You don't need me anymore. God will provide from here on."

"Forget that. We need you, Olisa. Otherwise, we might as well close shop. It's not God that they see; it's you!"

"Are you listening to yourself, Noel? Your reaction is exactly what I'm talking about. It's not me! It's God working through me."

"Okay, okay, I know that . . . Come on . . . I was so discombobulated by what you said, my words got all twisted up. I apologize. Just try and understand. We need you to continue to do the Lord's work. You are the symbol. You know what I'm saying? You can't quit! Everything's finally in place. Why are you trying to ruin it all after all the hard work I put into it?"

I couldn't stay quiet any longer.

"*You* put in to it? Wait a minute, Noel. Did you hear a word your sister said? She just said she is burned out and she needs to break away from it all!"

"I got it! Okay? You know what? Let's forget about talking business today. I'm flexible. Besides, I was thinking about spending the day with this new honey I met anyway. Might even bring her up here so she can enjoy the outdoors. Huh? That would be a good thing. Olisa, go ahead; take some time for yourself. I'm totally down with that. We're all a little tired. Olisa, do what you need to do to revitalize and get your energy back so we can get ready for the cross-country shows."

"Noel, you're still not listening. Olisa wants it to end. Are you more concerned about her or your reputation?" I asked.

"*You* had something to do with this, didn't you?"

"Noel!" Grace scolded.

Some of the edge left his eyes.

"Daddy had nothing to do with it, Noel, except for lending his shoulder for me to cry the blues on."

"I bet he didn't try too hard to talk you out of it!"

"You're right about that! You see my investment in her as my daughter supersedes all the other crap. It's about *her* welfare, not mine or yours."

"You're saying I don't care about her?" Noel's eyes smoldered with indignation.

"Noel, let's take that walk," Olisa cooed, gently tugging on his sleeve.

"Excellent idea," Grace remarked. "Why don't you do that? It will give y'all a chance to really talk. Right, Joseph?"

I grunted my assent. Noel's eyes set on me disapprovingly before he and Olisa ambled outside into the woods. Several security figures followed close behind them.

"Everything might work out after all," Grace sighed.

"Maybe." I watched a tall figure silently interweaving between the trees like the legendary Bigfoot. Except, I don't ever remember the Sasquatch wearing shades.

"Things have changed," Noel announced as he marched into the boardroom of his Century City office days later, eyes red and jaws attacking his gum. There were twelve people present including Peter, Alton, Logan, Grace, and myself. The others were executives Noel previously hired to help run the corporation. He dramatically slapped papers down on the table and surveyed the room, his eyes eventually resting on Peter.

"Petey, you better cancel the ten-city tour. We won't need it."

A chorus of groans surged through the office.

Peter's body snapped to attention like a switchblade. "You're shittin' me, right? Do you know how long it took me to arrange some of these deals? I can't just *cancel!*"

"I know, Peter. I know, and I'm sorry. Olisa abruptly changed her mind. She's disturbed by all the attention being solely focused on her."

"I figured that might happen sooner or later. Okay, so what's the next plan?"

"She wants us to divert more attention toward the fundraisers and charities. Peter, c'mon, are you really all that surprised? You guys talk all the time."

Peter thoughtfully tapped on his laptop computer. His eyebrows arched as he quizzically stared at Noel. "Let me get this right. If Olisa has unexpectedly refused to do any more shows, then why aren't you on your knees clinging to a toilet bowl instead of looking like you're holding the winning lotto ticket?"

Noel chuckled. "Let's just say, Mr. Kaplan, that I was a little taken aback at first, but I managed to recover. Olisa and I worked out a little compromise. Savannah . . ."

"Yes, sir." Savannah, his longtime assistant, pushed her laptop aside and bounced to her feet as she passed out paperwork. Cute, brilliant, and very efficient, I always thought she would have been the perfect wife for Noel. Physically she was a little too heavy for his taste. I always suspected she secretly carried a torch for him, but being the consummate professional, you'd never hear it from her.

Be that as it may, no one was more loyal to him than Savannah. She was a homemaker without the sex. If Noel said the sun was purple, she'd buy purple sunglasses to enhance the scenario. She attended to his every need, fastidiously arranging his work life to his dating life schedule, to how much underwear he required when traveling.

"Olisa promised to do one more concert, my choice, after the Shrine Auditorium this weekend. Take a good look at the literature Savannah is handing out. It's a retrospective of all the marches in Washington, DC, dating all the way back to the legendary 1963 March on Washington for Jobs and Freedom. You getting it now? That's right, baby! OLISA, Inc. is going to the State Capitol!"

"Washington?" we gasped.

"Yep, Washington, DC. Can't you see it? Love and unity on the steps of the Lincoln Memorial. Black, White, rich, poor, young, old, male, female, LGBTQ, straight, anyone and everyone—standing together, hand in hand."

His eyes flashed with the grandeur of his inner epic.

"Every show Peter organized sold out the instant the public received word Olisa was coming to town. Look; it's not often that the venue itself considers canceling. The Shrine Auditorium actually reconsidered its invite to us, suddenly feeling ill prepared for the all the potential commotion and turbulence that might ensue. However, I was able to convince them otherwise, and we would be responsible for any damage or problems that might occur. Within a day of announcing UCSH will be in the House, they sold out! Their only problem now is the endless deluge for tickets and added shows in spite of all the propaganda and misleading information put out by Olisa's enemies trying to cast a black cloud over her extraordinary God-given talent and abilities.

"I view everything occurring as a sign. If this is to be our last show, then let's do it right! We can accomplish everything desired in a single event. The March on Washington was a seminal turning point in the civil rights movement and its battle for equal rights. None of the marches, thereafter, have come close to the impact of that march which has taken on mythic proportions in the history of this nation. Back then the country was engulfed in fear, anger, bigotry, systemic racism, divisiveness, incoherence, and worldwide turbulence. What's changed? We're still dealing with those same issues, except now the obstacles and injustices are better hidden by innuendoes and euphemisms. I envision the mission for OLISA, Inc. is to perform our last and most spectacular Universal Concert for Spiritual Healing on the steps of the Lincoln Memorial for over a million to attend and broadcast via every social media outlet we can gain access to throughout the world!

"Baby, believe it or not, we are going to provide food for every single person there. Don't shake your heads. That's right—we're going to provide enough food outlets to feed the masses, just like the *Sermon on the Mount!*

Hundreds of thousands, if not over a million, attendees will be feted by the world's top musical groups and speakers who have been clamoring for a spot on our board for months. Savannah, get a hold of Junior. Tell him he will be our musical director. I need him to pull together all the musicians. Let him know we've got the musical resources, a list of the very *best* that have clamored to be onboard any future show!"

"Will do." Savannah quickly jotted down notes.

"And make sure he balances out the more commercial music with some of the world music Olisa is crazy about. You know shit with that natural, traditional feel to it: East Indian, Native American, Japanese, African, Irish, Mexican folk music, and so forth. Just give me a mishmash of stuff. Tell him I trust he knows what to do!"

"Yes, sir."

"Logan, I need you to put together a camera crew. We're going to turn this into a documentary, you know the making of the Universal Healing Concert in the State Capitol. I'm sure we can get Nick Cavaliere to narrate."

"All right. I got it," Logan said, tugging on his goatee as he camped out in the corner of the room. "Anyone in particular?"

"Yeah, the best crew you can get. Don't worry about the money. This isn't a student film. We're talking history. I want every scene to be pure gold. You with me?"

"I'm there."

My hands got clammy. Listening to all this gave me cold shivers. Noel seemed way beyond himself, and it felt a little scary. We would just have to see how this played out.

"Noel, I've got Junior on the phone," Savannah said walking into the office, phone cupped to her ear. "He said he'll do it as long as he can debut the song he wrote for Olisa. He says it's a killer."

Noel laughed. "Tell Uncle Junior he can do whatever he wants. He's the musical arranger. He's got carte blanche on this one. Just get the music right!"

Noel stomped around the room pumped up as if he'd been shot with a caffeine-loaded dart. "Peter, as usual, you'll handle all the public relations arrangements and information."

"Aye, aye, *capitan.*"

"Folks, this is going to be a monster! We've got sixty days to pull it together."

"Sixty days! You're going to give us a whole sixty days? Wow!" Peter facetiously remarked rubbing his chin with both hands.

"Peter, Peter, Peter . . . what are you worrying about? This is destiny we're talking about. You can't stand in fate's way. Turn on the faucet, and let the water flow!"

"Sue, until DWP turns it off first."

"I know I'm not hearing negatives from you, Pete. You, more than anyone else, knows this was all built on a foundation of positivity."

"No argument here, Noel. My concern is how in the world are we going to pull this off in such a ridiculously short period of time? Isn't the grand opening for the new corporate headquarters around the same time?"

"Yes. According to my calculations, it's scheduled to open exactly one week after the concert. How do you like that for perfect timing?"

"Noel, that's impossible!"

"My father told me growing up, nothing is impossible! This is it, man. We've got to dig deeper so we can all reach the Promised Land. Olisa will see everything she wanted from agreeing to do this come to fruition."

"Olisa?" tumbled out of my mouth. I couldn't help the sarcasm even though the ice was beginning to thaw between Noel and I.

"Yes, Olisa!" Noel reiterated. He refused to look in my direction. Probably good he didn't; otherwise, we'd be headed toward another face-off.

"The UCSH is going to be the greatest statement on racial harmony and peace on this planet! It will be the penultimate event. No one has to feel alienated because of color or gender. No one has to worry about obtaining tickets. They won't be turned away at the door because they aren't celebrities or didn't dress right. Anyone who wants love, peace, and unity is invited to this extravaganza. All others stay home. Don't watch. Huh? C'mon, y'all, talk to me. What do you think?"

"What about security, cuz? It's gonna be *mad*," Gumbo pointed out, folding his arms nervously as he kicked back in his chair.

"Don't worry about security, big fella. We've got the A team in our corner on this one. Name your favorite: the FBI, Secret Service, CIA, military ... doesn't really matter. They'll all be there. I've already talked to some of the big boys from Washington. It will run smoothly; you'll see. It's destiny, baby!"

A feeling of dread shot through me. My hands started shaking. Grace's eyes were languid. She was not one to unmask any family grievances in front of people she didn't know at our meetings. She would air her feelings out privately with Noel at a later time. Even so, she already recognized it would be an exercise in futility.

"Noel, you may be right about all of this. It may turn out to be one of the most significant events in history but also be one of the greatest migraines," Peter grumbled.

"Give me some love, brother! This will be a concert for the ages!" Noel laughed, clinching Peter in a playful bear hug. "All right, everyone. We've got very little time. *Let's get busy!*"

Chapter 13

Grace and I were surprised Olisa was willing to conduct a phone interview with Eva Sanchez shortly after her appearance at the Shrine Auditorium. Usually, she was too exhausted to want to do anything except rest. I guess it was her concession to Noel. Still, I could tell it was a struggle for her to stay alert as Eva's voice blasted from the speakerphone as we drove back to her house in the Santa Monica Mountains.

"Olisa, thanks for granting me this interview. You must be exhausted."

"I am, but at the same time I'm energized by all the love I received this evening."

"They do love you, Olisa. They really do."

"I love them. Though as good as it feels, I don't want to be the only beneficiary. We've got to spread the love everywhere if we're going to heal the world."

"You certainly gave it your best effort this evening, devoting a large portion of it to touching and hugging people."

"Yes, I try and hug as many people as I can even though I know my cousin, Alton, who's in charge of security, greatly prefers that I don't for my own protection. It's just something I have to do," she sighed. "I really miss the day when I could just intermingle with people without being noticed."

"Olisa, I can't imagine you ever not being noticed, regardless of your gifts. You are such a striking woman."

"I appreciate you, Eva, but this is Venice Beach I'm talking about. It used to be pretty easy for me to get lost in the shuffle of characters."

Eva laughed. "True. Well, the word is your hugs go a long way. I've interviewed people who swear that, after hugging you, days later they find illnesses have disappeared from family members and friends they come into contact with."

"Eva . . . I think people underestimate their innate ability to be healers."

"There are some who vehemently oppose everything you are doing. They accuse you of being blasphemous. They claim you ridicule biblical stories and say inflammatory things that are anti-Christian. Your response?"

"I never denounced anyone's religion. I do contend that faith in God should not be measured by belief in Bible stories or memorizing all the truths from any religion. I encourage people to explore the true nature of God and not permit themselves to be sheep and easily led or dependent on someone else's work. I'm not sure what else I can say."

"I think you've said a great deal. There will always be those who disagree."

"True."

"On another note, I've been told you are planning a final UCSH event that will take you to the steps of the White House door."

"Yes."

"Why only one more?"

"There's too much attention on me and not on our Creator."

"Can you really step out of the spotlight now, Olisa?"

"I must. The message is getting lost in all the sensationalism. It's not about me."

"I understand, Olisa. I truly hope you can. Just keep in mind you're viewed beyond superstardom. You're an icon. Tonight at the Shrine Auditorium, thousands of non-ticket holders stood outside of the building, holding up traffic, waiting for the end of the show, and hoping to sneak a peek at you. The crowd was relatively peaceful, except for a breaking-news sketchy report that is yet to be substantiated. A minor skirmish occurred. It's alleged blows were exchanged between your security people and hecklers."

"I don't know . . . This is the first time I've heard about it," Olisa replied. She looked at me for confirmation.

I shrugged. I hadn't heard anything.

"Well, we only have a few seconds left. As always, Olisa, best of luck! This is an incredible undertaking. People are already speculating that this will be one of the greatest events in this millennium. Thank you for speaking with us. Please keep us apprised of your progress."

"I will."

A frown creased Olisa's forehead.

Little Oak greeted us at the door when we arrived with a smile. It quickly faded when she saw Olisa's face. "What happened now?"

"Laura, has Alton gotten back yet?"

"Not yet. He just called. Said he was on the way but needed to tie up some loose ends. Why? What's going on?"

"Uh, nothing . . . I guess I'm just being paranoid."

"Your paranoia is about as frivolous as dialing 911."

"I'm probably just tired. Everything is fine. I'll talk to him tomorrow."

I agreed. "All things can wait until tomorrow, kid. Get some rest before I dip a pen into those ink bags you got growing under your eyes."

"Okay, Daddy."

She kissed me and her mother goodnight before retiring to her room. The distress remained on her face. Whatever bothered her had something to do with this so-called "minor skirmish."

Gumbo was surprised to find Laura, Grace, and me waiting for him when he pulled up. He said the much-ballyhooed skirmish amounted to no big deal, just a bunch of hecklers they tossed out. Nothing out of the ordinary.

Later that night I tried to read but nervously kept pulling back the curtains and staring out the window into the pitch blackness of the mountains. Periodically, I spotted security wandering about like specters in the night. A couple of them nodded reassuringly to me all was fine. The anxiousness in my stomach told me different. In those rare prescient moments, I appreciated the blessing and curse that haunted Olisa her entire life.

"You too, huh?"

"What do you mean you too?" Wilma asked haughtily.

"Let's see . . ." I said, examining the draft of the new menu. "The cover art with platters of food on clouds is a nice touch. All right. Let me see . . . 'Seafood Gumbo. You'll know you've made it to the Promised Land when you taste this aromatic combination of crab, shrimp, chicken, and sausage, accompanied by a bed of rice. Especially suggested for an entire party because there's enough here to feed the masses.' Really?"

Wilma grinned sheepishly. "About that, I—"

"Hold on. This is a goodie: 'Holy Fried Chicken! After you take a bite of this scrumptious treat, you'll be ready for your heavenly rest . . . and don't forget to order the Sweet Low, Sweet Chocolate Cake'? Should I stop here, or shall I keep going?"

Wilma laughed. "Well, Joe, we did name this 'The Soul of Venice.' Don't you think it's about time the restaurant lives up to its name?"

"Hey, I'm down with that, but don't *you* think you're laying it on just a little thick?"

"Uh, uh. Customers will love it! They already think the food's been blessed. Just the other day this woman, who must have just come from a holiness service, jumped up during Sunday brunch and started dancing to the piped-in music *playing softly* in the restaurant."

"No, she didn't."

"Yes . . . she . . . did, honey. That church lady started doing a butt dance just like this."

Wilma whipped off her apron and waved it in the air. She mimicked the woman, dancing throughout the office, bumping the files, cabinets, chairs, and desk with her butt while screaming out, "Hallelujahs and Praise the Holy Ghosts." The look on her face had me falling out laughing. Before long, we were leaning on each other, tears streaming down our faces, on the ground in hysterics.

One of the kitchen staff burst into the office, worried. Five other workers stuck their heads in the door also concerned.

"What's all the noise? Is everything all right? Oh . . ." he uttered when he saw us sitting on the floor, giddy with laughter and holding our sides.

"Everything's good, Geraldo. Wilma just told me a funny story."

"Oh, you must have told *El Jefe* about the lady!"

"Yep, *that* lady, Geraldo."

"She was funny. Customers checked to see if they ordered the same thing."

That got us to giggling again, Geraldo too.

"Okay. Have fun!" he turned and ushered all the other workers out.

After he closed the door, I heard him laughing with his coworkers.

After a momentary rest, I could finally talk again. "So you're going to add to this fervor?" I asked, pressing my aching jaw.

"Damn right! See you've been away too long. That's the only thing that can be added. Not enough room in the restaurant to add more people. By the way, I've got a list of executives ready to play *Let's Make a Deal* with you. All you've got to do is say yes, and you'll instantly have a string of restaurants worldwide. You think I'm playin'!"

"No, I don't. Your nephew's been hitting me up about that for years before *the healing*." I rubbed the bridge of my nose. "Wilma, there was a time I might have been all over news like that. Now . . ."

"You don't even have to go there," she empathized.

The office door flew open with such velocity that Wilma and I jumped like the Holy Ghost entered the room.

"Alton!"

"Sorry, Mama. I didn't mean to scare y'all. Unc, we've got to go!"

He was breathing hard. The look on his face made my stomach drop.

"Gumbo, what's wrong? Where's Olisa?"

"She's fine, Uncle Joe. It's Ernesto. They got him."

"Got him? Who's got him?"

"The police—they arrested him."

"What?"

"Yeah. They picked him up at the Century City office. Police cars all over the place. They had so many guns drawn, I thought I was at the Alamo.' "

"What was he arrested for?"

"Murder. Cops said he killed two people."

"Mercy me," Wilma cried.

My voice dropped. "Gumbo, was Olisa there?"

"They roughly paraded him past her in handcuffs. Noel and Logan tried their best to talk her out of going down to the county jail, but you know..."

"Shit! Okay. Let's go!"

"I really didn't think it was any big deal, Unc. I mean yeah, I was kinda pissed off at Ernesto for losing his cool at the time, but I thought he had calmed down. I just can't believe it," Gumbo kept repeating as he drove his Ford Explorer down Olympic Boulevard. We weren't going to bother with the freeway traffic because we knew it would be packed. Fortunately, the street traffic was pretty light even though it was four in the afternoon. Thus far, we were making all the lights.

"Gumbo, slow down . . . What happened?"

"During the show last night, two ese's started heckling Ernesto for no reason, calling him every fucking name in the book, in Spanish and English. I mean they wouldn't let up. It's not like we hadn't encountered hecklers before; except these dudes had it in strictly for Ernesto. I thought they were from some rival gang he fought within his past, but Ernesto said he'd never seen these cats before."

"How did Ernesto handle it? Did he go off on them or what?"

"It wasn't like that. Ernesto laughed it off and tried to ignore them. I'm not even sure I could have been as cool as he was with the kind of bullshit they were dishing out, challenging his manhood and all that. We even sent Ernesto to another section, but those MFs followed, still bagging on him. We finally threw their asses out the auditorium."

Gumbo screeched to a halt a quarter of the way past a red light. He quickly backed up behind the line.

"Gumbo, will you fucking slow down? You trying to give me a heart attack? You almost ran the light!"

"I'm sorry, Unc. I'm just hyped."

"Well, un-hype. We don't need you getting a ticket or getting arrested."

"I'm good." He wiped his sweaty forehead.

"Were these dudes drunk or high?"

"I don't think so. My guys told me they didn't smell any liquor on them and they didn't look high either."

"So then what?"

"Ernesto was posted alone at one of the exits when the show was over. One of the guys walked over and bitch slapped him!"

"That's when he retaliated?"

"Yes and no. Despite all the bullshit, Ernesto still didn't throw down on him; at least that's what one of the witnesses told me. It wasn't until dude threatened to do harm to Olisa that he finally lost it. Before we could get to him, he stole on one of them and dropped him on his ass. To be honest, I was kind of happy he did after all the shit he took from those assholes. Ernesto knocked the jerk down and threatened to kill him if he saw him anywhere near Olisa. The worst part is he said this in front of a bunch of people."

"Damn."

"Let's go, idiot! Don't you see the light changed?" Gumbo barked at the car whose driver's head popped up from texting. "You know what's weird, Uncle Joe? Those punks backed away looking all pleased after Ernesto knocked one of them on his ass! They fled after that."

"Did Ernesto try to follow them?"

"Nope, especially with us restraining him. He felt horrible afterwards for losing his cool. I mean I didn't have to get on him. He beat himself up more than I ever could."

"Okay, so why did the police arrest Ernesto? You said they fled. I'm sure they didn't file an assault charge with all those witnesses around? Did Ernesto have a warrant on him or something?"

"That's the part I'm getting to. The police found Gary Mejia and Richard Alvarez around 5:00 AM, dead, lying face down in a Culver City alley. Someone shot them execution style in the back of the head. The police found the gun with Ernesto's fingerprints all over it a few blocks away in a trash bin."

"So, of course, with Ernesto's reputation and threat to kill them, he was arrested."

"Exactly. Uncle, I'm telling you it's bullshit! This was a setup! Ernesto and I grew kinda tight. I learned he's a pretty smart guy, despite all the trouble he's gotten into in his life. If he was going to do something like that, I can't see him being that stupid."

"Gumbo, anyone can do stupid things when they are in a rage."

"Yeah . . . In my heart and gut, I just don't believe it, Uncle Joe."

"Me neither, man. Were you guys with Ernesto all night?"

Gumbo swallowed hard. "No. After things calmed down, Ernesto told me he needed to chill, said he wanted to go take a walk on the beach. I told him it was fine with me and to do whatever he needed to take his mind off things. I should have gone with him."

"It's not your fault, Gumbo. You made the right decision. And if you really don't believe he did it, it wouldn't have mattered anyway. They still would have been killed."

"Yeah, but at least I could have been his alibi."

Gumbo's lip stopped trembling as he gripped the steering wheel harder.

"Did he get a chance to say anything to you before he got arrested?"

He tilted his head from side to side as his neck cracked loudly. "Not really . . . except when they were carting him away. He chuckled and said, 'At least I know now what happened to my automatic. I thought my grandmother found it and tossed it away with all the others. Somebody must have been watching her. Trip, huh, Vato?' he said before they shoved him into the police car. All I yelled to him was, 'Hang in there. We'll figure something out.'"

It was bumper-to-bumper traffic once we approached the county jail. News helicopters buzzed like gigantic mutant wasps in the sky. We were just a few blocks away, and reporters and camera operators leaped out of their vehicles and raced down the streets past the stalled cars toward the Men's Central Jail.

"Guess Olisa must be here," I muttered as I motioned Gumbo to pull into one of the parking lots.

We never got inside the jail even though we tried every gimmick we could think of—too much of a madhouse. The police wouldn't let anyone outside the department inside. We finally reached Noel on his cell phone and learned that he hired an attorney, got in and out safely, and were already headed back by helicopter to the Santa Monica Mountains. We climbed back into Gumbo's car, relieved that the way out of downtown Los Angeles was much easier than the way in.

I was relieved we didn't have any road rage incidents as I watched two men jump out of their cars and square off after a collision that occurred when they tried to do a Lewis and Clark and find exits out of the traffic that didn't exist. I made Gumbo go over the story again as we drove up Sunset Boulevard on our way to the mountains.

At the house we found a sullen Olisa sitting on a chair in the living room. She was deep inside her head and not speaking to anyone. We walked around her, discussing the problem among ourselves as if she was part of the furniture.

"How ignorant can you be?" Noel whined as he stomped around the living room wringing his hands. "We definitely don't need this shit right now! I knew it. We shouldn't have let Ernesto join us. You can take the gangbanger off the streets, but you can't take the street out of the gangbanger. That's just the way it is!"

"Ernesto didn't do it," Olisa enounced in a somber tone.

"Then who did, Olisa? Who else had the motivation?"

"I don't know yet."

"Look, sis . . . I know you love Ernesto. Maybe with more time he could have changed. We threw him into the water, and he wasn't ready to swim—too much pressure. Ernesto got smacked, but it was Chato who lost it. You don't do that to a dude with his history. The old ways kicked in. He couldn't control himself, you know?"

Olisa's eyes remained glued to the floor, her hands clasped to her head.

"You can't hold his hand forever, Oli. On top of it all, it was *his* gun!"

"That doesn't mean he pulled the trigger, Noel." She embedded her fingers into her thick hair.

"All right. All right . . . Even if someone else did it, maybe one of his homies has a vendetta. Why are only his fingerprints on the gun?"

"I don't have an answer. I just know he's innocent."

"How do you know that, Olisa? Seriously."

"Because he told me he is!" She continued to anxiously run her fingers through her hair.

"Okay, got ya—innocent til proven guilty, right? Stop worrying. I'll take care of everything. Sheldon Silver, the 'ol' gray wolf is on this. He's one of the top criminal defense attorneys in town. If anybody can get this kid off, Shel can."

Olisa got up and walked away. Grace immediately shadowed her into her bedroom. She held the door open for me to join them and then closed it.

"Mom, I couldn't even touch him," Olisa conveyed as she sat on the bed and unconsciously stroked her cheekbone with her fingers. I stood by the door. Grace sat down on the bed with Olisa.

"All I could do was stare as he walked out there all macho, ferocious gangbanger back in his body. And I understand why. In jail, he had to be Chato again for his own protection. But when he saw me, he dropped his head and barely talked to me through the heavy-duty glass partition. It was awkward to ask: 'Ernesto, did you kill him?' All it took was a gaze from those brown orphan eyes, and I received my answer. No way he did it. He talked to me about being at the beach, smoking a joint, and falling asleep in the sand. The morning sun woke him up."

Grace rubbed her hand supportively.

"I tried to assure him that we would find a way to get him out. He didn't seem to care. He said the only thing that mattered to him was that I believed him."

Olisa stopped talking. She was in her head reflecting on her conversation with Ernesto. I felt like I should say something, but what could I say? I would only be talking to fill a void. The room stayed hushed until Olisa spoke again.

"Just before his time was up, he said to me, 'Olisa, this may not be so bad, ya know? I've done some really ignorant things in my life. I've hurt people, Olisa . . . badly. I don't know if I ever killed anyone, but whatever I did, I did to prove I was *Him*, the Man! You know? All that shit was ignorant. It clapped back on me. You entered my world and changed my life. Now, I don't think that way no more. I never paid for any of my past crimes, either, 'cept for spending some time at a juvenile detention center. Maybe this is payback time. Maybe I deserve to be in here, you feel me? How do they say it, 'It's all come back full circle'? Please don't worry about me; it's all good. They were gonna catch up with me sooner or later, ya know?'

"'Ernesto, you have changed,' I told him. 'And in the process, you've changed a multitude of lives in so many outstanding ways with the drive-by blessings and initiating the truce between the gangs. I love you, Ernesto, and I love what you've become. Ernesto is the one who's living. Chato died a long time ago.'"

"Yes, he did," Grace echoed.

"Right about then the guards came in and forcefully led him away. I thought he might freak . . . Instead, he smiled, seemingly completely at peace with himself. I'm the one who couldn't stop crying."

I didn't say it at the time, but to me, there was no doubt Pocock's signature was written all over the incident.

I must have been feeling sadomasochistic. Once again, I decided to listen to one of Reverend Pocock's weekly radio broadcast while driving to the Soul of Venice.

"How about it? You believe me now?" Pocock implored from the speaker. "Are you starting to see what I've been talking about? Uh-huh. All may not be what we perceived it to be. They say this witch gal can do miracles. Do you believe all the hype? Or are we victims of mass suggestion and the biggest scam in history? Has peer pressure lured us into thinking we've witnessed a miracle when one really didn't exist? Talk to me, people!"

"Kiss my ass, muthafucka!" I yelled at the radio.

"Don't we love it when a magician, or master illusionist they call 'em nowadays, works their magic on us with a sleight of hand? We love to be fooled. We love to pretend it's magic. Yet, we're aware if we are allowed to go backstage, we might find out how they did it. Doesn't that mean it wasn't truly magic but a well-crafted trick?"

This man is unbelievable, I thought, as I accidentally rolled over a curb to make a right turn. Thank goodness no one was standing on the corner.

"Get hardcore and ask yourself, friends: have I been duped by an elaborate hoax? Nick Cavaliere is one of the finest actors of our generation. When he rose from that wheelchair, everyone screamed and hollered, 'It's a miracle!' Did we ever wonder if this man just pulled off his greatest acting jobs? Is it possible he was cured months ago? Listen to me; I'm not saying that's the way it was, folks. I really don't know. It just seems to me that you've got to ask tougher questions. You can't just accept things at face value.

"What we do know is that this ruthless character known as Chato, Olisa's closest friend, was arrested for a brutal double murder. That's what we know. Maybe we need to find a way to get backstage at Olisa's camp and find out what other magic tricks they've got up their sleeves or back pockets."

I cancelled my doctor's appointment for later that afternoon. After listening to Pocock, I was sure my blood pressure soared sky high. I didn't want my doctor to see it, so I rescheduled it for the following week.

Although Pocock's voice rattled my eardrums, he was only a catalyst. The media partnered with him in what I termed the "crucifixion plot." Ever since Ernesto was arrested, the news hounds, particularly the right-wing and fundamentalist press, probed into our lives with a vengeance, particularly since we refused to talk and disclose any further information to the press. The arrest gave them the green light to go full blast after Olisa who, up to this point, was inviolable. The gates were open for any scandalous matter they could gather up. They were all competing to outdo each other. Can't say I really blame them. It wasn't exactly like we discouraged the initial publicity.

It's the price you pay for getting too damn famous. Time to put Olisa in her place. Some relished it, primarily because she never followed media protocol. The tabloids could give a shit; they made up their own headlines. One linked her to a recent mass cult suicide of two hundred people who believed that an alien vessel would restore them to life and they would all metamorphose into Gods in the afterlife. The connection to Olisa? One corpse was discovered clutching a magazine to her breast with Olisa's face on the cover.

Olisa met with whomever she wanted to and for however long she wanted to regardless of their status in the media hierarchy. It frustrated the hell out of Noel. He was acutely aware of how vicious the press could be if they felt they were being snubbed.

For example, Theo Balanis, considered one of the most respected investigative reporters in the nation, got only a thirty-minute interview with Olisa. He was constantly peeved whenever he saw local-street-reporter-turned-celebrity-anchor Eva Sanchez flashing that "stay bright" smile in her Olisa interviews. He'd been looking for an opportunity to skewer Olisa ever since. He recognized she was virtually untouchable in many people's eyes. After things began to unravel in her inner circle because of the Ernesto incident, he couldn't believe his luck, chiefly after receiving an anonymous phone tip while researching information for a feature article on corruption in the record business.

When I returned to Noel's office from the men's room, Noel paced back and forth in his office. I thought he was talking to himself until I saw him wearing a headset.

"La Tisha, why do I feel like I'm having such a hard time communicating with you? English is your native tongue, correct? . . . Yeah, I'm being a smart-ass. I'm too busy to put up with your shit! Something unexpected came up. I need to take care of it, got it? . . . No. You fucking calm down! I know we planned to go to the play for weeks. Get it through your head—it ain't happening tonight. I'll have Savannah send you an email scan of the tickets. Take a girlfriend, boyfriend, whoever. I don't give a shit! Later!"

He ripped off the headset and flipped it across the room. He clutched papers stiffly in his other hand as if he had rigor mortis. Noel stared at the fireplace in his office like he wanted to toss the papers in it. First, he'd have to light the logs. I don't think he wanted to bother with it. His face was so pale his skin looked discolored.

He shook the papers at me. "Dad, can you believe how these assholes are trying to fuck me after all I've done for them? What horseshit!"

"Son, that's why I rushed over here. I saw you made the news today for all the wrong reasons."

He gestured for me to sit down. His leather couch was so plush, it gratefully hugged me when I sat down. It was going to be difficult to stand back up.

"I'm the only representative for RPM who made the papers. Technically I don't even work there anymore as an employee!" he yelled at the ceiling. He threw the papers down on his mahogany desk that was about as wide as a landing strip. He eased back into his chocolate-brown leather recliner, laying his feet on the ottoman. He crossed his hands behind his head as he stared at the ceiling showcasing a dour expression.

"Yeah, I read the *Los Angeles Times* this morning and came across the five-page article by our friend, Theo Balanis, the first of a three-part series detailing corruption in the record business. And your picture is prominently displayed as one of the key suspects offering kickbacks to programmers encouraging them to add songs to the radio playlists."

"Dad, tell me something I don't know."

The way he looked at me, you would have thought *I* wrote it.

"Noel, I'm just worried for you. They're saying RPM and other record companies pay independent consultants like yourself millions of dollars to dangle money, audio equipment, prostitutes, luxury vehicles, exotic vacations, and leased houses to station personnel."

"Pops, the deal is that RPM records confessed to the existence of kickbacks in the company when they realized the criminal investigation was headed for their doorstep," he replied, averting my gaze.

"So you already knew about this."

"Oh yeah. Everyone associated with the industry knew about it. The investigation about payola scandals has been going on for a long time. I'm expecting a subpoena at my door any day now."

He stood up with his back to me. He distractedly traced his fingers along an elaborate wooden frame that housed a magnificent painting of Paul Robeson presiding on the wall.

"Noel, why didn't you say anything?"

He seemed irritated that I broke his concentration. For a second, it looked like he wanted to smash his fist through the painting. "Like what? RPM didn't sweat it because they appeared to be focused on the dinosaur companies, not the independents, that is until a tip was made to both the fraud section of the Justice Department and the criminal investigation unit of the Internal Revenue Service to expand the probe to independents like RPM Records. A partner of mine over there, Luther Simon, informed me they fully cooperated with the governmental investigation to avoid being smacked with a payola offense. That way, they might receive a more lenient sentence."

"This is unbelievable."

"Tell me about it. I'm sure you read that promotion chief Jalisa Miller paid a $100,000 fine and received two years' probation. Her brother Patrick Miller was fined $250,000 and also given a two-year probation for a tax violation related to bribery."

The whole thing confounded me. All I could do was shake my head. Noel's hands quivered as he lit up a cigar and slumped down in his chair.

"Luther says everyone in the Urban Music division is shittin', knowing executives are being convicted left and right. All they have to do is follow the money trail to the program director for each station. And that shouldn't be too difficult, considering the Millers rolled over on everybody to protect their own asses. Moreover, there's a ton of talk that it would never have happened if I hadn't exhibited such a high profile because of my sister."

"So they're pissed off at you."

"You got it, the one they begged to stay on as a consultant. You know how it is. They need a scapegoat, so I got branded with the label. Figured I can afford it."

"So what are you going to do now?"

"My attorney, Sheldon, told me to blow it off and concentrate on the concert. He told me it's going to take a long time before they actually get to me if they ever do. He suspects that the worst that can happen is I'll have to pay a fine and/or get a couple of years of probation."

"Hopefully it won't come to that."

"Hopefully. I did what they paid me to do, although I can cause a little grief to some of the folks there if I talk, as well. I really don't want to go there but will if it comes down to it."

After he said that, a half-smile manifested seeming to buttress his emotions. "But pushing all that aside, you know what's really a pisser? Knowing that Pocock's ass is behind this in some way."

"No doubt."

"That son of a bitch will do anything within his power to stop us from going to Washington. That's all right . . . I've got something for his ass." He literally cackled at the thought of it. "Just think—all eyes will be on Olisa. Our girl will be a goddess for modern times. And we can be proud because we helped to put her there."

I refrained from commenting; my insides were too queasy.

Noel slapped his hands on the desktop. Looking determined, he pushed himself up from his leather chair. "Let's get some breakfast, Pops!"

He nonchalantly grabbed his car keys and extended a hand to me. I was glad he did because his couch didn't want to let me go.

And that was that. Though his smile was a bit more strained, he seemed fine. I agreed with Noel on one issue. Pocock was pulling the strings on this. I was convinced even more after seeing his Grandpa Walton act on a *Fox News* interview. He, naturally, was horrified by the disturbing reports about fraudulence, bribery, the harlotry, and other evils emanating from the Olisa Timmerman camp.

Nevertheless, Pocock's mendacious statements and propaganda didn't bother me to the same degree anymore. Like someone wearing a KKK hood, his stance remained transparent and I never had to guess where he stood. More worrisome to me was my son never really refuting the reports leveled at him about his scandalous activities at RPM records. A day later, it was like he was almost apathetic to it, justifying it in conversation with, "Hey, I'm a promoter and I sell music. The public buys what they like if they hear it. If you've got to wax a few palms to get your consumers to play it, what's the big deal? This has been going on for decades. It is what it is."

"The big deal is it's against the law, Noel! You told me yourself it's only legal if you disclose the amount you paid to listeners."

"Yeah, but that's bull, Dad! The listeners could care less about all that. Our society's foundation is based on capitalism. Whoever has the most dollars wins. If I pay you more than someone else to get you to play my song, hey, get over it! That's what capitalism is all about in this land of free enterprise."

"It's illegal, Noel."

"So was Prohibition. Anyway, why are we even debating this? Thank goodness I've got more than enough money to fight this. Let's not worry about this any further. This ain't nothing. Besides, they may be paying *me* to drop the whole thing before it's over." The statement tickled him.

Power does corrupt. It may be an old cliché, but for me it was a fact. Noel's attitude about this scandal caused me many sleepless nights and many door-slamming arguments, mainly because I dared to question *whom* I should really fear.

I was half asleep when Beverly Fairchild, a former model-turned-activist, materialized as a talking head on my television screen. I used the sofa arms to push myself up from my slouched position. I glanced at my phone: 2:05 AM.

"If she were a man, would you have been as quick to judge her, Mr. Sorenson?" she asked with a perky flip of the hair.

I pressed the Info on the remote. It was the *Chase Sorenson Show*. I had never watched his half-hour program before, although I was fully aware of his politics. He was cloned from the same factory that produced the Walter Pococks and Biscuit Heads of the universe. Speaking of factories, the small homogenous studio audience, no matter what age, looked like they'd all been manufactured from the "Wonder Bread" industry.

"I don't think that would have anything to do with it," said another talking head, a jowly man who spoke as if he had a grapefruit stuck in his throat. He sat behind his talk show desk and tugged on his yellow bowtie.

"Sure it does," Beverly fired back from her chair to the side of his desk. "All of this has been blown out of proportion. Why should Olisa's character be tainted because some people around her have gotten into trouble? Ernesto Padilla has yet to go to court, and likewise, her brother is being investigated and nothing has been proven yet."

A sprinkling of boos and catcalls from the audience could be heard.

Sorenson sneered. "You forgot to mention her uncle Junior, that musician fella. He's been in rehab so many times, they ought to name an alcoholic beverage after him. Then there's that Indian gal, her best friend they say. I heard she's had her own battles with drugs and alcohol."

"You mean the same woman who was physically and sexually abused as a child?"

Sorenson rolled his eyes.

"The same woman who devoted her life to helping young women find direction and purpose in their lives? And you mention her uncle Junior who has performed free concerts to assist the homeless? That's the same person you just belittled. If you're going to tell a story, Mr. Sorenson, try telling it in its entirety."

"Hmmph . . . That's what you say. Come on now, Ms. Fairchild; you're not so naïve to believe that Olisa doesn't hold some responsibility for her group's actions. After all, they do work for her."

"Yeah!" someone shouted as the audience cheered.

Fairchild was oblivious to the hostile crowd. She was cognizant of what she was up against and prepared to do battle as she locked eyes with Sorenson. "Oh, so in other words, if a disgruntled employee marches through the office shooting employees, this is the supervisor's responsibility. Do you hear how ridiculous you sound? Moreover, both of the individuals you referred to dealt with those issues when they were much younger. Both have been sober for years."

"Ms. Fairchild, how can you ignore the criminal element encircling her?" Sorenson jiggled his newspaper at her.

"Conservative talk show hosts like you and your crony, Reverend Walter Pocock, have tried to rip her down ever since her rise to national prominence. You can't handle a beautiful and powerful African American woman making an impact on the world. You can't control her, and it drives you batty! The only way you and your constituents can empower yourselves is to discredit her and nail her to your manmade cross."

A loud barrage of boos greeted her.

Sorenson milked it with a dramatic pause before rising to his feet with righteous indignation. "That is utterly reprehensible, Ms. Fairchild! I'm appalled you'd stoop so low as to squeeze the race and gender card into this discussion. Why don't you top it off by addressing your lady saint as Jesus Christ while you're at it?"

The boo birds rose to their feet, screaming and yelling. Beverly Fairchild remained cool. She folded her hands with a grin and waited for Sorenson and his crowd to take their seats before she calmly asked, "Are you absolutely sure she's not, Mr. Sorenson? You can sneer all you'd like. Wouldn't it be interesting if the omnipresent God decided to come back as a Black woman to challenge people like you to look beyond gender and ethnicity? My question is, if it were true, would you still accept Jesus as your Savior?"

"I would if there were a kernel of truth to it. You're just being silly, Beverly!"

"You mean like all those people who continue to ban women from assuming an active role in church leadership, similar to the group you're affiliated with, Chase," Beverly replied facetiously.

"Incredible, just freakin' incredible," Sorenson grumbled, shaking his head and looking bemusedly at his devotees. "Everyone around this woman is being investigated for something, and yet people persist in following her."

Boos and hisses filtered the air again.

"I read a poll that stated 80 percent of Americans believe in miracles. In Olisa, people have discovered a breath of fresh air and a sense of hope. They are not going to give up on her that easy. We don't need more corrupt politicians, police officers, sports figures, or supposed men and women of God falling down on their knees and praying for forgiveness because of their sins. We need more Olisa Timmermans. To me, Olisa is the balm for healing a cynical society that has somehow lost its innocence."

"She's not Jesus Christ!"

"No one said she is. She doesn't have to be to spread the message of love and peace."

I turned off the tube. I didn't care to hear the response.

The night air was chilly and breezy. It felt good to me as I pulled my jacket tighter and sat on the patio bench to admire the full and radiant moon. It shed light on the patio like a night sun. I spotted a shadow leaning against the wall in the corner, studying the luminescent orb just as intently. He took notice of me and walked lightly my way. When the moonlight unveiled his presence, I was relieved to see Logan's handsome face. While I bunched my jacket to stay warm, he wore only a T-shirt. I felt old.

"I thought I was the only one who loved cold weather. I was going to drive home until I spied this effulgent moon. Beautiful, isn't it, Joe?"

"Yes, it is. I was going to write a little in my diary, but I got sidetracked."

"Pretty cool you keep a diary. So do I. Comes in handy during my travels."

"I bet."

"I can recollect camping out in the African veldt listening to the earth-shaking roar of lions contrasting with the silence of the moon. There was a natural symmetry to it all that was just awesome . . . Man, talk about a moon. You ever been to Africa?"

"No, I never have. I'd sure like to go one day."

"You'd love it. The night sky can be spectacular in various regions. Africa is imbued with this fascinating and ancient aura that encapsulates the entire continent. Yet, there is a dangerous edge that tops it all off. You owe it to yourself."

"I will, although I think I can forego the dangerous edge part. I've got that now."

"I hear you, boss," he chuckled.

We both gazed at the moon a little longer.

"The way you're grunting, you've either got a sore throat or more to say."

"Um, yeah, I do, Mr. Timmerman. You got a minute? I don't want to intrude."

"Must be important. Suddenly my secret identity as Mr. Timmerman is being called up. Wasn't but only a few minutes ago you and I were just Joe and Logan. Pull up a chair, man."

"Sorry. I'm a little nervous, that's why." He cleared his throat again. He grabbed one of the lawn chairs and scooted it next to me.

"Been there. Let's wing it. Tell me what's going on."

"Cool." He hesitantly sat down. "Joe, you know how I feel about Olisa."

"Let's say I've got an idea."

"I . . . I love your daughter. I really do."

"You don't have to convince me. Judging by the way you look at each other, that's not breaking news. Why does it seem like it is to you?"

He gave it some thought. "I'm sure Noel has already given you an essay on my background. My history with women . . ."

"It has been on broad blast a couple of times."

"I'm sure. I can't say I've been real successful at maintaining lasting relationships. The love of my life has always been a camera. The women in my life have been more like mistresses, then girlfriends. I never ever thought that would change until I met Olisa . . . and I'm speaking of the first time at my exhibition."

Me and the moon stayed motionless.

"The first time I saw Olisa at my show, it was over. I fell so hard, I'm still bouncing off the mat. I've shot thousands of images in my life, none more ravishing and arresting than her. If I'm being biased, I'm good with that. When it comes to Olisa, objectivity was thrown out the proverbial window a long time ago. I feel kind of weird telling you, her father, all this . . . I just wanted you to know."

"I don't mind. I like hearing good things about my daughter."

"Mr. Tim—uh, Joe . . . I'm going to straddle a cliché, but I truly feel Olisa and I are meant to be, like, soulmates. Am I being too corny?"

"Remind me to tell you about Grace and me one day."

"Good. I'd love to hear about it. Your family is great. I sometimes envy the bond you guys have for each other."

"Thank you . . . But like any couple, we're not perfect. We have our ups and downs."

"Yeah, but it looks like you manage to work them out."

"We do our best."

"That's something you can't take for granted. I never had that. My family is originally from Jamaica. My father was a hustler and a primetime womanizer. They moved to New York the year I was born. He disappeared when I was around three years old. We didn't see him again for another year. He claimed he'd been working wherever he could, though we never saw a dime."

Logan chuckled, even though his face was impassive.

"Those early years, I remember us spending most of our lives like fugitives, moving from city to city. My mother professed she was trying to find better jobs. The reality was she was running away from him. The perfect job for him would have been as a private investigator. He always seemed to find us whenever he wanted to. I was twelve years old when he was fatally shot by the police in an armed robbery attempt at a liquor store."

"I'm so sorry . . ."

"Not me," he replied curtly, nearly stepping on my words. "I was scared to death of him. If the cops hadn't killed him, I would have." He drew in a deep breath. "He used to beat the hell out of my mother. I've wrestled with that guilt ever since." He scratched behind his ear as his mouth twisted into a wry grin. He suddenly rubbed his lips with his fingers, and the grin disappeared. "My mother raised me in the best way she could, but it wasn't easy. Eventually, she settled down and married a really good man, but me—I got the running genes. I was always dreaming in school, wishing I could escape to all these faraway and exotic places I saw in the pages of encyclopedias. Man, I spent so much time in detention in high school, they should have created a nameplate for me."

This time a real smile evolved from his lips.

"So after all that, how the hell did you end up in photography?" I inquired.

"Luckily, this one art teacher saw something in me no one else did. She became my mentor. She delighted in how much I loved pictures and turned me on to photography. Man, that did it for me. It opened up a whole new and exciting universe. I was so into it, I even finished high school. Photography helped make sense of the world for me. I guess that's why I have this thing about abuse in my work. It took me to all those places inside of me I only dreamed about. Photography was the only thing I felt I had a grip on and the only thing I trusted to never fail me. I loved women, except I couldn't even spell commitment, let alone act upon it. There was too much world to see out there. Then I met Olisa, and all I wanted to do was share the world with her."

"Logan, you don't have to seek my approval, if that what's up. I'm there. I think it's great how you feel, but shouldn't you be discussing this with Olisa?"

"I have. However, I took a longer route than intended to get to something Olisa insisted I speak with you about, something that's come up."

Things got quiet. I waited.

He rubbed his hands and gazed at the moon as if he were waiting for a cue card to come to his rescue. He took a deep breath and exhaled. His gaze shifted to me. "There's this woman who had been kind of showing up lately wherever I've been shooting. I'd see her at the concerts and in the malls at Santa Monica Place. Quite honestly, I couldn't help but notice her. She's real attractive and always smiled at me," he commented, his face pinched, like it was painful. "And always alone. One day she finally approached me and struck up a conversation, said her name was Barbara Redding and she was an aspiring photographer. She mentioned she knew all about my work and attended all my shows. I never recalled seeing her at any of them. A standout presence like her I wouldn't have missed if she was present at all my showcases. Even so, she claimed familiarity with all my works and even rattled off pieces I did, plus titles. I'd be lying if I didn't admit I was impressed and flattered."

"Of course. Sound to me, though, the underlying thing here is she had a thing for you."

"That's what I discovered later."

"What about you?"

"No. It was a hell of a test, but I resisted the temptation. I did talk to her. It was just shop on my part. I swear to you on my mother's soul—nothing happened, sir. Sure, I get lonely sometimes sharing Olisa with the world, but I came to grips with that. I love her way too much to do *stupid*, you know?"

"I believe you. And?"

He rubbed his hands on his knees. "Well, I did something close to stupid. I was alone at a bar downtown when she magically appeared. So I had a drink with her. Now you're looking at me funny . . . I swear that's all it was going to be. She knew where I stood with Olisa. Olisa means the world to me."

"Uh, huh. You already made that clear." The look I gave him inferred, *Whatever you say next will determine the extent of our relationship.*

No comment was immediately forthcoming.

"Okay . . . Well, we were just talking films, and then unexpectedly, before I had time to react, she flung her arms around me and kissed me hard. I damn near fell off the barstool. When I shoved her away, she slapped me hard in the face and stormed off, making sure to yell loud enough for everyone in or outside the bar to hear, 'I'm tired of you treating me like I'm your personal whore!'"

I closed my eyes for a few short seconds.

"Simultaneously, I saw a guy concealing his camera follow right behind her out the door. I thought I was gonna die. I chased after them. By the time I reached the streets, a red Porsche screeched around the corner."

"They got you."

"Yes, sir. Got me good."

"So we can expect to look forward to seeing you on some front pages."

"Guaranteed."

"Uh-huh."

"Joe, I'm so sorry for the additional flare-up of grief headed toward Olisa and your family in the saga of Olisa's journey. I didn't expect everything to get this convoluted. I accept the blame for—"

"Stop. Welcome to my world, Lo. My only question is, did Olisa believe you when you told her the story?"

"Yes."

"Then so do I."

He heaved an uneasy sigh of relief. "She told me to talk to you and you'd understand."

"I do . . . although I'll expect you to make better decisions in the future."

He hung his head and muttered, "Definitely."

"By the way, was Olisa okay with it all?"

"Ha, a little too okay. She could have shown a hint of jealousy."

I laughed. "Olisa doesn't do jealousy well. Too forgiving."

"No kidding," he grinned. "Joe, I know I shouldn't ask, but would you mind . . . ?"

"Bringing everyone up to date about your screw-up? No, I don't mind."

"Thanks. And Noel too? You know him and I don't . . ."

"No worries. I'll take care of it."

He looked like he still wanted to crawl inside a deep hole.

"*So* stupid! I love Olisa. It would kill me to lose her. You do believe me, right?"

"Son, you wouldn't have moved past the woman was 'really attractive' if I didn't believe you. Now, tell me more about those gorgeous African skies . . ."

Damn! Tabloid magazines don't waste time. Within a couple of days, *Idol Gossip Central* magazine featured Logan's picture on its front cover along with Olisa's photo pasted in the upper corner shedding tears. The picture was unrelated to the tabloid story. She was crying because of her joy after healing an individual. They made it seem like she was torn up about Logan betraying her. The magazine was available in every newsstand and grocery store across the country, including England and other countries. They set Logan up like a tea party.

The following day, in a different magazine the headline read, "Psychic Holy Woman and Healer, Olisa Timmerman, Should Have Seen It Coming!" In the foreground, the picture portrayed a distraught woman whose face was partially buried in her hands rushing out of the bar. In the background, a stunned Logan held the side of his face. Under the photograph was the caption: "A Lover's Quarrel! Mystery Girl-on-the-Side of Celebrated Photographer, Logan Matthews Breaks Down Crying 'I'm tired of being treated like your personal whore!'"

In all of the planted compromising photos strewn throughout the magazine, remarkably, the woman's face was never clearly shown. I speculated she was a high-class call girl who got paid very well to do her big-time performance job on Logan. The story captions accompanying each picture read like trashy romance novels. They made up stories wherever they deemed necessary. In order to be in all the places they claim he was rendezvousing with her, he had to have been able to split in two like an amoeba. Didn't matter to them; getting millions of readers was the objective. It was evident to me that many of the shots were gleaned from some of Olisa's concerts and then graphically treated through the computer to look like he was somewhere else. By always standing close to him, she made it easy for a photographer lying in wait to snap shots of them talking. They were then scanned into the computer to produce "graphic whoopee."

Surprisingly, Noel handled it fairly well. Naturally, his first response was the requisite, "I'm gonna beat his ass!" After cooling off, he agreed with the rest of us it smelled like a well-planned setup. He was more disgruntled that Logan didn't immediately recognize that anyone closely associated with Olisa was a prime target and potential weapon to be utilized by her adversaries to discredit the movement. It didn't take long for him to move on from the issue. He was much too occupied and ensconced with promoting the final Universal Healing Concert in Washington to waste energy on another scandal, particularly in the process of dealing with his own.

Chapter 14

Two weeks remained before the big event. Grace and I planned to stay another night at Olisa's mountain retreat before returning home to Venice. As the concert neared, we were eager to spend more quality family time with Olisa. She needed us to be around, and likewise, we needed to be near her. It had been almost a month since we had been home. Security people were posted at the house and around the walk street, but Grace was still anxious to get back and check everything out.

That evening, Grace went into Olisa's bedroom to assess how she was feeling. She complained earlier about suffering from a severe headache. About a second after entering Olisa's room, Grace screamed out my name. I sped into the bedroom. Olisa was violently thrashing around in her bed, amazingly still asleep but eyes opened wide and stricken with terror.

"Joseph, help me!" Grace cried out as she struggled to restrain her, but it was futile. Olisa's arms flailed about like a broken helicopter blade. At last, we subdued her. Her head continued to swing from side to side. Abruptly, her body went still. She awakened, but her eyes darted wildly, looking disoriented.

"Honey, you all right?" Grace brushed her hair back and wiped her damp forehead. "My God, you're burning up, girl! Joseph . . ." She placed my hand on her forehead. "See how hot she is? Please dampen one of the wash towels and give it to me. Hurry! She feels like she's got a fever."

By the time I returned with a cold washcloth, Olisa's eyes were more lucid.

"How's my girl? Looked like you were auditioning in your sleep for a martial arts film."

"Daddy . . ." she smiled faintly.

"The dreams again, Olisa?" Grace asked, her face taut. She dabbed her face tenderly with the cloth. Olisa pressed Grace's hand to her face.

"We were sitting in front of the fireplace, and Daddy fed a log into the fire when it exploded into flames. The sparks leaped onto the curtains, and before I could do anything about it, the entire house was an inferno. I ran outside, but the flames beat me, jumping onto my clothes, my hair. I felt the intense hotness even though it was only a dream."

"Okay, honey, don't talk about it anymore. It's causing you to perspire again. Let me get you some different clothes; you're soaked."

I continued to wipe Olisa's face and neck.

"The dreams have been coming at me nightly, Daddy. Tonight was the worst. The minute I shut my eyes, they start up again. What's it all mean? Some kind of omen?"

"I don't know, sweetness. You either missed your calling as a fireman, or you're under too much stress."

She squeezed my hand and held it until Grace returned with a change of clothes.

Olisa's phobia about fire was nothing new. She had been dealing with it since childhood. Nothing else frightened her: snakes, spiders, heights, enclosed spaces—nothing. The first time I noticed her fire phobia was when she was around four. One morning she pranced into the kitchen naked waiting for Grace to find her some clothes. I accidentally left the burner on after cooking bacon. A small grease fire erupted like a geyser in the pan. Man, you'd have thought it was raining fire and brimstone the way she bolted out of the kitchen!

At first I cracked up because the flames died out immediately. Olisa wasn't around to see it. I peeped out the kitchen curtains and saw her running down the street butt naked and howling at the top of her miniature lungs! I had to chase after her for almost two blocks, pajamas and robe flying behind me before I caught up to her. She was in absolute hysterics and wrestled to get free. She wanted to run some more. People gaped at me like, *What in the world did you do to that poor child to make her act like that?*

It took some time for me to coax her to come back inside the house. I think everyone has a boogeyman they fear in life. Hers was fire. Lighting a match too closely when she was a child was traumatic for her. During Halloween, the carved-out and candlelit pumpkins grinning savagely with their glowing teeth unnerved her. A counselor assured us she would outgrow this paranoia. She did to a certain extent. Nonetheless, fire dreams tormented Olisa every so often and became like an Achilles heel to her.

Mama Willis theorized that the ghost of her late husband Reverend Willis, who perished tragically in a church fire, was trying to communicate with her. She constantly chatted in Olisa's ears telling her to look for the hidden message beyond the fiery nightmares. I had my own theory. I think she had an aversion to fire because she was born in the midst of the Los Angeles Riots.

The phone jolted me out of my reverie. As I picked up the receiver, Olisa sat up rigidly in bed intently watching me. The expectation in her eyes made me nervous.

It was my mother-in-law, Katherine Willis, sounding completely distressed. I could barely make out what she was saying.

"Slow down, Katherine. I can't understand you!"

"Joseph? Is that you? Praise God!" Hysteria erupted again. "Where's Grace? Is she there? Tell me she's with you, Joseph. Please don't tell me she's in that house!"

"Katherine, Katherine . . . calm down. She's right here with me and Olisa."

"Thank you. Thank you, Lord . . . Noel too?"

"Noel's at his office. I talked with him only an hour ago. What's going on? You're scaring me. What are you saying about a house?"

In the background I heard Papa Willis yelling, "They all right, Kath? Goddamn it! Tell me something, shit! Ask him where's the kids!"

"They're fine, Harold," she yelled off the line. "Thank you, Jesus. Let me talk to Grace. I want to hear her voice."

Grace had already grabbed the phone. "Mama, what is wrong? Joseph told you I'm fine . . . We're all fine . . . No, I don't know anything." Grace's eyes ballooned, and she gesticulated at the television.

I fumbled with the remote control. Emerging from the black screen appeared an aerial shot of a house swarmed by angry flames. Firemen ran around frantically battling the flames, trying to contain them and prevent them from spreading to the other homes on the walk street. It looked like they pretty much had it under control. Thus far, it was only one house on the walk street consumed in flames . . .

Our house!

The remote dropped out of my hands as Grace gasped. The camera panned the gathering crowd. I recognized many of the faces. There was Fred and Nancy Schafer, talking to Wesley Guillory. Behind them were Cedrick and David, shaking their heads, faces contorted in disbelief watching our house burn. A newscaster said something about a pipe bomb detonating as I snatched my car keys. Everything's kind of fuzzy after that.

The next day we had no choice in sharing our plight with the whole world. A battalion of cameras observed Grace and I sifting through the smoldering ashes of our house for salvageable belongings. Reporters shouted from behind the ropes protecting our privacy, begging us to say a few words. Overall, the firefighters did the best they could do. Olisa's stand-alone studio building, where we later found out the explosion started, was completely burned to the ground. The exterior of our main house was still fairly intact. The interior damage was irreplaceable. A surreal sheen lay in the hazy air as ashes floated above ground. I discovered a pair of dress shoes I'd never taken out of their box, untouched in what used to be my closet. My eyes stung torturously accenting our reality.

At least family was there. The Willises, Peter, and Laura sorted through the rubble for valuables. Thieves had picked off what they could earlier. Gumbo grimly interrogated the security officers assigned last night and the police chief who informed us as to what steps the department intended to take regarding this vile deed. Wilma supplied food to make sure we all ate something. A solemn Noel fielded calls on his phone as he traipsed through the damage.

Olisa tearfully pleaded to come with us. No way. I didn't care how persistent she was. Logan stayed with her. He told me later it turned into quite a wrestling match, but he prevailed. With her there, it would have become more of a circus than it already was—too dangerous. That was verified when the police lieutenant handed us a note left in our still-standing metal mailbox at the front gate. It was written in bold cryptic letters:

TO THE PARENTS OF OLISA TIMMERMAN – THE NIGGER WITCH. IF YOU CAN'T READ THIS LETTER, THEN SMELL IT. THIS IS YOUR FIRST AND FINAL WARNING, NIGGERS AND NIGGER LOVERS. NO ONE GOT HURT THIS TIME. WE CAN'T BE RESPONSIBLE FOR WHOSE BLACK ASS GETS BLOWN AWAY NEXT TIME! FOLLOW THIS ADVICE – DO NOT GO TO WASHINGTON! KEEP YOUR FRIED CHICKEN, WATERMELLON EATING BUTTS AT HOME AND EVERYTHING WILL BE FINE. IF YOU GO TO WASHINGTON, THE TRUE MESSENGERS OF GOD WILL SEND THAT COCKSUCKING BLACK BITCH

TO HER ETERNAL REST IN PICKANINNY HELL! ALL THE REST OF YOU FAT LIPPED DARKIES WILL BE RIGHT BEHIND HER IF YOU FUCK WITH US! THERE IS ONLY ONE GOD AND HE IS THE WHITE LIGHT! NOT A GODDAMN INK SPOT. HAIL TO THE TRUE AND FAITHFULL MESSENGERS OF GOD!!!!

Anger seared my insides. I wanted to rip the letter to shreds and raise hell with all those ignorant, demented, and unconscionable idiots out there staring at our tragedy like it was some bizarre form of theater. I wanted to call out the coward who I'm positive was in the audience, watching and grinning, and I wasn't going to stop until he or she materialized. That was what I wished I could do. Instead, I simply handed the letter back to the police lieutenant because it was evidence they wanted to examine further. They assured me they would not only give it a thorough looking over but the FBI would also be contacted. As it turned out, they were already there on the scene.

This wasn't the first death threat we received; there were countless. They started coming almost instantly after Nick Cavaliere was healed by Olisa. They were as common as the junk mail we received labeled "Resident." Be that as it may, this was the first time someone succeeded in committing a domestic terrorist act upon us. Gumbo and his crew actually prevented numerous terrorist activity against Olisa and family from occurring. He refused to tell me how many and what types of methods they had contained and prevented from happening, although he did indicate there had been many. Even more of a downer was we had no idea who planted the bomb. Like I told the police and FBI many times over, 'Investigate Pocock and company.' My gut and just pure logic and common sense told me Pocock had everything to do with it. And the problem, again, was, no proof! Though he acted like a virulent strain of the late Rush Limbaugh in his public tirades, he had no visible history traceable of violent acts despite all his mouthing off. His dog whispers were enough to incite his sycophants to mobilize and take action on his abominable behalf.

My gaze fell on Grace, alone, sitting on the charred divan, unmindful of the crocodile snapping photographers pressing against the ropes. I huddled beside her, shielding her from their penetrating stares like a veil. She shocked me with a smile so warm that it lulled me into her aura of intimacy. We were alone in our living room one more time. An entire stack of photo albums stuffed inside a footlocker had been preserved. Giddy laughter sprang forth as we perused the photos that became one of our most valued possessions on earth. Soon family and some close friends who arrived to help out surrounded us as we passed the books around, all of us caught up in this lunacy.

"Look at this," Grace held up a sepia-toned photograph, "Ironically, Grandfather Willis managed to survive this fire."

Papa Willis, his eyes moistening, looked over Grace's shoulder. "Ain't that something?"

There he was, the Reverend Odis Willis, dressed to the nines, arm in arm with his pretty young bride, Sharlisa, displaying a smile a yard wide. They proudly stood in front of their new church, ready to tackle an unknown frontier they believed was filled with promise. I held Grace closer to me as warm tears rolled down my cheeks. In that blurred moment, I was so grateful to have my family and friends around to love. Damn the material things; they were replaceable—not so with family.

Nick Cavaliere phoned me a day later. His voice was choked with guilt. "Joseph, I . . . I . . . I don't know what to say to you . . . I am so very sorry about what went down. I truly wanted to be there with you guys . . . I . . ."

"Nick, stop acting like you set the time bomb. I know that, if you had showed up, it would have been a zillion times crazier than it already was."

"That's what Lena told me. Still, I'm broken up about this . . . I feel so bad."

"Stop! If it wasn't for you, we wouldn't be sitting in this house in the mountains right now, either."

"I guess, but if it wasn't for me, you might not be in this predicament, either."

"And if it hadn't been you, I guarantee you it would have been someone else," I stated tersely. "Man, you're starting to sound like an insecure actor."

"Can't help it. It's in my blood." His mood finally lifted.

"No. It was the last movie piece of shit you did before the accident. Makes me think you faked the whole thing so you *could* go into hiding."

This time I heard that full-throated signature laugh. "Okay, you found me out. Just don't mention it to Theo Balanis."

"Depends on how much he's willing to shell out."

"I should have known from the first time I met you, you were only in it for the money."

"Now you know my secret!"

We both laughed.

"Joe, can I be frank with you for a minute?"

"You can be Ted, Shirley, or Zachariah if you want. I know how you actors like to change their names."

"Seriously, Joe."

"All right. I was on a roll . . . Go ahead."

It seemed like forever before he spoke again. "You can't let her go to Washington, Joe. You just can't."

That caught me off guard. What was I supposed to say?

"Are you listening? I'm afraid for her, for you and Grace, and for your family. No matter what they tell you, no matter how much security you have been promised, they can't protect her. Look what just happened."

"It's different now, Nick. We've got the big guns in on this."

"So did Kennedy. So did King. So did Sadat. So did Indira Gandhi . . ."

"Uh-huh." I knew Nick was looking out for us, but I was getting irritated. I didn't need the added pressure.

"Screw the concert, man! Please forgive me for saying this, but there are motherfucking bastards out there who don't give two pennies about offing your daughter. They'll approach it with a sense of duty and kill her for the Glory of God!"

"You don't think I know that, Nick? You don't think that shit fucks with my head every goddamn day?! You tell me: how the hell am I going to stop her? Her mind is made up. She's more determined now than before. The fire pissed her off. She refuses to let a bunch of assholes prevent her from doing the work she feels destined to do."

"There's more than just a bunch of assholes out there."

"You're preaching to the choir, Nick. Olisa is a grown woman who makes grown-up decisions. You know I'm sorry, too. Let me ask you: what's with all this sudden concern about her going to Washington? Huh?"

"When all is said and done, no matter how big the event is, the world has proven it is not ready for Olisa. Why sacrifice her to the wolves for nothing?"

"Yeah? Well, you didn't mind, huh, Nick? And now that you're healed, fuck everybody else! Is that the mentality you're talking about?"

Nick's voice barely rose above a whisper. "You're right. I am a perfect example of how fucked-up and selfish a person can be. That's why I'm reiterating: don't let her do it! She will not be truly appreciated. In the end, it's human nature; we're all in it for ourselves. Some people profess a belief in God out of fear Hell might actually exist. We want to make sure we cover all our bases. The *only* shining soul among us is Olisa."

I felt like the biggest jerk for what I had said to Nick. Even so, I couldn't stop. "Nick, do you realize what this is doing to me and Grace? I doubt it. How could you?" I felt the veins sticking out of my neck. They always do when I'm screaming.

"You're right, my friend. I cannot possibly know how you feel in such unusual circumstances. The only reference I have are my three grown-up children. I know how *I'd* feel if it was one of them possessed the gift. I'd do anything I could to stop them."

"You'd have to kidnap Olisa."

"I'm willing to do that if you are."

Did he have shit for brains? The man was dead serious. I sat there holding the phone, speechless and growing increasingly tired.

"Joseph, I've had a long and prosperous career. During that time I've been lucky to have worked with a very loyal and remarkable film crew that has been with me throughout the majority of my career. They trust me, and I trust them with my life."

Why we segued into the "Lifetime Achievement Awards" I had no idea.

"Some of these guys I worked with, particularly in my action films, are absolute geniuses, hands down the best in the business regarding special effects."

"That's great."

"They are great," he pressed on, ignoring my indifference. "Consummate professionals. Man, these guys can do anything. If you asked them to drop an elephant on my head and make it believable, they could do so without me getting a scratch. It's all about trust. Any stunt can be inherently dangerous. I rarely used a stunt double because I trusted them. That's why people believed it when I walked out of a burning airplane that crashed. It's because I really did, thanks to their well-conceived acts of wonder."

"I see."

"Do you? Mark Baylor, who is head of those special production units, is a very close friend of mine. I can call him any day or hour, and he'd be at my door. He's willing to work independently if necessary, strictly as a favor to me."

"That's pretty cool."

"Yeah."

The silence on the line was excruciating.

"Listen, Nick. I've got a call on the other line. I better answer it. Probably the FBI. They still have questions for me."

"I understand. Do what you have to do. Again, in the meantime, please let me know if there is anything I can do. If so, don't wait too long, okay? Call me."

"Oh yeah, for sure. I'll be in contact. Give Lena a kiss for me."

I quickly clicked off the call. I was hyperventilating. Just then, Grace walked into the living room from the kitchen. I guess the expression on my face betrayed me.

"Joseph, are you all right? You look like you're having a stroke or something."

"Me? Nah, I'm good. I drank some water. It went down the wrong way."

She looked at the full glass of water on the coffee table that looked untouched. I braced for her to say something, but surprisingly, she didn't call me on it. "I'm going to check back on the food I've got on the stove. Sure you're okay?"

"Yes," I lied, again, as she reticently returned to the kitchen.

I didn't know why Nick freaked me out so much in that conversation. He was a good dude. All he was trying to do was offer his help, and I acted like a jerk. My nerves were just frayed. I told myself I'd call him after all this was over and apologize. *It's just stress.* The household was frazzled after the fire episode. Our entire family had been targeted, and the pressure that came with it had us all snapping at each other. Furthermore, the tension was substantially heightened with our upcoming event in DC.

As I sat in the living room, alone, waiting for dinner, my brain started randomly associating. I thought about an interview I recently saw on television conducted by a young brother named Jason Collier. His local program was called *Meet the People*. The program entailed him traveling around Los Angeles County each week and hooking up with interesting people and cultures to interview on a variety of topics ranging from drugs to knitting quilts. This week his topic revolved around Olisa and the upcoming Washington event. The interviews were held on the Venice Boardwalk.

Collier, with his hair in intricately designed cornrows, wore a dark-gray Nike warmup. He stood poised with his microphone next to a short, stocky Black man wearing a tank top and shorts. Despite being on camera, the man seemed distracted as his eyes darted around with all the goings on at the beach.

"Hey, everybody, I'm Jason Collier, and I'm here with Dimitri Quarles. Dimitri was recently released from Soledad Prison. What they lock you up for, brotha?"

"I was, uh, incarcerated for carjacking and armed robbery."

"Then you must be happy to be outside with us here on this nice sunny day at Venice Beach."

"Fo sure, Mr. Collie." He lasciviously eyed a voluptuous girl skating by.

"Uh, Collier."

"Exactly, Mr. Collie," Dimitri said, clapping his hands enthusiastically. "I just want you to know, Mr. Collie, that I'm happy to be on your show."

"We're pleased to have you," Jason remarked, scratching his head. "Listen. We're not formal out here; why don't you just call me, Jason?"

"All right, Jace," he replied, clapping the very slender man a little too hard on the back, causing him to bobble his microphone.

"Cool. Okay, so moving on. It's my understanding you've met Olisa Timmerman before?"

"Yeah, yeah, that's right."

"So are you going to be in Washington for the Universal Healing Concert?"

"Hell, yeah! I would love to participate and support the sista if I can find a way to get there. Ya know what I'm sayin'?"

"Yes. So, Dimitri, what can you tell us about your experience with Olisa? Dimitri?"

Dimitri was busy wrestling his eyes away from a couple of female body builders that passed by. "Okay, um, yeah . . . I've never met anyone like her before in my life."

"You are talking about Olisa, correct?"

Dimitri looked at him like he was crazy. "Of course, man! The holy woman? Yeah, I used to know her back in the day. Well, let me explain. I didn't really know her. I just used to see her hanging out in the Venice hood. She was always involved in all these good-works programs. You know charities, that kind of good shit.

"And let me tell you something, all that shit they say about her, it's true. I seen it for myself. She did all that healing stuff back then. It just wasn't all over the news like it is nowadays, like what you do. Everybody in the hood knew she was different. None of my homies fucked with her. She was always nice, but like Cameo sings, 'She's strange . . .'"

"You mind elaborating on that a little?"

"Huh?"

"Explain it to us."

"Oh, okay. Got ya. You know all that stuff they been talking about on July the Fourth?

That ain't nothing. I saw her take on Pookie Reeves."

"Who is Pookie Reeves?"

Dimitri eyed Jason like, "How could you not know that?"

"PR was the baddest muthafucka—oops, can I say that? That's right; this is like cable! Anyway, muthafucka controlled all the shit going down on the Westside. You could travel one hundred miles away, all you had to say was that you know Pookie and you were covered; deal that? Nobody messed with my boy, Pookie, except for Olisa. You lookin' at me all funny. Okay, then check this."

Dimitri started gesturing with his hands like he was in a hip-hop groove. The music we could faintly hear in the background on account of being near the rollerblading area must have influenced him.

"Some of Pookie's boys were thumping on this dude who was trying to get by without paying his respects. Boy didn't have no money, so they had his ass surrounded. I remember thinkin' they was about to turn him into a punching bag until I sees this skinny-ass chick with wild flying hair come walking up and stepped in front of dude."

Jason pointed to a spot on the boardwalk. "Well, I'm not surprised because she proved that right over there."

"Oh yeah? They were even talking about that in the joint. So she gets all up in Pookie's face starts talking all this crazy shit. You hear me? In Pookie's face, bro! Righteously dressing his ass down, preaching the shit to him like no minister I've ever seen. All this mess about him not respecting himself or the neighborhood, or God. It ain't like Pookie never had no one preach to him before, but not with their finger all in his face like she did. I was like, whoa, man! What the fuck is he gonna do to her? I got scared."

"That is incredible."

"Fo sho. The whole neighborhood started gathering around them. I'm thinking if she had a chance to walk away she done fucked up. Now it's gonna be all about his manhood in front of everybody. Even dude who was about to get jumped was trying to restrain her, but she wasn't going for it. I'm like, oh shit! Oh shit, cuz Pookie is an equal opportunity muthafucka! He'll slap a bitch down and try to fuck her in broad daylight. Muthafucka didn't have no conscious.

"'Cept, he fucked me up on this one. She said her piece to him and turned her back on him and walked away. Pookie didn't do didley-squat! Ya know what I'm sayin'? He walked away, too. Nobody said shit to him about it, 'cept for me. He kind of respected me. Still, I had to be careful what I said, too, depending on his moods. When I caught up to him, I was hoping he wouldn't try to take his shit out on me."

"So what did you say?"

"I says to him, 'Hey, Pookie, why you let her get away with that? Was her shit that good?' He turned very slowly toward me. I got real scared, not because I thought we were gonna be tusslin'; I got scared cuz I saw something in his eyes I'd never seen before. Fear! The muthafucka looked like he'd seen a ghost. He says, 'Yeah, she talked some good trash, but that ain't why I didn't do nuthin'. Did you see that big Black muthafucka floating behind her? That's why I didn't do nuthin.' And PR stares at me real hard. Then he looks around all crazed and shit like he's worried about somebody following him. I'm looking at him like maybe this is a joke, but I can see he's as serious as a

James Brown perm. So I says my goodbyes, and I take my ass on out of there. I ain't gonna question his sanity because I value my life."

"What a trip, man," Jason said to the camera. "So what happened to Pookie Reeves?"

"Never saw Pookie again after that. Last thing I heard is he moved out to West Covina. Tell you the truth—I don't even know if he's around anymore. Somebody told me they found him in the streets with a knife sticking out of his back cuz he owed money to some dealer. Cold world, ain't it?"

"Yes, it is," Jason solemnly agreed. He gave Dimitri a brotherly handshake and winced a little because Dimitri obviously had a strong grip. "Dimitri, I hope to see you in Washington."

While the theme for the show played and before they could turn off the audio, Dimitri yelled, "Hey, Mr. Collie, you know any way I can hitch a ride to DC?"

To say tensions were festering a week before the grand event was the greatest understatement of the year. A slamming door validated this as Olisa tore past us, her face hidden.

"What in the world!" Grace exclaimed.

Olisa whistled for Free, and I saw them treading up the crest of the hill, followed by a couple of bodyguards despite Olisa angrily waving them away.

The front door opened as Peter and Logan walked in with hangdog expressions.

"Anybody care to let us in on what the hell is going on?" I inquired looking from one to the other.

Neither seemed particularly anxious to begin. Peter reluctantly spoke.

"I guess I'm partly to blame for the whole thing."

"Pete, it's not your fault. You thought she already knew. This was the first time I heard about Noel's deal."

"Logan, what was Noel's deal?" I was afraid to hear the answer.

Logan smirked, glancing at Peter. "This one's on me, Mr. T. Usually, I don't discuss general business matters with Olisa, per her request and Noel's.

She doesn't need to be bothered with extraneous day-to-day details unless it involves something that directly impacts her personally. Having said that, I assumed it was important enough for Noel to confirm with her before greenlighting it."

Folding my arms, my eyes widened.

"This morning I innocently asked Olisa which colors she preferred I use to complete her online shopping site."

Grace's eyes narrowed. "*What* online shopping site?"

"Uh, oh . . . the look you and Joseph are giving me says you guys don't know."

Logan lowered the lid on his cap and shook his head. "Okay, here we go . . . Ever since Olisa announced this would be her last event, Noel decided to plan a major launch of Olisa's Universal Healing products to coincide with the concert."

Peter winced seeing our reaction.

"He *what*?" Grace and I asked in unison.

"Greeting cards, posters, cosmetics, soaps, protein powders, tableware, and other related gift items—it's a long list." Peter took a deep breath and exhaled before adding, "His slogan is, 'All designed to bring out the Goddess in you.'"

"Oh, no," Grace groaned, bowing her head.

"That was Olisa's reaction, multiplied by ten," Logan asserted. "Let's just say she ain't real happy about it."

"I don't believe Noel. He didn't talk or consult with anyone?" I could barely talk I was so angry.

"No, Joseph," Peter corrected. "He did consult with people, major companies and suits."

"He just didn't consult with us," Logan added as he peered out the front window. He spotted Olisa in the distance standing on top of the hill with Free. "I'll be back." Logan hurriedly walked out the open front door.

"Anyway, Olisa asked me to drive her to Malibu so she could be a part of the pre-tour."

"Pre-tour?"

Peter self-consciously rubbed his chin. "Yes. Ever since the OLISA, Inc. building has been completed, Noel decided to give a pre-tour to some of the big executives before it officially opens in two weeks. He somehow failed to mention it to Olisa, but I did."

"My son, what a guy!"

"Joseph, don't," Grace chided. "And thank you, Peter."

"My pleasure. Noel wasn't real happy about it, seeing Olisa standing next to me in the lobby while conducting his tour. He played it off, but you should have seen the look he gave me, like I had shot him in the back."

"He is a piece of work," I huffed.

"Nonetheless, Noel being the consummate professional recouped fast. He instantly flashed that award-winning smile and wrapped Olisa into his arms and told her, 'You spoiled my surprise. I wanted to make a private presentation to you. That's okay. I want you to meet some people.' He then introduced her to all the suits who were already oohing and aahing as . . . How did he put it? Oh yeah, as 'the one who makes this gorgeous new building pale in comparison like a light bulb to the sun.'"

"Nice comeback . . . Still, why do I think Olisa was unimpressed?"

"Because you know your daughter well, Mr. T. I've got to say, though, quite a scene observing twenty-five suits rushing her like she was selling hot stocks for the lowest price. Olisa tried her best to recover from her annoyance and be nice, but she was just too angry. She's no good at faking her emotions. She hinted to Noel that they needed to talk in private, but he was too into his flow to perceive what she was getting at. Finally, enraged, she yanked him aside and yelled, 'Noel, get these people out of here, *now!*'

"'Okay, sis,' Noel said reassuringly, still trying to smooth things over. 'My goodness, what has Peter been telling you? Let me converse with my associates for a bit and then we'll talk, all day if you want.' Olisa wasn't having it. 'Uh, uh, Noel. I'm not waiting. Apparently, there has been far too many discussions without me present. Bottom line is—this is not the direction I want to go in and certainly not what you promised me would be the goals, values, and objectives of our organization! You betrayed me and deceived the people who have placed their faith in what we are all about!'"

"*Deceive* is a good word."

"Joseph, please . . ." Grace admonished me again.

"Got to give Noel credit though . . ." Peter recounted. "Nothing fazes him when he's in his zone. Without skipping a beat he said, 'Hold on, Olisa. Don't make up your mind until you talk to Frank Pellegrino and Cheryl Roberts.' Frank and Cheryl are VPs of sales at one of the largest Fortune 500 companies in the nation. He called them over to give Olisa a brief synopsis about what they planned to do with the products and all the millions that they could potentially make. They made sure to add a portion of the proceeds will go to charities of her choice. They seemed very proud of themselves after informing Olisa of all the good that could happen from this. Noel put his arm around her and said, 'What I tell you? This is all going to work out beautifully.'

"While everyone gathered were bumping fists and giving each other high fives, Olisa was furious! She pushed Noel's hand off her shoulder and yelled at him again to get them all away from her. This time he got the memo but had a hard time accepting it. He cried, 'Olisa, what are you doing? Don't you realize these people are here out of devotion to you?' Olisa cut him off. 'No, Noel. They are here to make a buck! I'm just the platform for them to jump off of. Get them out of here!'

"Frank and Cheryl hastily ushered their people out of the building. Noel followed behind assuring them it will all work out. 'Olisa's just having a bad day.'

"When he walked back in, he was irate. 'Oli, what is wrong with you? Those people you just kicked out represent the fruit of entrepreneurs across the country! I flew them here on your behalf. Everything they do will benefit you. Let me do my job! This is how an organization is run!'

"'Noel, don't you see what you're doing? Money begets money. That's all you're talking about!'

"'No, it's not, Olisa,' Noel argued. 'Look at how many people we're going to help here. You're making this out to be a bad thing, and it's not. It's all good. Wait til I show you all the ideas and products we've come up with: oils, perfumes, soaps, paints, floor wash, candles . . . Wait—I've even got a prototype here.'"

"I don't know if I can stand to hear the rest," Grace commented as she stared out the window at the dirt road leading to the house.

"I can. Keep going, Peter."

"All right, Mr. T . . . Well, Noel went and grabbed a candle out of this briefcase that was a miniature image of Olisa and handed it to her saying, 'Don't you see it, Oli? OLISA, Inc. products for those seeking a little magic healing in their lives. What do you think?'"

"Oh no," Grace gasped.

"Uh-huh. Olisa held the candle and gaped at Noel in disbelief. Noel's eyes were so wide it made mine hurt. He was so caught up in the creation of this candle, he failed to be cognizant of how Olisa was looking at him. 'This is where you need me, sis,' he stressed. 'I'm going to make it all right. We're going to change the world, baby, just like we said. And we can do it without you taxing yourself to heal another soul.'"

"I think I can fill in the rest. Olisa broke the candle in half."

"Nope. She may have wanted to, Joseph. Instead, she handed the candle back to Noel. I think what broke was her heart. All that rage dissolved into tears. She whispered, 'No, Noel, no. This is not the way. This is a bastardization of everything we sought to accomplish. I feared this might happen from the very beginning, and here we are. Don't fool yourself. You're not helping people. You're helping you.'

"'Olisa, that's not true,' Noel fought back. 'I'm not harming anyone. I'm making them feel good! These are feel-good products! If you're uncomfortable about me using stuff with your image on them, we can easily change that. Actually, I get what you're saying. It's a good observation. Here's another thought. I'll commission some of the best artists in the country, and we'll design new images, ones with rainbows, stars, suns, moons, oceans, and so forth. Give it an environmental focus, you know. That makes sense. It was on the key issues currently, global warming and all that. There you go; see how much we need your input. That was stupid on my part. I should have gone to you from the very beginning. I was just afraid with all the stress you've been experiencing, you might not see the concept objectively and shoot it down. That's why I didn't tell you. You've had enough pressures coming at you to add weight on those delicate shoulders."

"How did Olisa react?" Grace's voice was clogged with emotion, so much so I could tell Peter felt guilty about saying more. I nodded for him to go on.

"Her exact words were, 'Congratulations, Noel. You have made yourself God.' Noel was totally flummoxed by her statement. She patted him on the shoulder. 'How does it feel to be God and fashion a world in your own image?'

"'C'mon, Olisa. That's not cool. You know that was not my intention.'

"'It's not? Name one time you mentioned religion, spirituality, or God in your entire explanation.'

"Noel was speechless."

"'Noel, you are guided by enormous aspiration but not the type I want to live by. You are consumed by the spirit of greed. It's clawing at you, choking you, and it's eating you alive.'

"The crazy part is Noel acted like he hadn't heard a thing. He hurled right back in with the sales pitch like a man possessed. Olisa let him rant for a minute and then sealed it up with, 'Noel, I'm sorry. It's over.'"

"Noel fell backwards like he'd tripped over something. 'Olisa, what do you mean it's over? Anything can be worked out, like for instance—'

"'Noel, I told you one day it might all have to end when I got tired of it, and you agreed. This is that day. All I wanted out of this was to help people, to heal them, and to find a way to help them be at peace with each other. You convinced me I could use my gifts to uplift society in that way, but things have changed. I will not be a part of a system that will tyrannize them or prey upon their spiritual weakness. I will not be another version of Walter Pocock.'

"'See, you're still not getting it, Olisa. What I'm trying to do is—'

"'You are the one not getting it,' she retorted. 'True spiritual healing comes from inside. It doesn't come from the purchase of a product on Amazon. It comes from deep in here,' she emphasized, planting her hand to his chest. 'Buying products is easy and convenient. It's safe. It allows you to go home and feel good about yourself. It's cosmetic healing without all the work. The downfall is it doesn't teach you compassion.'

"After that she walked away. He trailed us, furious and shouting, 'How are you going to do that to me, *your brother*? No! No! It's too late now. You can't quit on me like that! It doesn't work that way, sis. We've got people to answer to now. It's way beyond I want to do something else in my life. Do you fucking know how much I've invested into all of this? There are some very important people involved now I didn't tell you about! They're not going to take this information too lightly. They're not the type you can fuck over. Do you hear what I'm saying? We're in this together, baby! Who's betraying who now, huh? It's not over, Olisa. *Do you hear me?*'"

I could barely look at Grace's tear-stained face. Both of us were crushed and at a loss for words.

Didn't matter. We would have had no time to discuss it. A car hauled ass up the road, waves of dust spewing from underneath the tires. We didn't have to guess who it was. Noel drove so recklessly that a security guard dove into some shrubbery to get out of the way. Noel sprinted into the house like a posse was on his ass. If the front door hadn't been wide open, I believe he would have crashed through it.

"Where's Olisa?" He was breathing hard, damn near panting and perspiring heavily.

"Hello to you, Noel. How are you? Why don't you sit down and have some tea?"

"Dad, I'm not in the mood. I need to speak with Olisa right away!" His eyes skimmed to Peter standing in the corner of the room. "Oh, is that my pal over there?" he uttered derisively. "I'm sure he couldn't wait to tell you the latest news. He likes to do that. Makes him feel good."

"You know it's not like that, Noel."

"Really? So break it down for me, sweetie; what's it like?"

"Noel, you're being really ugly. Sit down and relax so we can have a civil conversation. Olisa took a short walk. She'll be back."

"Can't, Mom. I'll just go look for her."

"No, Noel. I don't think that's a good idea," Grace emphasized more firmly.

It was easy to understand her concern. Huge bags sat under Noel's sleep-deprived eyes, coupled with a frenzied, ungovernable look in them, one fueled by fear. The person standing before me was a stranger. He didn't resemble our son.

"What?" he asked, registering we were all gawking at him. "I'm fine."

Just then, Logan walked in from the rear of the house.

"Oh, my bad. Maybe it was Pretty Boy that spread the news."

He started to walk up on Logan, but I moved in front of him. He locked eyes with me for a second but then backed up against the bookcase behind him. Incensed, he folded his arms tightly. "So what'd did you tell them, Lo? Did you tell them how you turned my sister against me? You've known her for six months; kind of coincidental she doesn't trust me anymore. What do ya think?"

"I didn't have to say anything to her, Noel. You did that all by your lonesome."

"Fuck you, man, and fuck you!" He furiously pointed at Peter. "At least I thought I could trust an old family friend, but I see who you side with."

"I'm not on anyone's side, Noel. I've never given you any reason to doubt me. I'm not so sure about you. You gave me the impression that Olisa knew all about the merchandising campaign."

"Oh yeah, sure, we're supposed to believe the muthafucka whose ancestors killed Christ!"

Peter with a half-smile started to respond, thought about it, and made a better decision by walking out the front door.

Grace arduously walked up to Noel who glared defiantly at her and whacked him hard across the face. "Noel, how could you be so cruel and insensitive to anyone, let alone Peter. You know he's family!"

Noel clinched his jaw, working hard internally to maintain a stone face, but it soon crumbled as his body wobbled and he fell into Grace's waiting arms. A little boy's voice I hadn't heard in years trickled from his lips. "Mama, I'm sorry . . . I'm really sorry. I didn't mean it. I promise I'll go apologize to Peter. Don't worry; I'll make it up to him. I'm just feeling a lot of pressure right now. You guys just don't know."

"Then tell us, son. There's no way we can understand or help you the best we can unless we know what's going on."

My eyes were on the verge of welling up as I watched him holding on to Grace like he did as a little kid.

"You guys can't help me. Only Olisa can. If she doesn't go to Washington in a couple of days, that's it for me. They're going to kill me."

At first I didn't think I heard him right until I saw Grace's reaction.

"What?" Grace pulled back as she cupped her hands to his face. "Noel, who's going to kill you? My God, who are you in business with?"

He clapped his hands to his head as if it were about to burst. "I'm hooked up with all kinds of people, Mom. That's all you need to know." He began wringing his hands and pacing about the living room. "When Olisa told me she'd do one more event, I hustled around to get some fast backing. I didn't have time to check resumes. I just went to some big-money people I worked with through some contracts in the record biz. We had one shot. I wanted to make sure we reaped the max on this whole venture."

"Give them their money back."

"It's not that easy, Dad."

"Why not, with all the money that's in OLISA, Inc.?"

"These people are expecting to get twenty times what they paid out. I had it all worked out. They were just loans, not a partnership. They were going to get paid back easily after this last concert."

"And they never would have left you alone. Don't you know that?"

"Maybe, but Mom, I'm telling you: I had it planned to perfection. I could have paid the loans back and still accomplished our mission to help people. It would have worked out." Noel started bawling again. "I'm so sorry . . . I just did what I thought would work best for everyone involved. I got in over my head and tried to move too fast. I wasn't trying to hurt anyone. Please believe me. If I could just talk to my sister, I know she'd understand."

A voice that entered the room like a gentle breeze said, "I believe you, Noel. I know you tried your best even though I disagree with your methods. And that's why I'm not going to let you down."

Olisa stepped into the living room from the rear where she left the back door open for Free who came trotting in and immediately ran into the kitchen where we heard him lapping water from his pan. Olisa stood stoically beside me.

Hearing Olisa's voice made all the swelling in Noel's face practically disappear. He was so relieved and buoyed by her words. He grabbed her so tightly I thought I'd have to use the Jaws of Life to spring her loose. She said, "Everything is fine here. I need you to go to Peter."

He held her a minute longer searching her eyes one last time, and then he was gone.

And so was Olisa. She left the room before we had a chance to talk with her. But I saw her eyes when Noel hugged her. It will haunt me for the rest of my life. They were disconnected from reality, yet resolute. They spoke of love, self-sacrifice, and something that filled me with dread. Grace noticed it, too.

It was conspicuous by the look on her face she had a premonition. She also had the look of someone prepared to die.

Chapter 15

U nable to fall asleep, around midnight I decided to take a walk and stretch a little bit. I was too tight and rolling about the bed like tumble weed, I'm sure much to Grace's chagrin. She was asleep but periodically groaning. I had a feeling she was wrestling with her own sleep demons.

"Mr. Timmerman, I don't think it's a real good idea for you to walk around out there alone. I'd be happy to accompany you," offered Franklin, one of the guards, as I stepped out the door.

"I've got it covered, Franklin. I just need some fresh air. I'll make it short."

"Okay, Mr. Timmerman. I'll keep an eye out for you."

"Good enough. Thank you, Franklin."

Maybe I should have had Franklin accompanying me. It was a little creepy walking on one of the mountain trails as crickets chirped. I slapped my neck as the mosquitoes treated me like I was a fast-food restaurant on two legs. As I shined my flashlight on the path, grotesque shadows leaped wildly about me. When the incessant sounds of the crickets died, I knew I was no longer alone.

It was him.

He receded into one of the giant shadows. I might have missed him if not for the gleaming polar cap of hair and golden trumpet hanging loosely at his side.

"You're here."

"You knew I would be," he responded in that voice.

The light of the flashlight made all the shadows dance at my feet as I jiggled it nervously. "It's that time, isn't it?"

Silence.

"You're getting ready to take her away, aren't you?"

Still nothing.

"Well, I won't let you. We need her in our life more than you do."

I gazed into his shadowy essence, and I felt him taking me in as well.

"That's it? No answer? All my life I've prepared to be there if my daughter was in trouble. And here I stand, utterly helpless. Don't you even understand a little bit? She needs me. Please don't let me be powerless in her time of need. I'm begging you with all my heart. At least give me a solution. Tell me what I can do."

My shoulders sagged with exasperation. "Oh, that's good. Thanks for the advice. I'll tell you what. I'm *not* going to sit back and let my daughter be murdered. I'm gonna do something. To hell with destiny. If this is my fate, then let it be. No matter what, I guarantee you I'll play a part in how it ends."

"That's what you should do, Joseph Timmerman," he rumbled in a detached voice layered with emotional overtones.

Once again, I heard the crickets and the pesky mosquitoes.

He was gone.

I walked back to the house and was zapped in the eyes by the crisscrossing tactical flashlights of the security patrol.

The second I lay back in bed, Grace rolled over and said, "I saw *the* lady tonight, Joseph. She appeared at the foot of our bed. No words, only a smile."

"Hmmm . . . I guess it's old home week again."

"You too?"

"Yes, he made his presence known."

We kept each other company talking all night. When the morning sun flashed upon us, I still wasn't tired. That's why I had no problem answering the bedside phone on the first ring.

I knew who it was. He was returning my call. I nodded affirmatively at Grace as she studied me with anticipation. Her head fell back into the pillows as she briefly closed her eyes and breathed deeply. I saw her mouth moving and realized she was saying a prayer. This was it. We agreed there would be no turning back.

With three days left to go before the DC concert, it was like a tomb inside the house. There was still a security team watching the premises for trespassers, but the rest of our family, Noel, Peter, Wilma, Gumbo, and Little Oak had already flown to Washington. Logan was still around, but he was at home in Echo Park packing and tying up loose ends in his studio. Aside from security, the only ones currently left in our mountain retreat were Grace, Olisa, and me.

The atmosphere surrounding us was tense and oppressive. We were fully aware of what lay ahead of us and dealt with it the best way we could. Olisa spent most of her time alone, meditating in her room. Grace read a lot, and I wrote in my diary. We took several long quiet walks together, at all times escorted by security.

At around 5:00 PM, I took a call from Noel checking in. His voice was barely audible.

"Hey, Dad. How's it going?"

"Hanging in, man. How about you? How's the weather out there?"

"Great. About seventy degrees . . . Got a nice little breeze."

"That's what I'm talking about. Make sure it stays that way when we arrive."

"I'll do my best. Um, look; everything's arranged."

"Perfect. So what time can Olisa do a final walkthrough in the new building?"

"She needs to be there 8:00 PM sharp! The door will be unlocked. If she's not there by that time, Savannah has instructions to lock it up by 8:15."

"I'll let her know. She's very excited. As you know, she didn't really get a chance to thoroughly check it out last time."

"No she didn't. Dad?"

"Uh-huh?"

"She absolutely sure about this?"

"Without a doubt. It's something she needs to do, alone, before leaving for Washington. You agree?"

There was a long pause before he answered, "Yes".

"Good."

"Dad?"

"I'm listening."

"Do me a favor. Please tell her how much I love her, okay?"

"She knows, but I'll relay it anyway."

"Thank you. I'll see you guys in DC. Be safe."

"Likewise. Goodbye, son."

I held the phone to my ear even though Noel hung up minutes ago. Grace gently took it out of my hand and clicked it off.

It was about seven forty-five in the evening when we made it to the OLISA, Inc. building in Malibu. We were escorted by a fleet of police and security officers. As I turned to go uphill, I noticed Danny Cavaliere with another man sitting in his jeep cruising onto the highway, but he never looked my way as he turned in the opposite direction.

The office was tucked in an isolated area off Highway 1 not far from the Pepperdine University Malibu campus. The building's back side faced the hills peppered with expensive houses. You had to park the car and walk up steps to the modest but elegant three-story structure. We parked on the lower level, which meant we had to walk up a small grade to get to the establishment as the caravan of vehicles followed suit.

"Why aren't we driving all the way up to the building, Mr. Timmerman?"

"My son told me they have been doing some resurfacing, so he wanted to be sure no cars are parked on the grounds before next week's official opening, Officer Akins."

"Makes sense to me." Akins signaled the other cars to park.

Grace and I watched Logan help Olisa out of the Lincoln Navigator. "Come on, old lady. How are you going to make it up the hill if you can't even get out of the car?"

Olisa smiled crookedly as she reticently accepted his hand. When she got out of the vehicle, she gave him a tender, loving kiss. "Thank you, kind sir," she intoned softly.

"You are certainly welcome, lovely one."

"Almost eight," I hated to interject.

It took a moment before they wrestled their eyes away from each other.

Olisa sauntered over to us, her spirit rising as she said, "Oh, it is such a beautiful evening. And I'm here with the people I most love in the world. You can't ask for more. This will be the nicest walk I've had in a while. Look at that magnificent building. A whole new beginning."

"Yes, it is." Both Grace and I had a difficult time letting go of our daughter when we embraced.

"Olisa, Logan is going to take your picture, so be sure to give us a big smile when you reach the crest of the hill."

"I will, Daddy."

"Wait a minute," Officer Akins interrupted, frowning. "My understanding is we all are going up there together, correct?"

"Would you mind if I take a few minutes on my own, officer?" Olisa asked sweetly. "I just want to get a feel for the place on my own."

"I understand, ma'am, but I really think we ought to check it out first, for your safety. You never know."

"No one knows about this site, officer." I glanced at my watch. "We haven't released the address yet."

"What about your construction crew? People talk, you know, especially in regard to this young woman. No, I don't think we should take a chance. We'll accompany you, and once we find it is absolutely safe, then we'll give you the privacy you desire. Okay?"

"Sarge, look what we got coming our way!"

"Oh shit! Who the hell invited *them*?"

Barreling up the road like NASCAR racers were several news vans, reporters hanging out the windows like college kids on summer break. In the distance, you could hear the whirring sound of an approaching helicopter.

"I thought you said no one knows about this address, Mr. Timmerman? What would you call that?"

I shook my head. "We must have a mole. Someone tipped them off. You were right. People can't keep their damn mouths shut!"

"Olisa, looks like you're going to get a little time to yourself after all. Try to make the best of it while we try to control the hounds."

"Thanks, Officer Akins," Olisa replied, waving as she headed up the slope to the building.

After she reached the top, before opening the door, Olisa turned and gave us the most beatific smile as Logan snapped the photographs. A second later, a flurry of cameras went off behind us as the officers worked diligently to keep the clamoring paparazzi corralled.

Ten minutes passed since she had gone into the OLISA, Inc. building. It was eight thirteen. One of the paparazzi broke through the human barrier of police and raced up the hill. Fortunately, Logan tripped him and he flew headfirst into the brush. He poked his head out and started cursing, except no one heard a word he said over the two horrific explosions that were so deafening it sounded like the apocalypse had come to fruition.

Grace and I clung to each other as we fell face down into the dirt. When I dared to look up, the OLISA, Inc. structure had converted into a gigantic bonfire. All around us, reporters and camera operators darted and skirted every which way, some toward the fire to get a better shot. Phones were whipped out and glued to their ears as they babbled with shock merged in with excitement. Only seconds passed before we heard the faint sounds of sirens penetrating the air. I heard them, even over our own mournful wails. Outlined in the blaze, Logan was on his knees, camera dangling from his neck, convulsing with tears. All was vague after that. Grace and I were heart-wrenchingly buried in each other's arms.

My daughter, Olisa, my heart, and my soul, was gone. To imagine never seeing her again was a pain far too unbearable.

Eva Sanchez tearfully announced on the nightly broadcast, "No one, not even the extraordinarily gifted Olisa Timmerman, could have survived such a catastrophic fire. Our hearts truly go out to her family. In this reporter's view, she was truly an angel sent down from heaven to make this a better world for all. She was our one shining soul on this planet. Now it's back on our shoulders to love and forgive each other and to do our best to carry out her mission and heal the world. I'm told the Universal Healing Concert will go on as planned as a memorial to Olisa Timmerman. She will truly be missed. If you can't be there, at least be there in spirit. Thank you and goodnight. God bless us all."

Not long after that news report and that there would be a major arson investigation because Olisa did have enemies, the most important call of my life came in. I pounced on it like a cur to scraps. My in-laws, my parents, and my sister all joined us in the house. I don't think anyone breathed, even as I fell to my knees, tears streaming and cradling the phone.

Needless to say, we never made our scheduled flight to Washington. Instead, Cecilia Moss, the Malibu lady, chartered a private jet for us. Nick and Lena Cavaliere joined us on the flight.

Grace and I did not want to go, but we had to do it. It was for Olisa. I'm glad we went. In many ways, it helped to soothe the agony. We all participated in a spontaneous unity march, arm in arm: Grace, Noel, Little Oak, Gumbo, Logan, Peter, Nick and Lena Cavaliere, Cecilia Moss, James and Katherine Willis, Uncle Junior, my parents, and sister Wilma.

The president spoke and so did many world leaders whose hearts she touched; poets, and motivational speakers, including Beverly Fairchild, who in her particularly eloquent speech said, "For all of you that thought you had it together, think again. If Christ had come back to earth as a woman, we proved with Olisa Timmerman that we aren't ready because she's the closest thing to godliness we may ever see in our lifetime. Maybe next time we'll be able to see past gender, race, religion, physiological, and philosophical differences, and straight to the heart."

Olisa would have treasured it and loved seeing the millions of people, of all ethnicities and religions who showed up in her honor with their heartfelt and sincere pledges to devote their lives to bringing peace and harmony into the world.

The top international musical groups and individuals performed with a vehemence that many of them never matched again in their own concerts. It was the most uplifting and incredible thing I had ever seen short of Olisa's miracles. Man, it would have lifted her heart so high. I could envision seeing her joyously and unabashedly dancing to the outpouring of eclectic music that rocked the nation's capital.

Uncle Junior finally did it. Accompanying himself on a twelve-string acoustic guitar, he sang his newly written soulful composition, "A Song for Olisa." It had them crying from DC to Paris. Noel broke us up again in a moving tribute to his sister: "Olisa retained a childhood innocence we adult lost years ago. A yearning, a hunger, a zest for living that if it could have been bottled would have set us free. No one is going to miss her like I do . . ." There was no more to say as he broke down in tears.

Grace and I were so proud of Noel and the way he gallantly stood on that stage and faced the audience, even more so when he scrapped the merchandising campaign. Now that she was dead, it would have made fifty times more in profit than when she was alive. It is what it is. In fact, Noel went so far as to make sure street vendors illegally hawking products with her image on them were unceremoniously removed from the event, even though, realistically, he would never have been able to stop it overall in the days to come. People were going to do what they did to make money off of her fame.

Did Olisa's existence and death ultimately change the world? That's something I've pondered for quite some time. The memorial concert was one of the most phenomenal events ever. The mood and ambiance of the ceremony lasted for quite some time, coloring, at least in philosophy, the future direction of international politics and legislation for at least a decade.

Olisa touched an innumerable number of individuals literally and figuratively in ways that significantly changed their lives. Even Eva Sanchez eventually admitted in a televised interview that she lost all objectivity after Olisa embraced her for the first time after an interview. She went to her mother's house afterwards and upon leaving gave her a great big hug. Her mother suffered from stomach cancer. Coincidentally, the next day in her scheduled medical exam, the stunned doctor announced to both her and her mother that all the tumors had completely disappeared and she had a healthy prognosis.

I can't begin to say how many people sold their souls to publishers for lousy book deals in an effort to capitalize on their shared and, in many cases, imagined experiences with Olisa. The only one we endorsed was a beautifully written book by our other son, Peter Kaplan, who lovingly wrote about his friendship with Olisa. There were numerous book proposals received by publishers covering every angle of the story. This included all the competing television movies and feature films that were either directly about her or a similar character. After Uncle Junior's "Song to Olisa" stayed on top of the charts for months, record companies tried to duplicate the effort commercially. Naturally, they lost sight of the significance behind the song and the fact that Uncle Junior donated the majority of his profits to the Olisa Timmerman Scholarship Fund.

What can you say? Olisa always forewarned us to be prepared for this.

A religious group cult known as the Olisians was formed who compiled all of her speeches, interviews, and anecdotes about her and used them for worship like they were gospels. The group never acknowledged this was exactly what she preached against. It didn't help that one radical faction of the Olisians claimed in a vision that Olisa came to their leader Charise Favreau and ordered the cult to commit mass suicide because the world was not listening. Fortunately, the majority of the devotees ousted Favreau as the leader for about ten other reasons, including for her thinking she was the reincarnation of Joan of Arc.

Yes, the world changed—good and bad. At least I never heard the apocalyptic blast of a trumpet, not yet anyway.

One positive change was that Alton and Laura had a child a year later. They named her Sage. To date, I haven't been notified as to whether she has any extraordinary powers except for being so damn cute.

The Soul of Venice continues to be packed every night. In fact, Wilma and I have opened up two more locations in Oakland and San Diego. The lines are just as long as the one in Venice. We have special days each month in which we serve dinners solely for the homeless.

After the Universal Healing and Unity Concert, Noel also personally transformed. He devoted himself to carrying out Olisa's dreams and making them a reality. All of his energies went into operating OLISA, Inc. the way it was originally intended. He reconstituted the institution and turned it into a truly philanthropic organization. It was renamed Olisa's Institute for Healing and Social Change. Millions of dollars were donated to charities and social organizations dedicated to erasing racism, gender discrimination, violence, poverty, and pandemic diseases.

Evidently, Noel wasn't the only one committed to change. A major upheaval occurred in the Glass Cathedral. Some of the loyalists in the Walter Pocock camp elected to turn over a new leaf a day after the concert. Given complete anonymity and immunity or reduced sentences, they confessed to being paid by people in Pocock's employ to discredit Olisa and her associates by any means necessary, including revealing information on who actually planted the bomb in our Venice home.

Former Pocock associates also stated that the two young men, former gang members and drug dealers, who were found dead in a Culver City alley had been paid cash by Pocock's organization to taunt Ernesto Padilla and goad him into fighting. Consequently, a hit was placed on these same individuals. The damning evidence came to light when a handwritten note by Pocock was given to one of the conspirators. It read: "After they do their job, please be sure to dump out the garbage, so it doesn't stink up the place!"

Walter Pocock and his henchmen, featuring the irrepressible Mr. Furhman (a.k.a. Biscuit Head), are now facing trial as co-conspirators to first-degree murder, amongst other eleven counts including extortion, bribery, and the imminent possibility of federal indictment for defrauding his parishioners over $180 million! Many believe he was responsible for giving the order to bomb the OLISA, Inc. new building, which would tie him to Olisa's death, but no substantiation has been found to support that allegation.

Furthermore, it currently appears that one of the main witnesses against Walter Pocock was his wife of thirty years who, while rummaging through his personals, found out that not only was he engaged in an affair with the musical director of his television show but that her three-year-old son is his. Moreover, during the process, she decided to rummage a little more and found some additional items she could turn over to the state as proof that the good Reverend Pocock moved people to Christ via his television and radio shows in addition to fraudulently transferring money from their pockets and life savings to his ministry without their knowledge, particularly elderly people. I'm reminded that "Love is a many splendored thing" as his ministry is in the process of being completely dismantled.

Ernesto Padilla was eventually freed from jail as a result of the planted murder weapon (the knife), lies, and false allegations by Pocock and company. Grace, Gumbo, Little Oak, and I were there to greet him for a bittersweet reunion. Lamentably, I was unable to revel in envisioning Pocock and Biscuit Head in prison garb. We became victims of another tragedy only weeks later. Noel was discovered severely beaten and left to die in a vacant lot in Venice. Someone sprayed his car with bullet holes and left a note in his lapel that stated: "We Never Forget!" Many of the locals used the lot as a dog park and someone found Noel that morning. He had already lapsed into a coma.

Chapter 16

race squeezed my clammy hand as we confronted a sea of flashing lights that gradually merged into one harsh glare. The tension in the air was stifling, making my head pound so hard it felt like a percussionist was trapped inside.

Meanwhile, security attached themselves to us like a piece of lint. I didn't mind. There were still crazies floating around out there.

As we stood near the front entrance of the Santa Monica UCLA Medical Center, we were instructed to make all our statements short and sweet, then proceed to get the hell out of there. *A real stretch*, I thought facetiously, *like I want to be here*. All I could think about was how they had beat Noel down. They tried to kill him! For all we knew, as we stood awaiting the start of our press conference, he could be dead. We were advised to conduct the press talk—forced, I maintain—because the questions refused to go away. Our son was near death, in a coma, and we had to talk to these imbeciles just to secure a degree of privacy. One of the organizers signaled to press corps they were ready to start. Naturally, Eva spoke first.

"Mr. and Mrs. Timmerman, once again I offer you my deepest sympathies for your great loss, which is ours as well. Olisa's impact on our society during the short time she shared with us, publicly, could never be measured. It seems like we were just getting to know her."

Grace and I nodded to her in appreciation.

"That's why I ask you to please forgive me for asking this, but if I don't, then I'm not properly doing my job. Is there any possibility Olisa Timmerman is still alive? As you well know, her body was never found. Many people refuse to believe she has truly left us."

I closed my eyes, took a deep breath, and exhaled slowly. "Eva, nothing would bring us greater joy, but please . . . let it go. Grace and I were there. Olisa is dead. And we are going to have to live with that final vision every single day of our lives. Our only comfort is knowing she has finally been rewarded with the love and peace of mind she has always strived for."

Of course, it wasn't enough. They wanted, needed more.

Dissonant voices roared at me. The press was anxious, obnoxious, bullying, asking sugarcoated questions but looking for hard-core answers.

We endured their screams, watched them vie for attention, ducked when they volleyed grating interrogatives, gawked as they climbed over each other like crabs in a bucket as they fielded ego-spawned inquiries before the bright lights.

"Please, folks. One question at a time," one of the organizers shouted to the media.

"Mr. and Mrs. Timmerman, who was Olisa Belle Timmerman?"

"Who was Olisa, you ask? Who was Olisa Belle Timmerman?" I echoed sharply. "Are you referring to before or after the media intrusion?"

Whoever asked the question chose not to elaborate.

"You still don't get it, do you? To you, she was a phenomenon, a spectacle for the modern age, a 'freak of nature' as one of you so eloquently quipped—"

Grace gently tugged my coat sleeve.

"To us, she was a gifted beautiful girl who grew up to be an even more incredible woman. First, above all else, she was our daughter. Do you understand that? Our daughter . . . I will never be able to convey to you how much we love and miss her."

I had so much more I wanted to add, but my throat felt like it was populated by wads of cotton as I labored to breathe. My heart beat rapidly. I was beginning to hyperventilate as anxiety swirled through me like a centrifugal force, causing my body to shake involuntarily. If not for Grace's warm and caressing hand, I would have met the floor headfirst.

It was so terribly difficult to disguise the bitterness ravaging my body. These people made our lives impossible. Somehow, I had to transcend it. That's what Olisa would have wanted. I grappled emotionally to compose myself as tears ran mercifully down my cheeks.

Sliding protectively in front of me, Grace took over, addressing the press in a voice that was as calm as mine was frantic.

"Olisa was one of the most wonderful, compassionate, and caring persons the world has ever known. We were richly blessed to have her be a part of our lives and us as a part of her existence. And maybe, somehow, now that she's gone, possibly, there is still hope that the love and healing she tried to deliver us will continue to find a home in our hearts."

No one said a word for some time.

Nonetheless, someone left the gate open. The silence was jarred by, first, one question, followed by an onslaught of others.

"That's it. We're done." I hugged Grace and waved my hand tiredly. "I'm sorry we can't answer all of your questions, but right now our son is in desperate need of our attention. We ask that you please keep us in your prayers. Thank you. Love and peace."

I was aware our words were in danger of being swept away as soon as we backed away from the podium.

Pandemonium broke out, and we were swiftly sandwiched by a wall of bodyguards herding us back inside the hospital.

In that moment of chaos, all of life fragmented as rabid photographers and jabbing microphones assaulted us from all sides. Luckily, security blocked the press from moving on us any further. We rounded the corner and walked down the narrow white Spartan corridors. Our police escort halted at the door to Noel's room. I knocked three times on the door, and the crack in the door grew larger as it slowly opened. Two behemoth security guards eased out the door, bellies rubbing against us as we squeezed in like alley cats through a gap in the fence.

"Thank you, gentlemen. We'll be okay now."

"Are you sure, sir? It's no problem if you want us to stay inside with you."

"No thanks, Gerald. You and the crew get some coffee or something. It's all right. We're good. Thank you."

"Call us if you need us, Joseph. We've always got a couple of people posted outside the door."

"That works."

"Ma'am."

"Thank you so much, gentlemen. Bless you."

The second I closed that door and heard the lock click under its own accord, in the room, I felt it . . . *the* presence.

My chest instantly constricted. My breath shortened as though invisible fingers began to close around my throat. I froze. I didn't even realize how hard I gripped Grace's wrist until she winced. Even so, that wasn't why she sank to her knees. It was in reverence to the giant figure looming over our son. It wasn't long before I followed suit, head bowed.

It was *Him*.

He didn't stir or flinch when we entered the room. He seemed to be only focused on Noel as he took off his dark glasses and gazed down at him. The angel's massive hands swarmed over his face.

He had never been the one to fear.

Soon Noel's body violently flip-flopped. The air in the room transformed into a living, breathing entity as a powerful earsplitting sound assailed our ears. And then, just as suddenly, it was over, and the air quieted.

Dispassionately, he covered his eyes with his shades, turned, and studied us for a long moment, then passed by us—no, correction—through us.

It felt like a sudden gust of warm Santa Ana winds. The hairs on my arms bristled as if an electrical storm hovered overhead.

I spun around, but in a blink, he was gone.

And we were alone, alone with our hysterical tears, tears of unbridled joy, an elation that left us hugging and laughing and unable to fathom whatever in our lives could have caused us such sadness.

That is until Noel groaned, "Oh, God . . ."

Confused as I was, I didn't know if he meant it as an expression or if he really meant . . .

Regardless, we got up and rushed to this bedside ignoring the jungle of irritating wires and intravenous cords that had been keeping Noel alive. We embraced him and each other in sheer jubilation.

At that moment in time, I recall thinking, *I thought he wasn't supposed to intervene?* An answer ripped through my conscious mind: *True, but it doesn't mean I can't, Joseph Timmerman. Nothing is impossible.*

Hospital personnel and security burst protectively into the room as clarity began to emerge from the murkiness of Noel's eyes. He groggily asked, "What happened?"

"What happened?" I yelled repeatedly, eyeing Grace as both of us giggled like little kids sharing a big secret. We were on a high that would make a drug addict envious.

"The question is, what has *not* happened, boy?"

We had to quickly step aside as wide-eyed doctors and nurses raced to his bedside absolutely shocked to find him sitting up comfortably, legs crossed and smiling.

Dare I say it was a miracle?

We let the doctors have their time to examine him and let him rest for a precautionary couple of hours. The next time we saw him, he had improved so rapidly he was sitting in bed and scrolling through his phone. He looked up and said, "Man, I've been missing out on all kinds of fun stuff."

"That's what happens when your lazy behind won't get out of bed, son."

"I'll try to keep that in mind, Dad," he replied grinning broadly. "So, what else is new?"

"Even with so much sleep, you're still pushy," Grace said, kissing him on his forehead several times as she sat on the bed with her arm around his shoulders. "Be patient. We have plenty of time to talk."

Noel's eyes widened anxiously. I asked the personnel moving about and occasionally gaping at Noel in wonderment to give us some time alone with our son. They willingly obliged as we waited for them to empty out of the hospital room. We gave Noel an update on everything that occurred while he was in a coma.

"So where's Logan?"

"Logan? He's down in Mexico right now. Said he's always wanted to spend some time there because the country is so culturally rich for his photography." I kept my eye on the door as I spoke.

"Is that right?"

"Yep, said he may never come back. He's got an opportunity to buy a house from a good friend there on several acres of land in a very remote area. He mentioned the house is large enough for him to construct a huge photography studio there. Since Free is now his dog, he took him down there with him."

"Yeah? I'm glad to hear it. That's cool . . . It really is."

"Definitely. Hey, Grace, show him that article you've been saving."

Grace retrieved a newspaper from a folder in her purse. She removed the paperclip on the second-to-last page of the newspaper. She pointed to the article circled in red for him to read. Noel's face brightened as he read the Mexican paper.

He was far more fluent in Spanish, like his mother, than me. After perusing through various newspapers in Mexico, Grace and I discovered a small article that was particularly interesting. My Spanish may not have been that great, but I knew enough of it to notice the word "*milagro*" sprinkled throughout the story. With Grace's help and getting the Spanish translated to English online, we read that this miracle happened in a small-town hospital in which three patients on their deathbeds terminally ill from cancer were miraculously cured overnight—no explanation for the diagnoses. The doctors and specialists were completely baffled. The locals were on their hands and knees testifying they had witnessed a miracle! One patient swore they saw the Dark Virgin of Guadalupe visiting the patients' bedside the night they were cured. She was brown skinned, hair braided, and wearing a multicolored robe coat.

"I knew there was a reason I had to come back to the living!" Noel laughed, clapping his hands enthusiastically. "Some things never change!" He began reading the article again.

"No, they don't." I laughed heartily.

"So, Mom, Dad, when are we going to take a Mexican vacation?"

"In time," Grace acknowledged in a low cautionary voice. She hugged Noel with one arm and held my hand in the other. "We just have to exercise patience. Let things die down a little more. In the meantime, we carry on with our lives. The right time will certainly present itself."

"Where have I heard that before?" Noel teased.

Damn, it felt good to laugh again.

The End